PETER CLARKE

An Ocean Away

A Journey of Hardship and Survival

- The William Stewart Saga -

First published in Australia by Aurora House
www.aurorahouse.com.au

This edition published 2020
Copyright © Peter Clarke 2020

Typesetting and e-book design: Amit Dey
Cover design: Simon Critchell

The right of Peter Clarke to be identified as Author of the Work has been asserted in accordance with the Copyright, Designs and Patents Act 1988.

ISBN number: 978-1-922403-26-1 (paperback)

All rights reserved. No part of this publication may be reproduced, stored in a retrieval system, or transmitted, in any form or by any means without the prior written permission of the publisher, nor be otherwise circulated in any form of binding or cover other than that in which it is published and without a similar condition being imposed on the subsequent purchaser.

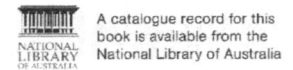

A catalogue record for this book is available from the National Library of Australia

Distributed by: Ingram Content: www.ingramcontent.com

Australia: phone +613 9765 4800 |
email lsiaustralia@ingramcontent.com

Milton Keynes UK: phone +44 (0)845 121 4567 |
email enquiries@ingramcontent.com

La Vergne, TN USA: phone +1 800 509 4156 |
email inquiry@lightningsource.com

DEDICATION

To my great grandfather.
A man of his time, a time for a man.
And to all those who followed.
A credit to him, a credit to themselves.
And particularly, to Cherie, Vi and Jean who gave
me so much information and so
many happy memories.

Acknowledgments

The idea of the book first came to me, many years ago. I was intrigued with how people of the mid 1800's lived. How they worked and loved and died. I started to research and found nothing was in one place. I became adept at following ideas and words through a myriad of sources to determine how they were used, and what people said and meant nearly two hundred years ago.

My father originally set out to research the family, travelling by train all over the state to libraries and government offices, like Births, Deaths and Marriages. Some of the history I used was his hard-won information. To my family and relatives now passed, I am eternally grateful.

Now, one can surf the Internet, chasing down leads like the gold-diggers of old. As they found, not all hunches pay off, nor is all information valuable. However, every bit helps to paint the picture.

Books are still a source, be they fact or fiction and they often help to resolve an issue. Books on steam, sailing, gold hunting and Ireland litter my desk and library. To the authors of the hundreds of books I have read and the thousands of on-line articles I have browsed, I am grateful.

Contents

1. The Beginning — 1
2. The Decision — 13
3. It's Done — 21
4. A Mother's Loss — 33
5. The Journey Starts — 39
6. The Road to Belfast — 43
7. Belfast — 53
8. Liverpool — 69
9. Portsmouth — 87
10. Signing onto the Steamship — 111
11. Planning the Crew — 123
12. Joining the Steamship — 129

13. The Captain	139
14. A Leading Fireman	147
15. Becoming Part of the Crew	163
16. Armstrong's Crew	169
17. Hall's Crew	171
18. Setting Sail	179
19. The Captain's Ship	187
20. Setting the Sails	193
21. Hall Shows His Hand	205
22. It's My Watch	209
23. The Officer's Ship	215
24. The First Storm	223
25. The Ship in a Storm – the Deck	227
26. The Ship in a Storm – the Helm	237
27. The Ship in a Storm - the Boiler Room	245
28. The Ship in a Storm – the First Officer	261
29. The Ship in a Storm – the Chief Engineer	277
30. The Ship in a Storm – Sailing as Best they Can	281
31. The Storm Passes	289
32. Trouble in the Boiler Room	299
33. The Ship's Surgery	305

34. The Confrontation	313
35. Another Storm	323
36. Some Trouble with the Ship	331
37. The Fight	339
38. Melbourne at Last	347
About the Author	361

1

The Beginning

William didn't see the blow coming. It caught him on the side of the head and knocked him to the floor.

Don't hit him back, he told himself. *He's your da.*

"Damn ye," yelled his da. "Why do ye no listen?"

They stared at each other for a few moments. It was now a battle of wills, but it was a one-sided battle and short-lived. His da was muddled by whiskey. Anger showed clearly on his face, his mouth moved to form words, but nothing more was said.

His da slumped on a stool by the fire, his back against the wall, staring absently at the embers. The fire glowed on his da's face, smoothing the wrinkles. The anger was gone. It was clear there was no fight left in him.

They lived in a one-roomed cottage, typical of those of peasants in rural Ireland. It was night, so the one window was of no use to light the room. All the light came from the fire that had been used to prepare their evening meal and would be left going to heat the room.

William's siblings and mother were still seated at the table that was mostly used for eating, but also provided somewhere to be when they were not in bed. There was no sound or movement from any of them. The light from the fire glowed around them, and they looked like a painting in the corner.

His da stirred and looked at William. There was no contrition in the look, only confusion. "I don't mean to hurt ye. Ye should listen."

William already knew his da meant him no harm, but still resented the blow. Life was not easy for his da, life wasn't easy for any of them. There was no laughter in the cottage. He always wondered why his da and ma were so remote from each other. They seemed only to talk through the children. "Ask your ma," or, "Ask your da," was the usual line of communication.

His da closed his eyes again. The rest of the family were still motionless as though afraid to reignite the conflict. Even though William sat up cautiously, he knew from experience his da was unlikely to hit him again, certainly not now that it looked like he'd gone to sleep. The blow really hurt, and he wanted no more of it. He wondered if it was time to move on. Some of the boys in the town had already left their families.

William's ma quietly shushed and shooed the little ones to bed. They had no distance to go. Only one or two steps from the table to the bed which was laid out on the polished earthen floor, in front of the fire. They all slept together on straw, mostly naked, under an assortment of coverings. Bits and pieces of rags and cloth stitched together that had been acquired, or so worn as to be no longer useful as clothing.

"Are you coming to bed, too?" whispered his ma.

William shook his head and took one of the stools vacated at the table. He sat, folded his arms on the table and laid his head on them.

His ma got up from settling the little ones who glanced fearfully at their da and put her hand on her son's arm. "Take your time, William. He means you no harm. You know it's all about your Mary. He'll be sorry the-morrow."

William watched his mother get into bed with the little ones, and his thoughts turned to Mary. He loved thinking about her. It seemed of late, he was always thinking about her. Perhaps he could just take Mary and leave.

Mary had lived nearby for most of his life and until recently, neither had been interested in the other, even though they had sometimes met in children's games. Not that William or anyone he knew had much time for games. Most children went to school, and they were busy enough before and after it. There was always something to be fetched or disposed of for the purposes of daily living. A mouth to feed, an errand to run, a little one to be cared for, or a belting to be had.

Most games were played after dark and in one's own place when supper was finished, and beds or the hearth not yet occupied. There were never any games at William's cottage.

Then, not so long ago, William was seated beside Mary at Old Patrick's wake. He noticed things about her he had never seen before. He liked the tilt of her chin, her sparkling eyes, and her sense of humour. Why hadn't he noticed these things before?

"It's so sad Old Patrick has died," she said. "My da said he was a very good worker, and it will be hard to find someone else who'll work as hard for the touch of a farthing." She looked at him and smiled. William had no idea what to say, so he remained silent.

"Of course, I'm pulling your leg. My da wouldn't know hard work if he fell over it. But I'm glad for Patrick. He's with God now, and I'm sure He'll be glad of a good worker." She smiled again.

William had no idea where this colleen drew the line between being serious and being funny. He loved it. He thought he'd try his hand at this game. "I can't remember the last wake, even though there have been plenty that have died. My ma says we do dying better than anyone." He paused, then said, "I suppose not everyone can afford a wake."

"And that's a good thing. Why, if everyone had a wake, there would be a wake almost every day, and no work would be done. I'm glad they're having this one, though."

Once again, William was delighted to see the same wonderful smile. He looked at the people in the room. Some of the men were already drunk, and many were well on their way. The wives looked on. Most of the children played games.

The little ones played Hide and Seek, Corners, Jump-a-Rope, or such games as could be played in the house. He didn't doubt there would be more play in the yard. They jumped, skipped and shouted wherever space was available. Some of the adults chastised them, 'Have some respect for the dead.' But the games went on, and the adults were mostly ignored.

William knew there were two rooms in the house, one upstairs and one downstairs, even though he'd never been there. Many houses were like this one. Everyone was in the downstairs room which was bigger than the same room at William's. It allowed for beds against the chimney on both sides, behind the fireplace. The house belonged to Mrs Murphy, not long a widow, who lived there with her two children. They didn't use the upstairs room, as the children were small and shared one bed downstairs, and Mrs Murphy used the other one. William overheard her say she didn't like to sleep alone. He couldn't see what the beds were like, as the curtains, that allowed some privacy when they went to sleep, were drawn.

The men had put in a little money to cover the cost of whiskey. Those who didn't had brought some of their own, and men tasted it and declared it was as good as the bought stuff. All the women had brought some food. It was by no means a lavish affair. It was more about getting together. Old Patrick was just the excuse.

Some of the men had already drunk too much and looked angry, causing some sidelong glances. William saw Mary's father was one of those and resolved to avoid him.

The boys, who were not little and not adults, seemed to be much more interested in the girls and vice versa. A game of Kiss in the Ring had just started in a corner, providing a legitimate excuse for a kiss for those involved. William thought he and Mary too old to join, but if that was all that was on offer, he decided he would have to take it. "Would you like to join that game?" he asked, instantly red in the face and very embarrassed when Mary smiled, as though onto his motivation.

"Let's go outside. It's too noisy in here, anyway," she said.

William's heart skipped a beat. The very thought that he could be outside, away from prying eyes and find some privacy was more than he could have expected. He knew that carts, stables, even a turf stack, would provide some privacy. Any privacy that could be had, while others of all ages were engaged in their own pursuits, would be enough.

When they went outside the sun was near to setting, and there was little warmth in its rays. It cast long shadows off the haystacks, turf stacks and outbuildings. Apart from the occasional call from a lamb or a calf, separated from its mother, all the noise came from the wake. The ground was moist underfoot, and Mary walked carefully in what William thought must be her best shoes.

William was dressed like any village lad. Woollen shirt and pants, no shoes and the pants held up by a piece of rope. Mary wore a simple calico smock with a coloured ribbon around her waist and a floral bonnet that held the curls off her face. He wanted to ask about her shoes, but lacked the courage. She might think him forward, but it was unusual to see a girl of her age with shoes.

Mary broke into his thoughts and asked, "Do you know why they called Patrick *old*?" Taking his silence as ignorance, she went on, "My ma says he was so kind, he must have been related to St Patrick. My da said that he was so old, he might have *been* St Patrick. I think that when we started to call him *old*, everyone did. Do you believe that story?" She stopped, looked at him and said, "No? I wouldn't either." She laughed again, and he delighted in the sound as they walked on.

Mary continued, "Ma used to give me food for him in the famine. I'd bring it to him, and he was always so grateful. He used to say that God would prepare a special place for us in heaven for our kindness. I asked him once if he'd been married. He answered that he was once, but his wife was killed in the fighting. I asked him about his eye, and he said he lost that in the fighting, too. Then he said he missed his wife every day, but he never missed his eye. He said he could see all of the world he wanted or needed through the one eye he still had. I asked him, 'What fighting?' He said it didn't matter because people always found something to fight about."

They walked in silence for a few moments, before she went on, "Here's one for you, William. He asked me once, 'What has eyes, but can't see?' Do you know?"

William thought about the puzzle as they tried to find somewhere to sit together. Everywhere was taken, but it did feel good to walk with Mary and share the fun of finding every place taken. For a while, anyway. He had become so absorbed by the idea of being alone with her that finding nowhere suitable became frustrating.

Without waiting for an answer to the puzzle, Mary said, "I don't see you in school, William. Where do you go to school?"

He was embarrassed, hesitated and said, "I don't go to school."

"You sound like you go to school. I think you speak very nicely. Much better than some of the boys in my class."

"My ma has always made sure I speak like her. I don't know why." However, he thought, if it made him better in Mary's eyes, then whatever the reason, he would always be grateful to his ma.

"How old are you?"

The flush of embarrassment again. He had no idea how old he was. He couldn't read, write or count. He had some idea of small numbers where his fingers were of reliable assistance, but a thing like age? Who knew?

"Did you ever go to school?"

"Yes, I did before the famine. Then I stopped."

"Why? It seems like a waste. A smart boy like you should go to school."

Relishing the compliment, he replied, "I didn't like it. Besides, during the famine, I could help my ma and da, and I could earn some money."

"When were you born?"

Was there no end to this? he thought.

He'd have to ask his ma and get some answers to these questions.

They stopped and he looked at her, held up one hand and spread his fingers. "I think it was this many years before the famine," he said, once again crimson with embarrassment.

Mary put her hand on his arm. He couldn't remember when he'd last washed his arm, but he knew he'd never wash it again. He was amazed Mary couldn't see or hear his heart beating. His blood roared in his ears, his eyes couldn't focus. All he wanted was the hand and his arm to remain locked forever. This colleen, this creature - so beautiful, so interesting, so wonderful.

She leant close and whispered, her breath light upon his cheek, "I think it makes you about fourteen, and you were born around 1840. Do you believe in God, William? Do you think He has a plan for us all? Do you think He has a plan for you and me?"

Just then, Mary's da stumbled out of the wake and called for her. He sounded angry, muttering about Protestants.

"I must go now," said Mary. "It's never a good idea to keep my da waiting."

He watched her walk to her da who was talking to himself and didn't notice Mary turn back to William and say, "I like you, William. I hope you like me, too."

⁓

The fire glowed, his da stirred, muttered something unintelligible under his breath and returned to his snoring.

William looked at his ma and da, both asleep and welcomed the moments alone to think. Perhaps he had always liked Mary, but he hadn't thought much about it. The difference now was, not only had she told William she liked him, she wondered if God had a plan for them. He'd never understood how someone else's interest changed a person and was surprised at how good it was to be liked by someone. No, it was more than that, this someone was a girl. And she wasn't really a stranger. Why, she'd been his neighbour all his life. Again, he asked himself why he hadn't noticed her before.

Was he now grown up? Was he now, like his da, on the next step of his life where he would take a wife and have little ones? What would Mary be like as a wife? Thinking on it, he really didn't know what a wife did. He really only knew what his own ma did, and he was not too sure how she rated.

He smiled to himself. He liked to look at Mary's breasts when he thought she wasn't watching. There was a lot to think about. It was the first time he knew he'd have to give better attention to the difference between boys and girls. He'd seen his own sisters and mother naked often enough to know they were different. He just didn't know why they were different. Sure, he'd seen farm animals mating, but there was no way people would do that.

He'd asked his da once why boys and girls were different. His da mumbled, "If someone hasn't told you yet, they will one day." His da seemed really uncomfortable, so William didn't pursue it again. He did sometimes wonder if he should ask his ma, but always thought better of it. He didn't have any friends he could ask, so it all remained a mystery, but he might have to solve that one soon.

His head hurt less when he thought about Mary. He liked the freckles on her nose. "Kisses from God," she called them. He didn't know if that was right, but he was pleased God liked Mary. Her eyes sparkled, too. It seemed she was always just about to say something really interesting. It seemed to him everything about her was interesting. He thought he should give her a present, but he didn't own anything. Even the clothes he wore had once belonged to someone else. He remembered he had found an interesting stone a year or so ago, that he had kept. He hoped he would be able to find it in the morning, and if he could, he would give it to her. He didn't know how or when, but he was so excited about the prospect, he couldn't wait for the morning.

The loud snoring that he really hadn't noticed much, after it started, stopped abruptly. His da stirred and crawled into bed. William took off his own clothes and got into the bed too, and it wasn't long before he was sound asleep.

William woke and knew from the sounds in the room, he was the only one awake. There was little sound from its occupants, except from his da, who was snoring again. That wasn't unusual and was a good sign that he wouldn't wake until morning. All the family were jumbled together in one bed. He had to be careful of little Jimmy, his brother and the youngest. William was always worried he would roll over and crush him. He loved his sisters, but Jimmy was his favourite. Jimmy was the only person who called him Willie. He was William to everyone else.

It was still dark outside, but he could no longer keep his excitement under control. He crept out from under the covers, put his clothes on and began to search for the stone. Then he spotted it by the light of the remaining fire, on a shelf of sorts, in the corner. He didn't remember putting it there, so he knew his ma must have done it. He felt an irresistible surge of affection for her.

The room was so small, it wasn't hard to lean over from collecting the stone and place a gentle kiss on his ma's cheek. Her eyes opened briefly, a smile appeared, and she settled back into sleep, as though to put off the inevitable chores of the day. It all happened so quickly, he wondered if he had imagined it.

Turning the stone over in his hand, he was terribly disappointed. It wasn't as good as he remembered, even though it was hard to see in the half-light. Worries that Mary might not like it, crowded his mind. He had wanted to give her something nice, but now it had lost its appeal and seemed like just some old stone. He knew it was all he had. So, if he was to give Mary a present, it had to be the stone.

He slipped out of the room through its only door and went outside. He shivered a little as his feet touched the cold ground. It was unusual to be outside at this time of night, and he wondered if he should borrow his da's boots, but decided against it, as his feet would get used to the cold soon enough. Most children of his age went without shoes, so he'd look silly in his da's boots. Besides, if he didn't get back before his da needed them, there'd be trouble. Anyway, he was excited as he thought of Mary and his excuse to see her again, so walking on the cold ground was neither here nor there.

It wasn't a long walk to Mary's place, and he was lucky the moon was out. There was a light breeze blowing, and the night was colder than he expected. He hugged himself in a useless attempt to be warm. Clouds flitted across the moon, casting shadows from the trees and hedges which made him jump. He'd heard stories about witches and fairies being about at this time of night and of children that had disappeared. Shivering, nervous and afraid, he nevertheless continued on his journey.

He was halfway there before he realised he had no plan as to how to give her the stone. The whole venture had become so silly, so pointless. He couldn't knock on the door or hang about waiting for her outside her house. No one did that, certainly at this time of night.

Resentment gripped him. Resentment for everyone and everything. All he wanted to do was to see Mary and give her a present, yet it seemed to be the hardest thing in the world. He clutched the stone tightly in his hand, and it was all he could do to prevent himself throwing it away. Still he had come this far, and not knowing what else to do, he continued the journey to her house.

When he got there, he could see no one was about. Mary lived in a bigger version of William's cottage. He'd been told Mary's da owned it, but he didn't know how that was possible. His da didn't own their cottage. As far as he knew, the viscount owned everything in the valley. It had several windows, all of which stared back at him, refusing to give him any hint of what was behind them. He was about to turn away. Then, he sensed someone was watching him. He looked at her cottage again, and there she was, watching him from a window. How did she know he would be there? His heart skipped a beat. Would she come out? Was she waiting for him to come this morning? Did she know he might come?

He stood undecided. Then, her face was gone. He waited for a while, hopeful she might come out. She didn't, and he wondered if he had imagined her. He knew it wasn't a smart move to be found outside someone's place with a stone in his hand, so he turned and headed back to his own cottage, disappointment gnawing at his heart.

The sounds of nocturnal animals, the whispering of the breeze through the trees, and the fleeting shadows caused by clouds across the moon, made him fearful he was being followed by someone or something he couldn't see. He regretted his fruitless trip with every step. His heart raced, and it was all he could do to stop himself running as fast as he was able, back to the sanctuary of his cottage and the bed.

2

THE DECISION

James heard his son leave the cottage. *Where's the boy off to? And before the sun is even up?* He dreaded the answer to the first question, but knew it in his heart. His son was in love and had probably gone to Mary's, though what was he hoping to do? Experience told him love and common sense didn't go together, so there'd be a reason for the trip that would make sense to no one else.

The rest of his family lay quietly. Good. It gave him time to think, but immediately the wrong thoughts crowded his mind. Regrets, mostly.

He regretted hitting his son last night. He'd tried to warn him that soon enough there would be trouble with Mary's family. The damned Catholic-Protestant divide was never far beneath the surface. The boy tried to argue he and Mary were different, it would be all right for them. Why did anyone think they were different? No one was different. There was never any understanding or sympathy. The poor, bloody young ones had no choice other than to fall out of love. He'd been lucky. Like him, Margaret was Protestant. Not everyone was lucky.

The whiskey didn't help with his side of the argument, and in frustration, he'd cuffed William on the side of the head. He didn't do it very often, and it was only William that he hit. It was just that the boy wouldn't listen. What the hell was a father for if it wasn't to teach his son? William had such a determined streak. He was sure it came from Margaret. She'd sometimes set her jaw, and James knew the argument was lost, even if he was right. Oh, hell. What was he thinking? He was never right.

When he first met Margaret, he didn't drink whiskey. Then, when life was hard during the famine, he'd pop into the pub every now and again. That was a long time ago. Now, he went there whenever he could. There was hardly a night when he didn't come home with at least a few whiskeys on board.

He didn't need to see the room where he slept to know the money spent on whiskey could be much better spent on other things. They'd been lucky to hang onto the one-roomed cottage when he'd wasted all his money on drink and couldn't afford the rent. He knew Margaret couldn't forgive him for his stupidity. He couldn't forgive himself. Another regret.

There were still a few embers glowing in the fireplace that cooked their meals and was the only source of heat. Winter was coming, and he'd have to find and store more fuel. If he couldn't find any, they'd all freeze. If he'd kept some of the money, he'd be able to buy it. Now, he'd have to find more work, or find fuel in the hills and carry the damned stuff home.

A table and a few stools where they ate was all the furniture in the room. No need for anywhere to hang the spare clothes. There weren't any. No need for a bathroom. They didn't wash. No need for a toilet. There was plenty of space outside.

Many of the Irish peasants allowed the pigs to live in the cottage with them. They helped to heat the room. Margaret wouldn't have it. "I might have to live like a pig, but I don't have to live with them," she'd say. He didn't like to hear her say it. It reminded him of how bad he was at being a husband and father.

There was daylight in the one little window. It was time to get up. He'd been promised some work on a farm nearby, and it was best to get there early. Margaret had been shocked by his argument with William, the little ones were just frightened. It was best to avoid his family this morning, so he decided to head off without eating. He hoped another worker would bring some food he could share for breakfast. As he rolled out from under the covers, he thought how much he missed the intimate moments he used to share with Margaret. It hadn't happened much since Jimmy, the youngest was conceived. He and Margaret weren't always nice to each other. Melancholy threatened him. He sighed. Another regret.

He found his boots by the bed where he had dumped them last night. *Always in the same place*, he thought. "A place for everything, and everything in its place," Margaret always said. Well, at least he got that right.

He crept out of the cottage before pulling them on, which wasn't easy. His feet were still warm, and the boots were cold. It didn't matter. Just one more discomfort to endure in the daily business of living.

The sun was a faint glow on the horizon. There was a little frost about, and it was cold enough to draw his jacket about himself.

His boots clumped on the dirt road that led to the farm where he would find work. There was comfort in the rhythm of his footsteps. He stayed away from the grass to keep his feet and boots as dry as possible. The crisp air nipped at his cheeks and hands, but there was nothing he could do about it. He had no scarf, gloves or pockets where he could find temporary relief. He looked around to take his mind off the discomfort.

Everything was green, even though winter was coming. The grass, the trees, the hedges. The sun added a golden splash where it fell. This was the Ireland that he loved. Further north, it was wild and unkempt, but his valley was a paradise. It was only the people that ruined it. No, that wasn't true. Only some of the people. There were a few cottages he passed on the way, but no one was stirring. Not even a wisp of smoke from a chimney.

There were only a few landlords, but many farms, each with an overseer. Workers would come from cottages nearby, so sooner or later, there would be more men like James tramping the roads, seeking or going to work. Overseers had their favourite workers, so established relationships were the best source of work as was the case for James this morning. He'd worked on the same farm many times. He'd been there the day before, and he'd been asked if he would come back again. It was a foolish question. Of course, he'd come back again. He always needed the money.

Approaching the farm, he saw a wisp of smoke above one of the outbuildings, and his nostrils delighted in the smell of burning turf. He loved the smell. It brought images of fireside, cooking, laughter, stories, music and warmth. His parents were long gone, but he missed them every day.

The farmer provided a simple kitchen for his workers, and someone was already using it. There'd be a dozen or so men working on the farm today, so it was no surprise someone was there before him. He stepped into the room through a doorless opening and was pleased to see his friend David cooking at the fire.

"Bout ye?" he asked.

"Well enough," said his friend.

"Do ye have enough to share?"

"Aye that I do. Thought ye might need some, so I brought extra. Ye in the shite?"

"Aye, that I am. How did ye know?" He envied his single friend who answered to no one.

"Ye look like a dog that's expecting to be kicked. There's more trouble brewing if I'm a judge. I think ye did well to avoid a fight with Mary's da at the pub last night."

James warmed his hands at the fire.

"I think it's just the beginning," added David. "He's a nasty piece of work and can't hold his whiskey."

"I know. I know."

The men stood in silence to eat the cooked potatoes, some pieces of cold bread and to drink their tea.

"What'll ye do?" asked David finally, as they waited for the overseer to allocate their work.

"Thinkin' on it."

"Like I said, Mary's da is a mean one. Don't tangle with him, James. Can ye talk some sense into William?"

"Have ye ever been in love?"

"Lots of times."

The men laughed together.

James thought back to when he fell in love with Margaret. It wasn't that long ago. Perhaps just the blink of an eye. Time is a funny thing. So quick looking back, so slow looking forward. Yes, he'd been lucky, all right. Would he have listened to his da if Margaret had been Catholic? Who knew? Who knew the truth about anything? No one knew he and Margaret weren't married. She'd been pregnant with William even before he found out she was Protestant. They delighted in each other then, and the rest of the world didn't exist.

Her da had found some work near to where they lived now, and she had come with him from Belfast. He knew nothing about her or her family. Not like the village and the nearby town, where everyone knew everything about everybody.

When she found she was pregnant, she and her da had gone back to Belfast. James followed her there, returning with her and William a few years later. It had been easy to let people think they were married.

As though reading his thoughts, David said, "It's not much of a life here, is it? I mean, for a family man like yerself - a wife and the little ones."

He was glad his friend couldn't read his thoughts. The past was a good place to leave the past.

"It's not all bad."

"It's not all good, either. People ask why I don't get married. It's too hard, I tell them. My ma used to warn me about love on a shoe string. She said it's fine at first, then the little ones turn up, and you have to feed and clothe them. Then ye can't do anything that doesn't get yer wife mad at ye. I was glad I was single during the famine and that's for sure." Other men started to arrive and the conversation turned to other matters.

He and David were given a task to stack rocks into a wall.

"Not too high," said the overseer.

"How high?" asked David.

"Christ! Don't I pay ye enough to do the thinkin' as well?"

"We don't want to get it wrong, is all," said David and shrugged.

"Well, about this high," said the overseer, signalling with his hand and then stomping off.

"Don't push him," said James. "I don't want to lose the work."

"He likes ye, so ye'll be all right. I think I got the job because ye've got it."

"He likes ye right enough. Let's get on with it."

It was warm now, and soon the men were stripped to shirt sleeves. There was a fair walk to the pile of stones they would load into wheelbarrows and move to the wall. It wasn't long before they were a sorry looking pair, soaked with perspiration and puffing and panting over their job.

"I think we need to slow down," said David. "He's not here, so we don't have to impress him. Besides, there'll be none of last night's whiskey left if we work too hard. We'll sweat it all out."

They stopped for a rest, sitting under a tree enjoying the view, watching the small flocks of sheep graze. The sky was a brilliant blue and cloudless. There was no wind and a crispness in the air. It was easy to see the river and the town in the distance. There were cottages scattered about the landscape in groups of two or three. It didn't work to put them too close together. The refuse of daily living needed to be spread about. The town? Well, that was a different matter. It had the river.

"What happened to Duncan's boy?" asked James.

"The one who got Mack's daughter pregnant?"

"Yes, that one."

"Went to Belfast."

"Do they hear from him?"

"Not a word."

"What about her?"

"I heard she went looking for him."

"Did she find him?"

"Dunno. Mack doesn't hear from her, either. His wife is terrible upset. Duncan avoids her. I heard she spotted Duncan at the church, and she yelled and screamed at him so much all the dead couldn't stand it and left the graveyard."

The men got up and started back to work.

"Are you thinkin' to send William away?"

"Thinkin' on it."

"Will ye come to pub, the night?"

"Thinkin' on that, too."

3
It's Done

Dawn broke as William headed back from Mary's, so he didn't go home. It wasn't unusual for him to wander about, trying to earn a little money for odd jobs. He was big for his age and strong. He had a lively smile and a good sense of humour, and anyone who hired him once would hire him again. Of course, it was a bit of a cheat because the employer got the size and strength of a man for the wages of a child. But William didn't mind. He was accustomed to being paid a pittance, and his ma always welcomed the money. It never occurred to him to keep it for himself.

The village wasn't big, so he noticed his da's friend and then his da heading off to work. He would sometimes walk with them, turning back when they reached their destination, although he had stayed with them occasionally when the farm overseer didn't mind. There was a lot to learn from them as they worked, and he had recently found work himself using those skills. He was a quick learner, and he knew he was good with his hands and was practical like his da.

Not today, though. It wasn't time to talk with his da just yet. He was unhappy about what his da tried to say last night, even though he didn't understand all of it. There was no doubt his da was trying to help, but the whiskey talk made no sense. And the disappointment at not being able to give Mary the present still rankled. Perhaps he could find another way to see her. He might be able to get some odd jobs near her cottage, then seeing her would be easier.

He walked past Mary's place several times, but didn't see her again. Wandering about was easy, so he kept at it, but failed to find any work. He thought some more about running away with Mary. The idea appealed to him because they would then have all the privacy they wanted.

At last, he decided to go home. Maybe his ma had some work for him, to take time off his hands and his mind off Mary. He thought about Mary as he walked along. Things were different now. He wanted to be with her, but it wasn't possible. He had his place, and she had hers. He had no idea how to change things, nor who to ask as to how he should go about it. Life was confusing now.

He saw his ma at the fireplace as he entered the cottage. Of all the ma's, his fussed over making things as clean as possible. She told him once she thought that if things were clean, people using them were less likely to get sick. He didn't understand how such a thing was possible.

He went to ask if she had any chores for him, but before he could say a thing, she said, "Your da has been home, but went out again. He'll want a word with you, later, when he gets back."

This was a surprise, and he was taken aback. It was more usual that she would tell him something to tell his da. He was also worried the discussion might result in a belting, although it hadn't happened for a while. "What about, ma?"

"You'll find out soon enough."

Realising the futility of any further questions, he went out to the garden and worked with the plants there. He knelt amongst the vegetables. They'd soon be ready to harvest. Even though the warm earth smelt of animal dung, the smell was not unpleasant. His ma had a good way with the garden. The tricks and the methods for success were all hers. He only provided the labour, but it didn't diminish his pleasure on seeing how well the garden grew. He sought the weeds, pulling them out mercilessly.

His mind kept drifting back to his da. Nervousness made his hands shake and gripped him like a knot in the pit of his stomach. He kept looking up to see if his da was coming. He tried to convince himself he'd find out soon enough, and it did no good to wonder what it was about, but it didn't stop him worrying.

Finally, when he saw him in the distance, he marvelled that his da must have left his friend at the pub and continued on home. *Oh, no. It's bad*, he thought to himself. He knew it would be foolish to hide and doing so would only put off the inevitable. So, he resolved to stand by the door and wait for his da who didn't take long to arrive.

"Wait here," was all his da said and went inside.

William knew that in spite of the previous evening's argument, his da hated serious talk in front of the little ones and would be fetching William's ma for a private chat somewhere. *This is really, really bad.*

It was only a matter of moments when his da re-emerged with his ma beside him. They weren't talking, but it looked like they didn't need to. It looked like they had already done all the talking they needed, even though his da had been inside only a few moments. His brother and sisters peered through the doorway, showing as little of themselves as possible, to be told by their ma to stay in the cottage. Tiny, worried faces scuttled away, only to reappear when they thought it was safe.

James walked down the road in front, with William and his ma slightly behind. No one spoke. He and his ma were shoeless, so only his da's boots made any noise. William was a little surprised his ma didn't ask him to ask his da about his day. His da was full of purpose, as though he knew exactly where they were going. He was relieved they were not heading to Mary's, although he was not sure why. He wondered if Mary's da had heard about him and Mary. Mary's da was bigger than his own da, with a greater liking for the whiskey. He didn't relish the thought of any fight with Mary's da.

His da suddenly stopped and turned. He looked straight at William and said, "Ye have to go."

William was stunned. "Go where?" he asked, after a few moments. He'd never been outside the village or the town nearby. He just stared at this da. He wondered what his da was talking about and after a few more moments, asked again, "Go where?"

"Ye have to leave here," his da said, turning to his ma, saying, "Be quiet now, ma. Ye are not helping. Besides, someone will notice."

The noise subsided, but his ma remained still, face buried in her hands, sobbing.

His da looked back at William. "It's because of this thing with Mary."

What? What thing? Does he know something about Mary that I don't know?

Before William could say a word and with his ma weeping now almost silently, his da barked, "William, ye can't stay here. I won't let ye stay. If ye become involved with Mary, ye'll never get away. This is a hard life for anyone. Ye have a chance to get away, and ye have to take it. We've all made the mistake of doing what our parents did. Everyone in this cursed valley is here because their families have always been here, doing the same things their parents did and their parents before them and theirs before them."

His tone softened. "Yer ma will miss ye, and yer brother and sisters will miss ye, but ye can do better than staying here. Ye're young. Ye are big and strong for yer age, so ye can go before ye get involved with someone like Mary and have to stay."

"But, da."

"Just listen to me for once. It's not because Mary is a Catholic, although like I told ye, Protestants can't marry Catholics. No lad, it's because ye have to give yerself a better chance in this world."

His da wanted him to leave the village? Only last night he'd thought he might leave, but thinking and doing were two very different things. Then his heart skipped a beat. For just a moment, he actually liked the sound of it, but what about Mary? He also realised his ma was still weeping softly. He didn't like that at all, because it meant the decision had already been made.

"But da," burst out William, realising while the idea sounded good at first, there were many questions to answer. "Where will I go? I have nowhere to go. I only know the village and the town. Who will look after me? You and ma have always looked after me. What will I do with no one to look after me?"

He was having trouble breathing and was afraid his legs would no longer hold him. His ma still hadn't said a thing. Is this what she meant by his da having something to tell him when he got home? He hoped there wasn't more, because he wasn't sure he could take it.

"Forget all that," his da said. "There's a cart with produce from the farm going to Belfast tomorrow, and I've arranged for them to take ye as well. I've paid some money, so they'll be sure to take ye. We'll all go home now and get yerself ready to go. The cart goes around the middle of the day, and ye can't miss it. I won't get my money back if ye do, and I don't want to pay a second time."

"What will I do in Belfast?" asked William, already dreading being on his own. "I've never been to Belfast. I don't know anyone in Belfast." He wasn't too sure about standing on his own two feet, just yet. "Perhaps I can go in the cart, have a look around and then come back? That might be a better idea."

His ma was still sobbing quietly, but William was more worried about himself at this point.

"No, ye don't know anyone in Belfast, but people in Belfast know ye. Ye were born in Belfast."

William was shocked. His sisters and brother had been born in the village. He thought he was born in the village, too. His curiosity overcame his fear. He sensed he was calmer, but didn't understand why. He was born in Belfast? How did he get to Belfast? Then he realised he didn't get to Belfast - his ma did. He looked from his da to his ma, and nothing made sense any more. He was nervous all over again.

"We lived in Belfast once. The driver of the cart will take ye to a house there. The people there will look after ye, but not for long. I know they are not expecting ye, but they will be pleased to see ye. There are plenty of ships leaving Belfast for places all over the world. The people will see ye get on one of those ships. Don't be afraid, son. Many Irish are doing it, so ye won't be alone. Keep yer wits about ye, don't trust anyone, and stay away from the girls, at least for a while."

His da then turned and started walking back towards the house. William thought he might keep going and head for the pub, but he didn't.

He and his ma hesitated for a few moments, then they too, started back. He whispered to his ma, "Ma, I liked the sound of it at first, but I'm not sure now. What was it like in Belfast? Who are the people I will meet? Do you know them? Are they good people?"

"William, you are not a child anymore, although I wish you still were. You have always been a good lad. Your da is sometimes wrong, but not about this. It's for the best. So, do as he says, and I'm afraid it's time to grow up and to be a man." She didn't say any more, and William realised she couldn't. She had lost control of her voice and was weeping again.

They all reached the cottage, bringing a sombre mood with them that affected the little ones too. His ma prepared a simple meal at the fireplace, and they ate in silence. William realised he was hungry in spite of being nervous. He hadn't eaten all day, apart from some late season apples he had found. He ate what was put in front of him. His da and ma didn't speak to each other at all, but he noticed his sisters and little brother looked at them all as though they knew something was wrong but had no idea what it was.

They were all in bed soon enough and after a while, William thought everyone was asleep. He crept out of bed and the cottage, with no clear plan. As he went through the doorway, he heard his da ask his ma, "Is he running away?"

"No," she replied. "He'll be back soon."

William headed for Mary's. The moon wasn't as bright as the night before, but there was enough light to find his way. He had no idea what to do when he got there. They could run away. It wouldn't be easy, but he could do it. He'd get some work, look after her and show his parents he could be a man like his da. His da said he was big for his age, and he was, wasn't he?

The grown up feeling from last night returned, along with the knowledge he was already different. He was confident, that was enough. As his confidence grew, he knew that with Mary by his side, they could do anything. Why, he might even own a farm one day. That would show his da, and his ma would be proud. Once again, the sounds and images of the night leant speed to his journey, and it was not long before he reached Mary's.

He stood outside amongst the trees on the other side of the road and saw only the dark windows staring back. It was so dark where he stood that even if Mary was waiting for him, she would never see him. He moved out onto the road and hoped she might appear as she did last night. The stones on the road pushed into his feet. He was aware of them, but they didn't hurt. His feet were so hard, he could almost drive nails with them.

What would he do if he saw Mary? What would she do? Would she come out? He prayed, begged for her to see him and come out. He waited, but saw nothing. He was going away and wouldn't even get to say goodbye. A picture of Mary came to his mind as clearly as if she was standing in front of him. He reached out, and as his hand swept the empty space, the tears started to flow. Silent sobs wracked his chest, and he sank to his knees where he stood, overwhelmed by grief and loss. Finally, the storm of emotion and longing passed, and he sat back on his haunches.

"You are not a child anymore," his ma had said.

"Then I suppose I can't behave like one," he said to the night and stood. He knew standing there, that his going away was inevitable, and his parents had probably always planned he would go. Perhaps his interest in Mary wasn't the reason, but it was reason enough, and there was the added threat of Mary's da. He was confident his da wasn't scared of him, but was likely afraid of what might happen to William.

Turning slowly, he walked home. The dread of the unknown meant he wasn't looking forward to the next day. Despite realising there was nothing he could do, he still hoped something might happen to prevent his going away.

He crept silently back into the cottage and into bed. As he drifted off to sleep, he thought he heard a sigh. Perhaps it was his ma's sigh of relief because she was right, or his da's sigh because his son's departure was now inevitable.

William was shaken from sleep by his da and told to be ready immediately. The other children were still asleep, and his ma was by the fire with some bread and some tea for them both.

"Are the little ones awake?" Margaret whispered quietly to James, once they had finished breakfast.

"No," he replied gruffly, "but they will be soon enough, I'll warrant."

William and his da were ready to go, but his da sat as though reluctant to move.

"Well, get them," he said with a sigh, after a few moments. His ma went to the bed, weeping again. William and his da went outside and stood silently. There was a lot to say and no time to say it.

His ma appeared with his brother in her arms and his sisters, staggering more than walking, behind her. He wondered if all three were still asleep.

"Well," his da said. "Let's get it done."

His ma shook Jimmy gently and gave him to William. She turned to the girls and said, "Say goodbye to your brother."

"Why?" the two girls said in unison. "Where's he going?"

"Away," his ma said.

Jimmy just looked confused. William tried to hand him back, but he wouldn't let go, holding William's neck so tightly, it hurt. Jimmy's curls brushed William's face, and the realisation hit him that he might never again see his brother. Once more, he wondered how to prevent his leaving.

Finally, his mother succeeded in pulling Jimmy away, and as soon as she did, his da started walking. His da stopped, looked back and said, "C'mon, lad, time's wasting."

William joined him.

"Bye," the girls called again in unison, waving.

As though he now realised what was happening, little Jimmy called, "Willie? Willie! I want to come too!" Then, he went quiet, as though he knew how foolish that was because his ma wasn't going, and he wanted to stay with her. He held her tight around the neck and started crying. Then, the girls and his ma started crying, and it became almost too much for William to bear. He hoped his da might change his mind, but the rhythm and set of his da's step showed that was never going to happen.

William tentatively reached out and took his da's hand. He nearly shouted for joy when his da took his hand and held it firmly. They walked down the road together, father and son, their feet crunching the remnants of last night's frost, side by side, until the sound of crying had nearly disappeared. William looked back briefly. The girls clasped their ma's skirt, faces buried in it. Jimmy fought to loosen his ma's grip, now desperate to join his brother and his da. William knew it was only his da's grip that prevented him from turning and running back.

Then, the morning mist enveloped his ma and siblings, and he and his da were alone on the road. William thought his heart was breaking. He tried to ask his da to pick him up and carry him like he used to, but couldn't find the words. Then he realised it was a waste of time, as he was too big, and his da wouldn't find the strength.

It seemed little time had passed when they saw the farm where his da worked and there outside the gate was a cart and driver. William's da noticeably slowed as though to delay the moment, now he saw the cart was still there.

"I told the driver ye would help him to load the cart. If ye help him, he'll take ye to Belfast."

"I thought you paid him some money?"

"Never mind that. Just help him."

The driver nodded to his da.

"Mornin'," said the men in unison.

It took some time to load the cart, but when it was done, the driver looked at William with kind, but sad eyes and said, "Hop on, lad."

William looked to see where his da was and was surprised to see him standing not far away. His da held out his hand, and William took it. He still held his da's hand, and both were reluctant to let go, when the driver noticed and said, "No time to waste. I must be away."

William tried to look at his da's face in the hope eye contact might give him a last-minute reprieve, but his da grabbed him around the middle and put him up on the seat beside the driver. He could tell his da was surprised at how heavy he was.

His da held him for a while. Before he let William go, his da looked him in the face and said, "Remember what I told ye."

William was astonished to see his da was crying, but doing his best to hide it.

Then his da said to the driver, "Do ye remember where to take him?"

"Aye."

"Then get on with it," said his da and turning on his heel, walked away.

The driver shook the reins and clicked his tongue, and the cart moved off. William didn't think he could hurt so much without breaking an arm or a leg. His da turned and waved briefly, then continued walking.

4

A Mother's Loss

Margaret watched her husband and son walk away, until she lost them in the morning mist. She hadn't realised how hard it would be to say goodbye to her son. Eventually, her crying stopped, but the babies continued to fret. She had forgotten sadness was catching. Well, it was time to get back to the cottage and settle the little ones.

Walking into the cottage, she looked around, realising the hopelessness of it all. The miserable sticks of furniture, the polished mud floor, the hearth with its wretched cooking pots. With a sigh she knew James was right to send William away, but she would miss her little man and hoped it wouldn't be for the rest of her life. As he had become older, he had replaced James in many ways. She relied on him to do the things around the cottage that James was often too drunk to do.

Something had to be done about James' drinking. It consumed valuable money and strained their relationship to breaking point. She sighed again. Many of the men drank. She understood their need to spend time in the company of men, to find laughter where there was often only sorrow, and to hide from the harsh reality of everyday living. But, she was running out of understanding, and knew she and James were heading for a confrontation. It would be worse now with William gone, and she would no longer have what little money he earned.

Putting the little ones to bed seemed like the best thing to do. They had all cried themselves to sleep anyway, so it was only a matter of laying them all out. In the midst of her pain, she found a little smile. It was unusual for someone who wasn't sick, to be in bed at this time of day. Well, she was sick. Sick of everything, so she lay down beside the little ones and was soon fast asleep.

There was a sound and Margaret woke to find James kneeling beside her.

"Are ye all right?" he whispered.

She nodded, but didn't say anything, not finding the strength or the will to say, "No, I'm not all right. My heart is breaking for the loss of our love and the loss of our son."

James lay down beside her, and rolling over to face him, thought it wonderful to be lying in bed with her husband and no smell of whiskey. She reached out to touch his face and was surprised to find his cheeks wet with tears. There was no need to ask what was wrong, but she was still surprised to find the tears. Men didn't cry.

"Can we talk?" he asked.

She nodded. He still had the bluest eyes she had ever seen. They were somewhat lost in the craggy, hairy, life-worn, lived-in face, *but at least his eyes have not been touched by poverty*, she thought. Then noticed there was something else in his eyes this morning, a look she hadn't seen for a long time.

"Will ye tell Mary?" he said.

"Tell Mary what?"

"That William is gone."

"She'll know soon enough."

"She might follow him."

"She won't."

"She might."

"She won't."

"Why not?"

"Mary is not stupid, and she's not pregnant. Besides, there's her da to deal with, and she'll not want to make him angry. Not even our William is worth that. She's a fine girl, and will make someone a fine wife one day. She'll always wonder about our William, but there's no harm in that and wondering is not following."

James was silent for a while. Margaret thought he had gone to sleep.

"Margaret, I was thinkin' the day 'bout my da and ma. I miss them. Their home was filled with fun, music, laughter. I was thinkin' might be my fault it doesn't happen here."

Where's this going? she thought. *What's got into the man?*

"Margaret, will ye marry me? I know I'm not much of a husband, but if I promise to be a better one, will ye marry me?"

"Oh, James. What will you do to make yourself a better husband?"

He was silent for a while, and she wondered if he had heard her, or didn't know the answer. Their faces were close, but she could still see his eyes. She could sense the delay was deliberate on his part, as though to make sure she would hear and understand. She waited.

"The biggest change, Margaret, is no more whiskey. I've been so stupid. I know I hurt my son, and I will never have the chance to apologise. But I can apologise to ye. I am sorry for everything." He moved his head forward and kissed her on the cheek.

"The second change is that, if ye will let me, I'd like to be a good husband to ye. I will need to do the chores until the girls and Jimmy are old enough to help. They will miss William too, so I will have to fill that hole in all yer lives. If ye will have me, then I hope ye will find again the love we once had. I miss it Margaret, but I didn't realise how much until I put William on the cart this morning. We have to realise our little ones are only on loan from God. We expect them to stay and look after us when we get old like we looked after our parents when they got old. But if ours will have a better life than us, they will all have to go like William has gone."

"Oh, James, please don't do that," she whispered, anxiety in her voice and eyes. "Isn't one enough? This is a hard life, James. Please don't make it any harder." She started to cry again.

He looked thoughtful for a moment. "I may not be strong enough when the time comes, so let's see. But if they want the chance, we have to give it to them."

"Ireland doesn't have to lose all its children, does it? What will our country become if our children aren't here to help it to grow strong?"

Instinctively, he reached out and piled all the little ones between them and held them and his love fiercely. "Way too young to be discussing it now, anyway. What about my proposal?"

Margaret laughed.

"There it is!" said James. "How long since I have heard that?"

"Four children and then a marriage proposal? What kind of a girl do you think I am?"

"The best, Margaret, the best."

"I think we'll have to let marriage still be the step we have missed, but I like that you asked me. My love hasn't gone anywhere, James. It was always there for you, although you have sorely tried it at times. So, hold us all close, and let's be a family again. If I have lost a son but found our love and regained a family, then my loss may not be so great." They lay silently for a while. "James, do you remember the day we met on the road?"

"Of course, I've never forgotten it. How could I?"

"I was reminded of it when you lay down beside me. I thought again, you have the bluest eyes I have ever seen. But, that day on the road, there seemed to be something wrong with them. I worried you might not be completely sane. They seemed bigger and rounder then, like you sometimes see on people that aren't all there." She laughed again, and he smiled at the sound. "Now, we'd best be up and about. I'm sure it would be seen as slothful to be in bed at this time of day," she said.

They held hands as they stood and looked down at the little ones. "May they never grow up," said Margaret. "And I hope and pray God will always watch over our son."

"Oh, Margaret," said James as he held her fiercely. "I hope so, too. Do ye know on the road that day, I hoped ye'd see and like my blue eyes? My ma had told me one day a lassie would fall in love with my eyes, so I tried to make them as big and as round as I could."

"It worked James, but you did look strange," replied Margaret and laughed again. *Can this be true,* she thought. *Is there a chance our cottage could be a home again?*

5

The Journey Starts

The cart moved so slowly the driver worried William might jump off and run home. "Now, don't be thinking ye might jump off. Yer da's asked me to take ye to Belfast, and take ye to Belfast I will. If ye jump off, I'll just have to fetch ye back, and that will get me angry, and lad, ye don't want me angry."

If William had been thinking to jump, he looked at the driver with respect and settled back in the seat as if he had no intention of getting the driver angry.

"Do ye know any songs, lad? Perhaps we could sing a song together to pass the time." Without waiting for an answer, the driver started to sing. He didn't have a good voice, but he'd been told it was pleasant enough. The events of the morning, the sound of the driver's singing and the gentle swaying of the cart all had their effect on William, and he soon fell asleep and collapsed back against the fully laden cart.

The much-travelled road wound its way into the distance, following the river and climbing slightly as it took them out of the valley. They would cross a stone bridge further on when they swung east to follow the road to Belfast. If the driver fell asleep before the bridge, and anyone came the other way, the horse would stop and remain there until the driver woke and got the horse moving again. The driver could fall asleep if he wanted, but not until they crossed the bridge. The horse had done the trip many times and would walk obediently at the same pace regardless of anything the driver did. It was warm in the sun, there was a gentle breeze blowing, and puffy white clouds chased each other across the sky. There was no other traffic, and the driver could let his thoughts wander as he sang of lost love, leprechauns and loneliness.

He had performed this task before, and the children would always fall asleep. He gently eased William into a more comfortable position and continued singing. "Big lad," he muttered between songs. "Good looking, too. There'll be a few hearts broken before he's done."

William's da and the driver had talked about what to do when the driver and William reached Belfast. The boy's da and the driver had agreed to pretend there was a predetermined destination for the boy, but the truth was there was none. The da had made it sound like the boy would go to friends or family, and the driver didn't disagree. It made as much sense as any other plan. They hoped the boy's size, self-reliance and quick wit meant he would be better off at the docks, but the men on the docks were a tough lot, and the boy could come to harm. However, the driver had told the da that as much as he liked the boy, it wasn't his problem, and once the boy was in Belfast, his job was done.

The driver's wife had asked him once if they should send their children away. He replied he didn't know where parents found the courage to send their children into the world. He wasn't sure he could do it, but was glad of the money he sometimes earned to do this job. It helped them keep their own children at home, and he was glad of that, sure enough, even if she wasn't.

He stopped singing as he reminisced. The threat of anger hadn't always worked. There was a girl once who became so frightened by his threat she did jump off and broke a leg. He heard later she had died from the injury. Even though it was some time ago, he didn't feel too good about that. He was sorry for the children he took into Belfast. Most of the boys finished up labouring in the mills or around the docks, while others went to sea. Most of the girls finished up in the mills. It was hard work and didn't pay much, but it was better than starving to death.

He wondered how many children he had taken. He'd never bothered to count them, so he thought it might have been twenty or thirty. Belfast made lots of children of its own, so not all the children that were sent to Belfast stayed. He did sometimes bring one or two home, often the worse for being away. He glanced at William again. *This lad is different*, he thought.

There was a farm house where a woman lived where he could stay on his journey to and from Belfast, and he wanted to reach it before nightfall. *Best to get moving*, he thought. He got off the cart, took the horse by the bridle, walked a little faster and clicked his tongue to get the horse moving.

He liked the woman at the farm house. He would give her some of the produce from the cart, and she would cook a good meal for both of them. He couldn't always do this - the produce he took to Belfast wasn't always edible. She liked it when he had a child with him because she had none of her own. A boy would be put to work in the yard and a girl in the house.

If he didn't have a child with him, he would sometimes get to share her bed. He liked that too, although neither of them ever talked about it afterwards. He wondered if others might share her bed and was sometimes nervous he might bring more home than the commercial results of his journey to Belfast. If he did have a child with him, he and the child would sleep in the stable, along with any animals that happened to be there. His own horse would be left outside, even in winter. The stable wasn't big enough, and the horse would stand against the stable on whatever side was out of the wind. The horse handled it well enough, but there was no choice. Horses didn't get choices. People sometimes didn't get them, either.

6

THE ROAD TO BELFAST

William stirred, woke and saw a farm in the distance. There was a cottage on it with smoke climbing skywards from the chimney. The air was still and fresh, so much so, the smoke fell down again after a few moments and formed a skirt around the cottage. It looked to William like an upside-down white tree.

The driver pointed to it. "That's where we'll stay the night. Won't be a moment too soon. It's getting cold out here." They were both quiet for a while and then the driver asked, "How old are ye, lad?"

Not this again, thought William and tried to remember what Mary had told him. *Oh, Mary, what are you doing now? How I wish you were here to help.* Unable to remember, he made up a number.

"Twenty-five." He hoped the driver would be happy with the answer.

Instead, the driver laughed. "If ye're twenty-five, I'm the Pope."

William wasn't sure what he meant as he'd only ever heard of the Pope and not met him. Nonetheless, the driver was laughing at him, and he didn't like it. "Well, how old do you think I am?" he asked testily.

"I figure fourteen or fifteen," said the driver, softly as though he knew William's feelings were hurt.

"Which one is older? Fourteen or fifteen?"

"Fifteen," and this time William committed the 'fifteen' to memory. He thought it might be useful later.

They had been late getting away, so it was almost dark as they pulled up outside the cottage. The woman had a shawl pulled around her shoulders and a lantern in her hand. She held the lantern up to improve her view.

"Well, what do we have here?"

William thought she looked disappointed he was there and wondered if she had a task for him that she thought he would not be able to do.

"Brought someone to help with the chores."

"Aye, that ye have. There's turf to be fetched and a stable to be mucked, but it's nigh on dark, so I doubt much will be done the-day."

"Well, he'll fetch some turf for ye in the morning, but we'll need to be gone early, so the stable will have to wait for another time."

"No matter," said the woman, as though the chores were incidental to some other purpose. "Get yerselves down from there, bring me some things from yer cart, tend to yer horse and come inside where it's warm. It'll be cold soon enough, and a full belly will be yer best guard against the chill." The woman handed a basket to the driver and went back inside the cottage.

The driver selected some of the produce from the cart, put it in the basket and gave it to William. "Here lad. Take this inside and come back out to help with the horse. Any chore is easier done by two than one."

William took the basket inside, and the woman took it without a word. She still looked upset about something. He went back out, and the driver stood beside the cart. He hadn't moved since William went inside.

"Here," said the driver. "I'll show ye how to do this. There's no point in having a dog and barking yerself."

William wasn't sure what he meant, but he figured somehow, he was the dog. Anyway, it didn't matter because he liked the driver and thought it would be good to learn something about the horse and the equipment.

The driver set about undoing all the ties on the harness. William was astonished the horse stayed still and quiet during the whole process. He'd not been this close to such a large horse before. It was big compared to him and not a little frightening, but he really liked the way it smelled. It behaved well enough, even though he was there, and his confidence around it was growing as the driver removed the harness and collar.

"Why don't we leave it on overnight as we'll be using it early in the morning?" asked William.

"Well. Horses aren't like people who leave their clothes on all the time. If we leave all this on, it'll get sores on its neck and back, and it'll be too sore to pull the cart. Always look after a horse, and it'll always be there to serve ye. Now, we need to feed it."

"What with?"

"I leave some feed for it here in the stable. I sometimes bring it back from Belfast, or sometimes I can bring some with me. If ye look inside that door, ye'll see a big basket and a smaller basket.

Put half a basket-full in the small basket from the bigger one and put the small basket by the stable wall, on the side away from the wind. Come back when ye've done it."

William did as he was told and returned to the driver who got a piece of rope from a hook on the cart. "All right, lad. Now, watch me make what's called a halter and put this over the horse's head like this."

William was nervous, but was surprised the horse didn't object when he did the same.

"Now, tie a knot like this, so it won't come off."

It took William two tries, but it was done and looked fine. They led the horse across to the basket with the food. The horse started to eat immediately.

"Won't it run away?" asked William.

"If it does, it won't go far. It thinks the halter is tied to something."

"Then, why don't you tie it to something?"

"Then, if it really needs to get away, it can't."

William stood beside the horse thinking about the logic of what the driver said, watching it eat and thought he had never seen an animal so beautiful.

"It likes ye," said the driver. "That's good. It normally doesn't like strangers."

William was secretly very pleased with the compliment. He was glad the horse liked him because he really liked it.

With the horse settled, William and the driver went inside. They went into a single room with a fireplace and a low table and some stools. The driver wasn't tall, but he was hunched to avoid hitting his head on the ceiling. It was dark apart from the light from the fire, and the woman fussed with some pots hanging over it. The room smelt wonderful, and William was instantly hungry.

"There's a dish over there, and ye two wash before supper. I'm not having the likes of ye two sitting at my table after messing with the horse."

William was confused, but the driver winked at him and whispered, "Follow me." The driver rinsed his face and hands in the bowl and dried them on a cloth near to the dish. William did the same. They returned to the table and took a place each, as indicated by the woman.

In front of William was a bowl and a spoon. William hadn't used a spoon before and didn't know what it was for. He wondered how to eat the contents of the bowl. He thought it might be a big cup and was about to grab it, to drink from it when he noticed the woman and the driver sat quietly, watching him. He sat quietly too, his stomach desperate for the contents of the bowl.

The driver said, "Bless us, O Lord and these thy gifts, for ever and ever. Bless this house, this woman and this boy. Amen." William wondered about all of this and continued to watch and wait. He was glad he did as the woman and the driver picked up the spoon and began to eat from the bowl. William did the same and was soon making such a racket the woman and the driver stopped eating and watched him.

"There'll be none of that in my house," said the woman. "Anyone sitting at my table will watch their manners, and if they make as much noise as the pigs outside, then they'll be going to join them."

William felt himself turning bright red and wondered if he could make a dash for the door and run from there as fast as he could.

"Now, woman, go easy," said the driver, softly. "He's a village lad that's probably never eaten anything but bread and potatoes. Now lad, pick up the spoon, put some food on it and put it in yer mouth. The trick is to make as little noise as possible. It's not hard, and people will be grateful and think better of ye for it. There's nothing worse than the sound of a person enjoying their food. Here, watch me, and ye'll soon get the hang of it."

William did get the hang of it quickly and realised he hadn't thought about his own home since waking up on the cart. Not only that, he hadn't thought much about Mary, either. Even though he learned new things all the time, and the driver and the woman appeared to like him, and seemed to care about him, he still missed his home and Mary. Sadness threatened to get the better of him. *What's to become of me,* he thought. *Is there anything I can do to go back?*

Once they had eaten, they thanked the woman for her kindness, and both left for the stable. The woman thanked the driver for what he had given her for the meal and told him she would have something special for him on his return, especially if he was on his own.

"I'll have some porridge and tay for ye for the road the morrow, so come inside before ye leave." The driver assured her he would. William wondered if they would both come in for porridge, or if the driver would come back on his own. He hoped the assurance was about them both getting porridge.

The stable was dark, but the driver knew where everything was. He spread out some straw and covered it with canvas and sacks for beds for them both. It was rude, but comfortable. It seemed to William he had hardly closed his eyes when the driver shook him.

"Wake up, lad. It's late, and we must be away."

As they went outside the stable, William noticed the horse was already in its harness and ready for the journey. He was disappointed he didn't get to help. They both went inside the house, and the table was already set with bowls, spoons and cups. Without a word to the woman, the driver went to the dish on the table by the window and William followed. They washed their faces and hands, dried them and sat at the table. William liked this process and liked how his face and hands felt.

He waited for the driver to talk to the Lord again. He thought he would ask about this later. Once that was done, William enjoyed the taste of porridge for the first time in his life. The driver abruptly finished and said, "We'll be off, now. We're both grateful for yer hospitality."

William started to thank the woman too, and she said, "No need, boy. Ye are always welcome here. I like ye, because ye listen, ye learn and ye try." Then she said with a slight smile on her face, "And don't worry about fetching any turf. Yer driver will do that on his way back."

I guess he won't have a dog to do the barking on the way back, William thought, but he did notice the driver didn't seem to mind.

As they pulled away from the cottage, he saw the woman standing at the front, unsmiling and arms folded. From a distance, he couldn't see the expression on her face, but he did appreciate what she had done, so he waved. Tears pricked his eyes, and he felt sad. After just having met her, he doubted he would see her again. He thought she waved back, but he wasn't sure. The sadness added to his loneliness, and he thought again of home and Mary. In the moment, all sense of being grown up disappeared.

He turned and looked at the road ahead, and the fear of the unknown came back. It was the same fear he felt yesterday as his da put him on the seat of the cart. There was too much happening, and he struggled to find a way to handle it all. He struggled to control his tears, and the more he tried, the harder it became.

The driver, as if sensing William was not at ease, asked, "All right, lad?"

William was glad to be asked a question. It gave him something else to think about. Since they were talking, he thought he'd ask about the Lord. His da and his ma had rarely mentioned God, other than to attribute to Him all the ills and rarely the good in the world. He had grown up thinking God wasn't particularly nice to anyone, yet the driver and the woman had been grateful to Him. He said, "I have a question," and felt the driver stiffen.

"All right, lad. What is it?"

"How could you talk to the Lord in the woman's house? Does the Lord live there with her?"

The driver looked grateful and relieved.

Then William thought how silly his question sounded and hoped the driver didn't make fun of him again. He was glad of the driver's simple answer.

"The Lord is everywhere. Why, has no one told ye about the Lord yet?"

"I don't know. Maybe I'm too young, and no one has got around to it. I asked my da once about why girls and boys were different, and he told me someone would tell me some day. Maybe they'll tell me about the Lord at the same time. Can you tell me about the Lord and about boys and girls while we travel?"

"No, that's not my job. Someone else will have to tell ye. Just be patient. I had a boy like ye in the cart once. He asked those kinds of questions. I didn't answer them for him, and I won't answer them for ye. I worried the boy might be in for some serious teasing at some point. However, he was big like ye so when it happens, only yer pride will be hurt, and it's more likely any broken bones will be suffered by the person doing the teasing."

"Who are the people you are taking me to?"

"Some family of yers," said the driver, but he shifted uncomfortably, so William wondered if he was lying. Who he was going to see had been a mystery from the beginning.

The sun wasn't up yet, and the chill of the morning made William shiver. In spite of it, William dozed again. There was something very comforting about the slight sway of the cart and the clip-clop of the horse's hooves. Before he fell asleep, he thought the driver looked relieved not to be asked any more questions.

7

BELFAST

William woke and noticed the driver once again walking beside the cart. "What's that smell? Where are we? Are we there yet?"

"The smell comes from the tanneries," said the driver. "There's a lot of curing of hides in Belfast. Animal hides come from all around here, and it seems every house, yard and shed has a tannery. It's always been that way." The driver turned and looked up at William. "It's all right. We're nearly in Belfast. That's why you can smell the tanneries."

In spite of everything, there was an eagerness about William. And he opened and closed his mouth several times, trying to ask questions. He'd never seen a place like Belfast and certainly didn't remember being there before. How could he? The town was wedged between the mountains and the river, and there was now a lot of traffic of every conceivable type sharing their road. There were people on horseback as well as sulkies and carts like the one William rode. People of every size and shape were walking or riding - some people with animals, some well-dressed and others in rags.

A hundred questions burst into his mind at once, but it was impossible to articulate any of them. He didn't realise his eyes were like saucers and his mouth wide open. He stammered and stuttered so much the driver burst out laughing. William didn't mind. He knew the driver enjoyed the moment with him.

"Where are the people my da knows?" he asked at last.

"Down by the docks," answered the driver, not looking at William.

"What's the docks?"

"See there, where ye can see the ships," replied the driver, pointing and now looking at William quizzically, as though to ask "Does this boy know anything?"

They came to the top of a rise, and the town was spread out below them. The river split the town, with less of the town on the far side, and it wound its way along, rather than being straight. He could see three bridges across the river. On the left side of William's view, all the ground was flat, but there were hills of varying sizes on the other sides. Like the river, the road they were on wound its way down to the town, joining a maze of buildings and roads running in every direction. The biggest buildings were down by the river, on each of its sides. The river looked packed with craft, moored on both sides and moving wherever space was available. Smoke was coming from chimneys on many of the large buildings.

There was a lot of noise from both the town and from fellow travellers, some of whom were angry and resented the slow pace of the traffic, demanding they be allowed to pass. The driver did his best to accommodate them, but most took it as a personal affront when his response was not immediate.

William thought he'd best be patient, since he didn't understand any of these things. He thought he had no choice other than to trust the driver, even though his da had told him to trust no one. His anxiety grew again due to the noise and the size of the town. He wished himself away from here and preferably back home. The cart kept swaying, the horse went clip-clop, and the din and the smell were unbearable. There seemed to be more of everything the further they went, and his senses struggled to cope.

The driver explained that the man his da knew had helped previous boys, too. He had always found his contact in a pub nearby, but it was too early for the contact to be there yet. He explained he would usually drop the boy and his produce and collect what he had to take back. Then he would have a drink at the pub and start back home. If it was too late to get to the farm, he would sleep under the cart once he got outside Belfast. The docks and the markets weren't too far apart, so there was still time to do both, but he needed to find his contact quickly. They were close to the docks now, and William became very anxious.

The driver asked a man who directed traffic, if he knew his contact.

"Aye," was all the man said, pointing to a building nearby and adding, "Ye'll find him in there."

"Is the man you want my da's friend?"

"Yes," said the driver, but the look on his face said otherwise.

Leaving the cart, the driver said, "Wait here," and turned before he received an answer.

The man directing traffic yelled, "Ye can't leave that there!"

"I'll only be a moment," he yelled back, heading for the building and again not waiting for a reply. He ran into the building.

Without hesitation, William jumped down and followed him. William saw him wave to a man just inside the door, near to some desks. The man was red in the face and clearly angry.

"This is not a good start," he heard the driver mutter to himself. The driver didn't wait, though and strode straight up to the man. "I have a man for ye," he said, before the red-faced man could say anything.

"I hope he's better than the last," was all he replied. But he seemed to relax a little, as though the arrival of the driver might help in some way, or perhaps another man would make a difference. "If he's any good, ye've come at the right time. We're short-handed and need every man we can get. Fetch him in," and he went back to the heated discussion the driver had interrupted.

The driver turned, and William hurried back to the cart before he was seen. The driver appeared in the doorway, signalled to him and gruffly called, "Come on!" and turned back to the building. The man directing traffic yelled at him again, but he ignored him and waited. Once William joined him, he turned and walked quickly into the building, so William had to catch up and couldn't ask any questions. A glance at the driver's face showed there was no sentimentality on offer.

As they approached the contact, William shrank back. The contact was still red in the face, but the man the contact talked to was even redder. William was frightened, even the driver looked frightened. The contact turned and yelled in the same tone he had just used with his antagonist, "What's this? I thought ye said a man?"

"Well, that's the end of it," the driver muttered to William. "Back on the cart we go, and I'll try to find someone else to take ye."

"I am a man. I'm fifteen," said William to the contact.

The contact hesitated. "Well, then, if ye think ye're a man, then perhaps ye are a man. But there'll be no favours or squibbing. Ye'll do a fair day's work for a fair day's pay, or ye won't last. Ye don't look like much of a man, but I've seen smaller men than ye pull their weight. Besides, I'm in no position to quibble. We need every man we can muster at the minute, so ye'll have to do."

He turned to the driver and said, "We don't need ye. I'll bet yer cart is on the street outside here like ye leave it outside the pub. It's in the way there, and it's in the way here so get yer money from the cashier and clear out before I change my mind." Without another word, he turned back to his previous conversation, and it seemed to William he picked up where he left off.

William made eye contact with the driver and hoped he could leave with him. "My da's friend doesn't seem very friendly. Are you sure this is the man my da told you about?"

"Ye heard the man," he said, without further explanation. "I have to go." He turned on his heel and left in a hurry to get his money.

William didn't like any of it. He seriously doubted the man was his da's friend. It just didn't seem right. He didn't like the way the man treated the driver, either. He suspected the driver had lied to him and putting him with this man was a way of not only getting rid of William but getting some extra money for his trouble. However, he decided to make the best of it and wait. He couldn't think of anything else to do.

After what seemed like a long delay, the man turned to him and said, "Are ye from Belfast? Do ye have a home to go to here?"

"No."

"All right. Let me tell ye how it works. Ye'll need to find somewhere to stay. Ye'll have to find it yerself. I can't help ye with that. Be back here at six in the morning. I'll give ye some work to do, and if ye do it well enough, then ye can stay on until either the work finishes, or someone better turns up. That's all. See you the-morrow." The man turned away, then turned back. "What's yer name?"

"William."

"Ye can't be William here. Call yerself Bill." Again, the man turned away, and this time he didn't turn back.

William turned and walked out the way he had come in. He was lonely and ached for his family. So much had happened so quickly. He had no idea what he was going to eat, where he was going to sleep, much less the many other things humans need to do. Perhaps he could find the driver and get him to take him home. There was no money to pay him, but having received some money in exchange for William might mean the driver would at least help him.

When he got outside, there was no sign of the driver or the cart. He was alone. No ma, no da, no family, no friends. He started to panic. What would he do now?

There were people everywhere rushing about, and no one was interested in him. He wished he had kept the money he earned from his last job. Well, at least he had a job. He had just got one, hadn't he? If he could find out when it was six in the morning, so he could be back by then, he'd get some money.

The driver should have given him some. His panic gave way to anger. The driver was supposed to leave him with some people his da knew. He was sure his da would be good and mad about that. Maybe, if he looked around, he might find the driver and could ask him for some money or at least tell him how mad his da would be.

Wandering along the docks, he was shocked at the terrible noise. Men shouted to each other, at each other. Ships of all types were tied to the docks, produce being loaded off and on. Animals were bellowing, baaing, neighing and braying, depending on whether they were being used as beasts of burden, or being loaded or unloaded from the ships. There was chaos everywhere. Any number of times, William was cursed for being in the way.

Then a man called, "Here lad, help us with this, and I'll give ye threepence!" Several men were trying to load a barrel onto a cart and making a mess of it. William stepped up and helped. He'd done it often before and knew exactly what to do. The barrel was safely on and William put out his hand for his money.

"Be off with ye!" the man laughed and turned away.

William was confused. "You said you'd give me threepence!" he called at the man's back.

"Ye heard me!" shouted the man without turning.

A big man detached himself from a group that had been enjoying the mess the men made of loading the barrel. He put a massive hand on the man's shoulder, gripped the man's jacket and turned him around.

"Give the lad his money, or I'll tip ye upside down and shake it out of yer pockets!" he bellowed in the man's face.

The man was overwhelmed and couldn't produce the threepence fast enough. He jumped up onto the cart to join his equally shaken companions and left.

The big man turned to William, a smile on his face. "Ye should ask for yer threepence first."

William nodded.

"What're ye doin' 'ere?"

"I'm working for a man in that building there." William pointed at the building he had come from.

"What's 'is name?"

William realised with surprise he had no idea. He hadn't even asked.

"Dunno."

"No matter. Where are ye off to now? Will ye need some grub and somewhere to stay?"

William nodded.

"Then come with us. We're off for a pint. Molly'll see ye right."

"Who's Molly?"

"She's got a pub."

William trailed the group. He was very out of place with all these big men. They all soon stopped at the pub and went inside. William started to follow, but the big man put up a hand and said, "Wait 'ere," and went inside without waiting for a response. He returned after a few minutes with a woman. "'Ere 'e is."

"So, what can I do for ye, lad?"

"Are ye daft, woman?" the big man muttered. "I've already told ye."

"Aye, ye 'ave at that, but maybe the lad has nought, and it'll come to nought." She stared at William, and he thought she might be smiling.

"I'll leave youse to it!" exclaimed the big man and went back inside.

"Now, lad. I hear ye'd like some grub and somewhere to sleep? Do ye 'ave some money?"

"Aye. That's what I want, and I have threepence."

"Ye speak well. I should ask where are ye from and what're ye doin' 'ere? But, no matter, that's yer business, and yer money is good no matter where ye got it."

William wondered if he needed to answer.

"Come with me, lad." She turned and went inside. "And I'll take one of yer pennies for some grub and a place to sleep."

William followed. He could hear the men talking, but William and Molly walked away from the noise.

"Out 'ere's the kitchen. We'll get ye some grub, and I'll show ye where to sleep. I can't spare a room, but I'll warrant that'll not be a problem to ye. If ye want to do yer business, then ye go through that door. Ye'll find a bucket. If it's full, ye'll find another nearby. Keep yer aim straight, no matter what ye'r doin'. Try not to make a mess, though there's plenty that do, so watch where ye tread." She stopped. "Do ye need to go?"

"Go where?" asked William, confused.

Molly tutted in exasperation.

"Why, do ye need to do ye'r business? Take a piss, for example?"

William nodded.

"Then off ye go, remember what I said, and I'll have some grub for ye when ye get back."

He went through the door, into a courtyard. It was open to the sky, and William wondered what people did when it rained. There were buildings on both sides with windows open to the courtyard affording a view to anyone that bothered to look. He found a bucket with some space in it, all the while taking care where he walked, realising that Molly was right. Some people's aim was bad.

Pulling down his pants, he hovered over the bucket as best he could, and when he finished, looked for something to clean himself. He realised he should have thought of that first. There was another bucket nearby with a brush poking out of it. Perhaps it was the right implement for the purpose. He hopped over to it, pulled the brush from the bucket, realised it was the correct implement when he saw what a mess it was in and used it nonetheless. Pulling his pants up, he headed back inside.

Molly waited with a plate of bread and potatoes. There was a mug of milk too.

"Sit there," she said, pointing at a stool near a small table. "And I'll thank ye for one of ye'r pennies. It'll cover yer grub and yer sleepin'."

William would have given her all his pennies and in spite of what his da had said, he trusted Molly. William set to with the food. He was really hungry. Molly came back with two pennies.

"'Ere ye go, lad. Now, when ye'r done with ye'r eatin', ye see those sacks? Pull a few together, make ye'rself as comfortable as ye can and ignore anyone that comes in. They'll be lookin' for grub, or a place to do their business." She started to leave.

"Molly, when's six in the morning?" William said.

"Why?"

"I've some work on the docks, and I need to be there by six in the morning."

"Aren't ye the one!" said Molly, laughing. "So ye'll be wantin' some grub in the mornin' then? And a wake-up service that we don't provide. I'm thinkin' I've short-changed myself only chargin' a penny!"

William blushed.

"I'm just havin' some fun. Don't pay me no mind, lad. There's a man comes by before six to empty the buckets. I'll tell 'im to wake ye. Find ye'rself some spuds and some milk before ye go."

She started to leave, then turned back.

"Lad, they're hard men on the docks. Ye've been lucky to meet some good ones today, but ther're bad'uns, too. Ye be careful now. Hide those two pennies ye still have left, or I'm thinkin' they'll not be yer's this time the-morrow. If anyone thinks ye've got some money, they'll be workin' out ways to take it from ye, and they're not above stealin'. So, when ye get to ye'r job, listen only to the man in charge, don't be fooled by the others. They'll all make fun of ye if they can. They're always lookin' to have fun, 'cause there's not much to be had on the docks."

Molly left the room, William finished his meal, pulled some sacks together, lay down, and tried to sleep. He heard Molly talking to the men in the bar. He guessed it was the men who brought him to Molly's.

"Can ye keep an eye on the lad the-morrow?"

"I'll try," said a voice that sounded like the big man.

Molly stood in the doorway, looking at William who pretended to sleep. He heard her sigh and say out loud to herself as he drifted off to sleep, "Stupid woman. Now 'e thinks I'm soft. It might also be that 'e thinks there'll be trouble, and it'll be too 'ard to stop it. No matter, it's just one lad, and Lord knows there're plenty wanderin' the streets. No point in bein' sentimental, but I do like this lad. In a town where so many die before they even get to 'is age, liken' is no excuse for carin'. Anyway, there's work to be done and standin' and talkin' to meself won't get nothin' done."

William was awakened by a kick. He looked up and saw a wild creature standing above him. He couldn't be sure if it was man or beast. Could it be a fairy? He'd never seen one but had been told about them often enough. Fear and curiosity caused him just to stare.

"What're ye'r waitn' fer? Molly said to wake ye'r, and wakin' yer I am."

"Are you the bucket-man?" asked William disappointed, no longer thinking it was a fairy.

"That I am, and if ye be wantin' to use a bucket 'fore I take 'em, be quick."

William found a bucket with some space and used it while the man busied himself collecting the buckets to one spot. He didn't seem to mind rampant inaccuracy and walked without looking.

William went back to the kitchen, found some potatoes, some milk and a piece of bread. The milk didn't taste too good, but no matter. He knew he would be grateful for it later.

He walked out the front, past several men sleeping either inside or outside the pub and snoring loudly. It was just light enough to see, and he headed for the docks. He'd gone out from home early in the morning, looking for work in the village, so it was not new to be up and about early. However, he'd never arranged to be somewhere for work at a certain time before and was nervous about how it all worked. He was also nervous about Molly's warning and what he had overheard. Well, if things didn't look right, he'd run and try to get back home somehow. He knew his da would be disappointed, but he also knew his ma would be glad to see him.

William had no trouble finding the building, but stood staring at its size. There'd been too much happening with the driver and his contact when he was last there, and he hadn't taken any notice. Opening the door, he stepped inside.

The building was immense in height, width and depth. There were a number of people-doors like the one he had just used. There were also a number of large doorways to his left and right, big enough for at least two or three horse and carts, side by side. The doorways were so high, a man as tall as three men on top of each other, could walk through.

There were goods of all types stacked in front of him. Horses and carts stood nearby in various stages of being loaded or unloaded with bags, barrels, packages, and stacks of timber. Horse dung was everywhere, and several men struggled to gather it into wheelbarrows, take it through the doors to his left and tip it into the river. While he watched, they interfered with the working teams, and there were shouts and curses. The floor was wood near the river and stone elsewhere. The horses' hooves clumped or clattered depending on whether they were on wood or stone. To his immediate right were people seated at desks, and then he saw his man standing nearby, once again angry with someone over something.

"Ye're late," said the man when he saw William.

William shrugged.

"No matter," said the man and pointed. "See 'im. Do what 'e says. Patrick! 'E's 'ere."

William was relieved to see the big man from yesterday and walked over to him.

"Bout ye?" asked Patrick with a smile. "Ye'll be workin' with some tough boys, so ye mind yerself, now. We pays the team at the end of the day, and the team pays ye, so ye'll get only what ye earn. There's a team there that needs another." He pointed at a group of men loading bags onto a cart. All but one man worked in pairs. "So, off ye go. No. Wait. What's yer name?"

"Bill," William replied and joined the man working on his own.

"Bout ye?" William asked.

"Better now. Ye look strong enough, but let's find out. I'm Martin," and held out his hand.

William took it, shook and said, "Bill. So, it's these bags here on that cart there?"

"Yes."

"What's in them?"

"Bird shite. Let's get on with it."

For the rest of the day, William worked when Martin worked and stopped when he stopped.

At first, it looked like there weren't too many bags, but more continued to arrive. Carts would come loaded with the bags, and teams would unload them for William's team to reload them to other carts. He wondered why they didn't load them onto the final cart in the first place and asked Martin when he had an opportunity.

"Ones comin' are from a ship, so they have to get them all off as the ship wants to leave. Costs them money to stay in port. Ones goin', well they've been bought, so someone has to buy 'em first. Nobody buys 'em, we've got nothin' to do."

"What do they use it for?"

"Fertilise their fields. Good for that, they say. Makes everythin' grow better, they say."

"I think I've smelled it on the viscount's fields at home. I suppose he uses it. Doesn't half smell awful."

"Aye, it's only for the rich folk and aye, smells bad, but I've never known shite that didn't."

They'd occasionally stopped for a drink of water, or to take a piss in the river, but most of the time the work went on.

William was sorry for the horses. None were in good condition like the one that brought him to Belfast. Most of the horses were skin and bone, with sad faces and heads hanging down as though it took all their effort just to drag the carts into place. Once, when a cart had been loaded, and the driver clicked for the horse to get moving, it looked back at the load and then at William as if to say, "They don't expect me to pull this, do they?" The driver took a whip and beat the horse several times across its back. Its hooves clattered on the cobble stones as it tried to get purchase. At last, the cart started to move, and the driver put the whip away.

One time they stopped, and Martin asked, "Did ye bring somethin' to eat?"

William shook his head.

"Did no one tell ye?"

William shook his head again.

"They should have," said Martin and pulled some potatoes and bread from a small parcel and ate it all while William watched.

"Next time, ye'll know better," said Martin when they resumed the work.

As the day and the work went on, William worried he hadn't enough strength left to help with the next bag, but somehow, he always managed. As they loaded one cart, another arrived. When they finished one pile of bags, another arrived. There was no end to the carts and bags.

At last, there was a whistle, and they stopped for the day. William had no way to work it out but thought if he got threepence for one barrel yesterday, then he would get a lot more for so many bags today.

Martin sat on a bag and said, "Now, we wait. See that feller? 'E's our team leader. 'E'll get our money."

The team leader walked over to Patrick, got a piece of paper from him and walked to another man who took it and counted out some coins. The team leader came back, handed eightpence to Martin and fourpence to William. William couldn't hide his disappointment.

"'Bout ye?" the team leader asked William.

"I got threepence for moving a barrel yesterday and fourpence for moving all those bags today."

"Then ye can go back to moving barrels," said the man in a harsh tone.

Patrick walked over. "Anyone need me?" he asked.

"The lad thinks fourpence isn't enough," replied the team leader, not looking directly at Patrick.

"I thought it was eightpence for a day's work."

"He's only a boy."

Patrick turned to Martin. "Did he work like a boy or a man?"

Martin flushed. He looked at the team leader.

William saw the team leader mouth, "A boy," with his face turned away so that Patrick couldn't see.

"A boy," whispered Martin.

"Youse are both full of it!" shouted Patrick. "Now, give the lad another two pennies and clear out, both of ye. I'll see both of ye the-morrow and don't expect an easy day of it!"

The man gave William another two pennies and the men hurried off.

"Ah, lad, I'll need to find another team for ye if ye come back the-morrow. Ye might be better to find somethin' else to do. It's a lot of hard work for very little money, but that's how it goes on the docks. No one is yer friend, and they're all out to cheat ye. Will ye come back the-morrow? Ye're welcome if ye want. I watched, and ye worked well, well enough not to be cheated of some of yer money."

William nodded. He didn't know what else to do. He was glad of the extra two pennies and thanked Patrick.

"Think nowt of it. But I've made no friends for us both in that team, and that's for sure!" he finished, laughing. "So, be off with ye, and I know Molly'll welcome ye if ye wish to go to hers again."

William walked off, clutching the pennies in his pockets to stop them jingling. He saw a pile of bags, didn't see anyone working with them, and the exhausting day caught up with him. The bags were stacked in such a way they looked like a big chair, and he decided to have a rest. He sat on a bag, leant against the pile behind it and in seconds was sound asleep.

8

LIVERPOOL

He woke to the sound of, "You! Boy! Are you listening?" The voice sounded like the viscount's wife back home, but it wasn't Irish. A lovely, soft voice. His ma sometimes sounded like that singing to him when he was much younger. It reminded William she didn't sing anymore. Worse, it reminded him of home and how much he loved and missed his ma.

He opened his eyes, blinking against the light and trying to remember where he was. He shook his head to clear his vision and saw a well-dressed lady standing in front of him and hitting him on the leg with an umbrella. He'd seen ladies in the town using them but never as a weapon. He stared at her. She was young and very pretty, wearing a dress that was more colourful than anything he had seen, with frills at her neck and wrists. There were splashes of red and green and other colours he didn't know. The dress flowed out from her waist and was so wide at the ground that he couldn't see her feet. There was rarely anything like her in the town and never in the village.

Her blonde hair was pulled into a tight bun at the back of her head, but some tendrils had fallen loose at the front, and she tried to blow them off her face. She had a faint line of perspiration on her upper lip, and her mouth was set in a straight, severe line as though she was angry.

There were two children holding onto her skirts, peeking around the side as though frightened of what William might do when he woke. She had a baby under one of her arms, held against her hip. Her pretty face was framed by tiny ears and a pert nose that were perfectly in place. The colour, the clothes, the small, rounded body and the perfect face helped William to decide she was the most beautiful lady he had ever seen.

"Well, are you listening?"

"Aye."

"I need some help. That fool of a coach driver has dumped me and the little ones here, and I need help to carry my bags to that ship." She pointed with her umbrella at a ship moored to the wharf. "Well?" she asked. "Will you help?"

William said nothing, still absorbing the sight of her, her children and for the first time, he noticed a smell coming from her. He'd never known anything to smell so nice and didn't know if it was her, or something she put on. It reminded him of the flowers in the garden in the town square back home.

"All right," the lady said. "I'll pay you. I'll pay you sixpence. How does that sound? I won't pay you any more than sixpence and don't expect that I will. It's probably too much, but I can't stand here waiting, and if I don't get aboard soon, the ship will leave without me. So, make up your mind. I don't have all day, and I'll get someone else, if you don't help."

William looked around. There was no one else. The only people he could see were the ones getting ready to board, and no one paid the lady any mind. He'd worked all day for sixpence, and he was about to get another one for a few minutes work helping the lady with her bags. "Of course, I'll help," he said, holding out his hand.

"I'll give it to you when we get on board. I know what you urchins are like. I'll give you the sixpence and off you'll go!"

William decided to trust her in spite of his recent experiences and his da's advice. She looked like a nice person, and she was definitely in need of some help. "Are these your bags?" he asked, pointing to three bags nearby.

"Yes, and you'll have to carry them all at once. I'm not leaving anything on the dock to be stolen the minute my back is turned."

William shrugged, put one bag under his arm, took a bag in either hand, and nodded to the lady.

They set off, the lady leading. She had a great deal of difficulty walking with the babe under one arm, the umbrella under the other, and the two little ones refusing to let go of her skirts. Eventually, they reached a type of bridge leading up to the ship. William put the bags down.

"What do you think you're doing?" asked the lady. "I'm paying you to help me onto the ship, not to bring the bags halfway."

"Do we walk up this thing?" asked William.

"It's a gangplank, and yes, we walk up it."

The gangplank was a rickety affair, and it didn't seem right to call it a plank as it had five or six planks laid side by side. It didn't look safe. There were gaps between the planks, and one or two of them looked loose. To William, it had already seen too much use.

It was wide enough to accommodate the lady and her children, and there was a rail to hold on one side only. Part of the ship's railing had been removed, and the gangplank was the only obvious way to get on the ship. William was nervous that it might break, or he might fall off.

The lady transferred the babe and the umbrella to the side away from the rail, got her children to hold her dress front and back on the same side and started up the incline, gripping the rail as she went.

It wasn't easy going, trying to make sure none of her little ones fell over the side, every now and then checking William followed and hadn't disappeared with her bags.

William picked up the bags again, but was glad of the short rest and started up the incline too. His heart pounded with fear. He had no free hand to hold the rail, and he would need to maintain his balance all the way up. Still, if she could do it, then so could he, but what if he fell, bags and all, over the side?

When they reached the top, he saw a man in what looked like a uniform, put out his hand and say, "Tickets!" The man was short with a belly falling out of his shirt. He'd secured a jacket at the front, with the only button William could see, above his belly. The jacket was stretched so tightly, it looked like the button wouldn't last much longer. He had a peaked cap and smiled broadly as though such a welcome would ensure the comfort of his customers. A grubby hand hovered expectantly in front of the lady.

"Has everyone in this God forsaken country taken leave of their senses? You stupid man. How do you think I can present you with our tickets when I have a babe in arms? Do you think I can put the babe down? Or, shall I give it to you?" She clumsily tried to give the man the baby while holding the umbrella under her arm.

The smile vanished from the man's face. At this point, the baby started screaming. The man shrank back and waved the lady on board. He then stopped William. The smile returned as though he was glad to be able to resume his job. "Yer ticket!"

The lady stopped and turned. "Do you think those bags are his? They're my bags, you idiot, and if you let me on, you have to let him on, too!"

People started to queue, and there were shouts of, "What's going on? Why are we stopped?"

The uniformed man decided to take the easy way out and waved William on board.

The baby still screamed as the lady, struggling with the children and the umbrella, got to a seat on the open deck and collapsed onto it. William put the bags on the deck in front of her and held out his hand.

"Yes, boy, you have earned your money, and I'll give it to you shortly. Before I do, let me ask if you'll come with us and help me again when we arrive at Liverpool?"

"Will I get another sixpence?"

"Of course," said the lady quickly.

"How long does it take? How will I get back?"

"Why, all night and you'll find someone to help on the way back, so you'll earn more money."

William stared at her, his mind a tangle of doubts and questions. *Well,* he thought, *I've worked all day... and now I have the opportunity to earn two more sixpences and the work was easy.*

"I've got a job here, and they expect me in the morning. I've never been on a ship. I don't know what to do," he said finally.

"You'll be with us. We'll stay out here. The first- and second-class passengers can go inside, but that's not us. It's all right out here provided it doesn't rain. They'll give us some food once we leave the docks. The children and I will sleep in the chairs. You can sleep on the deck."

"What's the deck?"

"You're standing on it."

There were now lots of people gathered all around, most with bags, many with children. Most people were well dressed, like the lady, but there were some poorly-dressed country people like William. He was pleased to see some of his kind, and he didn't feel so alone.

There were not enough seats, so while many people were seated, many also stood. He thought about the job he had here in Belfast where he earned sixpence for a day, compared to helping the lady where he got sixpence to carry a few bags.

As William thought on the lady's proposition, the man in the uniform called, "All aboard!" and the gangplank was pulled away.

The lady gave a triumphant smile and said, "It looks like your mind is made up for you."

They were about to move away from the dock. There was a swishing sound coming from both sides of the ship. Its horn blew loudly. It trembled, then shook as the men on board and those on the docks released its moorings. The ship moved slowly at first, taking its time to get away. There was little excitement from either the ship or the docks. The passengers looked bored, as though this was a familiar trip. William wasn't sure whether he was scared or excited. Then the bow was out into the river, and she picked up speed, leaving the docks behind, the noise from the side becoming louder, and the ship moving faster.

There were no sails, and a lot of smoke came from a large pipe above them, flowing over the back, causing distress to the animals in pens and some of the passengers in its path. The animal pens were all at the rear, and there were mostly sheep and goats, although William could see a few cattle as well.

He was surprised to feel calm, even though he was leaving Ireland. He'd never been away from Ireland and never on the water before and didn't know what to expect. He'd seen boats on the Lough Neagh and Six Mile Water but had taken only passing notice. The ship shook a lot more now, and he wondered at the cause. It picked up even more speed as it went down river. He shivered as the wind caused by the speed, freshened.

The lady noticed and speaking loudly to be heard over the noise from the sides, said, "You'll be cold. There are blankets over there, and we are allowed to use them. Be a good boy and fetch some for us."

William picked his way carefully through the crowd gathered on the deck, took two blankets from a pile and returned to the lady. She had her children sitting in chairs on either side of her, but both resting against her. The baby was asleep in her lap.

As William sat, a steward came around. "Biscuits! Tay!" he called, and people helped themselves. There was an immediate crush as though passengers were afraid there wouldn't be enough.

The lady nodded at William. "Be quick, boy. We'll all need some, or we'll go hungry and thirsty."

He got up, joined the throng and fetched mugs of tea and biscuits for them both. He saw the lady break hers in half and dip the halves in her tea before feeding them to the children. William did the same. The biscuits were about as big as his hand and as thick as his thumb - hard, dry and not sweet. It wasn't much, but he was grateful for it.

William heard the lady's little girl ask, "What kind of ship is this, Mummy?"

"Why, darling, it's the same type as the one we used last time."

"I forget. Tell me again."

"Well, it's called a paddle steamer and that's because it's got paddles on each side that turn and pull the ship along."

"How do the paddles turn?"

"There's a big engine underneath us that turns the paddles."

"I don't think this ship is as big as the last one."

"You might be right. Daddy told me this one is about two-hundred feet long, twenty-five feet wide and ten feet deep."

"The engine can't be that big, then. You said it was big."

"Why do you think the engine isn't that big?"

"You said the ship is ten feet deep. If they put the engine underneath us, then they have to fit it in ten feet. Ten feet, isn't much. Daddy is ten feet tall."

"Why do you think Daddy is ten feet tall?"

"Grandma says he thinks he is, so I think he is, too."

"Will they use the sails?" asked her little boy.

"No, darling. They only use those if the engine breaks, and it's not going to break. Daddy said this is a new ship."

They were leaving the river and entering the open sea. It was dark now, and William struggled to see anything in the direction of the land. There was nothing but blackness in the direction of the sea. The ship started to move up and down as well as roll. He didn't feel at all well and wondered if the biscuits and tea had made him sick. As he thought about it, some people moved to the rails at the side and were sick into the sea. The smell came to him on the breeze. He thought he might be sick himself.

The lady noticed and said, "Lie down, boy. Flat on the deck and the feeling should pass."

"Why?" asked William, stretching out. Others did the same and space to lie became scarce.

"It's seasickness. Not everyone is affected, but many are. Depends on how rough the sea is. I'm told that if you are out on the sea for a few days, you get used to it. My longest trip is to cross the Irish Sea, so I don't know the truth of it."

William didn't feel a lot better lying down, but in a few minutes, he was sound asleep.

He woke to daylight and the blast of a horn. He looked around in surprise, remembering where he was and was pleased to have slept through the night. It was cool, so he kept the blanket pulled around his shoulders. A beautiful blue, cloudless sky formed a cobalt canopy above him. Sunlight sparkled off the waves. Seagulls wheeled about, calling their anger and distress about the lack of something to eat, some settling on the ship and others on the waves.

The ship still bounced about, but not as much as last night. Many of the people around him were asleep. The lady and her baby were asleep, too, but her children were awake, sitting quietly, waiting for their mother. The uniformed man appeared from a room nearby.

"Liverpool!" he called out. "Make yerselves ready to get orf at Liverpool!"

The passengers started to stir. William was desperate for a piss, but had no idea where to go. He saw a man bring a bucket from a room and go to the back of the ship.

"Look out!" the man called. "Bucket man."

The people standing nearby shrank back and moved well away from the man. He threw the contents off the back of the ship, and William could see and smell what it was. Some of it blew back on the breeze and landed on the man's jacket. He brushed it away absently and brought the bucket back to the room. Once he had done so, William noticed some people forming a queue at the door.

"You can join them," said the lady. He hadn't noticed she was awake. He got up, dropped his blanket and stood in the queue. When it came to his turn, he went into the room and pulled the door shut behind him, as the others had done. There was a lamp hanging from the ceiling, so he could see, and it swung back and forth slightly as the ship moved. The no longer empty bucket was also set in something, so even though the ship was moving, the contents moved only slightly.

The room was dirty, like at Molly's, where someone's aim had been off. Standing carefully, he pissed as well as he could despite the ship's movement. He finished and left the room. The queue was bigger now, and the bucket man hovered nearby, as though expecting to be of further service shortly.

He got back to the lady. She fed the children with a biscuit she had kept. Once again, she broke it in half, but not to dip into her tea as she had none. She gave them half each, and they gnawed at their pieces like a dog with a bone. Once the children were occupied, she drew her blanket about herself and breast-fed her baby. William was surprised. He'd not ever seen anyone do that in public, although he'd seen his mother feed his brother and sisters and thought nothing of it. Not that he or anyone else could see anything, so the feeding went unnoticed by the other passengers.

The Liverpool docks were very close now, and they looked like Belfast, only everything was bigger. There was frantic activity accompanied by all the noise, to which he had become accustomed. The ship slowed, and there were men on board and on the docks, standing ready. Suddenly hitting the docks, the people on deck stumbled when the ship stopped abruptly. Men on the docks threw ropes to the men on the ship, and it was tied securely.

Two men removed a section of the rail, the gangplank was dragged up from the docks, and a few people were quick to leave.

Others queued patiently, talking loudly to each other and shouting and waving to people on the docks. It was more exciting to arrive than it was to leave.

The lady wasn't in any hurry to move and remained sitting with her children. There was now a spare seat beside her, and William took it.

"What's your name, boy?"

"Bill," replied William and liked the sound of his new name.

"Bill, you may call me Hannah. Now, I have a further proposition for you."

Hannah noticed the look on William's face and said, "Now, now. I know I owe you two sixpences. I'll give them to you soon, but I am going on to Portsmouth, and I wonder if you'd like to earn another two sixpences to go with me?"

"Are we leaving now? Where's Portsmouth? Is it back in Ireland?"

"No. It's still in England, like here, so you'll have to come back to return to Belfast. We'll go tonight and be in Portsmouth tomorrow. You can help someone to come back here, then help someone else to go to Belfast." Hannah looked thoughtful for a moment.

William thought she looked uneasy and wondered to himself if she wasn't telling him everything.

"Do you have a family, Bill? Where are your mother and father? Will they be worried about you if you take a few days to help me before you go home?"

"No," said William. "They won't be worried." *Is that why Hannah is uneasy? She's worried about my family?*

He looked at Hannah and the children. His life had been so simple before coming to Belfast. His ma and da had made all the decisions, but now he was on his own. Once again, he missed his ma. He remembered sitting on her knee once and asking why his da drank whiskey.

"That's his decision," she had said. "Life is all about making decisions, and we don't always get them right."

Hannah waited. He would need to decide. If only his ma was there to help. He'd earned some good money for easy work. After his day on the docks, he thought this was a much better job. Yet, he did worry Hannah was never going to give him his money. There always seemed to be further jobs to be done with payment only on finishing them all. Then there was the worry that if she did give it to him, and he put it in his pocket, he might lose it. The eight pennies already in his pockets were awkward enough.

"You've trusted me this far, Bill. Won't you trust me a little further?"

The uniformed man stood beside them.

"Youse gettin' orf soon?" he asked. "The animals will be taken orf shortly and youse can't be 'ere then," he said, jerking his thumb over his shoulder at the animal pens.

William looked at the pens. The animals darted about, the sheep and the goats calling to each other nervously at the sight of a dog pacing up and down outside. The smell was dreadful, since the wind now blew over the pens towards them. William wondered if anyone ever cleaned up once the animals left.

"Aye," said William, looking at the man and shrugging his shoulders. He could get off and leave Hannah to find someone else to help. The extra two sixpences sounded good, but he'd have to travel to Portsmouth to earn them. He was on his own now and had to make decisions for himself. He'd had a job in Belfast, and Patrick had said he could stay with Molly. No, he'd best get back to Belfast. He hoped it was the right decision.

"Aye," he said again, as he stood and picked up Hannah's bags. Hannah stood, putting the umbrella under one arm and the baby under the other. The two children grabbed her skirts again, and they all struggled down the gangplank.

Hannah looked at William when they reached the dock.

"He's a nice boy," whispered her son. "But mummy! He smells!"

Hannah blushed, then hesitated, as though wondering if she was foolish to ask him to come to Portsmouth. However, she shrugged and said, "Now, carry the bags to that hotel over there, and I'll give you your money at the door. Are you coming to Portsmouth with us?"

"No," said William, shaking his head. "The man asked you for a ticket when we got on the ship. You pushed him around, and he let you on. How much will it cost me to get back to Belfast on another ship?"

Hannah blushed again.

She's not told me everything, thought William.

"It's three shillings," she stammered.

"So, you're about to pay me one shilling, and it'll cost me three to get back to Belfast?" William hadn't spent much time at school, but he'd been doing odd jobs and knew how to count small sums of money.

William found his new world much more difficult than the one he had known before. Everyone was trying to take advantage of him - the driver, the man with the barrel, Martin, even Hannah. He'd been warned, but was now very annoyed, mostly at himself for being so stupid.

He must have looked it, because Hannah reached into her purse, took out two sixpences, held them out to him and said, "Well, here's your money. I got you here for free, didn't I?"

William now looked at her in astonishment. "Why would I want to come here?"

Hannah looked surprised. "Why Bill, didn't they teach you anything in school? From here, you can get to anywhere in the world! So, since you are not coming, you may leave, and I'll find someone else to help me with my bags."

"No, Hannah. You paid me to help you at this end, and help you I will." He picked up the bags and headed for the hotel, not putting them down until he reached the door.

The hotel was a modest affair, not much wider than other houses in the street. It might have once been a house and was now a hotel. The doorway wasn't very big, but there was a man standing there who said, "Ah, missus. Welcome back." He picked up the bags and disappeared inside.

Hannah stood still, her children waiting quietly. She looked like she had something she wanted to say. Moments passed. William waited.

"Thank you, Bill. Good luck," was all she said at last and went into the hotel.

William stood for a while, shrugged, then turned to walk away. He had taken only a few steps when Hannah called after him.

She stood in the doorway. "Bill, I'm sorry, very sorry."

"Why?" he asked, turning to face her.

"I suppose because you didn't want to come here. Anyway, I know you'll be hungry. If you go around the back of the hotel, they'll give you something to eat and drink." She pointed to a laneway beside the hotel.

"Go down that lane and knock on the first door you see. It's the kitchen. Also, the people here said they have some guests going to Belfast tonight, and someone might need some help with their bags. They said to come back here later today. I know it's not much, and I am sorry." She waved and went back inside.

Nodding to signal his gratitude, William headed down the lane and knocked on the first door he found. Nothing happened for a few moments. He wondered if he had the right door. Then it opened, and a stout woman filled the doorway. She wore a white scarf wrapped around her head and a white apron that covered her front completely. She looked as wide as she was tall and had a very stern look on her ample face.

"Might ye be Bill?"

"Aye. Did Hannah tell you I'd be here?"

"Aye, that she did."

She studied William for a few moments. Then she shrugged her shoulders, stood back and waved him inside. He walked past her and didn't fail to notice her wrinkle her nose. She closed the door behind him.

He'd not ever been in a hotel kitchen before. Pots and pans hung from hooks on the walls and above the stove. Two pots on the stove were both steaming. A long table with some stools stood to the left of the stove and opposite that was a series of cupboards. Between them was another door that he presumed went to the hotel. To the right, on a bench, there were piles of plates that looked like they needed washing. Apart from the stacked plates, everything was neat and tidy. It wasn't a big room. There was just enough space for either the woman or him to walk around. Light for the room came from a long window above the cupboards. There were some unlit lamps on the walls.

"Sit there!" she commanded, pointing at a stool. William sat on the stool. There was a glass of milk on the table, and he thought to drink it, but was afraid it wasn't for him. The woman went to the stove, ladled some stew into a bowl and put it on the table in front of him. She turned her back and walked away to fetch something from the cupboards.

William picked up the bowl and began to slurp its contents noisily, forgetting what he had been taught recently. The food was delicious, especially for a village lad who mostly ate potatoes. There was a loud bang! The woman brought some bread and slammed a spoon on the table in front of him.

She glowered at him. "Why're eatin' like a pig? There'll be none o' that in my kitchen! Ye pick up that there spoon, and if ye make any more noise, then I'll be chasin' ye out, and there'll be nothin' more for ye!"

Embarrassed to have forgotten how to eat properly and afraid of the threat, William tried hard to eat without noise. Again, it was difficult at first, but he got used to it. He was glad when the woman stopped staring at him and went to the pile of plates. Watching her while he ate, he saw her pump water into large tubs into which she piled the plates. He wondered if she worked alone and what it would be like cooking and cleaning for the hotel guests.

She brought the pot over and ladled some more stew into his bowl and put another piece of bread beside him. William was relieved she'd at least decided he could have more to eat. He was hungry enough for two boys.

"That there is yer milk," she said pointing at the glass. "Where're ye from, boy?"

"Belfast." He drank some of his milk, being careful to make no noise.

"Why're ye here?"

"I came with Hannah. She needed help with her bags."

The woman laughed. "That's reason enough, I suppose. How come ye speak like ye do? Ye've got an accent, but ye don't sound like ye're from Belfast."

William looked at her. He didn't know what she meant.

She returned the look for a few moments and when William didn't reply, she said, shortly, "Well, it's not as if I care!" She looked and saw he had nearly finished his meal. Her face softened and kindly she said, "Finish up, boy and be off. I've work to do."

William jumped up and headed for the door.

"'Ere, take this," said the woman as he passed by, handing him more bread. "And good luck to ye, boy, if it's goin' back to Belfast ye are and better luck if ye're off to somewhere's else! Oh, and take a bath sometime." She pushed William out the door and closed it behind him.

William stuffed the bread into his shirt and wandered back to the docks, wondering what she meant by the comment about a bath. *Why would I want to take a bath?*

There was even more activity than there had been before. The noise of the animals, the men, and the machinery was deafening. Perhaps, if she hadn't been busy, he could have stayed longer with the woman. She was friendly enough and at least took some interest in him. He liked the kitchen. It was warm and much quieter than the docks. It reminded him of home and a wave of nostalgia gripped him. He shook it off.

Looking around, he saw people dashing about or working in groups, and he might not even have been there for all the notice they took. Men were busy loading and unloading the ships with animals of many types, big and little boxes, and bags like those he had moved in Belfast. He also saw stacks of timber, bales of wool, stacks of hides, and many sizes of tubs and barrels. Some goods were moved by men carrying them, and others by slings attached to tripods where they could be hoisted on or off the ship. There were little machines with steam coming from them that were used to hoist the slings. Orders were shouted, mostly by men who looked angry. There were carts everywhere. Some moved, pulled by tired-looking horses and others were waiting, their bored-looking horses standing on three legs and swishing their tails. No one was the least concerned by all the animal dung spread about.

There were so many people, and no one to talk to. He was lonely. He would even be glad to see Hannah, in spite of the fact that she had brought him here only to serve her own needs. Still, he had one shilling and eight pence in his pocket, and while it wasn't enough to get him back to Belfast, it was more money than he had ever had at one time before. He needed to be careful someone didn't steal it but had no idea how to protect it. If only his ma was there. She'd always been in charge and managed those kinds of problems. He had to stop thinking of his ma. It only reminded him of how far he was from home.

He thought about his situation. It wasn't hopeless. He could go back to the hotel later to see if they had someone needing help to go to Belfast and even try Hannah's trick to get on the ship. Or, go to Portsmouth with Hannah when she was ready to go. Both those things were for later, so he decided to have a look around.

He stopped every now and again when he saw someone struggling with bags or goods and asked if they wanted help. Everyone chased him away with, "Och! Be off!" After a while, he decided it might be harder to get back than it was to get here.

Sitting down on a bollard, he thought about Hannah's comment, "From here, you can get to anywhere in the world!" He didn't know a lot about the rest of the world. A lot? No, he didn't know anything. During the famine, he heard many people had left Ireland for England, America, Canada and Australia. Where were those places, and how long would it take to get there? Of them all, he knew he was in England now and looking around, wondered how it was better than Ireland and why people came here. He guessed it would be by ship to get to those other places but had no idea what it would cost. So while he could get to anywhere in the world from here, it didn't look like something he would be able to do. "So, it's back to Ireland I'll be going," he muttered to himself.

9

Portsmouth

Completely lost in his own world, he neither saw nor heard a man approaching.

"Boy! Are ye deaf, boy? I've been yelling at ye from over there. Don't ye listen?"

"My da says I don't listen, but I'm listening now," said William, smiling, looking at the man. He was well dressed, much like the viscount at home. Tall hat, waistcoat and coat, a watch chain across his middle, well-fitting pants, shiny, buckled shoes and a cane. He looked out of place in the refuse, stink and clamour of the docks, but he talked like he belonged there.

The man stared at William, his belligerence blunted. "We're tryin' to load that ship with coal," he said, pointing with his cane at a ship nearby tied to the dock. "We're late. We need some help."

"Where's it going?" asked William, wondering if he wanted to help. Helping people hadn't been too successful so far.

"What's it matter to ye?" demanded the man, his belligerence returning. "I only want yer help to load some coal, not pick the ship up and take it somewhere."

"No, it doesn't matter at all," replied William, wondering why the man was so upset. "But if you don't tell me, then I won't help."

The man seemed to recover his composure, once again getting his attitude under control. "Look, boy, it's off to Dublin. There's a storm comin', and we have to get out of port before it gets here! I need all the help I can get. Will ye no help?"

"Will you pay me?"

"Of course," shouted the man in exasperation.

"And will you take me when the ship goes to Dublin?"

"I will if ye earn yer way. We can always use an extra man below, but I'll not take a man that won't work."

"I'll work, if you pay me and if you will, let's go and show me what you want."

"Och! Boy! I'm glad to be done with the talkin', with the storm comin' and all. Do ye always talk so much?" It wasn't a question that needed an answer, and they set off for the ship.

The ship was about the same size as the one he had taken from Belfast, but there were no passengers or animals on board. William guessed it was because there was some time before the ship sailed, and the men working on her were scattering coal and coal dust about.

The man jerked a thumb at the workers on the deck. "Help them," he said, turning and walking off as he spoke.

William used a ladder and climbed a short distance to the deck to see what he had to do. Baskets of coal were hoisted from a barge moored beside the ship, and men on the deck poured their contents through holes along it. It looked like hard but simple work, and he decided to at least have a go. *No harm in trying,* he thought.

One of the men called to the others, "Good. Some more 'elp."

A few of the men waved to acknowledge him, and William stood in turn to take a basket and pour its contents into the ship. Once he got a basket, he wasn't sure which of all the holes deserved the coal, so he just followed the man in front and always poured the coal into the same hole as him. It was the second time he'd been on such a ship and decided he wanted to find out more about them.

They'd been at work for several hours when a man called, "Bunkers're full! We're done!"

Most of the men left the ship, but four or five sat down on the deck, backs against the deck structure. Another man appeared with some mugs and passed them around. William was surprised there was one for him. He thought it was tea and took a tentative sip. It wasn't tea at all. It was sweet water, and it tasted wonderful.

The man sitting beside William turned to him and asked, "What's yer name?"

He was a tall, thin man who looked like he would blow away in a gentle breeze. There was a rag tied around his head, his shirt was a torn, wreck of a thing. His pants were full of holes. Thin legs that looked like they were nothing but bones, finished in a pair of worn and battered boots, with no laces or buttons. His clothes were smothered in coal dust, grease and oil and looked and smelled like they'd never been washed.

"I'm Bill. And yours?"

"I'm Isaac. They said ye're comin' to Dublin?"

"Aye. Is there a storm coming?"

"There's always a storm comin'. He never hires enough men, and it's always a rush to get ready on time." The man looked at the sky. "But he might be right this time. Sky doesn't look good." Heavy black clouds gathered, and there were flashes of lightning in the distance. Seagulls dipped, swooped and cried about the ship. "Hope we get away soon, but nothin's ready. Boiler's fired, but steam's not up."

"Tell me about the ship," asked William. "I came over from Belfast on one like this, but it was night time."

"Aye. I've the time. She's called a steamer. They're two types of ship - sail and steam. Lots of types within the types, but this un's a paddle steamer because of the wheels or paddles on the sides. You can't see 'em because they're covered by those boxes you can see half way along the ship on each side. The coal we loaded is burnt in furnaces that heat water in boilers and turn it to steam. That goes into an engine that turns the paddles and pulls the ship along. Steamers're good because they don't need the wind, and even if the storm comes along, it won't matter if we're out at sea 'cause she'll push through. This un's a good ship. I've been on her since she started. She's already been through a few storms, so another won't matter."

"Why does she have posts?"

"They're called masts, and they put sails on 'em. She can sail as well as steam. They'll only use the sails if the engine breaks down. Happens sometimes, mostly when you least expect or want it. The paddles on the side make it hard to sail. It's like tryin' to sail a box."

"What's she made of?"

"Iron."

"Are they all made of iron?"

"Most are, now. Some are still wood."

"What's your job?"

"I'm a greaser. I know I look like one. I have to make sure all the moving parts have lots of grease. Stops them seizin' when they get hot. I check on the pressure dials, too and make sure there's enough water and not too much steam so she doesn't blow up."

"They blow up? How do they do that?"

"Too much pressure in the boilers will do it, or if the boiler has a fault. My brother was killed in a boiler explosion two years ago."

"What happened?"

"Story goes a tube plate burst. They'd just docked at Woolwich. The ship had been made fast when there was an explosion in the boiler room, and fire and steam poured out. Other crew tried to get to the men workin' in there, but the heat was too great, and they were forced back. They started throwin' water down, tryin' to stop the fire. Everyone was surprised and relieved when my brother crawled out, but relief turned to horror when they saw how badly he was burned. He'd lost most of the skin from the top of his body, and he died soon after. No one else got out."

"Why didn't he get out straight away?"

"They said he'd lost his eyes in the explosion and was blunderin' around tryin' to find the ladder. He followed the water when they started throwin' it down."

"Aren't you scared it might happen to you?"

"Maybe, but a man's got to do somethin'. Besides, bein' a greaser is all I know."

William reached inside his shirt and pulled out the piece of bread. It was soggy from his sweat and dirty from the coal. He offered Isaac half, thinking Isaac would not be interested.

Isaac muttered, "Thanks" and stuffed most of it in his mouth. William decided he too, needed a scolding from the woman at the hotel.

A man in a uniform appeared in front of them. "Get a move on," he shouted. "You're not paid to sit and talk. New boy, go with Isaac. He'll show ye what to do."

"This way," said Isaac and headed for a room on the deck. He opened a door, went inside and then climbed down the ladder through a hole in the deck.

There were a few lamps below, and in spite of how dark it was outside due to the coming storm, it took William several moments to accustom his eyes to the gloom.

It was hot and noisy. William had to suppress a reaction that was 'get out, now'. He didn't know he was at the bottom of the ladder until his feet found no more rungs. When he reached the bottom, he was only aware of Isaac as a shadow beside him.

There were layers of noise. He could hear men shouting, something hissing and something roaring. When his eyes became accustomed to the darkness, he saw three men other than Isaac. The room was the width of the ship and about twice as long as it was wide. There was a large box in the middle of the room with four holes and open doors in the front, and William could see fires burning in the holes. Behind the box and towards the front of the ship was another large shape. The roof was a few feet above his head.

Isaac cupped his hands around William's ear and shouted, "Congratulations, ye just became a trimmer. There are two trimmers on this ship and ye be one of 'em. Ye take one side of the ship each. Ye'll fetch the coal from the bunkers for the lads to stoke the furnaces." He pointed at the fires.

"Come and I'll show ye about trimmin'."

He took a few steps into the darkness. William followed and found himself stumbling on the uneven floor. He glanced down to see there were lumps of coal lying about. It wasn't long before he saw the lumps had fallen from holes along the sides of the ship.

"Ye'll need to keep the deck clean, or ye'll be falling and hurtin' yerself, so make sure if the coal falls, ye clean it up right smart.

Ye can't stop these from fallin' from the bunkers, but ye can pick 'em up. Ye should have boots, but no matter. Ye'll get used to it."

It was still very hard to see. The lamps were all but useless. He heard Isaac chuckle in the dark. *"Ye'll get used to it,"* did little to reassure him.

"Yer job is to take that there shovel, fill a basket with coal and carry it to the furnaces. Ye'll see the boys there shovellin' it into them. The boys're called firemen. Drop the coal onto the deck where the boys're shovellin' from. Pick the spot careful. Too far and they'll have to reach for it, too close and they can't swing the shovel. If ye make a mess of it, they'll reverse their shovel and belt ye on the 'ed with the 'andle, so ye be right careful."

William wondered if he had made a terrible mistake. The big men with the shovels looked like they wouldn't care if it was a trimmer or coal they put in the furnace. The trip with Hannah had been much easier, and he wished he had checked for bags to carry to Belfast. He shrugged, grabbed the shovel and looked for where he might find coal to start filling a basket.

"Houl," shouted Isaac. "Not yet. They might need a wee bit before we get under way, but not much until then and if they want some, they'll ask for it. Now, your bunker is along this side of the ship. Ye can see them 'oles." He pointed to a hole about half as high as a man.

"They be every few feet along the side. They open into the bunker. Stick yer shovel in there and fetch the coal. It'll be harder to get out after a while, so move to another 'ole. If they're all empty, ye have to go into the 'oles and move some from the pile inside it, so it falls, and ye can then get at it. Ye'll get the hang of it, but have a mind if the ship is rolling. The pile can fall on ye and kill ye, so ye better take care when ye're in the 'ole. And there's no point in shoutin' fer 'elp in there, there'll be none that'll 'ear ye."

"If ye need to do a piss, just do it where ye stands. It'll find its way to the bilge and get pumped out in good time. It's not the worst of things that finds its way there. If ye need to do the other, just do it on the shovel and throw it in the furnace. The boys'll know to give ye space when ye arrive with a shovel. They know there's only one reason ye'll be doin' it. Make sure ye hold the shovel by the right end after," he said and laughed.

He motioned for William to follow, took a few steps, stood beside a barrel and picked up a mug hanging on a rope at its side. "This 'ere barrel has sweet water. Ye'll need a lot of it when we get underway, but don't be stoppin' fer a drink if the boys need coal. Ye must keep the coal up to 'em and 'ave yer water when ye 'ave the time."

Isaac motioned again for William to follow. They went to the other trimmer who sat with his back to the wall. He didn't stir when they approached. "This 'ere is Pat, 'e's sleepin'. Ye should, too. Ye'll get none when we get underway, and we steam all night, so ye'll be busy. If the storm comes, it'll be 'ard down 'ere, and ye'll want yer wits about ye."

William cupped his hands and placed them near Isaac's ear. "What if they want coal at the furnaces, now?"

"Let's check with 'em now and if they want some, fetch it, then come back and have a sleep."

They walked together over to the furnaces. Isaac pointed to the coal on the floor, and the two firemen shook their heads. William found he was getting used to the gloom, because he saw all that had just taken place. Isaac waved at them all and headed for the ladder. William went back and sat with his back to the wall beside Pat. He was asleep in seconds.

He woke to a terrible din. One of the firemen stood in front of him, banging his shovel on the deck. He guessed he was meant to be doing something and jumped to his feet. Once standing, he realised it wasn't only the fireman's shovel. There was a rhythmic pounding that was getting faster. The fireman pointed at the furnaces, and William headed back to his side of the ship, picked up the basket he had already filled with coal and carried it to the furnaces. The fireman pointed at the deck, and William tipped the contents of the basket where he thought the fireman wanted it. The fireman shook his head and pointed a little further away from the furnace. William nodded and at the same time realised the room was much hotter than it was before. The furnace doors were open, the fires visible, and the furnaces glowed redder and made a continuous whoofing sound.

He turned back to get more coal and saw Pat was now in action. Pat delivered coal to the other fireman, and William watched where he tipped the coal. He noticed the fireman shook his head for Pat too, and pointed to a spot a little further away.

The next half hour was a race between the trimmers, the firemen, and the furnace. There was never enough coal. As soon as the basket was tipped, the firemen started on it, and the pile was gone when the trimmers returned. The room became hotter and hotter, the din louder and louder and the race to feed the furnaces, faster and faster.

Isaac came back down the ladder carrying some pots.

William knew the ship had been moving. He could feel it, but now it started a different motion, just like it had after they left the river at Belfast - side to side and front to back. The deck was no longer level, and he found he had to walk closer to the walls, so he could fall into them, rather than fall over.

At first, the new motion was imperceptible, then it became violent. He started to feel seasick, but was glad he was working as it took his mind off it. He saw the firemen were struggling to stand, open the furnace door and then deliver the coal to the mouth. They often had to wait for the motion of the ship to be right before they emptied their shovels into the furnace. There was no letup in the pace, though. Shovel, carry, and tip.

Isaac was everywhere, working around the room putting grease on anything that moved, and there were plenty of such things. He also left the room from time to time, so William guessed there were other moving parts on the ship that needed his attention.

Then, William realised there was no coal near the mouth of any of the bunker holes. He dreaded the idea of crawling inside to free more coal, but knew he had no choice. Isaac had said it would happen, but he wasn't sure what he would find inside. Looking about, he hoped to see Isaac so he could confirm with him, but couldn't see him anywhere. He stuck his head through a hole and couldn't see a thing. He started to crawl inside, feeling around with his hands, all the while expecting to be buried under a mountain of coal. By feeling with his hands, he could tell the coal was jammed above him, and he was in a cave. Then someone grabbed his britches and pulled him forcefully from the hole.

Once outside, he turned, saw Pat shake his head and motion for William to follow him. Pat picked a long bar from hooks on the wall, returned to the hole and jammed it inside. There was a rush of air as the falling coal filled the entrance to the bunker.

Pat cupped his hands and yelled into William's ear, "Too soon. Ye can't go in there until the level of the coal is way lower than now." He wondered how Pat knew his help would be needed. Pat's hand was on his shoulder. He nodded his thanks, Pat nodded too, removed his hand, and they went back to work. Shovel, carry, and tip.

At one point, the firemen stood near the barrel and motioned for William to join them. One of the firemen made a motion of wiping sweat from his brow and smiled. He filled the mug and passed it to William who drank it all and thought he had never tasted anything as good. The moment of camaraderie was over. Back to work. Shovel, carry, tip, hour after hour in the darkness, noise and heat.

Finally, the ship wasn't pitching as much. When he carried his basket to the fireman, he saw Pat.

"Dublin," mouthed Pat in the darkness. They carried their baskets to their respective firemen, who both shook their heads and pointed to the barrel. They all went for a drink.

It was every bit as good every time, thought William, who had, like Pat, taken a moment for a drink at times during the voyage.

The engines slowed, and the firemen motioned for everybody to sit. The work was done, and the waiting began. William started to doze, but Pat shook him awake. There was more light in the room, and William realised the light came through the companionway above. Pat shook his head. He leaned across to William and said, "Don't ye be sleepin'. They might want more coal. Ye need to wait 'till she's docked."

William was startled that Pat's face and arms were completely black. He hadn't realised Pat was a black man. He hadn't seen one before, and had only heard about them.

It was some time before Isaac came down the ladder and motioned to them all to climb out. William had spent the whole time trying to stay awake. They followed Isaac up the ladder. It was not long after dawn and cool and grey outside. It was only a few moments before William was very cold after the heat below. He looked at the others and burst out laughing when he saw Pat wasn't a black man at all. He was black from the cold dust. William looked at his own hands and arms. All four men might have been painted with pitch.

The decks were cleared. All the passengers and animals were gone. Some men still worked with the cargo, loading it into slings. There was the customary din from the docks, but anything was quieter than what they had endured overnight, so it was a relief to be outside.

Isaac said, "I have yer money."

He counted out two shillings each for the firemen and one shilling and sixpence each for the trimmers and an extra threepence for William.

"Bill, the extra money is fer loadin' the coal. Now, youse lot, we're off to Southampton the-night, so be back before then. Don't go gettin' drunk in the town either. Bill, boss'd like to see ye. The rest of ye, go."

He pointed at the docks where the belligerent man was in heated conversation with someone. They all walked down the gangplank. Pat said, "I'll wait for ye. Off ye go. I know ye won't be long."

The belligerent man stopped talking when he saw William. "Ah! Boy! Isaac said ye did a fine job. If ye've a mind to come to Southampton, then we'd be pleased to have ye. Not many last in the job, but the money is good, so what say ye?"

William replied, "I came to Dublin to get back to Belfast. Do you have a ship going to Belfast?"

"Och! Boy! Here ye go again! Do ye think I put on ships for yer convenience? No, there's no ship of mine for Belfast, so if ye want to earn some more money, it's on this ship to Southampton, or be off and stop wasting my time!"

"Will you come back from Southampton?"

"Of course! One day there and we come back! Ye could just do this one and see what ye think. It's a good ship, and many aren't. Isaac'll tell ye if ye ask and even if ye don't!"

The belligerent man's face beamed with anticipation.

"Well, boy? I don't have all day!"

"Aye," said William. "I'll be back." He turned and joined Pat.

Pat wasn't dressed in rags like William. His clothes were dirty from the coal, but William could see his shirt and pants were in good condition. His pants were held up by a belt, and he wore heavy, laced boots. He had a peaked cap on his head that was sweat stained, but it too looked in good condition. William looked at his own rags and bare feet and was embarrassed. He looked again at his feet and saw various small wounds where he'd stepped on or bumped into pieces of coal.

They walked together.

"What's yer name?" asked Pat.

"Bill."

"Well, Bill, let's go and get cleaned up, get some grub and some sleep and by then it'll be time to come back. Have ye been to Dublin before?"

"No."

"Then, I'll show ye where to go. There's a place not far that looks after the likes of us. By the looks of what ye're wearin', ye need somethin' better. We'll get that on the way. Mind that money ye just got. There'll be plenty wantin' to take it from ye. Where're ye from?"

"Belfast."

Pat nodded, and they walked in silence for a while. They stopped outside a shop. "Ye'll get some things here. Boots might be a good idea too. I see ye 'ave sore feet from the coal."

"Will you come with me? Do you know the people? They might try to rob me."

Pat smiled. "Aye, they might, but if they did, the word'd spread, and they'd go broke. Ye'll be right, Bill. They've seen me already, so I know ye'll be all right."

William went into the store. It was narrow with a large glass window at the front. Inside were a few tables and stools and a desk at the end. There were shelves stacked with clothing, shoes and boots from floor to ceiling down both walls. A bespectacled old man, seated at the desk looked up.

"Is that Pat, outside?" he asked.

"Aye."

"Pity," said the man and shrugged. "I don't need to ask what you want. It'll be everything, is my guess. Come on boy, let's measure you." He measured William and fetched shirt, pants and boots from shelves along the walls of the store and gave them to him.

"Thanks. How much?" asked William.

"Don't you want to try them on?" asked the man, tilting his head to one side.

William blushed. "Yes. Where do I do that?"

"Where you're standing would be as good as anywhere."

William took off his old clothes and put on the new. He sat on the floor to pull on his boots, just like his da.

"You'll need this," said the man and gave him a belt. William grinned broadly. Now, he'd have one like Pat.

"Here," said the man and showed him how to fold his pants over it so the belt worked. "Feel all right?" asked the old man. "They look good. There'll be some hearts fluttering on the street, no doubt."

"Yes. How much?"

"Sixpence to a friend of Pat," said the man, holding out his hand.

William retrieved his money from the pocket of his old pants, gave him sixpence, transferred the rest to his new pocket and was about to leave the store.

"Just a minute," said the man. "You might need these."

The man wrapped the old clothes in some paper, tied the parcel with string and gave it to William who thanked the man, put the parcel under his arm and left the store. He had a smile from ear to ear. He'd never shopped before and found he liked it.

"They charged me sixpence," he said when he emerged, expecting Pat to laugh. Pat nodded. William decided sixpence was a good price.

After a few steps, William wasn't sure about the boots. They were uncomfortable and made a clumping sound as he walked. He'd borrowed his da's a few times, but these didn't feel as comfortable.

"Don't worry," said Pat. "You'll get used to 'em and them to you after a while. Eventually, your feet will soften, and you won't be able to walk without 'em."

They hadn't walked far when they entered another building.

"Ye'll need threepence," said Pat, "and they'll give us some grub, a bath, a bed, and they'll wake us in time to go back to the ship. Will this do ye, or shall we find another?"

"A bath?"

"Well, not a bath. A scrub. Like a bath. Ye might even enjoy it."

William was exhausted, but nodded his agreement. He'd prefer to sleep right now, but the idea of being clean intrigued him. They approached a man, gave him threepence each and he pointed through a door.

"We'll have a scrub first," said Pat. "Some don't bother, but I think the dust can make us sick. Makes me feel better, anyway. Ye can try it this time and decide for yerself the next. Don't let yer clothes, yer parcel, or yer money out of yer sight in 'ere."

They walked into a room with tables and benches. There was a barrel of sorts, at the far end of the room with a fire under it, and steam coming from the top. There were some men in various stages of undress, standing at the tables, washing themselves from basins lined up on the table or the floor. Their clothes were on the tables, on the benches or hanging off hooks on the walls behind them. Nakedness was nothing new to William, so he paid it no mind.

It was easy to find vacant spots as there weren't many customers. A man walked up and put basins in front of them. He went to the barrel, ladled hot water into a bucket, added some cold water from another barrel and poured some of the water into each basin. Without a word, he put some soap and towels beside the basins and walked off.

This was all new to William, so he watched Pat who smiled and said, "Looks hard the first time, eh?"

William nodded.

Pat took off his clothes, put the basin on the floor and stepped into it. He had his back to William who, shocked to see a big scar on his back, thought to ask about it and then thought better of it. Pat reached for a towel and soap and began to wash the dust away using the towel, the soap and water from the basin in which he stood. The water was dirty in seconds. He stepped out, walked the basin over to a trough near the wall and poured the contents into it. Then he walked back to his spot, signalled the man who brought the bucket of water over and said, "Last one," pouring some water into the basin.

Pat shrugged. "It's only water."

"Aye. But it's our water."

He continued washing and when he finished, he dried himself on another towel.

William did the same and was clean enough not long after Pat, who put on some clothes from a parcel he had carried under his arm and then wrapped the dirty clothes into the parcel.

Pat looked at him and smiled. "So, 'ow do ye feel now?"

William smiled too. "You're right, Pat. I'm glad we had a scrub."

"For a penny, they'll wash yer dirty clothes, and they'll be ready for ye and by your bed at the end of the day. Not too sure about those things ye were wearin'. They might refuse to wash 'em, but I suppose they'll get a penny regardless. Anyway, it's a penny if ye wants to do it." He took his parcel to the man and gave him a penny. William shrugged and did the same.

Pat motioned with his head, and William followed. They walked through a door and came into a room with tables, stools and a kitchen at the end like the one William had seen at the hotel, but this one was bigger.

They sat down at a table, and a stout lady dressed like the cook at the hotel, put bowls, spoons, bread, and mugs in front of them. William started on the bread, but Pat waited until the lady returned with a pot and ladled stew from it into both bowls. Pat pushed all his bread into the bowl and set about his meal with enough noise for ten men. The lady returned with another pot and poured tea from it into both mugs. William preferred his new way to eat and tried again to master the process of silent eating. Pat was done first, belched unapologetically and waited.

When William was done, they both got up, and William followed Pat through another door. He looked back and saw the lady staring after them as she cleared the bench. *She must get bored,* he thought.

The next room had a number of bunks along the wall. There was an incredible noise of snoring from only a few occupants. William was about to speak, and Pat put his finger to his lips. William wondered why he bothered when he thought he would have to yell to be heard. He laughed out loud at the thought, and a big man, lying on a bunk nearby, rose immediately to an elbow and bellowed, "Ach! Who's the eejit?"

Another yelled, "Ach! What's 'appenin'?"

Pat pushed a startled William onto the nearest empty bunk and whispered, "Lie there and be quiet, or we'll get our 'eds broken." Pat lay on the next bunk and was hardly prone before he started to snore. William whispered a silent prayer of thanks for Pat, and he too, went to sleep.

William was shaken awake by Pat, who stood over his bunk. "It's time," said Pat, turning and walking through the door.

William grabbed the parcel he guessed now contained his washed clothes and followed. They found their way back to the eating room. Pat turned to William and said, "They'll give us a meal for a penny, and it's worth it, but it's up to ye." William nodded. They sat, and the process of the morning was repeated.

As soon as the meal was done, they headed off for the ship. They'd hardly begun walking when Pat said, "Yer a good lad, Bill, so there's somethin' I have to tell ye. I'm gonna jump ship in Southampton and join another goin' to Australia. Ye can't be tellin' anyone this, now. If ye do, they'll not let me on the ship 'ere. There's a new regulation to be made soon that stops seamen from jumpin' ship, so I want to do it before that 'appens. They say there's easy gold to be 'ad in Australia, and I plan to get some."

Pat stopped and looked at William. "Cat got yer tongue?"

William was stunned, not at the question, but at what he had just been told. Jumping a ship? Australia? Gold?

"I don't understand," he said.

Pat looked at William like he hadn't really looked at him before. Sure, he and William worked together on the ship overnight, they spent the day together, but Pat was now studying him.

Pat started to speak and then hesitated as though he wished he had said nothing in the first place.

"What's to understand?" asked Pat. "There's a steamship leavin' Southampton soon, goin' to Australia, and I plan to sign on as crew. They need about ninety crew, so they'll take anyone that's seen the workin' part of a ship. In a few months, ye'll need a document co-signed by the captain of a ship to enable ye to be discharged, so ye can go to another ship. If the captain doesn't like ye, or likes ye too much, he won't sign the document, and ye have to stay on 'is ship until 'e's good and ready to release ye. Well, I'm not waitin'. I'm goin' to Australia, and I hope to come back rich. Anyway, don't let it concern ye. Ye'll be comin' back from Southampton, then off to Belfast, and I'll be wishin' ye good luck, as I 'ope ye'll wish for me." Pat started walking. William joined him, and they walked in silence.

They soon reached their ship. William was no longer surprised by the noise and commotion. The animals were already loaded, and the last of the passengers were being helped on board.

The belligerent man saw them and looked relieved. "Ah, there ye are. Get on board and get below. There's work to be done and little enough time to do it in."

They came on board and saw Isaac, who also looked relieved. "Ah, there ye are," he said, in mimicry of the belligerent man. "Coal's loaded, the firemen are below, and we'll be underway soon. I was worried about ye. Get ye down there, too. Time's wastin'." Then he stopped, stared at William and said, "Ye look good, Bill," and wandered off, shaking his head.

Pat and William scrambled down the now familiar ladder into the darkness, the heat and the din. They put their bundles in a corner and sat down to wait for orders to shovel.

William's mind was drowning in thoughts. He'd believed Pat was a regular crewman, but even if he wasn't, he planned to jump ship and head for Australia. How would he do that? Get off the ship, tell them he'd be back and just disappear? He wanted to ask Pat, but couldn't for fear he would betray him. The thought then occurred to him that he could go too. Pat had shown him what to do in Dublin. Perhaps he would do the same in Southampton? Did he really want to go back to Belfast? What would he do when he got there, anyway? And gold? Pat said there was gold in Australia. Perhaps, if he stayed with Pat, he could get some gold as well. But then, how did you get it? Pat said it was easy, but what did that mean? If he got some gold and went home, his ma, da and Mary would be proud, and Mary's da might even be friendly.

One of the firemen appeared and signalled for them to get started. William was surprised how easy it was to get back to work. He took his now usual side of the ship, took up his shovel and filled his basket. He was almost on automatic. The time passed very quickly, and it was no time at all before the ship slowed for Southampton.

They all sat and waited for Isaac to call them up and collect their money. They heard the warning to be back in time, gave reassurances they would be and walked off. This time, Pat didn't have to wait for William, and they left the ship together.

William was desperate to hear more of Pat's plans, but had no idea how to ask, so he walked along beside Pat in miserable silence.

For his part, Pat said nothing until they were some distance from the ship. He explained to William he was unsure of his next step. He hadn't jumped ship before but knew several men who had, and it didn't always work out well. Some spent time in gaol having been caught as deserters and lost money to their employers when they were restored to them by the authorities. No, he wasn't as sure as he might be as to his plans.

"Well, where are we going now?" asked William.

Pat stopped, looked around and confessed, "I don't know. I was just walkin'." He looked at William. "I know a place where we can wash, eat and sleep, but they know I'll do that, so that's where they'll be lookin' fer me when I don't get back. I have to find out about the ship to Australia, so I best do that first, then decide what to do next. I'll show ye where ye can go, if ye like."

"I've been thinking," said William. "I'd like to know more about what happens when you jump our ship. Will there be trouble for you?"

"Aye. Trouble enough, but only if they catch me. I aim not to get caught. I'll use another name. Got to think of one." His voice sounded nowhere near as confident as it had when they first started talking.

"And the ship to Australia? Where does that go from? How will you join it?"

"I have to find out about that. Fella told me it was due to leave soon. I can't join it until it's ready to go, or I'll be found and have to go back to our ship where it won't go easy for me."

"Will you have to jump from this ship, once you get to Australia?"

"I suppose so. Why are ye askin' these questions? What're ye thinkin?"

"Pat, I'd like to go too. I know I'm not as old as you, but I did all right on the ship, didn't I? And you said they'd take anybody who knew the working parts of a ship?"

"Bill," said Pat and stopped, as though he'd started speaking without yet knowing what he was going to say. "It's like this," and stopped again as though he realised he didn't know at all what it was like.

William waited, expecting rejection, getting ready to head back to his ship and wait for it to return to Dublin. There was a chance of change and adventure, but now it was gone. He was crushed and no longer wanted to wash, eat and sleep. He just wanted to go back to his ship.

Pat found his voice and his words. "It's a much bigger ship, for a start. It's got sails as well as coal. They'll be used, and ye know nothin' about sails. The seas can get huge. I've heard stories of ships settin' off, bein' caught in big storms and never bein' heard of again. They'll have trouble findin' crew, so there won't be enough, and everyone will have to do the work of two men. There'll be big, rough, bad men in the crew who'll make fun of the likes of ye. The ship ye've just been on will be a lark compared to this. No, Bill, wait until ye get more experience."

"But you said there'll be a paper soon, and it'll be harder to get off one ship and onto another? If everything's so bad, why're you going? Are you stopping me going because there isn't enough gold? Can't we all have some?"

"Ye're right about the paper. But I'm not stoppin' ye goin', ye can do what ye like. No, I'm just sayin' this won't be easy, and I'm tryin' to help. If ye want to learn about ships, stay where ye are. And no, I don't know how much gold there is, and it's not in my mind there may not be enough. I only know what I've been told."

William stood and stared at Pat. This had gone the way he'd expected, not the way he hoped, and he was disappointed. He couldn't help showing it.

Pat looked like he wished he had said nothing. "Don't worry, lad. Ye'll be all right. So, ye'd best be off, unless ye want me to show ye where to get some grub?"

William shook his head and walked off. He'd only gone a few paces when he turned and said, "I'm sorry I can't come with you, but thanks for your help, Pat. You've shown me a lot. Good luck and I hope you find your gold." He smiled, waved and set off, looking back briefly to see Pat watching him leave.

"Well, at least ye won't be on the *Lady Grace*. It'll be bad enough if I get on it," Pat called, watching William walk slowly back to the ship. William heard him, but didn't respond.

10

SIGNING ONTO THE STEAMSHIP

A cry of, "Hot soup! Hot soup! Ye'll get some bread, too! Be quick before it's gone!" made William stop and look. There was an old woman nearby with a cart. The refuse of the dock blew around it, and he wasn't sure if the cart was a permanent fixture, or if she wheeled it into place when she came. It was a rickety affair, with handles to pull it, big wheels with spokes, and food stacked on shelves under a battered canvas cover.

The woman noticed William looking and called, "Eels! Cakes! Tarts! Ye want it, I've got it! C'mon lad, spend a penny!"

William walked over. The woman looked sly. He didn't trust her. His da had said to trust no one, and he was sure his da meant people like this woman. She was dressed in shabby, dirty, brown clothes and a woollen shawl wrapped around her shoulders.

A large, dirty, once-white bonnet covered her head. He could only see her face when she looked at him.

"What's in the soup?"

"Meat and potatoes."

"What kind of meat?"

"Are ye hungry?"

"Yes."

"Then, what do ye care?"

"How much then?"

"A penny. Soup and bread, a penny."

"I've only got a penny left, so I can only give you half."

"All right," the woman grumbled. She gave him a lump of bread and a bowl of soup from a pot that had a large candle burning under it. William gave her a penny. She put it in her pocket and ignored him. This was a new world to William. In his old one, you struck a deal and that was the end of it.

"Ah! There's a policeman," said William, pointing. The woman didn't even look and hastily gave him a halfpenny. William finished his soup and bread. Whatever the meat, it tasted good. He put the bowl on the cart and walked off. The woman didn't even look at him.

William smiled and thought, *At least an old lady on the street didn't get the better of me. Unless the meat was rat.* He looked back. She looked at him and smiled, as though reading his thoughts.

There was no need to go back to the ship, not yet. They'd probably put him to work loading cargo or coal, and he'd had enough for the moment. It might have been better if Pat had showed him where to wash, eat and sleep. He realised he was dirty, although that wasn't unusual, as lots of people on the docks were dirty, but he was tired and did need to sleep. Maybe he could find the place Pat was going to show him. He liked being clean now he had found it, and like Pat said, he did enjoy the scrub and felt better for it.

There was a big commotion some distance down the docks, and it got his attention. There was a huge ship, and it struck William more than passing strange he hadn't noticed it before. A large crowd waved and shouted. A group of men tried to manage goods into slings and lift them onto the ship. William looked up in awe. The ship he just came from might have been big in Dublin, but it was a dwarf in Southampton. He didn't know much about ships, but it looked like it could use both sail and steam. It had a huge funnel and three tall masts.

A voice beside him said, "A splendid vessel. It's the one I've been talking about. I'm glad we came. A wonderful investment. Built by Mare of Blackwall. She arrived yesterday from the Thames. No expense has been spared, and passengers will be offered a comfortable and affordable voyage. I wish I could be on her, but too much to do here, I'm afraid."

William turned and saw the source of the voice was a very well-dressed and portly gentleman, not unlike the viscount back home. The gentleman was talking to a lady who was every bit as pretty as Hannah. They were both dressed well. He in a tall hat, coat and waistcoat, watch chain, tight pants and long, black boots. He had a sizeable belly nestled comfortably under his clothes.

She wore a long black dress which billowed out to the ground, pulled tight around a slim waist. The dress had beautiful white trim on all its edges that shaped and moulded her lily-white complexion and contrasted with her jet-black hair. Like Hannah's, this was pulled into a bun at the back of her head. She wore a small black hat with netting that fell around her face.

"But I would miss you, darling," she said. "You promised you would stay with me for a while. Isn't it enough I agreed to come and see it with you?" She smiled shyly, but William suspected with purpose. "Sometimes I think you are more in love with your silly ships than you are with me." Looking disappointed when there was no answer, she said, "Where is it going? It looks big enough to go to the moon!"

"Yes, it is big, isn't it? It's over three hundred feet long and fifty wide. And the masts? Why, they're over one hundred feet tall." Then the man laughed and said, "And, where's she going? Why, Australia, of course. It's booming with the gold rush. People pay well to get there, and a ship like this reduces their prospect of being lost in bad weather in the Southern Ocean, as so often happens. Mark my words my dear, a man would be a fool not to seek his fortune in Australia, and this vessel is his best way to do so. Of course, I don't really care if they use this one. Any one of our four will do."

He looked at her as though he doubted that she understood a word he said. He laughed again and took her arm. "Come, my dear, at least we should pay our respects to the captain." They started to walk away.

William called, "My lord," only guessing the same would apply to this gentleman as applied to the viscount, since they looked the same.

"Yes?" said the portly man, looking for the source of the voice. He saw William and smiled. "Street urchin," he said loudly to his lady. "Only after money." He turned away.

"Does she need crew?" William called to his back.

"What would you know about steamships?"

"I'm a trimmer."

"Then you might be needed. Come with me, but stay your distance. It looks like you've been trimming only recently." He looked at his wife, as though hoping she would appreciate his wit.

She was silent, her face showing nothing.

"Wasted," William heard him say, and then noticed him smile when William smiled. The portly man chatted to his wife as they walked to the company's offices. William could hear it all.

"A sense of humour will be an advantage for a trimmer, no doubt." He glanced at William, following a few steps behind. "Looks strong enough, but he'll need to be." He told her he had not ever worked, much less been below decks on a steamer, but he'd heard it wasn't easy.

William glanced at the man's wife who stepped carefully to avoid refuse of every type that littered the dock. Most of it was animal dung, but there were many other things that had probably come from broken produce containers - fruit and vegetables of all types, flax, cotton, and rice. Every now and again a large rat would ignore danger and scurry out of cover to retrieve something that had taken its fancy. The man's wife either didn't notice them or chose not to. There were different smells too. Rotting garbage, the sea, unwashed bodies and sometimes, the smell of different types of produce he couldn't identify.

"Perhaps it's unfair," he heard the man say to his wife. "Men such as myself profit well, while folk like the lad take the risk and face the danger."

"I wouldn't worry about such things, dear," she said. "I'm sure they're paid well enough for the work they do. We don't even need to discuss them. I have never given it a moment's thought. I'm sure it's just the natural order."

They arrived at the company's offices. There was a sizeable, but well-behaved group of men gathered outside. Some removed their caps or hats when they saw the portly man approach. Many had taken some care with their appearance, but in most cases, they had very little with which to work. They were all similarly dressed in cast offs and rags with their pants held up by cord or rope.

William wasn't surprised the portly man paid them no mind, not even acknowledging them as they parted to enable his group to enter the door. His wife adopted an air of complete disdain, stepping just as carefully through the group at the door, as she had through the refuse on the dock.

They went into a room that was spacious and big enough to hold the people and furniture in there. Inside there were three men in a queue at a table, the first of whom talked to a man seated behind it. Paper in piles covered most of the table. The room also had a lantern burning brightly, and there were several others around the walls. William thought the room uncommonly well lit.

"Is the captain inside?" the portly man asked. The seated man nodded. The portly man continued to walk, squeezing past the table, followed by his wife and William, heading towards a door at the back. They had taken only a few paces, when the portly man stopped, turned and spoke to the man at the table.

"Take care of the lad. He's a trimmer."

He looked at William and smiled. "And a good one, by all reports, so take care of him as soon as you finish with this one." He pointed to the man standing at the front of the queue.

William gave a brief smile and a nod of gratitude to the portly man and when he looked back, he saw the men standing in the queue staring at him with hostility. He looked away quickly and saw the portly man nod in reply, turn and leave, followed closely by his wife who appeared to be glad to leave them all behind.

William stood to one side, waiting for the man to finish. He watched the scene before him. The man seated at the table was hatless, and wore a long-sleeved striped shirt with bands around the sleeves near the shoulders. He had short, grey hair and sharp features as though his face had been chiselled from wood.

The first man in the queue appeared very uncomfortable, holding a cap in both his hands, wringing it nervously. He was tall and badly dressed and had to lean at the waist to be heard by the seated man who looked bored.

"How long have you been a sailor?"

"Three years, sir," was the stammered reply.

"Vessels?"

"Mostly barques, sir."

"Hmm. Any time on a steamer?"

"No, sir."

"No matter. She'll use sails as much as steam, so there'll be plenty for you to do. You'll learn about the steam soon enough. Sign here."

He pushed a piece of paper in front of the man and gave him a pencil. The man signed and stepped back.

"Take this, go to the ship and give it to the officer at the gangplank. He'll let you on board and tell you what to do next. Ship sails tomorrow, but there's plenty to do, so best you get on now."

"Thank you, sir. Yes, sir. Thank you, sir. But I don't want to get on board, yet. I have a wife and children, so I have to tell them I'll be gone for a while."

"All right, but be there dawn tomorrow. And don't lose that piece of paper. There's no job if you do." He waved the man away.

The nervous man nodded, turned and left. The next man in the queue stepped eagerly forward and the next man outside the door came in, squeezing past the nervous man as he left.

"Hold on, you two. You heard the man. He's next," said the man at the table, jerking his thumb at William.

The first man in line glared at William. He stepped back to allow William space to stand at the table and stepped on the toes of the man behind him who wasn't wearing shoes. The man's face turned red, but he didn't utter a word.

The man seated at the table ignored them and almost shouted at William, "Name?"

"Bill."

"Bill? Is that it? Just Bill?"

"Bill Smith," said William, remembering Pat said he would change his name.

"All right, Bill. How long have you been a trimmer?"

William flushed and whispered, "Two days."

The man sat back, no longer looking bored, smiled and said loudly, "Speak up, Bill, I can't hear you. Tell me again. How long have you been a trimmer?"

"Two days," said William, loud enough for those in the room to hear.

The three men in the queue and the man at the table all laughed heartily.

"Two days is long enough to be a good trimmer, is it, Bill? They say you're a good trimmer. Are you a good trimmer, Bill?" said the man through his laughter.

William had no idea what to say. Isaac and Pat said he did a good job. How hard was it to shovel coal into a basket? Shovel, carry and tip. Two hours would be enough, he thought, trying to work out what to say, his face red with humiliation. Pat had said they would make fun of him.

"Have you ever been one?" he asked the man.

"Been what?"

"A trimmer."

The man went quiet. The others behind William didn't notice and continued laughing.

"Shut up, all of you! Shut up, I say!" yelled the man at the table, glaring fiercely at the others.

The men inside stopped laughing immediately, but those outside spread the amusing tale and continued to chatter and laugh.

The man behind the table pointed to the last man in the inside line and shouted, "Shut the door. Yes, you, shut the door. We don't need to hear from those idiots outside." Then he pointed at the three inside. "Come to think of it, I don't need to hear from you idiots either. You lot get out and close the door behind you, like I told you. Wait outside. I'll tell you when to come inside again." He stood up and looked at William. "Stay here," he said, turned and walked through the door behind him, opening and closing it as he went.

William didn't know what to think. Was the man going for the police? Should he run? The men gathered outside pressed against the window, trying to see inside.

The door at the back opened, and the man came back, followed by the portly man. "So, what's going on?" asked the portly man. He jerked his thumb at the table man. "He says you aren't a trimmer. You told me you are. What's the truth?"

The table man looked uncomfortable. "I didn't say he wasn't a trimmer. I said he's only been a trimmer for two days."

"That true? Two days?"

"Yes, my lord," said William.

"What's wrong with two days?" the portly man asked. "How long does it take to become a trimmer? Have you been a trimmer?"

The table man went red and replied, "No, my lord."

"No what. You don't know how long it takes, or you haven't been a trimmer?"

The man went even redder and replied, "I don't know how long it takes, and I've never been a trimmer."

"Then, give him the job and stop wasting my time."

The portly man nodded at William, glared at the other man and left the room.

"All right, Bill, you're a trimmer on the *Lady Grace*. I don't care either way. I suppose I had some fun, but you be warned. Those outside won't like it you've got a job. Some of those that have more experience than you will resent you getting the job, and their friends will go out of their way to make your life on board as rough as they can. Do you want to change your mind? You can if you want. Just turn and walk out." He jerked his thumb at the men outside. "They're still laughing but won't be when you turn up on the ship. So, what's it to be?"

William hesitated. What could the men do to make it rough on the ship? He had no idea. He'd been teased in the brief time he was at school, but not so much since. The men laughing at him was humiliating, but he'd been humiliated before, and there was no lasting hurt from it. Then he thought of the gold. Pat said there was plenty, so he could at least go and get some gold.

"I'll go on the ship."

The man shook his head. "It's your funeral."

He pulled a piece of paper from a pile.

"Name?"

"Bill Smith."

"Where do you live, Bill?"

"Belfast."

"All right, Bill, sign here," the man said, gave William a pencil and pointed at a spot on the paper.

William flushed again. "I can't write."

The man looked surprised. "You sound like you might be able to. No matter, I'll write your name, and you put your mark beside it." The man signed the name William had given him and gave the pencil to William.

The humiliation continued. "What's a mark?" asked William.

The man sat back, looked at William and said, "I've no idea how you got two days experience at trimming if you don't know how to make a mark, but his lordship said to give you a job, and it's a job you've got. I hope for your sake you do know how to trim, or it will be worse than rough on the ship. I'll make the mark for you. Watch me, and you'll know how to do it the next time." He put a small 'x' beside William's name and wrote, "His Mark" beside it.

"You heard me tell the other fella. Take this and give it to the officer at the gangplank. That's the way you board a ship, if you don't know. You can go there now, unless you have a wife and children to see first," he added sarcastically. "And don't go jumping ship when you get there. Don't even think about it."

William took the paper. "Thank you," he said, turned and set off towards the door.

"Wait," said the man, walking out from behind the table. He put out his hand. William took it, and they shook hands.

"Good luck, Bill. You'll need it. You've got guts, and you'll need them too. I'd tell you how much you will be paid, but I don't think it matters. I think you'll go anyway. Leave the door open as you leave. Those outside will be keen to get on with it."

William had his hand on the door knob when the man called, "Push through them. They'll resent what happened, but ignore them. Just get yourself to the ship. And Bill?"

William looked back.

"Don't let them push you around on the ship. If you let them push you around, you may not make it to Australia. There are lots of dangers and lots of accidents. I don't want to read about you in the paper."

William opened the door and stepped out. He had to push through the men gathered at the door. On the way in, they had all stepped aside for the portly man, but no one moved for William.

There was some muttering from the men. "'Ow come 'e got a job? Who's 'e anyway?"

William ignored them, pressed his parcel firmly under his arm, shoved the piece of paper into his pocket and pushed until he was through. By that time, everyone had lost interest in him and were more focussed on ensuring their place in the queue.

He spotted the gangplank and headed for it.

11

Planning the Crew

The men pushed into the room and formed a queue at the table. The table man stood up. "I'll be back shortly," and raised his hand to stop the man at the front of the queue, then turned and went through the door behind him. The captain and the portly man were talking, but stopped as soon as he entered. He closed the door behind himself.

"How's my crew going?" asked the captain. He was about forty years old, well dressed with a white shirt and starched collar and tie. He had close-cut, sandy hair and a full moustache. His jacket hung off the back of his chair, and his cap was on the table. He had sharp, blue, steady eyes that bored into something rather than looking at it. His face was slightly round and while it didn't look mean, it certainly didn't look friendly.

"I thought I'd check with you," replied the man and handed the captain a sheet of paper. The captain pulled several other sheets of paper from piles on the desk and did some calculations. The other two men waited patiently.

"Not there yet," said the captain. "I make eighty-five."

"What's the monthly wage bill for ninety?" asked the portly man.

"Including me, about three hundred and forty pounds."

"Can you make the ship work with ninety?" asked the portly man of the captain. "Do you need more?"

"Ideally, I need about one hundred and twenty."

"But there's only one hundred and twenty passengers. You don't need a crewman for every passenger!"

"No, sir, but I need one hundred and twenty crew for one auxiliary steamship."

"Do you need more?" asked the table man after several moments of silence.

"We can't afford more," exclaimed the portly man. "We spent so much on the ship and getting it here. I thought we'd have more passengers."

The captain looked intently at the portly man and said, "There's a lot of competition. There are ships going from Liverpool and Plymouth, as well as from here. But I understand the problem. Maybe, if you get a few more stewards, so the passengers don't complain. You need them to say they had a good voyage, or the word will get around, and people will go to other ships."

Once again, there was a few moments of silence.

The captain continued. "Some of the men will jump ship in Melbourne. They're only signing on to get there. If I hold their wages for a day or so when we get to port, they'll jump ship and leave without their money. That'll save you some."

"But, how will you get back? If men are jumping ship, there won't be lines of men wanting to crew on the way home."

"There's a few now. The diggings are proving a waste of time for many gold seekers. They're down on their luck, so some of them are drifting back to the docks and looking to come home. We might also be able to get some from the prisons, where they are held for a day or so if they're caught as deserters, and the ship has already gone. Anyway, that's my problem, and you pay me to solve them. If you can get five more stewards, I'll make a go of it. I've done more with less before."

"What about the provisions? Have they all been paid for?" asked the portly man.

"No idea. You'll have to check with the purser. He'll be on the ship arranging passengers and stowage. Do you want him?"

"No. Leave him be. It doesn't matter, it'll have to be paid for anyway." He hesitated, then looked at the table man waiting patiently. "Get another five stewards and that will do. I have no idea why we pay these people so much. Most of them are lazy, worthless, good-for-nothings." He paused. "Did you hire my trimmer?"

"Yes, but he might have a hard time of it, especially now I'm only after stewards."

"Off you go then and finish the task. I'll warrant it'll not take you long, as the next five men are sure to be stewards."

The man smiled briefly and left.

The portly man noticed his wife fidgeting and looking restless. "All right, my dear," he said. "Only a few minutes more. Captain, will there be any danger if the ship's crew is light on numbers?"

The captain shook his head. "No, not necessarily. Everyone will have to work harder and being tired, they may make mistakes. Usually, if they're worked harder, they want more money, but they won't find out until we get to port that they're not getting it. Again, that's my problem. Then, she's a new ship, and things don't always go right with a new ship. If lots of things go wrong, then there certainly won't be enough crew."

There was silence for a few moments and the captain continued. "Lastly, if she's not running under steam, I'll have to take some of the boys from the engine room and use them on deck. They won't like that, nor will the sailors, who think the black gang don't know a thing about sailing." He shook his head. "And, mostly they're right."

More silence. The portly man was looking expectant as if he wasn't sure if the captain had finished.

His wife said, "Are you finished now, dear? Can we leave?"

The captain looked up. "They're all my problems, sir. You pay me to get your passengers, cargo and ship to Australia, and get them there I will. Your crew may not want to sail with me again, but that's happened to me before, and no doubt, it will again. So, you take your good wife and go home knowing that with God's help, your investment is secure."

He stood up and shook the portly man's hand then bowed to his wife, took her hand in his and kissed the back of it. "You are a most handsome and patient woman, and your husband a lucky man." She blushed and smiled shyly. He turned and opened the door for them to leave, bowing again as they passed through.

He closed the door after they left, returned to his chair and sat heavily. "I suppose if it was easy, anyone could do it, and I wouldn't have a job," he muttered.

He pulled a blank sheet of paper from a pile and started to prepare the watches. It took some time to produce the document. He looked at it without smiling and shook his head. "Best I can do."

He stood up, pulled on his cap and coat, put the paper in his bag and left the room. There was no one in the front room. The business of hiring was done. He headed towards his ship.

12

Joining the Steamship

William stopped some way short of the gangplank to look at the ship. There was the usual din associated with the departure of a steamer. Animals and humans alike protesting about their treatment.

There was a knot of people gathered at the gangplank, and one man in a uniform trying manfully to deal with all their issues. Anyone seeking assistance no doubt thought their problems and issues of greater priority and more deserving of immediate treatment. There was an incessant hiss from donkey engines loading cargo, the clatter of goods of all types as they were gathered or dropped, and the shouts of men attempting to expedite their tasks. William marvelled at the industry of man and was awed he had just signed on to be part of it.

He sensed someone standing near. He turned to see a man standing beside him also watching the activity around the ship. He looked like an all right type, maybe forty years old, thick-set but wiry. The man put out his hand. Slightly wary, William took it and received a firm shake.

"Eddie Ward," the man said. "He said to find you and go aboard with you, if I can."

"Bill Smith. Who said that?"

"Why the man that's done the hirin'. Said he didn't like what he did. Said he shouldn'a made fun of you. Anyway, I said I'd find you if I could. I know you're a trimmer, 'cause I heard you say it. Not much experience, you said. Well, I just signed on as a steward, and I've never been a steward. I'm a seaman, so I know how to set a sail, but that's about all. Haven't spent much time on these, but there's more of 'em around now, so I've got to try. Like you, I've done a bit of trimmin'. I was hopin' to sign on as a seaman. I've got a family to look after, so a man's got to earn what he can and how he can. So, now I'm a steward."

They stood looking at the *Lady Grace*. William didn't know what to say, so he said nothing.

"She's barque rigged," said Eddie. "See the three masts? The one at the front is a foremast, the next is the mainmast and the last is a mizzenmast. The ship is set up so it can use either sail or steam."

"The other ships I was on used steam."

"Sure, but sail is best at sea if the wind is right, and the captain will be hopin' for that. Wind is free, and he'll have only so much coal. She's supposed to get to Australia without stoppin', so he'll only use his coal when he has to."

"Do the men work with sails and steam? I only know about steam."

"Don't worry. They have seamen for the sails and others for the steam. I don't know how many seamen he has, but I'll bet they'll earn their money. Last one of these I was on, sails were up and down like a fiddler's elbow. Didn't matter what went up or down, the captain was never happy."

They stood watching for a little longer.

"You ready to go aboard?" asked Eddie.

"Tell me some more about the ship."

"Sure, but might be easier if you ask questions."

"I don't see any paddles."

"She's a screw steamer. Propeller out the back. Have you been on a paddle steamer?"

"Aye."

"She's not much different inside, they tell me. I'm a sailor, mostly. Did my trimmin' like you, on a paddle steamer."

"What's she made of?"

"Why, iron. They make most of 'em out of iron now."

"How come it doesn't sink?"

"Ye'll have to ask someone smarter than me. It won't though. At least, I hope it won't. I suppose it would have sunk by now if it was going to."

"How long will it take to get to Australia?"

"About seventy days. Depends on the ship, supplies and the weather. Ship breaks, sometimes you can fix it at sea, sometimes you have to pull into a port on the way. Same if you run out of supplies, like food, water or coal, you have to pull into a port. If the weather is bad, it can delay the ship or drive it off course, and again, you can run out of supplies. I've heard of ships taking over a hundred days."

"I've sailed only between England and Ireland, and we worked all the time. Do we work all the time on this ship?"

Eddie laughed.

"Not laughing at you, Bill. It's a good question. I'll bet they'd like to work you all the time. They have two watches or shifts, they sometimes call 'em. They're called port and starboard. Don't be confused with the port side of the ship which is the left, and the starboard side is the right. Each watch works four hours on, eight hours off. So, the number of sails, furnaces and passengers tells you how many men you need. I hear they have women crew on some ships, but I don't think there are any on this'n. Pity."

"If it's not left and right, why are the watches called port and starboard?"

"Dunno. They just are."

"Where do we sleep?"

"Everyone has a place to sleep. The passengers have the best of it. Well, maybe first and second class, but not so the steerage passengers, although I don't think there are any of those on this'n. Then the officers do all right, but us, the workin' crew, we'll share bunks. It'll be pretty bad by the end of the trip. You'll see soon enough. C'mon, Bill, time to see your home for the next few months. Let's go aboard and find out what God has in mind for us."

"Why God?"

"Why not?"

The officer was still dealing with some people, so they waited for a break, then approached him. As they did, the officer looked past them and said, "Good evening, Captain."

William and Eddie looked behind them and saw a uniformed man of about forty, walking briskly towards them. The captain ignored them and nodded to the officer.

"Good evening, Mr Patterson. I trust things are going well?"

The officer waved some papers and said, "Nearly all the passengers and their luggage are aboard, Captain. Mr Price is checking on the cargo, and I understand it's nearly all on board."

"Good, Mr Patterson, but be sure of it. We sail with the tide on the morrow. There'll be no passengers or cargo coming on board after today and no exceptions. Please tell the chief I want to see the officers, the surgeon, the bosun, the chief steward and the chief engineer in my rooms at 6 o'clock this evening."

The captain put one foot on the gangplank, hesitated, turned back and said, "And, Mr Patterson, no one to be late." He turned again and without waiting for a reply, started up the gangplank.

The officer called out, "Yes, sir" to the captain's back, watched him for a few moments, then turned to Eddie and Bill.

"Crew?" he asked. They both nodded.

"Papers?" They handed over the slips they had been given.

He checked the papers and handed them back. "Top of the gangplank, go amidships. You'll be told there where you'll be quartered." He turned to deal with some more people that had arrived.

Eddie and William headed up the gangplank. William was glad Eddie was with him. He had no idea where to find amidships. They arrived at the top of the gangplank. Three or four men stood talking, but no one took any notice of them. William didn't know if they were passengers or crew. The deck was big, bigger than any William had seen before. He wanted to stop and take it all in, but Eddie headed for the middle of the ship, and William didn't want to lose him. He hurried after him.

As they walked, William continued to take in the sheer size of everything. The coastal steamers were nothing compared to this ship. Not only did it have huge masts, there was a much, much bigger funnel. He couldn't imagine the fires that would need such a big funnel.

There wasn't much activity on the deck. There were some people down the back waving to people on the wharf. In addition to the men at the top of the gangplank, there were some more lounging about, some were even smoking.

Eddie stopped at a structure, like a little cabin, just forward of the funnel. Another officer said, "Papers," as though that's all he ever got to say and was bored with it. He took Eddie's paper first, checked it and jerked his thumb to the front of the ship. "Stewards for'ard," and handed the paper back.

William held out his paper and Eddie waited. The officer shrugged, took William's paper, jerked his thumb at the little cabin and said, "Trimmers here," then handed the paper back.

Eddie started to walk off, turned back, took William's hand, shook it and said, "Like the man said, be careful," then he smiled and walked to the front of the ship.

William nodded, turned and looked into the cabin. There were four doors, two on either side, all open. "Why are there four doors?" he asked the officer.

"Why, you use them to stop the weather getting into the ship. In bad weather, you close the outer doors before you open the inner ones."

All he could see inside was a ladder and a hole in the deck. He shrugged. A bigger cabin was a new feature, but the hole wasn't, so he presumed like the other ships, he'd climb down the ladder and get to work.

He stopped at the top, before climbing down. He could still change his mind. The officer behind him now ignored him, so he could simply head back to the gangplank, walk down and go back to the other ship. Without Eddie, his confidence was draining away. Was he ready to go down the ladder?

Certainly, it would be better if Eddie was with him because Eddie knew something about ships and would be able to help him. Luck had been on his side in finding people that helped, but if he knew anything, he knew such luck rarely continued. How long ago was it he planned to run away with Mary? He might not have been grown up then, but if he went down the ladder, he had no other choice than to be grown up.

"Scared?" asked the officer, breaking his thoughts.

"Aye, but who wouldn't be?" He smiled at the officer who smiled back. Then, he put his foot on the top rung of the ladder and started down, leaving his boyhood and family behind.

It was hard to climb down with his parcel under his arm, so he took his time. His eyes were almost accustomed to the dark as he stepped off the ladder at the bottom. He turned and saw he was in a kitchen. There were two men in there, arguing about where to store pots, pans and foodstuffs, piled on the floor.

"Are ye an eejit? No one would put that there."

"I'm not the eejit. Ye're the eejit."

There were already some pots and pans along the walls, a big table to his left and a big stove at his right. He could feel the heat from where he stood, so it was burning, but nothing was cooking. Perhaps the men would start cooking once the arguments were settled, or maybe their job was to store everything, and the cooks were elsewhere.

A number of oil lamps hung from the ceiling, but only two were lit. There was some light from a skylight also in the ceiling, but that would soon be gone with nightfall.

After a few moments, when neither of the men took any notice of him, he had to decide where to go next. Turning, he saw light and heard talking and laughter coming from a doorway beside the ladder. A few steps were all that was required for him to get to the doorway and to look inside.

The room was jammed with bunks and men. He stuck his head through the doorway, and he was stunned by the smell of unwashed bodies. Now he'd had a bath, he knew how good a clean body could smell. *Or, how bad an unwashed one can smell.*

There was a long, narrow table immediately in front of him that went from the doorway to the far wall, and he had to step around it to get into the room. Once inside, he noticed the table was in fact three tables with a small space between each one. This enabled the men to reach the bunks on the other side, without walking the length of the table.

The wooden bunks were flat, and extended in rows running from the doorway to the far wall, with three levels from floor to ceiling. They didn't quite reach the wall to his left and right, providing a narrow passageway to access them. They were jammed so tightly, there was barely enough space to walk between them or even to use one. The ceiling wasn't more than a foot or two above his head.

The oil lamps in this room were along the walls, between the rows of bunks, and again, there was a skylight. Neither the skylight nor the lamps provided much light, so it was hard to see anything beyond the tables. There were some men seated on benches, playing cards. They were mostly quiet, only murmuring about their cards or their bets. Other unseen men were talking loudly, telling stories or cursing others for wrongdoing.

Voices merged and overlapped, and he could understand only the odd phrase or word. The sounds bounced back and forth off the walls making it impossible to identify a source. The words about a sick friend, a stolen kiss, an unfaithful wife or a robbery could have come from the tall, thin man at the table or the short, fat man standing at a bunk, or the men he couldn't see. He decided it didn't matter.

The bunks and the darkness meant he couldn't tell how many men were in the room, but he'd never seen or heard anything like it. So many smelly, noisy, scruffy people jammed in such a small space.

Squinting in the gloom, the room reminded him of a village with all types of people - old, young, rich, poor, but here they were, all crushed together. He was wrong about rich. There was no one rich in this room. Hard, cold-hearted, life-worn, miserable men, forgotten to their families and scrounging a living. He'd seen them and worked with them on the docks. His heart sank. It might be possible to escape a village, but there'd be no escaping this. If this was to be his home for the voyage, then the voyage would be a nightmare. It was too late to back out now, but he'd give anything to be standing at the top of the ladder again.

No one looked to be in charge, nor did anyone take any notice of him. William was uncertain what to do, so he stood inside the doorway and waited, nervous and apprehensive, the comfort of his family now an aching memory. Confronted by the room, fear tore at his resolve, and loneliness threatened to overwhelm him.

13

THE CAPTAIN

The captain took a moment to study his room. It wasn't a big room, but then, it didn't need to be. It was big enough for a small gathering. The faint odour of timber and varnish gave the sense of newness, as did the fresh lines of the wall panelling, his bed and desk. The bed was double size as many captains took their wives to sea. He smiled inwardly. His wife hated the sea. The oil lamps cast long shadows and weren't effective if one wanted to read, or see detail. There was an unlit lamp on his desk for that purpose. As usual, he had committed to memory the details he was about to discuss with his men.

He looked at the six men gathered in front of him. It was always the problem with a new ship. Most of the crew had never worked together. He'd had some influence in the selection of the officers, but the other men were unknown to him. It was disappointing that Mr Patterson, the second officer, was not present. It didn't augur well for his sense of commitment and responsibility.

On the other hand, the men presented well. All were neat and tidy. That was good. A man who cared about himself was likely to care about his job. The officers' uniforms made them at least look professional. *That's a good start,* he thought.

Vincent Price, the chief officer was about the same height as the others, had a rather severe, long face and looked very serious. His hair was thinning, and his high forehead gave him the look of a university professor.

David Hosking, the first officer had a woolly mop of blonde, curly hair that looked like he might have tried, but abandoned the effort, to put it in place. Even in the dim light, his eyes sparkled, and he looked like he would always find something to laugh about.

The chief engineer, Alan Cave, stood as straight as if he was tied to a mast, hands behind his back, legs apart, looking very stern. He had collar and tie, a bushy beard with a large moustache and was the only one wearing a hat. It looked like it was stuck to his head.

Patrick Merchant, the bosun, also stood as if both feet were nailed to the floor. And a considerable floor it would have to be, judging by his size. The man was huge and was the only one that looked uncomfortable in the confines of the room. He was mostly clean shaven with a simple moustache, very bushy eyebrows, and his ears stuck at right angles to his head. His massive hands were clasped in front of him. The captain didn't doubt either one could be used to dispatch an unruly sailor to a prolonged state of unconsciousness.

Time to address the matters in hand. "Mr. Price, shall I begin?"

"Mr Patterson is not here yet, sir."

"I'm aware of that, Mr. Price. Shall I begin?"

The figure of an out-of-breath Albert Patterson filled the doorway.

"Ah," said the captain. "Mr Patterson. So good of you to join us."

Albert Patterson flushed a bright red and took the few steps necessary to stand beside Vincent Price. The captain noticed the other men shift uneasily, as though wondering what would be the repercussion for Patterson's tardiness. He was by far the youngest in the room and couldn't have been more than twenty-one or -two. His hair was combed flat to his head, an impeccable part on the left side. His uniform looked new, smartly presented and tailor made, with nothing out of place, despite the fact he had just been running. He looked like the son of a rich man sent to sea to learn about life.

Well, that won't be a problem on my ship, the captain thought. He looked around the room once more. "As I was saying, Mr Price, shall I begin?"

"Yes, sir. Of course, sir."

"Gentlemen. The *Lady Grace* is a new ship, but I believe a sound one. I have assured the owners we will take good care of her and her passengers. We will all need to be at our best to be sure we deliver on my undertaking."

He stopped and surveyed the men. Apart from Albert Patterson who was sure to be contemplating probable retribution and still very red in the face, none of the men showed any emotion.

"It's not a commitment I made lightly, nor without due regard for some of the difficulties involved. For example, the number in the crew."

He looked at the chief engineer, Alan Cave. "This will principally affect you and the engineering department, Mr Cave, so pay close attention to my proposal. You will divide your men into two watches. Each watch will work twelve hours a day in two shifts, one of seven hours and the other of five." He passed a sheet of paper to the chief engineer. "The details are on here."

Cave studied the paper, but was no doubt unable to read it in the half-light. The captain didn't need to look at the chief engineer to know that even if he couldn't see the detail, the news would be unwelcome.

"But, Captain," said Cave, then stopped when the captain held up his hand.

"Hear me out, Mr Cave. If you have objections or questions, then I would prefer to hear them when I have finished. You may find they are addressed in what I have yet to say."

Cave nodded and the captain continued. Cave appeared to study the sheet carefully in the dim light and waited for the captain to stop.

Once finished, the captain signalled to the chief engineer.

"I don't see any dog watches," said Cave, looking up from the document, referring to the usual practice of two shorter shifts around supper time to allow the men to eat and to vary their shift times.

How the hell can the man see that, the captain thought. *His eyesight is extraordinary. I must remember to compliment him at another time.* "That's right, Mr Cave, you don't. The engineering department will maintain the same shifts throughout the voyage. Of course, if the men wish to swap, it's their business, and you should accommodate them as best you can. Unfortunately, we don't have the numbers to do it any other way."

"Will they get extra money?" asked Cave. He looked disappointed when the captain ignored the question and continued.

"The firemen and trimmers will need to support the sailors, so I want all firemen and trimmers that don't know how, to spend two hours every day learning how to sail a ship."

The bosun shook his head. "The sailors won't like that," he said.

"It's immaterial to me what the sailors do and don't like, Mr Merchant," said the captain harshly. "If we get caught in a big blow, and it's all hands on deck, the sailors may be glad of some help. So you make sure the sailors not only like it, they do a good job of teaching the men how to sail. Our lives may depend on it."

"Yes, Captain, sorry Captain," said Merchant in his booming voice.

"Now, the rest of the crew will operate on a three-watch system." He noted the officers, the bosun and the chief steward all looked relieved. "I am assured most of the men will be on the ship tonight, so you'll need to sort out your port and starboard watches before we sail tomorrow. I suggest you do that tonight. I intend we sail the ship whenever the wind is favourable and conserve our coal. I want to buy only what I must for the return journey.

I have spoken with the pilot, and he has agreed to be on board so we can sail around noon tomorrow. I want every man to attend to his tasks, and there will be no mishaps. We shall go out under steam, but the rigging should always be ready for favourable winds."

"Mr Hughes," he said and turned to the chief steward and handed him two sheets of paper.

The chief steward was a short man with large ears and weak chin. He didn't look like he ate too much, so he wasn't into helping himself to the cooking. He didn't bother to look at the paper.

"I have also done a list of the watches for you so you can organise victualling. I believe you will find you will be able to schedule meals without difficulty. However, if you do have any difficulties, I expect you to overcome them. The men will not go hungry on my ship. A well-fed crew is a happy crew, so you must always remember that.

There are both crew and passengers who will need a meal tonight and again in the morning before we get underway, so you will need to see to that urgently. It would be unacceptable for a passenger to have any need unfulfilled, so you must hurry your team along if need be."

He looked around the room. "Any questions, gentlemen?" He sensed there might be questions, but perhaps now was not the time. "You may all go now and attend to your duties. I'd like the surgeon and the chief officer to remain."

Once the men had left, the captain continued. "Chief, you arrange your officers and lookouts as best you see fit. The ship is your responsibility when I'm not at the helm, and I will hold you accountable. Is that clear?"

The chief nodded and looked about to say something. The captain knew he had stated the obvious, and the chief would be glad the other officers had left. It would have been an insult to say such a thing with them present. Nevertheless, in his view, it was necessary to ensure the chief knew his role.

"And chief, you are to devise a suitable punishment for Mr Patterson. I want strict discipline maintained at all times."

The chief nodded and again looked as if he was about to say something. The captain hoped he wouldn't. It was always difficult working together in the first few days with a new crew.

The captain turned to the surgeon. He liked that the surgeon was a little older than the other men, and also liked that he looked like a surgeon. He was probably in his fifties with thinning hair and a large, walrus moustache and had kindly eyes that hinted at a good bedside manner. He already wore his surgeon's jacket - the captain also liked that.

"Mr Abrams, I wish to assure you it is not my intention to drive the men beyond human endurance. I suspect the chief engineer is concerned for his engineering crew on a two-watch system. The men will be required to work hard, and that's not unusual on any ship of mine. I would be concerned if the men feign illness or fatigue to avoid hard work, so I want you to consult with me before allowing any man to stand down."

He knew his request would be considered by some as unacceptable, but wanted to be sure the surgeon knew his position. He saw the surgeon's jaw line harden and was surprised the surgeon simply replied, "Yes, Captain." Perhaps the surgeon would raise the matter later when no one else was present.

"Let's see to our duties then, thank God for a fine ship and pray for fair winds. Thank you, gentlemen."

The chief and the surgeon walked out of the captain's rooms and down the passageway that connected the various sections of the ship. The surgeon was undoubtedly heading for the surgery to make sure everything was in place and the chief to the crew's quarters.

The captain watched them go and then headed for the saloon to check on the first-class passengers. He was always very careful to maintain good rapport with them. They had the most influence and paid the most for the privilege of being tested to the limit on the oceans of the world. He already had misgivings about this voyage. Often it was necessary to make adjustments to cater for illness and injury to the crew during a voyage, but it was rare to start off that way. Nonetheless, he expected things to turn out well. He wasn't an engineer, but he knew enough about the engine room and knew heat, noise and hard work would take their toll. A seven-hour shift for weeks on end may well test a man beyond his endurance.

When he reached the forecastle deck, he saw the chief go into the amidships hatchway to check on the crew's quarters.

14

A Leading Fireman

After a few moments, one of the card players saw William.

"Ah, 'ere he is. The best li'l trimmer in Southampton."

The men with him turned to look at William.

"'E's only a baby. 'Ow does a baby get to be a trimmer?"

There was a general commotion in the room as the story of William's hiring was passed from those who knew of it to those who didn't. The men who were behind the bunks and against the walls struggled to see the subject of the fun. William stood watching.

"I'll wager 'e's missin' his mother's teat," called someone, and the laughter began again.

"Well, boy," said the first card player, over the noise. "What do you have to say?"

"About what?"

"About how you learned how to be a trimmer in two days."

William shrugged. "I don't think it takes much to learn. I think it's harder to be a trimmer than it is to learn."

"Where'd you learn to be one?"

"Coastal steamer."

"They're nothing."

William shrugged again.

There was silence for a few moments when a voice called, "They're not nothin'. I cut my teeth on coastal steamers."

Other voices joined the chorus.

"What do ya mean, nothin'?"

"'E's right. May da died on one."

"And my brother."

Then, those near to the door went silent as the figure of the chief engineer pushed past William. The room became silent.

He looked briefly at William and said, "Put your parcel on the table and go below to the engine room. Bring back anyone you find there. Tell them the chief engineer wants to see them."

"Where's the engine room?" asked William.

The room erupted in laughter. William went red with embarrassment.

The chief engineer glared at the room, turned to William, his face softening. "Don't worry, lad. It's easy enough to find. Out the way you came, then down the ladder to the next deck. That'll get you to the boiler room. Walk from there down the passage to the engine room." After William had left, he looked at the card players and asked, "All right, so what's that all about?"

The men stared at him, the noise in the room died down as the others realised there was some action afoot.

He pointed at the men who had spoken. "You both had something to say a few moments ago, and now you won't obey a direct order. Answer me, or get off this ship."

The man that had first spoken said, "What was what all about?"

"Don't take me for a fool. You'll only make that mistake once and you've just made it, so you won't get another chance."

"All right. Some fellow said the lad was a good trimmer, then we found out he's been trimming for only two days. We thought it was funny. Turns out," looking at the other men around him, "We all think it's funny."

"Who're you?" asked the chief engineer.

"Who's asking?"

"I'm Alan Cave, chief engineer and I'm waiting for an answer."

"I'm Brian Hall, leading fireman."

"How long do you think it takes to be a trimmer, Mr Hall?"

"They said a good trimmer."

"All right, if that's what they said. How long do you think it takes to be a good trimmer?"

Hall sat still and quiet, looking very uncomfortable, clearly struggling for an answer.

"Well?" asked Cave.

The room was silent. Its occupants looking from Cave to Hall. Cave was tense, but controlled. Hall looked ready to explode.

"Well?" said Cave again. "It can't be that hard a question. Or, don't you know?"

Just then, William returned with six more men. Cave noticed them and beckoned them into the room. The room was filled with the men, and there was very little room to move. Those that were sitting on the benches, tables and bunks would consider themselves lucky. Others who were around the walls, couldn't see Cave, but they could all hear him.

Cave's eyes swept around the room. He spoke louder than he needed for the confined space, but the words carried his authority. His eyes fixed on Hall. "All right, Mr Hall, we'll leave that discussion for another day." He looked at the others in the room.

"For the benefit of those that have just joined us, Mr Hall was just explaining to me how much fun you are all having. I'm glad you're having fun, because what I'm about to tell you may not be as funny. Where's Armstrong?"

The other man sitting with Hall who had also spoken, said, "That's me. I'm Armstrong."

"Good. The engineering department will be split into two watches and you and Mr Hall are watch leaders. Each watch will work two shifts a day, one of seven hours and the other of five." He waited for the brief buzz of conversation to die down.

"Mr Armstrong and Mr Hall will now divide you into two watches, each taking their pick in turn." He pointed at one of the men who had come back with William. "This is Bruce Fletcher, the second engineer. Either he or I will be on watch at all times. If the leading firemen have any issues, they will address them to Mr Fletcher or myself." Cave paused and his lips firmed into a hard line.

He turned to William. "You a trimmer?"

"Yes, sir," replied William.

"Good. You'll be on Mr Hall's watch."

He looked at Fletcher. "Mr Fletcher, you and I will go below. We have some work to do, and these men need to select their watches. Mr Hall, Mr Armstrong, get on with it. We'll be back shortly, and we'll expect you to be finished."

Cave and Fletcher stepped through the doorway and went to the ladder to go down to the engine room. When they were a few steps away from the door, Fletcher said, "What do we have to do?"

"Nothing. I want to leave them alone for a while."

"Was it wise to put that man on Hall's watch? It looks like there's already trouble between them."

"I hope not. Let's wait here. I want to hear what happens."

The room they had just left was silent for a few moments, then the first to speak was Hall. "What's your name?" he asked William.

"Bill Smith."

"Well, Bill we're off to a bad start, but we'll try to remedy that. We don't usually start with the trimmers, but let's keep going. If there are trimmers that can't be seen, come out to where you can be. Raise your arms. Good. Mr Armstrong's turn next."

Outside, Cave smiled at Fletcher and said, "Good. Let's go. Maybe Hall's all right after all."

Hall and Armstrong went through the men alternately until all eight trimmers were allocated to a watch. They then did the same with the firemen and the greasers. The room was not only crowded, it was now very hot. Most of the men were sweating, some removed their shirts.

"It's getting hot in here," said someone.

Armstrong and Hall started laughing.

"Now, that was funny," said Hall. "It'll be a damn sight hotter where you'll be working for the next few months, so you better get used to it."

Fletcher and Cave arrived back, and the room was immediately silent.

"All done?" asked Cave to Hall and Armstrong who both nodded.

"Good. A few more things, then I think you should go and get a meal. I expect it's not yet organised in the galley, so don't all go at once. Mr Hall and Mr Armstrong will make those arrangements." He glanced around the room. Everyone he could see was listening.

"It's crowded in here, but it won't normally be, as half of you will be on shift. Decide before you go what bunk you will share. Mr Fletcher and I will share that one near the door. If you have money, see the purser who'll take care of it for you."

"Where're the 'eads?" called a voice.

"The heads are for'ard where the rest of the crew are quartered. You can use those or you can do what we normally do in the boiler room. Also, there's talk of baths on some ships, but there's none for you on this ship."

"What's a bath?" yelled someone. A ripple of laughter ran through the crew. Many of them had never had a bath.

"Well, for those of you that want one, go to the weather deck around dawn and find someone to throw a bucket of water over you. You can't go there if there are any passengers on deck, so be careful."

"If there's a lady passenger having a bath, can we throw a bucket of water over her?" someone called.

"The next man that asks a stupid question like that will leave the ship. Like I said, you can't go there if there are any passengers on deck. Finally, those of you who don't know how, are to learn to sail."

"What? Learn 'ow to sail? What the 'ell do ye think we're doin' 'ere?" called a voice.

"'E's right. We are sailors!" called another, and some of the men laughed.

"That might be, but you are to learn how to handle sails. Mr Hall and Mr Armstrong, this is an order from the captain. You will find out which of your men need to be taught, and they will attend training every day. And men, no pretending you know how to sail. If you are all called out to help the sailors and don't know what to do, you'll put lives at risk and not just your own."

He looked around the room, as though surprised there had been little fuss about the two-watch system. "Thank you, gentlemen. Mr Fletcher and I will see the cook and return shortly."

Armstrong and Hall sat back at the table. Other men were gathered around, but if they spoke quietly enough, they could have a private conversation.

"Shall we toss for the privilege of the middle watch?" asked Hall, referring to the midnight to seven a.m. shift.

"Aye, why not? It's as good a way as any."

Hall took a coin from his pocket and showed Armstrong that it had a head on one side. Armstrong nodded, Hall tossed the coin and caught it on the back of his hand with his other hand over it.

"Head or other?" queried Hall.

"Head," said Armstrong, and Hall removed his hand, then smiled.

"What are you smilin' about? You just lost. You've got the middle watch."

"I'm thinking our Mr Smith will enjoy the middle watch. I aim to see he does, anyway."

"But I heard you say you were off to a bad start? Smith looked relieved."

Hall laughed. "I'll bet a week's wages Cave was listening outside the door. That was for his benefit. No, I aim to see Mr Smith pays for making a fool of me. Man's got to have something to look forward to when he's working with the furnace twelve hours a day."

"I didn't see Smith make a fool of you."

"Cave's on his side. I don't know why. So, he's set Cave against me."

Hall looked up, smiled and continued, "No, I really don't care what Smith has or hasn't done. I just want someone to help me pass the time. Knowing that Smith has set Cave against me only gives me a reason. That's all. A reason."

The men were silent for a few moments.

"I suppose the captain's hopin' we'll spend a lot of time under sail, so we won't be workin' twelve hours a day for the whole voyage," said Armstrong.

"Captain can hope what he likes. I've done this trip before, and the wind doesn't do what anyone wants."

"I've heard it's good once we get to the Roarin' Forties."

"Well, so they say, but my experience says it's anything but good, and it'll blow hard enough to blow a dog off a chain. They lose ships down there when the captain tries to make up time with too much sail, so I'm hoping this fellow knows what he's doing."

"Let's just hope we won't be steamin' the whole way."

Hall shrugged.

Cave and Fletcher appeared in the doorway. The men near to the door went quiet, and the others then followed their lead.

Cave announced, "Cook's busy with the passengers at the moment. He said he'd let us know in good time." He looked at Armstrong and Hall. "Sorted out the watches?"

"Aye," replied Hall with a smile. "I'm middle watch."

"All right," said Cave. "Armstrong's port, you're starboard. Sorted out the bunks?"

"Not yet. About to do it," said Hall.

Caves eyes narrowed, and he looked from one to the other. He hesitated as though about to ask the men what was taking so much time. "Get on with it, then," he said tersely and remained in the doorway.

"All right, men, you heard the man," said Hall. "Port and starboard watches to share bunks. Find the man nearest to you from the other watch and share with him."

There was some commotion as the men tried to work out which watch they were on, and who was on the other watch. Some men were confused as to which leading fireman had chosen them. Then as partners were taken, others struggled to find men who were still available for partnering. Things settled down soon enough, and only two men refused to share a bunk.

"All right," said Hall. "What's the problem?"

"I'm a greaser, he's a trimmer. Bunk'll be a pigsty every time he uses it."

"All right," said Hall. "Who's the other greaser?"

A man put up his hand.

"What's your name?" asked Hall.

"Andy Couchman."

"Who're you sharing with?"

"Him," said Couchman, pointing to a man nearby.

"Which watch are you on, Couchman?"

"Yours, sir."

"And you?" asked Hall of the man sharing with Couchman.

"Yours, sir."

Hall was silent for a moment, then said, "Gentlemen, I'm sure you remember the idea was to share with a man from the other watch, so you wouldn't be in the bunk at the same time. Now, I could take a few moments and ask Mr Cave if it's all right for you to share the same bunk at the same time, or you could find another man. Which is it to be?"

Couchman was quick to say, "I'll share with the other greaser, sir."

"Good man," said Hall. "And you?" he asked, pointing at the man who was to share with Couchman. "What do you do?"

"I'm a trimmer, sir."

"Good, you can share with another trimmer, and neither of you will notice the other has used the bunk."

Hall and Armstrong leaned close to each other.

"Some of the men might ask to change watches later," said Hall. "I know Smith will ask to change when he realises that he's my target, but if I take my time, I can have some fun before that happens."

Armstrong tapped him on the shoulder and whispered. "Cave's lookin' at you from the doorway. I wonder what he wants."

"Mr Cave?" Hall asked, looking at Cave.

"Thank you, Mr Hall," Cave replied. "Please determine the men that will need to be taught how to sail."

Hall looked back to the men. "There won't be too many honest answers to this question," he whispered to Armstrong. "All right, the men on the starboard watch who need to learn how to sail, please raise your hand." He shook his head. It looked like all the men on his watch had raised their hands.

"Mr Armstrong?"

"Men on the port watch?" asked Armstrong. Again, it looked like all the men.

"It's everybody, sir," said Hall and Armstrong at the same time.

"Not everybody," called a voice from the shadows.

"Well," said Cave. "That man can help. It looks like the sailors will have their hands full." He nodded at Hall and Armstrong. "I'll send the bosun to see you, and you can add the times for learning into your schedule." He looked at all the men.

"We sail tomorrow around noon. Look to your job and no mistakes. This is a fine ship. I think if we treat her right, then she'll do the same for us. God's speed and a safe voyage, gentlemen."

Armstrong raised a hand.

"Mr Armstrong?" said Cave.

"Where do the men sleep tonight, sir? I mean, no one will be on shift tonight, will they?"

"What do you mean? You and Mr Hall will need some jobs done below to prepare for tomorrow, so some men will be working. Captain intends to leave under steam. As far as sleeping, as best they can, Mr Armstrong. The ship is designed for a bigger crew, so there will be some spare bunks in here. I don't think the full crew is yet up for'ard, so there might be some space there. Why don't you ask the chief officer? I'm sure you'll work it out."

"Well done, Armstrong," whispered Hall. "Glad you asked the question. Now, it looks like he doesn't like you, either."

Cave stopped and listened for a few moments. "That was six bells. Shall we see you and Mr Hall in the boiler room at eight bells?" Without waiting for an answer, Cave said, "Thank you, gentlemen," to the room, then he and Fletcher stepped through the door.

Hall turned to Armstrong. "Let's you and I check out the boiler room. Cave is right. We need to prepare for tomorrow. The men will be busy messing and getting to know each other, so better we're not here anyway."

They too, left the room, and as they stepped into the galley, they saw the cooking was well underway with stewards ferrying trays of food to the passengers. They took the ladder down to the boiler room. It was dark when they reached the bottom of the ladder.

"Better get a few lamps lit," said Hall. The room was warm, and there was the faint hissing of steam.

"Fires're still burnin'," said Armstrong.

"Hope so," said Hall. "There'll be trouble if they're not. Still burning from the trip from London, I suppose. They won't all be burning, though. Be a waste of coal."

The boiler room was really two rooms, one being for'ard and one aft and the boilers between them. They lit some lamps and distributed them around the walls in both. It wouldn't do to light too many, just enough to see. If they set too many or not enough, there'd be a reprimand from Cave.

There was enough space between the decks for anyone to walk upright who was at least a foot taller than the average man. The boiler rooms were as wide as the ship. A passageway on one side allowed movement, not only between the rooms, but along the length of the ship including to the engine room which was aft of the boiler room. There were six separate boilers above the furnaces, three for'ard and three aft and four furnaces for each boiler.

"Better check the gauges," said Armstrong.

All the gauges to control the steam pressure and water levels were near to each boiler. There were lamps nearby so the gauges could be easily read, but they left these unlit for the moment.

Armstrong pulled a lighted lamp from its gimbals and checked the gauges. As a leading fireman, he knew the safety of the ship depended on regular and accurate checking of the gauges for those boilers in use. They checked the furnaces. Only a quarter were alight with one boiler making steam.

"They'll want at least another boiler tomorrow. We'll talk it over with Cave. Be a good chance to see what he's like when he's not grandstanding for the crew. Not sure I like the man and pretty sure he doesn't like me," said Hall.

Checking around the bunkers and the furnaces, they found all the tools were in place. It would have been a surprise if they hadn't been, but it was worth the few minutes to check. Again, there was no point incurring a reprimand from Cave. They headed for the ladder to go back to their quarters.

"If Cave agrees, we'll get another boiler going overnight. We'll put a couple of men on shift tonight. I have one in mind already."

When they reached the galley, there were some stewards taking food to the for'ard quarters, and some of the engine hands took plates into the engine quarters. Hall and Armstrong pushed in front of the engine crew, getting some plates of stew, some bread and some tea to take back to their quarters. They stepped through the door. The tables and stools were filled with men, eating. They pushed the first two men off and told them to eat on their bunks. Some men grumbled, but Armstrong and Hall had priority, so the men had no choice.

One of the men that had sailed before saw it and shrugged. He turned to the man beside him who looked bewildered by the behaviour of Hall and Armstrong. "Life's like that on a ship," he said. "Some leaders are worried for their men, others aren't. There's all kinds."

Eight bells sounded, so Hall and Armstrong finished quickly and set off for the boiler room. Cave and Fletcher were already there.

"Shall we have a look around, gentlemen?" asked Cave and set off without waiting. "The chief officer said they came from London with one boiler, but he'd like another two when we set off tomorrow. Would you arrange that on your watch, Mr Hall? He'd also like the three boilers to be fully working, so the fires will need to be stoked. I believe that will also need to be done on your watch, Mr Hall."

"Yes, sir. Certainly, sir. Will it be you or Mr Fletcher on the middle watch?"

Cave turned and looked at Hall. He squinted as though he couldn't see his features clearly in the near dark and said, "Mr Fletcher. Why?"

"Oh, just wondering."

"I'll bet you are," said Cave quietly, but Hall neither moved nor spoke.

Cave had talked it over with Fletcher, and they agreed there was less chance for trouble if Fletcher and Hall were paired.

"For some reason," Cave had said to Fletcher earlier, "I don't trust the man, but he doesn't bother you. There's a long voyage ahead, and it won't pay to court trouble. Nonetheless, Hall wouldn't be on board if I had any say."

"I thought I'd put all the men on the middle watch, to make sure the fires are well stoked," said Hall. "It's still eight bells before my watch, so I thought Mr Armstrong and his team can get the fires started, and my watch can bring them up to capacity."

"That sounds good, Mr Hall, but will it need all of you? I thought you and maybe one or two others would be enough?"

"It's my plan to use all the men at first so they can get used to the ship. There won't be much chance for that once we get underway. Then, the watch can decide how many need to stay for the full shift, or if they want to rotate."

"Very good, Mr Hall. I'm sure that will work. Mr Armstrong, have you spoken with the chief officer about accommodation for your men for'ard?"

"No, sir. Not yet, sir."

"You'd best be quick. Those that aren't on watch tonight will be in their bunks soon and won't take kindly to being disturbed, whatever the reason."

Cave and Fletcher left. As they walked down the passageway, Cave turned to Fletcher.

"I wonder why those two fellows are slow to act. I always want matters to be addressed as soon as possible. I'm starting not to like Armstrong too. This is no way to start a voyage."

"I'm sure it will be all right," said Fletcher. "We'll have plenty of time to work them out."

"What do you think about Hall's plan? It sounds like a good idea, but I hadn't expected it. It will certainly give the men some rest before setting off tomorrow and will indeed give them a chance to get used to the ship. Still, I doubt Hall's motives, but can't find a fault in the plan."

"I can't see any problem with it."

"I'm worried, Bruce, and I don't mind admitting it. Hall will be trouble, mark my words."

15

Becoming Part of the Crew

William was still getting over the humiliation by Hall, but watched the crew selection and bunk allocation with interest. He'd not ever been through such a process before. The men stood or sat patiently waiting their turn. The last man of any group selected never looked nervous which he thought was odd. Even in children's games, anyone hated to be last. There was a sense of not being wanted.

Some of the men grumbled about sharing a bunk, but William was not the least troubled. He'd been standing beside a trimmer from the other watch, so the process had not been difficult. There'd also been some grumbling about the need to learn to sail, but he looked forward to it. It would be a chance to get outside in the open air.

He didn't believe Hall's offer to restart their relationship. He'd been looking at Hall when the statement was made and was pleased at first. Then he saw Hall's eyes disagreed with his words. William wasn't sure why he'd said that, and it made him nervous. Several times he'd been told about how the sailors would be hard men. Hall didn't look hard, just mean. Perhaps he should have turned and left before starting down the ladder, but nothing apart from teasing had happened yet, and he might be letting his imagination get the better of him.

Hall wasn't a tall man, but he was thickset. He wore a woollen cap that covered all his hair. He was clean shaven, and that was unusual. Most men had at least a moustache and often a beard. William knew there was little time or facilities for shaving. Hall's eyes were always on the move, first looking here, then there, as though checking opportunity and danger at the same time. William didn't like it when he looked at him. It was as though he was sizing him for a fight, or looking for weaknesses.

Armstrong, on the other hand, was taller and of lighter build. He wore a funny little hat at a rakish angle that seemed so out of place in the bunk room. He had a greying moustache, dark hair, a long, troubled face and an air of sadness. He sometimes smiled, and once he had laughed. It was not an unpleasant sound. He wore a jacket buttoned to the neck, that also looked odd in the heat of the bunk room.

The men started drifting out to collect a meal, and he followed them. No one took much notice of him, so he just went along with things. Each man picked up a plate, a mug and a spoon from a stack on a table near the stove.

"Come on, lads. Bring yer mugs and bowls. I'll fill 'em but bring 'em back when yer done, or ye'll go hungry for the rest of the voyage," called the cook, over and over like a street vendor. It reminded William of the soup lady. He had a high-pitched voice, and there was already a rumour he was really a woman.

The meal was some stew, bread and tea. If he got this for every meal for the next few months, it might become monotonous, but for now it was perfect. Almost every meal since he left home had been stew. He supposed it was easy to make and keep for men who would be fed at odd times. There was nowhere to sit in the galley, so like the other men, William took it back to the bunk room. The table was mostly occupied, so he put the bowl and tea on the floor and sat on his bunk. His back was bent at a horrible angle due to the narrow space between the bunks, but there was little choice. He started on the meal. It was delicious.

After a few moments, his bunk partner came and asked if he could sit on the bunk too. William was surprised and said, "Of course, it's your bunk, too."

The man sat, put his meal on the floor and put out his hand, "Jim Huston."

"Bill Smith," replied William, putting his mug down and taking the hand. It was as hard a hand as he had ever held.

Jim looked about thirty with dark, thinning hair, a moustache and a long face that looked like it had never smiled. William guessed he was also a man of few words as he said nothing further. They went back to their eating.

After a few moments, William became curious about his bunk partner and asked, "What meat do you think is in this?"

"I'd say mutton," Jim replied, amiably enough.

"Been to Australia before?"

"No, but I've been to America," replied Jim, with a mouthful of food.

In spite of the fact that it was hard to hear Jim with the general noise in the room, William wanted to know more and asked, "How long did that take?"

"Forty-five days out and fifty back. They said we were lucky both ways. The ship wasn't new like this one, and they say new ships aren't lucky."

In the silence that followed, William looked at the room in which they sat. Some of the men who had a top bunk had put their meal on the bunk and ate standing up. The ones at the table were most animated. Most of the noise and conversation came from them. The room was hot with the press of men and smelled of stew and unwashed bodies.

William nodded towards the mattress on which they were seated.

"What's this?"

"What's what?"

"What we're sitting on."

"Oh, that. A mattress."

"Do we have one each?"

"No, we share this one."

"What's in it?"

"Probably straw. It's mostly straw. It'll be comfortable enough for a man so tired he'll sleep anywhere." Still not the hint of a smile.

"What's the system of bells?"

"It's how we tell the time. One bell for 12:30, 4:30 and 8:30. Add a bell for every half hour after that until you get to eight bells, then you start again."

"Why eight?"

"Length of a watch is usually four hours."

"Where is it?"

"Where's what?"

"The bell."

"Oh. On the weather deck, just aft of the foremast."

"Who rings it?"

"Well, the sailors in the forequarters do. They've got an hourglass. Well, a half-hour glass, actually. They ring the bell when the glass is empty."

"What if they forget?"

"Happens a lot. They check with the officer of the watch each day. There are three clocks on board, so they check against those. Officer of the watch will give them a scoldin' if they forget or ring the wrong number."

"Three clocks? Why three clocks?"

"To make sure the captain always knows the correct time. They check them often. Two have to agree."

"How do you know if it's day or night?"

"Some rooms have skylights which help. In the boiler room, you don't. But now you've got a long middle watch, so when that finishes, it's mornin'."

Finishing their meal at about the same time, Jim stood and said, "I'll take your mess kit back if you like."

William was again surprised, and it must have showed.

"Your turn next time," said Jim, taking the kit and disappearing through the doorway.

William was very tired and wondered how they would handle the fact that they were both there and both needed to sleep. Jim might have an answer. He was back in a few moments, but before William could say anything, Armstrong appeared in the doorway.

"A bit of quiet, please!" he called. "All right, port watch, I want you all down in the boiler room. Mr Hall will want the starboard watch at eight bells which won't be too long, so you can sleep if you wish, but it may not be worth the trouble."

The port watch filed out. William stretched out on the bunk and was asleep in seconds.

16

Armstrong's Crew

It was quiet enough in the boiler room, so the men could hear Armstrong without him yelling. "Men, introduce yourselves. Once you have done that, we'll sort things out."

There was a general hubbub as the men moved around in the half-light shaking hands and introducing themselves. Most had already met, so there was some fun when pretending to meet for the first time.

Armstrong waited until the chatter died down and continued, "I want this to be the best watch of the two. Always on time and ready to work, no one leaves before the end of the shift and no slackin'. We get one long and one short shift each day, so make the most of your time off between." He looked around. All the men were quiet and paying attention.

"All right, we need to start two more boilers. They used only one on the trip from London, but we'll need three tomorrow. The firemen will do that, and the trimmers can take a walk around, find the tools and agree where and who you'll work with. You don't need me to tell you what to do. This is a short watch, so enjoy it. It's the last short watch on this voyage, I'll warrant. Step to, lads."

There was one trimmer for every two firemen, so they took a few minutes to work out which firemen and trimmers were partnered. Armstrong looked on and saw no need to help.

As soon as that was done, there wasn't much to do, and too many men to do it. They got another eight furnaces going easily enough by using coals from the ones already burning. The trimmers brought some coal, and the firemen stoked the already burning furnaces and nursed the extra ones along. It wasn't long before the idle men were yawning and grumbling.

"All right, no need to keep you all," said Armstrong. "One fireman and one trimmer to stay and the rest can leave. It's not eight bells yet, so don't disturb the starboard watch. There might be some spare bunks in your quarters and if there aren't then go for'ard, you'll likely find one there. If you can't be bothered, find yourself a piece of deck somewhere." He looked around. Everybody had been selected. "Good work, men." *These are good men,* he thought.

He nodded at the last two selected and said, "You two will be the handover, so we three will stay at the end of our watch and hand over to the next."

They went back to checking the fires. Some of the men removed their shirts.

The room is already hotter with the extra fires, thought Armstrong. *It's not going to be fun when we get to the Equator.*

17

Hall's Crew

Hall yelled, "All right, starboard watch. You're on."

William opened his eyes. Jim stood beside the bunk. William rolled out and pulled on his boots.

"Good luck," said Jim, rolling into the bunk.

Most of the port watch was already in the bunk room, making it hard for the starboard watch to leave. There was some irritable pushing and shoving and one man called out, "For Christ's sake, you can wait until a man's out, can't you!"

Eventually, the starboard watch assembled in the boiler room. Armstrong and two others from his watch were still there.

"All right, you Smith and you Coe, you two can do the handover," said Hall.

William didn't know Coe and hoped he might have some idea as to the handover.

Coe wasn't forthcoming, so William asked, "What's a handover?"

Hall smiled as though he was enjoying himself. He ignored the question and called out, "Coe? Are you here? Where's Coe?"

"Here, sir," said a voice in the semi-darkness.

"All right, you two. A handover takes place when watches change. You have to get information on any problems to be faced by the incoming watch. Coe, you talk to the firemen and Smith, you talk to the trimmers. If there's any problems, it's your job to make sure the men on your watch know about them. If you can fix them, fix them. If you can't, explain to the men how to live with them. Clear?"

William was stunned, surprised he had been chosen for the job. He looked around at the older, more experienced men on the watch. Then he looked back at Hall and wanted to say, "No sir, it's not clear sir. Pick someone else, sir."

Coe hadn't answered either. The only sounds in the room were the hiss of steam and the huffing of the furnaces. Hall looked from Smith to Coe.

William waited, uncertain what to do. *Well, if that's what Hall wants,* he decided. "Yes, sir," he said out loud and was surprised to hear Coe answer at the same time.

"Damn," muttered Hall under his breath, but loud enough all his men heard him. Most of the men looked at him in surprise.

William didn't understand what was happening. *Did Hall expect he and Coe would say no, and Hall could further humiliate him?*

"All right, off we go. Hand over with the port watch."

The three men from the port watch stood nearby. Armstrong indicated the men for William and Coe as their opposite handovers. The men shook hands.

"Everything all right?" Hall asked Armstrong.

"Yes," replied Armstrong. "Fires are well underway. They should be fine by mornin'."

"That was our job. Cave asked me to do it."

Armstrong shrugged. "I thought you'd be happy. Less for you to do."

Hall shook his head and waited while the men spoke. "Anything to report?" asked Hall in the silence that followed.

"No, sir. All good," said Coe.

"And you?" he asked William.

"All good, sir."

The port watch left.

"Well, men. Introduce yourselves. No one needs to meet Smith, do they? But just in case, Smith, tell us about yourself."

William hesitated. *What was going on now?* "What do you mean, Mr Hall?"

"Tell us the ships you've been on, the jobs you've done, the places you've been."

"Not much to tell."

"You let us be the judge of that."

Some of the men shifted uncomfortably in the long silence that followed. The boilers hissed and the furnaces huffed. It looked like Hall was losing patience.

"What are you doing, Mr Hall?" asked Fletcher, a voice out of the darkness. "Can't we just shake hands like we always do? I for one don't care what Smith has done. I only care what he's about to do."

Hall looked to find the man in the group who had spoken, but as he did, there was a murmur of assent from more of the men. "That's right, Mr Hall, we've a job to do. Mr Fletcher won't take it well if he finds us standing around talking, letting the fires burn down," said another voice.

"All right, all right, get on with it then, shake hands," said Hall, standing back.

William saw him peer into the darkness, clearly trying to find out who'd spoken, but Fletcher had already gone. The men muttered their names and shook hands.

William overheard a few whisper to each other, they were confused by what had just happened. They didn't know what Smith had done, nor why Hall had it in for him. *Hall didn't notice, or more likely,* thought William, *pretended not to.*

"Divide yourselves up then, one trimmer, two firemen," said Hall.

Coe stood near William and said, "You and me, all right?" He pulled another man close. "This here is Vince Alexander. He's a good man, and we'll make a good team."

"Yes," said William, relieved he had been chosen. He expected to stand alone and unwanted.

The men stood in groups, waiting.

Hall addressed them. "We'll only have three boilers and twelve furnaces going when we leave Southampton, so spread your teams across the stokeholes and the bunkers. You trimmers do your job now. Make sure you get the coal evenly from the bunkers. I want the full watch down here, so if you've nothing to do, get out of the way, but be ready if you're needed."

William saw Fletcher still watching from the shadows, and Hall hadn't seen him, nor did he see him walk off down the passageway to the engine room. William was glad he had helped, but knew now Hall was trouble.

The team quickly realised there were more men than were needed for the job, so the men took turns doing tasks. When they weren't busy, they stood out of the way along the bulkheads.

They used wheelbarrows instead of baskets. The sheer size of the room, the number of furnaces and the use of wheelbarrows were the only differences for William from his previous ship. Of course, there was another, more important difference. Hall.

During the quiet times, some of the more experienced hands allocated tasks like cleaning the coal spills, putting the tools back in place, filling the sweet water barrel and washing piss off the deck. No one went to the heads. The deck and the shovels were fine, and there was plenty of darkness if you wanted privacy, but no one cared. In spite of Hall, William decided the team had started off well and was pleased he had been chosen in the group.

Several times, William heard some of the men discuss that Hall might be the only problem, but it seemed to be all about Smith. So it was for Smith to worry, not them.

Six bells sounded elsewhere on the ship, and the watch was finished. They hadn't worked hard. William was pleased the watch was finished and nothing further had happened. *Maybe, he was worrying for nothing.* The fires and steam were building, and the men generally agreed Cave would be pleased with the handover.

Fletcher appeared from nowhere. Hall looked surprised to see him. Maybe he thought Fletcher would spend all the watch in the engine room. *That's good,* thought William. *If Hall doesn't know when he'll be here, he'll be less likely to start trouble.*

Fletcher addressed the men. "Have a meal and go on deck for your training at seven bells. Hurry, now. You'll need to get some sleep before you're on watch again. I understand Smith and Coe are to stay behind for the handover."

The starboard watch left, and the port watch arrived. There was a jumble at the ladder, but it soon sorted itself out. Coe and William did the handover with nothing to report. Hall and

Armstrong spoke with each other, as did Fletcher and Cave. Fletcher said nothing to report, and Cave looked pleased there hadn't been any trouble. It was all very friendly. *Nothing to worry about,* thought William.

William hurried up the ladder and got his meal. He was pleased to see there was room at the table with the other watch below. He finished his meal quickly, handed the mess kit back and went on deck. It was a cold morning especially after the heat below, but William stood and threw his arms about as though he couldn't have cared what the morning was like. The men who had gone on deck agreed it was wonderful to stand outside.

Fletcher was standing and talking with a knot of men. There was a huge, silent man beside him. One of the men was Eddie Ward, the steward William had met coming on board. William joined them. The group was engaged in small talk, mostly about the weather, and what it would be like when they sailed.

The big man said in a very loud voice, "Get on with it then, Mr Fletcher. It's a busy day, and there's much to be done. Those that aren't here now can learn about it from these men."

Fletcher spoke, "The captain thinks training is not a good idea today. He's concerned about the passengers and the effect it might have to see the men learning how to sail a ship on the day we leave port. Besides, there's plenty else to be done, so head back to your quarters and get some rest. You'll be back on watch soon enough. Captain wants all hands turned out at six bells."

The group broke up, all heading to the rear of the ship to their respective quarters, mostly agreeing it was good to get off the cold deck.

"Eddie!" called William. "What are you doing here? I thought you were a steward?"

Eddie laughed. "Didn't last long, did it? They found they had a sailor that knew nothin' about sailin' and a steward that knew nothin' about being a steward, so they swapped us. I don't mind. I know more about being out here, anyway. You here for the trainin'?"

"Yes. I'm disappointed it's not on, especially now I find you'll be teaching!"

They both laughed and agreed to see each other the next day.

William headed back for his quarters where he found many of the men already asleep. He lay down and went immediately to sleep.

18

Setting Sail

The captain stood at the helm, aft of the ship. The helm was open to the weather. It had a wheel for steering the ship, with a stand in front of it called a binnacle, for holding the compass. There were three clocks, another compass, and a barometer in the captain's cabin. The helmsman was an experienced able seaman and could work the wheel on his own, but if the ship was hard to control, the officer of the watch would assist.

"Damn the man!" fumed the captain. "We'd arranged a time. The wind and tide are right, the tug is ready, the ship is ready, the passengers aboard. He should have been here an hour ago. Where is he?"

The chief officer noticed a commotion on the dock. "This might be our gentleman," he said.

There was a hurried ascent of the gangplank which was then quickly pulled away, and moments later, the pilot appeared on the main deck, hurrying towards the helm.

The pilot was a portly man, in more than one sense of the word. He was portly in shape, and his face and his breath indicated that several bottles of port might have had something to do with him being late. He wore a very large, double-breasted suit with a white pocket handkerchief. His collar and tie were forced into his neck in a way that must have been very uncomfortable. He had scruffy, curly, receding hair with a part down the middle at least an inch wide. His fingers were like sausages and in his right hand, he clutched a long, fat, burning cigar. It was fortunate for those gathered by the helm that the smoke was whisked away on the breeze. In spite of the cold, he perspired profusely.

"Sorry," he said, upon arriving. "Delayed."

The captain stared at him. "Mr Vaughn, are you able to take the ship as we have agreed?"

"Of course, Captain, your servant at your service." He tried to bow, but was unable to bend at the waist. He nearly fell forward and was only prevented from doing so by the binnacle.

"I have serious misgivings, Mr Vaughn, but we are already late, and I defer to your judgement. Mr Price, you see to the tug and ask the bosun to see to the mooring lines. Mr Vaughn has the ship and will now give the orders."

The passengers and many of the crew were on deck. There were loud shouts and much waving between the ship and the shore. The pilot was now aboard, and the ship was about to sail. The breeze had stiffened, and smoke from the funnel drifted across the river.

"The breeze might help to pull the bow around," muttered Price, heading for the bosun. "Ready the lines," he barked, hurrying by and going to the side where he could see the tug waiting.

The pilot called, "Heave her around!" in a voice so low he might have been asking for another port.

"Damn the man is right," said Price to himself, signalling to the tug. "He's in no condition to be giving orders."

The tug pulled on the bow, and it started to swing into the river. The mooring lines tightened. The bosun ordered the for'ard lines released.

"We're committed now," muttered Price. "Other ships and careers have foundered at this point." His lips then moved as though in silent prayer.

The *Lady Grace* swung away from the dock, and the gap between the ship and the dock widened. The outgoing tide caught the ship, and the bosun signalled to release the aft lines. The linesmen struggled. There was a lot of shouting from both the ship and the dock. Still moored aft, the big ship kept turning. The current was strong. If the aft line was not released, the tug would not be able to hold, and the ship would keep turning in an arc and crush the boats moored at the wharf behind it.

The captain looked towards the dock. The ship continued to wheel, but made no movement away from the dock. The captain said nothing. He couldn't, as it wasn't his ship. The pilot was in charge.

Then, clearly no longer able to remain silent, he said, "Mr Vaughn, do you notice she's not moving?"

"Of course, she's moving."

"No, Mr Vaughn, away from the dock."

"You're right. They should let the aft lines go."

"I think they are trying to, but perhaps there's a problem. Would you like some help from the ship's engines?"

"Yes, yes, of course."

The captain blew into the communications pipe and called to the engine room. "Mr Cave, half ahead, if you please."

"Yes, sir."

The ship started to throb, and the swinging slowed. The ship was trying to head out into the river. The strain increased on the aft lines.

"Any moment, we'll break the lines, rip out the bollards or take a goodly portion of the dock and the bollards with us," said the captain to the pilot. The pilot said nothing. The next moment, the aft lines came free, and the ship headed quickly out into the river.

"Mr Vaughn, would you like me to order reduced revolutions from the engine?"

"Yes, yes, of course."

Once again, the captain blew into the communications line and said, "Slow ahead, Mr Cave."

The tug turned to take them down the River Test with the tide. The pilot directed the helmsman to sail in line with landmarks that showed him the right channel.

With the combination of the engines, the current and the tug, the *Lady Grace* picked up speed. All too quickly, the ship started to overtake the tug. As they neared the mouth of the River Itchen, the tide and the breeze started to push the ship to the western shore. It was only a matter of time before they ran aground.

The look on the pilot's face showed he was once again in a dilemma. If he took the power off the ship's engines to slow her down, she would be fully at the mercy of the wind and the current. The tug wouldn't be able to hold her.

The captain noted his dilemma and suggested, "Mr Vaughn, if we put the ship's engines astern and the tug on the port side, we'll hold her away from the shore. If we do that until we reach the Solent, then we can release the tug and proceed under our own steam."

"Yes, yes, of course," was the predictable reply.

"Mr Price, see to the tug."

"Yes, sir."

The captain picked up the communications tube. "Mr Cave, slow astern, if you please."

There was a brief hesitation, then, "Yes, sir."

The chief officer signalled the tug to the port side. The helmsman on the tug waved in response, and the tug valiantly tried to overtake the ship, but the ship's speed was too great. Then, the reversing of the engines took hold, the tug reached the port side, the tug line was detached and re-attached and the tug pulled the ship to the east.

"You'll need to hold your course, so the ship maintains its way," said the captain to the helmsman. He'd ignored protocol, but the pilot didn't notice.

They continued this way until they reached the Solent.

"Time for me to go," said the pilot, almost bounding away from his post. "Your ship, Captain."

"Certainly, Mr Vaughn. The course, if you please?"

"The helmsman knows," said the pilot.

There was a moment's silence and the pilot snapped: "She's on 130," and walked over to the side of the ship to await the tug.

"Thank you, Mr Vaughn," said the captain to the pilot's back.

Once again, the chief officer signalled to the tug and the sailors attending the line. The line was cast off, the tug turned and came alongside to leeward. The sailors rolled out the pilot's ladder. The pilot climbed down unsteadily and reached the tug. As soon as he let go the ladder, the sailors reeled it in.

The chief officer went back to the helm. "Good riddance," he said to the captain, who ignored him.

The captain picked up the communications tube. "Mr Cave? Slow ahead, Mr Cave."

The ship wallowed for a little, now being at the mercy of the wind and the current. Then it picked up speed and once more underway, the helmsman could control it.

"Five degrees to port, if you please."

"Aye, Captain. Five degrees to port," replied the helmsman, adjusting the helm.

"Mr Price, would you find the bosun and get a report on the matter of the stern line? And a report on the readiness of the sails, if you please? And instruct Mr Patterson to report on the boiler and engine rooms?"

The chief nodded to Patterson and they hurried away.

Once away from the helm, Price said to Patterson, "Off you go to the engine and boiler rooms, but report to me first, then the captain." Patterson didn't question the order and hurried away.

Price found the bosun directing some men who were working on the sails.

"Will you be needing these soon, sir?" asked the bosun.

"I believe so, Mr Merchant. More to the point, I need a report on the stern line."

"It was jammed on the bitt, sir. The sailor had used a clove hitch, so the line jammed as soon as it took the strain. I couldn't see clearly, but the line caused some grief amongst those that tried to free the other end too. Probably another clove hitch. Then someone appeared on the docks with an axe. Couple of chops was all it took. There was so much strain on it by then, they were lucky no one was hurt by the whip."

Price nodded and said to the bosun, "It's done now, and there's little to be gained by making an issue of it." He turned and headed back to the helm.

He met Patterson coming up from below. "Well?"

"All good, sir. Mr Cave says the crew and the ship are fine. He wondered what was happening. The orders were not what he expected."

"I believe none of us expected those orders, Mr Patterson. The less said about it the better. I believe the captain would not welcome an enquiry. They may find him responsible for permitting a drunken pilot to take the ship out of the harbour."

They returned to the helm in silence.

"Well?" asked the captain of Patterson.

"All good, sir. Mr Cave said the ship and the men performed to expectations."

"Expectations, Mr Patterson? Whose expectations?"

Patterson flushed and replied, "I presume Mr Cave's, sir."

The captain nodded. "Then, Mr Patterson, I ask that you go back to Mr Cave and ask him what his expectations were, so we can judge the performance of his crew and our ship."

"Really, sir? Is this a joke, sir?"

"Mr Patterson. I'd like you to look around. Do you see any reason for mirth?" He paused, then said, "I'd like you to reflect on the events of the last hour. Did anything happen that would cause mirth?" Another pause, then, "In the last twenty-four hours you have been late for a meeting, and now you suggest that an order may be a joke. Let me ask you, Mr Patterson, is it you that is joking?"

Patterson stood in silence.

"If you have nothing to say, Mr Patterson, please be about your business."

"Yes, sir," said Patterson and hurried off.

"Mr Price?"

"The aft line was jammed, sir, on both the bitt and the bollard."

"How would it be a rope can be jammed on both ends?"

"Bosun says there was a clove hitch on the bitt end. He didn't know about the bollard, but presumed the same fault."

"So, one of our sailors used a clove hitch on a bitt? An experienced sailor?"

"I don't know, sir. I didn't ask about the sailor concerned."

"Then you should make it your business to find out. That man's incompetence put this ship and all aboard her at risk. Please ensure the bosun drills the men in all the necessary aspects of sailing."

"Bosun says it won't happen again, sir."

"Mr Price?"

"Yes, sir. I'll speak with the bosun."

"Now Mr Price, I wish to take a tour of the ship. You take charge of the helm."

"Yes, sir."

"Mr Price?"

Price turned to the helmsman. "Course?"

"One hundred and twenty-five degrees, sir."

The captain left the helm and its occupants to their own thoughts. When the captain had gone, Price looked at the first officer, obviously daring him to say something. Hosking wisely remained silent.

19

THE CAPTAIN'S SHIP

The captain descended the ladder into the control room. He saw Cave sitting beside the engine controls and Patterson standing beside him. Noise assaulted his ears. One of the greasers worked nearby.

The captain stood for a moment and looked at the spectacle of the control room. He saw that the engine and its associated mechanics took two decks of the *Lady Grace*. There was a huge wheel protruding from the deck in front of him, but only half the wheel was visible, the other half being on the deck below. The wheel turned, driven by the engines which were also on the deck below. There was a drive chain around the wheel which made an awful clattering sound, and this delivered the revolutions from the engine to the screw.

Patterson hadn't seen him, and though the captain struggled to hear above the noise, he did overhear Patterson's question to Cave.

"Mr Cave, I reported to the captain that the crew and the ship performed to your expectations, and he wants to know, what were your expectations?"

Before Cave could answer, the captain appeared beside Patterson, who flushed with embarrassment. Cave looked at Patterson, waited until the captain would be able to hear his answer clearly in the noise of the room and replied, "I expected the crew to be quick and efficient with their tasks, and the ship not to give trouble, Mr Patterson."

The captain saw Patterson was sweating and thought it wasn't just the heat.

Patterson turned to the captain and began his report. "Captain, the chief engineer..." The captain held up his hand.

"Very good, Mr Patterson. Please join the chief officer. I expect to be under sail shortly."

"Yes, sir. Very good, sir," replied Patterson, turning and climbing the ladder with excess haste.

"Mr Cave, is all well?"

"Yes, sir, like I just told Mr Patterson. The ship and crew are good."

The captain nodded, turned and climbed down the ladder to the engine level. He stood for a few moments, then headed down the passageway between the engine and boiler rooms. It was dark in the passageway despite there being some lamps.

She's a good ship, he thought. He always enjoyed walking between the major work areas on a ship. He loved the fine lines, the purpose, and the commitment to that purpose. The best designers in the country dedicated to building bigger, faster and safer ships. He was proud and delighted to be captain but would keep that from his men. It didn't suit him to be thought human. *Yes, she's a fine ship,* he thought, again. *Built to carry freight and passengers. No more, no less.*

He wasn't too sure about the crew on this one, though. Perhaps things would improve if he kept the pressure up. He would need all his officers performing at their best before this voyage was over.

Patterson was too young and had a tendency to be flippant. Perhaps he would need more discipline sooner rather than later. There'd been the business of the meeting. It didn't matter Patterson wasn't there, but it was a problem if his orders and directions were not taken seriously. He would need to ensure Price would be able to take command when needed.

He considered Price too cautious, with a tendency to support the crew. *Supporting the crew is the bosun's and the engineer's job,* he thought. *They both seemed like good men. Something to be grateful for, although neither has been tested.* He didn't know about Hosking yet, but there was plenty of time.

The boiler room wasn't as well lit as the engine room, but it didn't need to be. The dull, red glow from the fires when the furnace doors were open showed the men moving about mechanically. None of the men were working hard, and some stood, leaning against the bulkheads doing nothing.

They can all spend some time learning to sail this afternoon, thought the captain. *Better than idling about in here, and it will be useful if we get fair winds.*

He continued on, climbing the ladder out of the room. He stopped briefly at the quarters of the engine-room crew. Apart from the usual snoring and other bodily sounds, all was quiet.

The galley was busy, that was to be expected. The cooks were always preparing, delivering or clearing meals. He passed the chief steward and the chef who were discussing some issue. Neither of them noticed him.

He went down the passageway to the bow of the ship. Best to check the other crew's quarters. Arriving at the ladder, he climbed down to the officer's quarters. There was no one there, as he expected. He climbed the ladder down to the next deck. Some of the crew were sleeping there, again as he had expected. All seemed in order. It would be unlikely he would be back here for the rest of the voyage.

The captain climbed the ladders back to the top deck. The breeze still came from the nor' nor' west at about ten knots. He'd like a bit more west in it, but was comfortable they could make use of what was on offer. A few of the passengers strolled on the deck, rugged up against the cold. The bosun and some sailors were also on deck, working with the sails.

"Mr Merchant."

"Ah, Captain, that was a right shambles with the aft lines."

"Indeed it was, Mr Merchant. Do you know which sailor was at fault?"

"Mr Price has asked me already, sir. I'm afraid I don't. It was undoubtedly done when the ship docked from London, so it was probably the crew that brought her down, and they left immediately."

The captain looked at the bosun. He was a big fellow, with a big voice, exuding confidence. He liked that. Sailors should always respect the bosun. *Be a mistake not to respect this one,* he thought.

"It's the little things that cause the trouble. If you take care of the little things, Mr Merchant, the big things will take care of themselves. Are you confident your men are up to their jobs?"

"Aye, sir. I've been working with them now since we got under way, and all seem to know their way around. I am worried we don't have enough sailors. I have them all on watch. I expect you'll want to set the sails soon."

The captain nodded. "I want to get further into the channel. I'll discuss it with Mr Price."

"Very good, sir. Can we start the training now we are underway? Everything is ready, and the lads have some time."

The captain nodded again. "Yes, Mr Merchant. See the chief engineer. I'm sure he can spare some of the men." The captain walked on. The bosun went below.

When the captain returned to the helm, Mr Price was studying the horizon through his telescope.

"Mr Price," said the captain to get his attention.

"Sir," said Price and lowered the telescope.

"What do you think the barometer is doing?"

"I think steady, sir."

"Yes, I think so too. What do you think if we hold the present course until we clear the Isle of Wight, go out into the channel then change course to 235? We've been underway for about two hours, so it'll be another two hours or so before dark, and before we make the change. It may not be advisable to set the sails at dusk, so we can set the sails at first light tomorrow."

"If the Captain wishes, we could use the sails once we clear the Isle of Wight. If we set the jibs and the driver first, then we can set the square sails later. We still have about two hours to dusk, but it's a fair wind even though it's aft. When we change course, if the wind holds, it will be aft of the beam. I expect the men in the boiler room aren't busy, so we can bring them up to help with the sails and do training at the same time. We may still need the engines, but the sails will help. Bosun says all his men are standing by to set the sails, so they can hop to it once we change course."

The captain was silent for a moment and appeared to be studying the proposal, but it was exactly what he wanted. "Very good, Mr Price. Do you agree with the heading, for when we change course?"

"Yes, sir. 235, sir."

"Very good, Mr Price. Mr Hosking, you take the helm."

"Very good, sir. Helmsman?"

"One hundred and twenty-five degrees, sir."

"Very good, steady as she goes," said Hosking, his smile showing him to be delighted to be in charge of the ship.

The captain and Price walked together. Perhaps Price had expected the captain to come with him, because he looked surprised when the captain said, "Mr Price, I'm heading to the saloon to meet with the passengers. You find the bosun and raise those sails when we clear the Isle."

"Yes, sir."

20

SETTING THE SAILS

The bosun took three men, one of whom was William, from the boiler room and went to the weather deck where they met Price, the chief officer. A group of sailors was standing amidships, hopping about and slapping themselves, trying to keep warm. There was a sharp edge to the wind.

William heard the bosun tell Mr Price he was glad all his sailors were on deck. He'd brought three men with him from engineering. He hoped he'd eventually get another three, so he could pair his men and the engineers, even though one of his able seamen was always on the helm. Not the best solution for a crew shortage, but not the worst, either. Price nodded in agreement.

"Sails, sir?" asked the bosun.

"Aye, but only the jibs and the driver at the moment."

"But the wind is aft from the port side, sir."

"I realise, but we'll change course in about two hours, and the wind will be aft of the beam."

"Then we'll have to wear her, sir."

"You're right, bosun, but the jibs and the engine will help."

The bosun nodded. "Very good, sir," and walked off with Price to inspect the rigging.

William took the chance to introduce the other two men from his shift to Eddie. "This is Vince Alexander and Alan Coe," said William.

The men shook hands.

"What's happening? What's it mean to wear the ship?" asked William.

"Well," said Eddie. "The wind is behind us and slightly on the port side now. Square-rigged ships don't sail at their best with the wind behind, but the captain plans a change of course. So the wind will go from being behind on the port, to being on the side or the beam, as we call it, and she'll sail better. It's called wearing when we change direction with a following wind, and it's not easy to do on a square-rigged sailing ship. We've got to move the jibs to the other side. If the helmsman doesn't get her right through the turn as we move the jibs, the sails will backup, and she won't sail at all. They'll have to turn her through a full circle to get her going again. You heard Mr Price say he thinks the engine will help, and I think he's right."

"What are the sails he's talking about?"

"The jibs are triangular sails that are attached at the bow. The driver is a rectangular sail attached at the stern. You'll see soon enough."

"All right, men," said the bosun calling to the sailors. "You know what we've talked about, and you know you have to do some training. "You able seamen take one of these men each," he indicated the engineers, "and make sure you show them what you are doing and tell them why you are doing it. Step lively, now. The captain wants to take advantage of the breeze."

Eddie Ward grabbed Bill immediately. "Stick with me, Bill. I'll do my best to keep you alive."

William hoped he was joking about a need to be kept alive.

Once the men were paired, the bosun called, "You three men aft, the rest for'ard."

An able seaman, an ordinary seaman and Alan Coe headed aft. Eddie started for the bow and William followed. The others stood and watched.

Eddie turned back and called to the ordinary seamen. "Come on boys, there's work enough for all." A group of three ordinary seamen, Vince Alexander, Eddie and William went for'ard. One able seaman stayed with the bosun.

"You tell me where to go and when to go there, bosun," he said.

The bosun nodded. "You'll be needed somewhere soon enough."

"It'll be crowded with the other men," said Eddie to William with a smile, "but you boys need to learn, and I'll certainly need some experienced help."

The jibs were all stacked and stowed at the side of the ship, along the forestays and the gunwales. The sailors had done this previously, readying the sails for use. It would only be necessary to remove or to replace the sails in a big blow, or if one was damaged.

They quickly located the halyard for the flying jib.

"This here is a halyard," said Eddie. "It's to pull the sail up when needed and to lower it when not. Like I said, the jibs are triangular sails at the bow of the ship, and each of the three corners of the jib is attached. The top or head is attached at the halyard to raise and lower the sail. The tack shackle hooks onto the forestay, and the clew is where we attach a rope called a sheet, to pull the jib on. I'll do it first, and you can all watch and practise later."

Working very quickly the flying jib was up, then he showed them how to set the sail to take maximum advantage of the angle of the wind. "It would be better if the wind came more from the east at the moment," he said, "but no matter. A good sailor works with what he has." Next was how to stow the ropes, so the decks were always tidy and how to set the other three jibs.

The experienced hands and engineers worked well together, with good direction and advice. William was enthralled by everything he learned.

Even though the jibs were filled by a breeze coming from behind the ship, the *Lady Grace* wasn't moving much faster. "The jibs aren't enough sail for a ship the size of the *Lady Grace* in this wind," said Eddie.

The bosun signalled aft, and the crew waiting there set the driver sail. This was a harder job, as it used both a gaff and a boom, but the job was soon done. The ship sailed better with fore-and-aft sails, although William could see the aft sail was doing most of the work, once Eddie showed him how to judge it.

The three able seamen conversed and fine-tuned the settings of all the sails in use. They weren't yet all filled with wind, and the *Lady Grace* floundered in the sea. The wind still came from nor' nor' west, behind and slightly to the port side.

William really enjoyed being on the deck despite the cold. The other ships he had been on punched against the elements. This one at least tried to work with them. Being on deck was much better than being in the boiler room. No steam, no heat and no dust. No Hall. The sails billowed and swung about in the following breeze.

Smoke from the funnel enveloped them every now and again, and even though it wasn't hot, it was gritty and uncomfortable.

The bosun approached Mr Price. "The square sails, sir?"

Mr Price hesitated. "What do you think, Mr Merchant?"

"Well sir, everything's been done from the decks so far. We've cleared the Isle of Wight and there's time before we change course. If we set the square sails, the men will have to climb aloft."

William and the others looked at each other, concern on their faces.

Merchant looked at the sky. "There's about an hour of daylight. If the men move quickly, they'll get the job done, but it will involve the engineers. They're excited about what they've just done, but I expect the excitement to diminish when they realise the sailors will need to climb aloft. There's seven experienced sailors and three engineers to get the job done. It's possible, sir."

For William and the others, their look of concern became a look of alarm.

"Yes, bosun. The captain will expect it, I'm sure. Tell your men to be quick once they start. Darkness is approaching, and we want to finish while they can still see."

"There's no harm if they don't, sir. The men will need to work in the dark sooner or later and better in these conditions."

"That may be, but we want to be finished before we alter course, and we'll be doing that soon enough."

"Aye, sir," he replied and called his men over.

"All right, men. That was too easy. You may find the next job harder. You worked well together, and that's good. Now, break into two teams, one of four and the other of six men. The four-man team will stay on the deck to work the sheets. Eddie, you take the three engineers and stay on the deck. The experienced sailors can set the sails."

He saw a look of relief on the faces of the engineers and smiled at them. "You'll get your chance soon enough, so watch and learn."

The engineers once again exchanged nervous glances.

"All right, lads. Daylight is our friend and darkness our enemy. Step lively. Foremast, if you please."

The six sailors scrambled up what looked like rope ladders. Eddie explained the process to his team.

"The ropes they're climbing are ratlines. They cross the shrouds which are the ropes that act as stays for the masts, holding them when they are under pressure from the wind in the sails. The spars are across the masts, and the sails hang from them. They'll climb to the top, and when they're ready, they'll release the gaskets that hold the sail when it's stowed, or 'in its gear' as the sailors say. Then we'll release the clewlines and buntlines that fold the sails. Next, we'll pull on the sheets that hold the corners of the sail until it fills. We'll then fix those sheets. Then we'll haul on the tye rope that moves the spar up, until the sail sets."

"What do they hang onto while they're up there?" asked one of the men.

"There are footropes they walk on, and jackstays they can hold on to," answered Eddie. "You need to keep your balance. You'll need your hands free to work, so you have to develop a feel for the ship. Hold on when she is tryin' to throw you off and work in between. Much harder in a storm, of course, when the ship is being thrown about, the wind is tearin' at you, and the rain causes everythin' to be slippery."

William looked at the men. Their faces showed apprehension about what they might be expected to do.

"We have to do our job down here and do it well. When they release the gaskets, we must do our job quickly, or the sail will flap about and can knock them off. You have to think about it like you are up there and they are down here and what you would have them do."

"Do the job and do it well," said William, out loud. The other men nodded.

"There are six square sails on each mast and four ropes for each sail comin' down to the deck here, so we have to pick the right ropes to release and tighten. Let me show you. They're held in place with belayin' pins, and there's lots of them." He pulled one out and threw it to one of the men who remarked how heavy he found it.

"Look lively. The lads aloft will be ready soon."

Eddie showed them how to work out the ropes. He allocated two of the men to the lines and two to the sheets. It wasn't long before he shouted, "All right, men, release the lines and haul in the sheets!"

One of the men let the line go completely. "No," shouted Eddie. "Hold onto the damn thing!" He tied off his sheet, grabbed the line and secured it and went back to the sheet, hauling on it until the sail was set, then secured it.

Two men folded and tidied the loose rope while Eddie and William hauled on the tye rope until Mr Price called, "Well!" The sail was in place.

The sailors above were already moving down to the next spar as Eddie explained to his men, "You can't let the lines go. If we lose the end, we'll have to get one of the men aloft to bring it down to us. Make sure you let it go enough for the sail to open and the sheets to be pulled tight. Then, it needs to be secured." He looked up. The men had cleared the spar.

"Now, sometimes we have to set the angle of the sail, so it catches the wind. These ropes are called braces. We pull on one and release the other to change the angle of the sail until it's set.

The boys above will wait until we do this, but normally they would expect us to have this done when they are ready to release the next sail. We don't do anything with them now, since the wind is behind us." Eddie noticed the next sail starting to open and called, "Lines and sheets!"

The process continued apace until all six sails on the foremast were set. The sailors arrived back on the deck from the foremast and headed for the mainmast. Eddie's crew had a few moments of rest, then the process began again on the mainmast. His crew became more proficient with practice, and the mizzenmast sails were set in half the time.

Now, the *Lady Grace* was sailing, but with the wind from behind, it would be uncomfortable until they changed course.

"Well done, bosun. Don't let your men go. The captain wants to change course, so we'll need to reset everything. I'll be back shortly. Have Mr Ward explain to his men what's involved," said Price.

The bosun stood for a moment, looking around. The men waited for their orders.

"What's going on?" William asked Eddie.

Eddie smiled and said, "I'll bet the bosun is enjoyin' the ship. The men have done a good job, even if the sails aren't yet set, but they will be when we change course."

William looked up. The mainmast towered over one hundred feet above the deck. He looked from the deck to the tops of the masts, then along the three hundred feet of the ship's length. There was a solid wall of canvas. The major sound was of the ship hitting the waves, but there were other sounds, like the wind in the rigging, and the awful sound of the sails flogging as the wind shifted. It was beautiful, and he wondered if this was why men went to sea and if that's what the bosun was enjoying.

Eddie watched William and said, "Mother Nature has her moments, and this is the best of them. I hope they change course soon, and we can set the sails to make better use of the wind. We might have raised them too soon."

"It takes so long to set all the sails. What if we have to do things quickly?"

Eddie laughed. "There's no such thing as quickly on a square-rigged ship. The officer of the watch has to keep his eyes open for any danger and make sure nothing needs to be done quickly."

"What do we have to do when we change course?" asked one of the men.

"Well," said Eddie. "We'll have to let the jibs go and move them to the port side. We can't do that until the ship passes through the wind. So, when we get the order, we'll go for'ard and get ready. The other team will do the driver sail aft."

Mr Price headed for the helm. Eddie and the men all stood nearby. The captain wasn't there.

Mr Hosking had the helm and he asked, "All well?"

Price nodded and looked at the sky.

"Time to change course?" he asked Hosking. "The captain said at two bells."

"I think we should ask the captain."

"You have the ship," replied Price.

William thought the look on his face said he relished Hosking's discomfort.

Hosking thought for a moment and said, "Then, change course helmsman. Take her to 235."

"Aye, sir."

"Mr Hosking," said Price. "Do you think it wise to take the ship through more than 100 degrees at one change? The men will need to reset the spars as well as the sails."

"I'm in charge of the ship, Mr Price."

"That you are, Mr Hosking."

"Bosun?" called Hosking.

"Sir?" replied the bosun who stood nearby.

"Ready about!"

The bosun turned to the fore and aft teams and yelled in his booming voice, "Ready about!"

Eddie and his team hurried for'ard and readied the jib sheets to be released. William looked at Eddie. "How will we know when to release the sheets?"

"Wait," said Eddie. "I'll tell you."

They couldn't see, but heard the helmsman loudly and nervously ask, "Sir?"

"Bring her about," yelled Hosking.

The helmsman turned the wheel, and the bosun watched the bow move across the wind. As the jibs started to flap, he called, "Brace about!"

"Now!" screamed Eddie at his team. They let the starboard sheets go and sprang to the port sheets to haul the jibs across.

After stalling on the move for far too long, the bow was through the wind, and the wind came at the ship from the starboard side. The jibs were pushed across by the wind. The jibs and the square sails lost their wind and began to flap loudly. The ship no longer slid through the water. She began to bounce up and down and heel left to right.

"Sheet home!" screamed Eddie at his team who pulled the sheets until the sails were taut and then belayed them.

The helmsman continued to turn the wheel to steer 235, and the ship slowly swung so the wind came aft of the beam on the starboard side. On deck, the men hurried to the braces to adjust the angle of the square sails.

They had to loosen the starboard sheets and tighten the port ones. The engineers left it to the experienced sailors, but watched carefully. They knew it would be their turn soon enough.

It was hard to bring the ship back under control. She would have lost her way completely if it hadn't been for the engines that helped to set her on the new course. As the braces were reset, the sails caught the wind again, and the ship started to sail.

They returned to the jibs and the driver to make sure they were set properly. The men had to haul on the sheets again and pull the jibs closer to the ship's side. The jibs filled, and the ship was now sailing. She sailed much better with the wind at an angle. So much better than when it had been from behind.

Eddie and his team returned to the helm for further orders. There was silence on the helm until Hosking spoke.

"Do you think the captain will have some advice on how that might have been done better?"

"Undoubtedly," said Price with a smile.

21

Hall Shows His Hand

William and the other two men from his watch went down to the engineering bunk room, just as the rest of his watch came off shift. The crew below had had an easy time of it. It was only a matter of keeping the fires going and enough steam to keep the ship moving while the sails were set. They were keen to hear how things had gone on the deck and if those on deck had worked much harder. There was a barrage of questions as they entered the room.

William saw Hall look around, then he saw William and asked, "What about you, Bill?"

William thought Hall was looking to make sure Fletcher was not in the room.

"Well, Bill? Can you trim the sails as well as you can trim a bunker?" He looked around the room, perhaps to see how well his sense of humour was received.

The men who had been on deck with William were quiet. However, some of the other men laughed. William ignored Hall and went out to get a meal. Hall said something else and more laughter followed.

There were very few men in the galley, so William grabbed some kit, got his tea, bread and stew and headed down the passageway to see if he could mess with Eddie. He hadn't been to Eddie's quarters and didn't even know if he'd be welcome, but it was worth a try to get away from Hall for a while. Before he got to the sailors' mess, he realised it wasn't a smart move. He couldn't let Hall get the better of him. He had to face whatever would come and probably the sooner the better. He turned and headed back to his own quarters.

When he got back, most of the men had also been to the galley and were seated at the tables eating. Hall was talking and stopped when he noticed William arrive.

"Did you get lost?" he asked William.

There was a spare space at the table opposite Hall. William took it.

William had never previously had a confrontation with someone like Hall. Before he left home, he always had support from his ma, his da or an overseer. Now, he was on his own, and he needed to work out a plan to deal with the obvious threat from Hall. He knew he couldn't go to Fletcher for help. No, he'd have to work out what to do on his own.

He put his things down and looked directly at Hall. The men all stopped eating, and the room was quiet.

"No, I didn't get lost."

"Well, we had a meeting, talking about our watch tonight and who will be needed. The sails are up, so we won't need much from the engines. You should have been here."

"I'm here now."

"I'm not going over things again, just for your convenience."

William shrugged and started eating.

"Did you hear what I said?"

William stopped eating and looked thoughtful for a few moments.

"Yes, I believe I did hear what you said," he replied and went back to eating.

All the others had stopped eating, and the room was now hushed. William's new-found way to eat quietly meant the only sounds in the room came from some of the men shifting uneasily.

Hall sat still as though he wasn't sure what to do next. He watched William, perhaps expecting him to make the next move. Then he looked uncertain, his eyes flicking about, looking at others in the room as though someone else might take part. William continued to eat, showing no emotion. If Hall had expected him to be humiliated and apologise, then he would be disappointed.

After a few moments, Hall said, "It's just you and me on watch tonight."

William nodded and replied, "Good. Is that all I missed?"

Hall glared at him, got up, picked up his mess kit and left the room.

There was quiet for a few moments, then the men started talking about the watch, the ship and their day. It wasn't long before they all ignored William who got up, collected his mess kit, took it back to the galley and returned to his bunk. He wondered what the other watch was doing and how it was handling the fact not all the men would be needed. He assumed Hall hadn't thought about how the two watches would use the quarters at the same time. He hoped Hall's abilities were not up to the task and smiled to himself.

A man appeared beside his bunk. It was Alan Coe. "You be careful, Bill," whispered Coe. "Hall's got it in for you. I've asked around. No one knows why. He left the room then like he's good and mad. I think he tried to humiliate you, but it didn't work. He'll try again, so you be careful when there's just you and him on watch."

William nodded, grateful someone had noticed and taken his side.

22

IT'S MY WATCH

Hall heard Jim Huston shake Smith awake. "My turn," was all he said.

William got up and headed for the boiler room.

Hall followed. He took a piss when he reached the bottom of the ladder. There was the familiar sound of the fires and the steam, but not as much sound from the engines. The ship moved with a gentle up and down motion. William and Hall stood by the furnaces.

"The ship is moving very well," William said. "The sea is calmer than I thought it would be. It was much rougher than this on my other ships. It might be like this all the way to Australia."

"Let's get to work," barked Hall, ignoring William's attempt to be friendly.

"Do you want coal?" asked William, shrugging his shoulders.

"Damn right I do and be quick about it. If the fires go out, I'll report you to Fletcher. I've a good mind to report you for being late, anyhow. It's your job to be here on time."

William said nothing, just turned, got a wheelbarrow, filled it with coal and returned to Hall who ignored him.

"Where would you like me to put it?"

Hall indicated with his shovel and William dumped the coal at the point of the shovel.

"Not there, you idiot! Here!" indicating another spot with his shovel.

William got a shovel and moved the coal to the new spot. Hall had to stretch to shovel the coal into the furnace. He was about to ask William to move it again, then realised he would look foolish. If Smith noticed Hall was having trouble shovelling the coal, he didn't show it.

William returned with another wheelbarrow, stopped beside Hall who continued to shovel coal into the furnace, and waited.

Hall walked to another furnace and pointed to the deck with his shovel.

William picked a piece of coal from the wheelbarrow and placed it on the deck at the tip of the shovel.

"When you want more, just let me know," he said and stepped back.

"I said here!" bellowed Hall. "Put the damn stuff here."

William put another piece beside the first one and stepped back.

"Put it all here!"

"You mean, put all of it where those two are? All of it?"

"Of course, all of it. We don't have all night."

"As you wish," said William and upended the contents of the wheelbarrow onto the deck.

"Are you stupid?" yelled Hall. "Not there, here."

William looked at Hall. Hall thought he saw a brief look of uncertainty cross his face. *Might be getting somewhere at last,* he thought. *It's taken long enough.*

It was dark in the boiler room, and the lamps and the furnaces sent flickering light around the bulkheads. The noise from the furnaces, the boilers and the engine were ever present. A shouted warning could readily be missed. It would be easy to have an accident down here. Hall hoped Smith wasn't able to work out what he was up to and why they were here alone.

"Mr Hall, perhaps I have done something that upsets you? You told me we were off to a bad start, yet that wasn't the end of it. Would you prefer me to work on the other watch?"

Hall mimicked William in a high-pitched voice. *"Would you prefer me to work on the other watch?"* and delighted in the look of surprise on William's face.

There was silence for a few moments.

Hall enjoyed pushing people around, enjoyed these moments of power. He'd done it often before. From the time he could walk, he'd been kicked and punched by his father. Even thinking on it now, Hall relished the moment when he had belted his father over the head with a hammer. His father had punched him so often, he hadn't realised his son was growing bigger all the time. They'd been working on a job together, mending a fence. He'd done something wrong. He couldn't remember what it was, but his father had hit him, and it was once too often. He didn't hesitate to use the hammer. One blow was all it took. His father fell, and Hall ran away. Now, it was his turn. It didn't matter that he didn't know his targets, or they didn't deserve it. There was a well of bitterness and resentment to empty.

On a few occasions, it had ended badly for the victims when they retaliated, and Hall was able to break a nose or even an arm. The captain always took his side. A position of authority had its advantages. Hall didn't know if Smith could handle himself, but he wasn't about to put that to the test. He didn't need to, but he needed to break Smith, and now was the perfect time as they were down here alone. He was figuring out what to do next when Fletcher appeared from the passageway to the engine room.

Fletcher walked up to Hall, "What's going on here? Where are your men?"

"We didn't need the full watch, so there's just me and Smith."

"You and Smith? What the hell are you doing? Why just you and Smith? There's work down here for more men than that! Did you not think to discuss the matter with me?"

"I couldn't find you. I tried to. I met with the men during mess. They'd had a long day, the engines aren't being used, and so all the men weren't needed. I was only thinking of the men. When I couldn't find you, I thought that's what you would want me to do."

Fletcher looked like he was about to call him out, but perhaps decided he shouldn't in front of Smith.

"Smith," said Fletcher. "Go to the quarters and bring all the men for this watch. I know there are a few up for'ard, forget about them. Just bring those from your quarters. If you need help, wake Mr Cave."

Smith headed for the ladder.

As soon as Smith was out of hearing, Fletcher asked Hall, "I asked you what the hell is going on here, and I want a proper answer."

"Nothing's going on! I told you what's going on! Smith and I are on watch."

"What's the business with Smith? Why are you really down here with him? He worked as hard as anyone topside today. If anyone deserves a night off, it's him."

"He's a very good trimmer. He's young. I thought they'd be good reasons. Aren't they?"

"You weren't working when I got here, just talking."

"We weren't busy as the fires were burning all right, so we were just talking."

They could hear the men coming down the ladder.

"I'm watching you, Hall. If anything happens to Smith, I'll hold you responsible."

Damn Fletcher, thought Hall. *Arrived at the wrong moment. No matter, I'll find time and opportunity to finish with Smith. Hold me responsible? Not likely!*

William returned and spoke to Fletcher. "The men are here, sir. I couldn't find Vince Alexander and Michael Webb. I believe they're for'ard."

"Very good, Smith," said Fletcher. "Men, there's a change of plan. It doesn't matter what's happening with the engines, you are to always stand your watch. Keep checking the furnaces. If we run into bad weather, we'll need them at short notice. I don't care what you do if you're not busy down here, you can sleep on the deck if you wish. You can work that out amongst yourselves. Mr Hall, they're your men, set them to work." Fletcher went back down the passageway to the engine room.

"What's that all about, Mr Hall?" asked one of the men.

"Nothing," said Hall. "Firemen, check on your furnaces and trimmers, supply coal where needed."

Once everyone was back at work, Hall found Smith. "I'm not done with you and don't for a moment think I am. We'll finish what's been started. It's a long voyage, and there's plenty of time."

He was pleased when he thought Smith looked frightened. He walked away. The shift settled down, and men went about their work slowly as there wasn't much to do.

Hall heard a few of the men talk about how he had made a mess of it by being down here with only Smith. If Hall hadn't been so stupid, a few of them at least could be back in their bunks. Nonetheless, they weren't prepared to make an issue of it. Hall thought he'd let it go this time.

Six bells sounded, the watch was done. The port watch came down the ladder. Cave was in the lead, followed by Jason Armstrong. The starboard watch left, except Hall, Coe and Smith. Hall watched Coe and Smith do the handover, then go up the ladder. Cave, too watched the handover, then headed down the passageway to the engine room.

Armstrong found Hall. "Everythin' all right?"

"Of course. Why wouldn't it be?"

"Smith came up and got the rest of the men. What was that all about?"

"Oh, Fletcher decided we needed all the men. They lost some sleep, is all. The men'll all blame Fletcher."

Armstrong shook his head. "I don't think so. There was a lot of grumblin' as they left the bunks. You'd better be careful, Brian. Some of the men like Smith. A few say it's all right for you to have it in for him, but most say he works well and hard, and you'd be better to leave him alone."

"Well, you know what they can do," snapped Hall. "Smith's on my watch, he's my man, and I'll do what I damn well like. And you'd be better sticking up for me, or you're not much better than the rest of these half-wits."

23

THE OFFICER'S SHIP

The captain came to the helm. Price, the chief officer and Hosking, the first officer were there already. The ship had gone well during the night, and the wind had continued to blow at about ten knots and was now from the west. The sailors had worked with the sails, and the ship now sailed beautifully. The good start augured well for the voyage.

"Who has the ship?" asked the captain.

"I do, Captain," replied Price.

"Why are both my officers at the helm?"

"I've just taken charge, sir."

"No matter, I'll take her now. Is all well?"

"Yes, sir, all is well."

The captain turned to the helmsman.

"Heading, helmsman?"

"235, sir."

Price was at something of a loss being asked to turn the ship over to the captain. He had shared the night with Hosking, four hours on and four off. He had only just come back to the helm.

"Would you like one of us to stay?" asked Price.

"Where's Mr Patterson?"

"He'll be here soon, sir."

"Good. Mr Patterson and I will take the ship. Be back in two hours, Mr Price. Have some breakfast, take a rest."

"Yes, sir. Thank you, sir."

The men walked off.

"What was that all about?" asked Hosking. "The man was almost human. And nothing about the ship tossing about during the change of course. He baffles me, Mr Price."

Price didn't answer. Hosking raised an eyebrow as though wondering if he had overstepped the mark.

Patterson was hurrying towards them. "Who's got the ship?"

"The captain," said Price.

Patterson hesitated. "Perhaps I should come with you?" he said, looking hopeful.

"No, you'll be all right. The captain would appear to have had a good night's rest."

Patterson headed for the helm. Shortly after, the other men separated, Price heading for first-class dining and while Hosking would dine in second class.

As they separated, Price said, "You get some sleep after breakfast. Come back to the helm in four hours."

Hosking nodded.

Happy captain, happy ship, thought Price.

He stopped at the entrance to the dining saloon. He didn't like joining the passengers, but knew it was his job. Same idle conversation, same stupid questions. Already, he knew the captain welcomed it. He envied men that did because for him, it was always hard work.

Each to their own, he thought as he entered the saloon, looking for an empty seat. The fact the saloon was nearly full was a credit to how well the ship was sailing. *No seasickness, yet,* he thought, *but there's still plenty of time. There's a lot of ocean to go.*

He finished breakfast and took advantage of the first-class washroom and water closets. The bathroom stewards kept those areas nice and clean, unlike the crew's areas that were often filthy. Bedsides, it was expected by the shipping company that he would be well presented in the passenger areas, and it was hard to deny him the facilities to achieve that goal. He went back to his own quarters to have a shave, though. He was careful not to wake Hosking who was already there and snoring loudly. He didn't bother waiting for the two hours to be up before he returned to the helm.

"Ah, Mr Price. Mr Patterson and I were just talking," said the captain.

Price looked at Patterson who by a subtle shake of his head indicated the statement was not true. He wondered what could be coming next.

"Mr Patterson has informed me he has yet to receive discipline for his tardiness."

"That's true, sir. We have all been busy since the ship left port. The opportunity has not yet presented itself, but I anticipate it will do so shortly."

"Have you yet determined what form the discipline should take?"

Price was very uncomfortable discussing the matter in the hearing of the helmsman, but the captain seemed not to care, and the helmsman seemed not to notice.

"No, sir. Not yet, sir, but if the Captain has any suggestion, I would welcome it."

"No, Mr Price, I have none and expect I will be informed when the matter is dealt with. Are you ready to take the ship?"

"Yes, sir. Is all well?"

"Yes, indeed it is. Very well."

"Helmsman?" asked Price.

"235, sir."

"Very good. Steady as she goes."

The captain left without another word.

Patterson started to say something and Price shook his head. "Later," he said.

Price could see the helmsman revelled in how the ship sailed.

"Good sailing, helmsman. She's a good ship, there's no doubt of that."

"Aye, sir. She's getting along nicely."

"Have you logged the speed, Mr Patterson?"

"Aye, sir. She's doing four knots."

"Best we can do with this wind, I suppose."

The three men stood near the helm and the *Lady Grace* sailed on. A lookout came and stood nearby. He scanned about anxiously as though to give Price evidence of his diligence. He started to climb the shrouds. An elevated position would give him a better view.

"What's your name, sailor?" asked Price of the lookout who stopped climbing and joined the men at the helm.

No harm in letting the crew know you're interested.

"Michael Wilds," he replied.

"You seem to know your way around the ship already."

"Not much to it, sir. Square rigs is square rigs."

"And lookout?"

"Not much to that, either. Watch the sea. Be careful of other ships and land. Raise the alarm if I see something."

"I've seen lookouts that never bothered to look," said Price.

"Aye, I've seen the same."

"Not your first time on a ship, then?"

"No, sir. Not my first time. About ten times, sir."

"Been to Australia?"

"No, sir. Been to America a few times. Long trip and long time away from family."

"You married, then?"

"Aye, and two little ones, as well."

"Where are you from?"

"Portsmouth, born and bred."

"What of your family?"

"Wife lives with her mother. She helps look after the little ones. She's angry that I go to sea, so I try to get away as often as I can. No point in livin' with the anger. Wife don't mind, just her mother. I don't much like living under another's roof, either, especially a mother-in-law. Wife's brother is on board with me. I met her through him. Right good lad, he is too. Not married, either. I sometimes think he's better off that way. You, sir, are you married?"

"What's his name?" asked Price, ignoring the question.

"Aart Jansen. He's from Holland. They're all from Holland, that is. When I met his sister, I thought I was the luckiest man in the world. I'm always glad to get home, of course. And the little ones, they make such a fuss. I suppose it's not that bad. Her mum wasn't always angry. Seemed to like me well enough before we got married. Now, there's not much I can do that's right."

"What's he do?"

"Who?"

"Aart Jansen."

"Oh. Lookout, like me."

"It's a noble profession," said Price, turning back to the helm, terminating the conversation.

Michael Wilds went back to the shrouds and commenced his climb. The men gathered at the helm watched him climb up the main mast and stop at the lookout.

Price thought how lonely it must be up there and how he must wish for bad weather so he could remain on the deck. Still, there were worse jobs on a ship. He couldn't see the other lookout, but knew he would be somewhere about.

Looking around, Price thought how much he enjoyed being in charge of a beautiful ship like the *Lady Grace*. There were times he was glad to be a sailor, and this was one of them. Price scanned the horizon and saw some dark patches to the west. It was time to check the barometer.

"When was the last barometer reading, Mr Patterson?"

"Just before you came on watch, sir."

"And the reading?"

"Thirty, sir."

"Mr Patterson, ask the captain to check the barometer and do so urgently."

Patterson hurried off.

Damn, thought Price. *And things were going so well. Who'd be a sailor?* He looked to the west again. *Only an idiot,* replying to his own question. Patterson returned with the captain within five minutes.

"Mr Price," said the captain. "Mr Patterson said there may be a change in the weather?"

"Yes, sir. Look to the west, sir."

The captain didn't look surprised at Price's statement. Price was sure he'd checked the weather on the way to the helm.

"Yes, Mr Price. And you asked me to check the barometer?"

"Yes, sir, that I did, sir."

"It's at twenty-nine, Mr Price. When I first looked it remained at thirty. I wondered why you wanted me to check it. I tapped the instrument and it fell to twenty-nine, so there is a change on the way, and it may be severe, so very good. Well done, Mr Price. Hold her steady, helmsman."

The captain studied the weather to the west through the glass, and his face showed concern. "Mr Price, you are indeed right. We have to prepare ourselves for a severe storm. Find the bosun, tell him to get all hands on deck and furl and stow all the sails. All the sails, Mr Price. And ask the bosun to see to the animals. Which engineer is on watch?"

"Mr Cave, sir."

"Then see Mr Cave and have the fires stoked. We'll want steam before long, I'll warrant and good steam at that. Also, tell Mr Cave I want all the lamps out that are not in the engine and boiler rooms. Mr Patterson will tell the chief steward I want all his lamps out, too. There's not to be a burning lamp anywhere on this ship that's not in the engine department. Hurry, Mr Price. I fear there is little time."

"Yes, sir," said Price, catching the captain's concern. "Is there anything else, sir?"

"Mr Patterson, see the chef as well as the chief steward. Tell them to stop all meals, to stow all equipment, to extinguish the cooking fires and any lamps. Send all passengers to their cabins with a warning they should carefully and firmly stow anything loose."

The captain paused for a moment, then called to Patterson as he and Price made to leave. "Mr Patterson, bring all our oilskins and fetch Mr Hosking."

"Yes, sir," replied Patterson as he and Price hurried away.

24

The First Storm

Price found the bosun sleeping in the crew's for'ard quarters and shook him awake. "I'm sorry to wake you, Mr Merchant," he said as the bosun looked at him quizzically. "Captain's orders. There's a storm coming and by the look of the barometer, it'll be nasty."

"Very good, sir," said the bosun, rolling out of his bunk and pulling on his shoes. "Any orders, sir?"

"Yes, Mr Merchant. You are to get all hands on deck to furl and stow the sails. You are also to see to the animals and make sure they are secure."

"Very good, sir," replied Merchant, moving to wake the other men in the quarters. There were only a few sailors and the overflow from the engine quarters.

Price hurried away to find Cave. He sat at the controls in the engine room.

"Mr Cave. There's a storm coming and captain wants to be able to use the engines on full, if need be. He also wants all lamps on the ship, not in the engine and boiler rooms, to be out."

"Very good, sir."

Price hurried away.

Cave turned to the greaser working on the engine. "Fred!"

The greaser continued working.

Cave walked over and tapped him on the shoulder. "Fred!"

The greaser looked up in surprise.

"Go through the ship and make sure there are no lamps burning other than here and in the boiler room. Be quick about it. Then wake Mr Fletcher and tell him there's a storm coming. We won't want his men until their watch, but tell him if any of my men are hurt during my watch then we may need his men. Also, tell him to wake the men that have learned how to sail and send them to the bosun. I'm sure he's going to need all the help he can get."

"Yes, sir. Very good, sir," said Fred Barret, hurrying away.

Cave got up and went into the boiler room. The men worked quietly. Several of them lay asleep on the deck. Cave went up to Jason Armstrong who was leaning on his shovel.

"Storm comin'?" queried Armstrong.

"Aye. Did someone tell you?"

"No. I can feel the motion of the ship. The waves are bigger, and they feel like they're comin' from the west. That's where storms come from, so I figure there's one on the way."

"Well done. Might use you as lookout."

Armstrong smiled and replied, "Not likely. Especially in a storm."

"All right. Stoke all the furnaces. Captain wants to be able to use all engines if need be. Are all the furnaces burning?"

Armstrong shook his head.

"I think you are shaking your head, Armstrong, but you'd be better to speak. I can barely see in the dark."

"Still only four boilers, Mr Cave. Do you want us to light the other two?"

"Yes, I do. If the captain wants full power, he won't get it from four."

"Even if we do it now, they won't be ready for four or five hours."

"I know, I know, but get on with it."

Armstrong turned to the men, calling out they should wake those sleeping as he wanted to talk to them. Cave walked away and headed back for the engine room. The men gathered around Armstrong.

"There's a storm comin'. Maybe it's here already, if I'm any judge. I need you to light the furnaces for all the boilers and stoke the others. Captain may want full steam, so we need to be ready. For those of you that haven't been through a storm, it gets dangerous. The ship will pitch about as though it knows when you are off balance. Be careful of the furnaces if the doors are open. You don't want to get thrown in. You won't be alive for long if it happens, but it won't be a good way to meet Davy Jones. So, hop to it, do your jobs, look after each other, and above all, be careful."

25

THE SHIP IN A STORM – THE DECK

William heard Fred Barret try to wake Fletcher quietly, but the movement of the ship made it impossible. He leaned over Fletcher, but as he did, the ship pitched violently, and Barret was thrown on top of him.

"What the devil!" cried Fletcher.

"Sorry, sir. I'm very sorry, sir. Mr Cave says to wake you, sir."

"Well, you've done that. What is it?"

"Storm coming, sir. Mr Cave says he might need your men if any of his are hurt. He also suggests you send the men topside that have learned to sail."

"Why is it so dark in here?"

"Captain's orders, sir. No lamps on the ship anywhere but the boiler and engine rooms."

"How are we to see?"

"Mr Cave didn't say, sir."

"All right, all right. Wake Alexander, Coe and Smith and send them topside."

"Where are they, sir? Like you say, it's too dark in here to see anything."

"All right. All right," said Fletcher, irritated. "Alexander, Coe and Smith. You're wanted topside. Are you awake?"

"Yes, sir," came three voices in unison.

"We're all awake now," called another voice from the darkness.

Barret took his chance to leave and was closely followed by the other men heading topside.

When William emerged from the companionway to the deck, his senses were assaulted. He hadn't expected anything like what he saw. The sky was full of green-black clouds. The wind howled through the rigging and stretched the sails to what seemed like breaking point. The waves weren't too big, but the wind whipped the surface of the sea into a frothing mass of white caps. Water from the sea lashed the decks. William was wet and cold within minutes. He looked for the bosun and saw him directing some men to get the sails down. He signalled to his companions, and they all hurried to the bosun.

Merchant looked at them and nodded. "Glad you're here." His booming voice was torn away by the wind. "We're trying to get the square sails down first, but I fear we may be too late. Eddie's got some men, but now you are here, they'll be more use aloft. Do what you can to help Eddie."

William and the others hurried over to Eddie, but it wasn't easy to do. The deck was slippery with water, and the ship was forced on its side by the wind, almost until the sails touched the sea. Then, when the wind slackened, the ship would come back up again. The men looked for hand holds, but there were precious few. It took several minutes to cross the deck.

Eddie saw them coming and signalled to his other men to go aloft and help those already there. The men started to climb, but it wasn't easy, and they were flung back and forth on the ratlines and shrouds as the ship heeled to its side and rose again. They worked on the mainmast which had the bigger sails. The sails went in size from smallest at the top to the biggest at the bottom.

Eddie waited until they were in position, then called to his men. "All right, we'll try to get the sail furled."

The noise was terrible, and the men could hardly hear him. William missed being in the boiler room where it was at least warm. He was not only almost too cold to work, he had a great deal of difficulty standing.

Eddie signalled the men to come closer. "Do you remember the clew lines and buntlines? I hope so. We have to pull on them to furl the sail. Once it's furled, those poor men up there will stow it. We can't furl it when it's filled, so we have to wait until the ship is on its side, then we'll let the sheets go, and the sail will empty. Then, we have to haul on all the lines and furl the sail before the ship is upright. Work quickly men when I give the signal."

William looked up as the ship started to fall on its side again. The men looked like monkeys hanging on for dear life - legs, arms and hands wrapped around anything that would give them purchase. The group looked fearfully at each other. *It was bad on the deck*, their look said, *but what about up there?*

"Let the sheets go!" called Eddie. The men let them go and looked at the highest sail, obviously hoping they had released the right sheets. The sail started flapping nosily.

"Haul on the lines!" shouted Eddie. William and the others started to haul on the clewlines and buntlines. Their hands were frozen, and the ropes were wet. They slowly hauled the sail in, frozen hands struggling for purchase on the rope. Just as they seemed to be getting ahead, the ship came upright, and the sail flapped with large, cracking sounds. There was no time to look up and see if those aloft were all right. The ship started to fall on its side again.

"Come on, boys!" shouted Eddie. "Put some heart in it!"

The men threw their backs into the task, and the sail folded into place, but there was still plenty of open sail to catch the wind. The men aloft fought with the sails to get the gaskets on. The ship continued to fall and rise. It seemed to make no difference to the men aloft whether the ship was upright or on its side. There was plenty of wind in the sail, and it took all the men and all their strength to get the gaskets tight.

Just then, there was a roar from behind. "Look out!" shouted Eddie. "Hold on! Wave comin'!"

The men on the deck had tied the lines off and fastened them with belaying pins. It was easier to wrap a rope around a pin than it was to tie a knot in wet, frozen rope. They all grabbed the lines as the wave poured across the deck. William was astonished at the force. It was all he could do to hold the rope against the force of the water. His hands had never known such punishment. The rush of the water across the deck, past the hatches and through the rigging drowned out all other sound.

He was thoroughly soaked now, but no longer cold as the energy he had expended furling the sail had warmed him. When the wave had passed, William looked up and saw the sail had been stowed. He had no idea how the men had done it.

"Next one!" called Eddie and showed the men which sheets to release and lines to pull.

The men aloft moved down to the next sail.

"Don't look at them!" shouted Eddie. "Look behind!"

Another wave towered over the ship. The wind drove water off its top, onto the deck. William was startled there were pieces of ice in it, then realised they had sailed into a hail storm.

The wave broke across the ship which was now upright. The wave had blocked the wind from hitting the sails, so the ship was hit with the wave from above. There was a loud crash as the wave hit the deck. Water boiled and roared around the men and the infrastructure on the deck. William hung onto the rope as the water frothed around him. As the wave subsided, he saw some pails, brooms and even a chicken, float off the ship.

"How many of these can the ship take?" William asked himself, again wishing he was below. He'd even welcome being on watch with Hall.

Eddie looked around. "All the men are still here, but I'm not sure how much more of this they or the men aloft can take," he shouted to William.

The bosun came over. "Eddie, the captain's worried it's taking too long, so we need more men. We need two teams on the deck."

"It won't work, Mr Merchant. The men aloft can only handle one sail at a time. Doesn't matter how many men you have down here, there aren't enough up there."

"Look out!" called one of the men as another wave boiled around them.

The wind had now increased and hurled itself at the ship. William had never heard anything like the noise that came with the wind. He'd been in storms on land, but this was different. The wind tore through the ship's rigging with a sound like a thousand squeaky wagon wheels. From time to time, it subsided, then came on harder and louder, screaming its anger and then venting its fury the ship was still afloat. Night was coming, and William thought it would be suicidal to keep working in the dark.

"All right, but we're running out of time," said Merchant. "I'll spilt the men above into two teams of four each and add two of the engineers to each team. I'll get you another eight engineers. Can you handle two teams?"

"I'll do my best Mr Merchant. Are you sure these lads are ready to go aloft? It'll be dangerous up there. One of the new men will have to go aloft too, if you want me to stay here."

"I have no choice, Eddie. They have to be ready."

There was another "Look out!" as another wave tore at them.

The bosun left, and Eddie turned to his team, screaming to be heard above the noise. "All right, lads, you heard Mr Merchant. You'll need to scramble aloft. Don't stay as a group. Mix yourselves with the others and watch what they do. There are two teams up there, so two of you to each team."

The men looked confused. Eddie held up a hand.

"Mr Merchant is bringin' up some more men. One of them will join with one of you to make a pair. Keep your wits about you, and you'll be all right. Make sure to hang on. It looks hard up there because it is. Bill, I think the lads up there'll know what we are doin' when they see you climbin', but if need be, let them know we're goin' to do two sails at a time. It'll be easier to do a mast at a time, but if they have problems, we'll sort it out when they finish the mainmast. Finally, get your shoes and boots off. Bare feet are best for this."

Another "Look out!" Another wave and the engineers removed their shoes and boots.

"Here!" said Eddie, taking them.

Just as the engineers started climbing, another eight men appeared on deck, one of whom was immediately conscripted to go with William and the others. He didn't look frightened. William decided it was because he didn't know what he was in for yet. Eddie opened the outer doors and dumped the shoes and boots into the nearest companionway. William thought that might be the last they saw of them.

William was astonished at the force of the wind. He hung on for all his worth, and he tried to master climbing the ratlines. He found it was better if he only allowed one of his feet or one of his hands to be free. He didn't know why, but it felt safer and hoped it was. He also decided it was better if he didn't look down. He'd never climbed anything in his life before and found being aloft downright frightening. This was no place for a boy from the country.

The men already aloft had worked out what was going on, had split into two groups going to the next two sails.

William realised he had made a mistake by climbing first as it was now logical he would go to the higher sail. The ship was still lying down and standing up, so the sail was sometimes higher and sometimes at the same level. It took longer to get upright, now the wind was stronger. William hoped it would stop getting stronger. It was strong enough now, as far as he was concerned.

The team he joined moved out along the spar on the footropes, so William and Vince Alexander could be closer to the mast and wouldn't have to go so far out. They hadn't been there long when the sail started flapping, and the men below tried to haul it in. They rode the ship up and down several times before the sail was in enough for William's team to apply the gaskets. William found it was easier to do when the ship lay on its side. He did this partly by watching and partly by trial and error. He also found it was every man for himself. None of the men tried to secure a gasket when there was any danger of being thrown off the rigging. William had no idea how to secure the gasket, so had to watch the sailor do a slippery hitch, before he could do the same. There was much to learn, and this was no time for learning. William cursed himself for a fool even to be on the ship.

Once the sail was secure, they moved over to the mast and went down past the team securing the next sail. The sails were bigger as they went down, so the effort from the team on the deck was greater each time. William had no idea who was better off. The teams on the deck fighting the pitching deck and thunderous waves, or the teams on the masts and spars fighting the wind. He decided no one was. He was so cold he could barely concentrate, but he knew he would need all his concentration just to stay alive. Finally, they were back on deck and ready to move to the next mast.

"Bosun has decided to do the last two masts at the same time. He's worried if we do one mast and have sails fore or aft, it will pull the ship around," said Eddie, dispatching the teams.

It was darker now, but the teams were more accomplished, so the work proceeded at a better pace. There was very little daylight when the teams arrived back on deck with all the square sails stowed.

The jibs were pulling the bow around more than the heeling that was taking place with the square sails, but the ship continued to bounce as well as being flung violently from side to side.

"Tell the sailors and engineers that have been aloft to go below and get some rest," yelled the bosun to Eddie. "Can your teams furl the jibs?"

"Aye, Mr Merchant. Their hands'll be sore, but they'll do it right enough. It's a miracle we've not lost anyone, but we're all owed a miracle every now and again."

"Leave a storm jib, Eddie. I warrant it'll be wanted to keep her bow up. There's more than one miracle. We've got all the sails in and lost nothing. Captain will be pleased, but I reckon he'll want them up again once the storm passes."

The waves were bigger than ever now, towering over the ship before falling and trying to crush everything in their path.

William and the other sailors needed no second bidding to go below. They were all utterly exhausted. It took several minutes to cross the deck to the companionway to go below. Then they had to wait and go in several groups, so the outer doors wouldn't be open when a wave hit the ship. Finally, they were all in the darkness below decks.

Someone called in surprise, "Here's our boots!" It was hard in the darkness, but they each got their own shoes and boots. Their feet were too wet and sore to put them on. The engineers went to their quarters amidships and the sailors to theirs in the bow.

William and the others made it to their quarters by feeling their way along the bulkheads or the bunks. Most men found their bunks empty. However, some found theirs occupied and had to look elsewhere. William was one of the lucky ones who found his bunk empty as Jim was on watch. He fell into it and went instantly to sleep.

26

THE SHIP IN A STORM – THE HELM

Price got back to the helm at the same time as Patterson and Hosking.

"Mr Hosking, double the watch," said the captain. "We don't want to run into another ship."

"Yes, sir," said Hosking.

The group on the helm watched as he staggered away. The ship was already unsteady and no longer had the wonderful gliding motion of even a few minutes earlier.

"Storm is coming quickly, Captain," said Price. His voice betrayed his nervousness.

"I believe we are about to be tested, gentlemen," said the captain absently.

"Would you check on the progress of the sails, Mr Patterson? I want to change course into the storm as soon as possible."

Patterson hurried off.

The sea now came at the ship in large waves that either slid over it or burst onto it, depending on whether it was heeled or upright. Water came onto the helm. The helmsman was lucky to have a wheel to steady himself. The others had to brace themselves against the binnacle or whatever purchase was available.

Patterson returned and reported the sails coming down slowly. The captain ignored the report, as though lost in some other more important thought. Patterson looked at Price quizzically, but Price shook his head imperceptibly.

The captain blew into the communications pipe. "Mr Cave?"

"Yes, sir?"

"How's my steam coming along?"

"Do you want to use the engines?"

"How's my steam coming along?" Louder this time.

"Very good, sir."

"Thank you, Mr Cave."

"All right, Mr Price, as soon as the sails are down, I want to head directly into the wind, but I don't want to make way, so we'll use just enough steam to hold her against the storm."

"Perhaps a few degrees off the wind, sir? That way, we'll make way and not be far off course, but still hold against the storm."

"Very good, Mr Price. Excellent suggestion. Would you think 260?"

"Yes, sir. I think that would be fine sir."

Price asked about the barometer.

"At last check the barometer was twenty-eight and a half. We'll get what we get, Mr Price. No more, no less. See the bosun and hurry the sails, if you please. I'm afraid it will be dark soon."

Like Patterson before him, Price walked off unsteadily, holding whatever he could to brace himself against the pitching of the ship and the waves bursting around and over it.

He found the bosun standing by the funnel, watching the progress with the sails. "Mr Merchant," yelled Price.

The bosun had to lean close to hear over the noise of the storm.

"Captain's worried it's taking too long to stow the sails. Can you make the men work faster?"

Merchant shook his head. "We need more sailors, sir. If we had more sailors, we could work faster. The engineers have had some training, but I don't think they're ready to go aloft."

As he finished, there was a huge rush of water, and a wave broke from above. They had not seen the wave building, and it caught them both by surprise. They grabbed at the funnel rigging and held on as the water thundered around them.

When the water subsided, Price said to the bosun, "Hurry, Mr Merchant, we need to get those sails stowed. The masts cannot take much more of this punishment."

"Aye, sir," said Merchant and set off to see Eddie who was managing the deck team.

Price headed back to the helm, now looking carefully at the sea before covering any open space. Arriving at the helm, he saw both Patterson and Hosking helping the sailor with the wheel. It was all the three of them could do to hold it as the waves battered the ship. The captain stood aft, holding the rail. Price joined him.

"Captain, the bosun is adding more men to the teams working with the sails. He is fearful the men have no experience, but hopes more men will make a difference. The storm came too soon, I'm afraid. The men would have more training in a few days," he shouted.

The captain's face showed no emotion. Price looked momentarily bewildered as though he expected a response but had failed to get one.

There was no further time for talking as another wave crashed across the deck. The ship continued heeling and rising, and as it did, the waves smashed across the ship from the side or from above. The men at the helm were constantly swamped with water. The howling wind and soaking water took their toll on spirit and strength. It was obvious the three men on the wheel were not coping, but it wasn't possible to add more men to the task.

The captain leaned close to Price after a wave had passed. "Mr Price, the four of you will need to manage the helm by rotation every fifteen minutes. There are no other hands we can use, so apply yourself to the task. One man can take relief back here. I suggest you replace the sailor first."

Price nodded and waited until a wave had passed before taking the few steps required to reach the helm. "Take a break," he shouted to the sailor. "Fifteen minutes."

The sailor nodded gratefully, waiting until a wave had passed and went to join the captain. He wrapped his arms around a stay, visibly cold and shaking. Price joined Hosking and Patterson at the wheel. Patterson and Hosking did most of the work until Price became familiar with when to fight and when to relax.

Darkness was coming fast now, but it was possible to see that only the jib sails were still up. There was only the crew left attending to the jibs. The others had gone below. The bosun emerged from the darkness, waiting for a wave to pass before crossing the deck to join the captain.

"Sails will soon be furled, sir. No sails or crew lost," he shouted to the captain. "Once the sailors have rested, I'll have them relieve the officers at the helm."

"No, Mr Merchant, have the sailors come on deck immediately and relieve the officers. Establish a shift of thirty minutes each so there are three sailors at the helm until the sails are stowed. Mr Hosking and I will go below and see to the passengers. Mr Price and Mr Patterson will remain on watch. Once the sails are furled, report to Mr Price who will order the wheel be lashed and all men are to go below."

"Very good," said Merchant and hurried away when the sea permitted.

He arrived back after a few minutes with three sailors who all looked exhausted, but were better dressed to manage the weather and had probably borrowed additional clothing. Despite this, they all looked like drowned rats.

The captain signalled to Price who joined him once the officers had been relieved. "Mr Price, Mr Hosking and I will go below to see to the passengers. You and Mr Patterson remain at the helm until all the sails are furled. Mr Merchant will report to you when it's done. Then lash the wheel on our agreed heading of 260, and all men except the lookouts are to go below. Advise the lookouts to be vigilant. I want two men, both on lookout of one hour duration until the storm passes."

"It'll be dangerous for the men," shouted Price. The captain ignored him.

"Then, go below and tell Mr Cave to keep her steady on course. The communications pipe is flooded and useless, so you'll need to tell him in person."

"How will Cave know if she's holding?" shouted Price.

"You will tell him, Mr Price. It's your job to tell him."

The captain and Hosking waited until a wave had passed and headed off to the companionway to go below.

Price and Patterson waited at the aft rail. It was too dark to see what was happening with the sails, and the waves now crashed across the bow of the ship and came at the helm through the darkness. The waves tried to tear the men away from the wheel and then crushed Price and Patterson into the stays and rail at the aft of the ship.

It seemed an eternity before Merchant once again emerged through the darkness to tell Mr Price that with the exception of the storm jib, the sails were stowed.

"Praise God," said Price. "Wait with us while we lash the wheel, then take your sailors and reset the jib."

"Very good, sir."

Price signalled to Patterson. They waited until another wave had passed, then turned the ship's heading to 260 and lashed the wheel. The sailors on the wheel looked totally exhausted, but had time to thank Price before they and the bosun, headed off to reset the jib sail, after waiting for another wave to pass. They had to go for'ard, and it would be a slow and dangerous trip as they waited for, then dodged the waves.

"Come with me, Patterson," shouted Price and headed for the engine room.

They found Cave sitting by the engine in the almost darkness, a single lamp providing the only light. It was dry and warm. Cave looked surprised to see them.

"I assume the communications pipe is flooded. Are you ready for the engine?" asked Cave.

"Aye, but the captain wants to hold against the storm and not sail too far off course."

"You tell me what to do, Mr Price."

"I think all ahead half, Mr Cave. It's only a guess, but I hope a good one."

"Yes, sir," said Cave, reaching for the controls. "All ahead half it is."

"Note the order, Mr Patterson," said Price. "I will stay with Mr Cave for a while. You head to your quarters."

"Yes, Mr Price. Thank you," said Patterson and headed off down the passageway.

"Mr Cave, keep her at that speed until I advise you otherwise. I'm hoping to fix her position at daylight, God willing. I know the shifts are out of order due to the storm, but I would appreciate if you could remain on watch until the storm passes."

"Yes, sir. I can do that, sir."

"Very good. I'll be in my quarters. Send for me if you need me. Don't hesitate."

"Yes, sir."

27

THE SHIP IN A STORM - THE BOILER ROOM

Armstrong had struggled into the for'ard boiler room to make sure all the furnaces were lighted. Shadows flitted around the bulkheads making it impossible to see corners and shapes. It was hard to move about without using the bulkheads to support himself, but just as hard to tell where they were. He groped along in the darkness. The ship heeled suddenly, and he fell into a trimmer who was waiting to deliver some coal.

"Sorry, sir," shouted the man above the hiss of the steam, the roar of the furnaces and the creaking and groaning of the ship.

"It's all right. It's my fault," said Armstrong. "You been through a storm on a steamship?"

"Only coastal steamers. I imagine it's worse out here."

Armstrong tried to see who it was in the darkness. It looked like Jim Huston. "That you, Jim?"

"Aye."

"It's worse out here because of the size of the waves. She'll heel so she's lyin' on her side. It's a long way to fall from one side of the ship to the other."

"It's the same on the coasters. They pitch and heel, too."

"I'll grant you that."

"I suppose the coasters aren't as big, so if you fall, there's not so far to go."

"Coal's bigger here, too. Pieces the size of a bag of potatoes. You'll get 'em from the bunker, and before you break them up, they'll be rollin' around the deck," said Armstrong.

"Aye, but coal doesn't have to be big to be a problem. We lost a man on my last trip to Scotland. Slipped and fell on a piece of coal and split his head open. He was dead before we reached port."

Argument's lost, thought Armstrong and returned his attention to the room. It was the opposite arrangement to the other boiler room. The aft room furnaces faced aft, the for'ard ones faced for'ard.

"All right, Jim. Let's hope that doesn't happen on this one. You've done it before, so keep an eye on the others, if you can. Pass the word around. Make sure they all know the danger. Are all the furnaces goin'?"

"Aye, just stokin' them now. Be a while before they are ready, though. We're findin' it hard with the ship heelin' and all."

They heard the banging of a shovel at the same time and saw John Cooper looking to Jim Huston to bring the coal. Huston judged the moment and hurried forward with his wheelbarrow. He dumped it on the spot that Cooper indicated, but it didn't remain in place for long.

"Damn!" shouted Cooper as the ship heeled, and his coal rolled away. He'd managed to get one shovel full into the furnace before the rest had rolled to the port side.

This is not goin' to work, muttered Armstrong to himself. *How are we goin' to deliver any coal to the starboard fires?*

The coal was dumped by the trimmers, but it rolled away soon after. There was a growing pile scattering about on the port side. It was dangerous for the men there as they tried to contend with the lumps rolling about.

Armstrong realised the noise in the boiler room was increasing as the coal rattled on the deck plates and against the bulkheads. The firemen banged their shovels on the deck to demand more coal, and the ever-present hiss of steam and thumping of the engines added to the cacophony. It would be hard to work out what to do by talking with the men, but he had no choice. He had to involve the men in the decision. He was sure the problem had been solved on steamships before, but what did they do? This was the biggest ship he'd ever fired.

He signalled to John Cooper, one of the firemen. It took a while, but he got his attention, and they went into the passageway, away from the noise. "I can see what's happenin' to the firemen," he yelled to Cooper. "The trimmers put the coal on the deck, but when the ship heels, it rolls away to the port side. When the ship rights, some of it rolls back again. The pieces that roll back again hit the legs of the men trying to stoke the fires, sometimes knockin' them over."

"Aye, that's it all right. We've had the trimmers wait until she's level before they dump the coal, but as soon as they dump it, she starts to heel again. There's not even time to get the door open. It's getting worse, too. She's hardly on the level, and she starts heeling again." The ship heeled as they spoke, and both men found themselves pinned against the bulkhead in the passageway.

"There's another problem, as well, Mr Armstrong," said Cooper. "The heeling means the coal is often heaped to the port side of the furnace and needs to be levelled all the time. There's not enough time to do the levelling."

"I know," said Armstrong. "It's no job in a storm. It's hot, tirin' and never-endin'. We have no choice, John. It's important to level the coal so it heats the water in the boilers evenly, or we'll get an explosion down here that will finish some of us anyway."

"I know. Maybe if we had more men? Each fireman's looking after three furnaces. It's too hard when each one requires constant attention for either coal or levelling."

Armstrong shook his head. "There aren't any more men. I wish there were."

"What are you going to do?"

"Think on it. We'd better get back."

As the men headed back from the passageway, the heeling was already longer and steeper.

"Storm's getting worse," yelled Cooper above the din.

They stood at the entrance looking into the for'ard boiler room. The trimmers were no longer servicing their own firemen. The coal scattered, and the firemen retrieved whatever pieces were closest. The men were doing their best, there was no doubt of that.

Armstrong turned to Cooper, "It's difficult down here, but what of the men topside?"

"I'm glad I'm not there," said Cooper. "Imagine trying to furl the sails, being pitched about in the wind and hanging on for dear life. The ship's heeling ever more violently, so some or all of the square sails are still set. It's taking too long to get them down. They've been at it for hours."

Armstrong tried to tell Cooper it was hard to hear what he'd said above the din in the boiler room, but gave up. They were done, anyway.

The lamps swung in their gimbals, and shadows chased each other around the walls. Nothing remained still for any time, and the men fought with a deck that was both leaning sideways and bounding up and down. The movements became more violent as the storm's intensity increased. Coal bashed against bulkheads and furnaces, and the firemen tried to retrieve it. If it moved too far away then the trimmers had to retrieve it again and put it in place once more. But it didn't remain in place long, and the chase began over.

Christ, muttered Armstrong to himself. *What the hell can we do?*

The firemen on the starboard side had the toughest job as the heeling meant they had to get back to their furnaces once the ship righted. Some tried to find purchase on the furnace handles and stay with their furnace until the ship righted, but after some burns and near misses, they elected to retreat to the port side as the ship heeled. Steamships were not designed to go through motions like the *Lady Grace*. They were meant to steam into the wind and waves, so the deck would be pitching forward and back, not sideways.

Armstrong looked and saw Cooper still with him. "It's only a matter of time before there's an accident," yelled Cooper over the noise.

"It's madness," yelled Armstrong in reply. "The trimmers are now workin' faster and harder and deliverin' less coal to the firemen on each trip."

"Tell us what to do, Mr Armstrong," yelled Cooper, reminding Armstrong of his responsibility, watching expectantly for a reply.

Only one thing we can do, thought Armstrong. "Get the men together in the passageway," he yelled to Cooper. "I'll wait for you all there." He turned and headed back to where he had met with Cooper. It was only a little quieter there, but he'd have a chance to instruct the men and have them hear.

The men arrived, and while he was waiting, Armstrong had devised a plan. He looked at the men gathered in front of him. They looked exhausted, and the watch had just started. He longed for relief from the noise and the movement, but the ship wasn't waiting for him to either start or finish his talk. Some of the men dry-retched every now and then from seasickness. The noise and the movement continued unabated. The little group were closely packed to hear Armstrong and were jostled and pushed about by the continuous movement of the deck.

"It'll be easier for the firemen to shovel the coal out of the wheelbarrow while the trimmer holds it," began Armstrong. The faces showed no emotion. Perhaps there was none left.

"It means all of you will work from the port side. The port trimmers will load their wheelbarrows and when the ship levels, hurry with their fireman to whatever furnace needs attention. The starboard trimmers place coal in the wheelbarrow when she levels, go to the port side and wait as she heels. Then hurry with their fireman to the furnace and go back to the port side as the ship heels. They go back to the starboard for more coal." He looked around the group. *Had they heard anything?*

"What about our shovels?" asked one of the trimmers. "We keep losin' them on the deck."

"Throw your shovel into the bunker when you've loaded coal. It'll be there somewhere when you arrive back for more."

"What about the starboard trimmers?" asked another. "We'll have to get past everyone to get coal. Our job will be much harder with your plan."

"I know," replied Armstrong, his voice hoarse from shouting. "I've thought of that. Trimmers to swap port and starboard every hour. That way, you'll all have a chance to see how hard it is." He looked around the group. They all stood waiting. "Let's get on with it, then."

They all went back to the furnaces and put Armstrong's plan into effect. Armstrong returned to the aft boiler room and arranged the men to do the same.

They'd been at it for several hours, and there were burns, knocks, bruises and bad language as the men fought with the storm, the ship and each other to do their job, but the plan worked. That was good. He didn't need to return to the for'ard boiler room. If it would work aft, then it would work for'ard.

Armstrong hadn't seen Hall and the change of watch. His team were tired, very tired, and tired men make mistakes. He'd been listening for the bells, but knew it was a waste of time. There'd be no bells. He didn't need to hear them to know they had worked past their shift time. He guessed the other shift was needed on deck and wouldn't be coming to relieve them. He decided he would need to tell the men, but didn't know what to say, nor did he want to leave his post to find out what was happening with Hall's watch, but he'd have to do it sooner or later.

Finally, he stumbled around to the for'ard boilers to see how the men fared. It might be better to send a man from there to Cave and find out what was happening. When he arrived in the for'ard boiler room, he saw Jim Huston leaning against the bulkhead on the port side and judged his moment to join him. It wouldn't pay to fall the full width of the ship if it heeled as he started his journey.

"Mr Armstrong," said Huston, as he arrived. "Is all well?"

"As well as can be expected, Jim. How goes it here?"

"Your plan is good, Mr Armstrong. Took us a while to get used to it, but it's workin'. The boys're tired, sir. Is our watch done yet?"

"Should be, Jim. Next time the ship is righted, go to the engine room and check with Mr Cave about the next watch. He'll know what's goin' on. If he doesn't, then find Mr Hall and ask him why he hasn't presented his team for change of shift."

"The lads are all very tired, Mr Armstrong."

"I know Jim, I know."

The ship righted and Jim Huston hurried away to the engine room, just making it to the passageway before the ship heeled again. Armstrong waited for a few moments watching his team with the for'ard furnaces. They appeared to be going well with the men feeding them coal as expected. He watched for a while, then took the next opportunity to hurry back to the passageway to the aft boiler room.

The ship's deck reached almost level as he approached the room. What he saw was like a Punch and Judy Show, shapes of men moving quickly about, trying to take advantage of a level deck. He knew it was his plan, but it made it no less comical to watch. Still, there was a doubt in his mind. He was still missing something. He wanted someone to share the moment, to discuss the doubt. Just then, Huston arrived at his side.

"What're you doin', Mr Armstrong?"

"Just watchin' my boys," replied Armstrong.

"Why?"

"I might want to remember this in my old age. What do you see, Jim?"

"Are you serious, Mr Armstrong?"
"Yes, Jim. Tell me what you see."
"The light's not too good and with the lamps swingin' to and fro, I can see shapes more than I can see people."
"How many shapes?"
"I can see the shapes of three firemen and two trimmers."
"And what are they doin'?"
"Well sir, the ship's just righted, so the trimmer for the starboard side has rushed to the starboard bunker, pushin' his empty wheelbarrow, racin' against time to find his shovel, fetch some coal and retreat to the port bulkhead before she heels again, and the deck's too uneven to move."
"Wait 'till she levels again and tell me what he does."
"But you know what he's doin', sir. Shouldn't we be helpin'?"
"In a moment, Jim. A rest will do us no harm."
"Well, sir. She's righted and the trimmer's deliverin' the coal to one of his firemen. He's opened the furnace door, shovelled the coal in, raked it over and closed the door. It's good work, sir. I didn't think he'd get it done in time. Is this why we're watchin'?"
"Could be. What's the port trimmer doin'?"
"Well sir, he's doin' the same, but it's easier for him. The firemen are closer to him. He's delivered coal to his fireman who's opened the furnace, shovelled the coal from the wheelbarrow, raked the furnace, closed the door, and they both retreated to the port side as she heeled again." Huston stopped for a moment and added, "It might be easier, but it's still hard work sir, and they're gettin' the job done."
"There's somethin' we've forgotten."
"And what's that, sir?"
"The trimmers aren't balancin' the coal taken from the bunkers. The starboard-side trimmer has the same time, but further to

go to do his job, so less coal is comin' from the starboard side. We'll have to allocate a fireman from the starboard side to the trimmer on the port side, in addition to the port firemen he already has. I should have seen it before. He'll work harder then and deliver less coal."

"Port trimmers won't like it, sir."

"I know," said Armstrong, "but it can't be helped. We've got to trim her properly. If we don't, she'll pitch and heel more, or maybe even roll over if we get it badly wrong."

They stood still for a few more moments, watching the scene.

"Christ, sir. She sounds like she's about to break up," said Huston.

Huston's comment brought him back to this reality. The heeling and righting, pitching and yawing meant the ship was stressed in every rivet, plate and joint. The stressing produced a grinding, groaning sound. The scattered coal on the deck rolled backwards, forwards and sideways, bumping the men, the bulkheads and rattling on the deck plates. The furnace doors were bashed shut by the firemen so there was no chance they would accidentally open, crashing into men hurrying by on whatever errand. When the doors were open, the furnaces roared and huffed. Sometimes, a mishandled wheelbarrow would scatter its load of coal to the deck, its owner would slip on the contents and fall cursing. Or a shovel would slip from its owner's grip, falling to the deck and clattering amongst the debris.

"You're right, Jim. Back to the job. The ship'll be all right. She's built to take this, and she's new. It's the men I worry about. How long can they work so hard in these conditions? Damned if I know."

"Do you want to know what I got from Mr Cave?"

"Ah, Jim. Of course. What news?"

"Mr Cave doesn't know what's happenin', Mr Armstrong. Says the communications pipe is filled with water. Some time ago, he wondered why he hadn't heard from the helm, picked up the pipe and got an earful of water. So, I went to find Mr Hall. He told me to tell you all his men are on deck helpin' to stow the sails, so he doesn't have a shift and can't take a watch. Says you'll have to keep goin' until his men are back. Says even then you'll need to leave some of your men to help, as his will be tired from workin' topside."

"Where was Mr Hall?"

"I don't like to say, Mr Armstrong."

"All right, Jim. Go back to your team."

Armstrong shook his head. No relief in sight, and the job still to be done. He would have to change the teams for both fore and aft boiler rooms to address the bunker balancing problem. He didn't believe for a moment all of Hall's team were topside, but there was nothing he could do about it. He wondered what Fletcher was doing, and why he hadn't seen him. He was probably in the engine room with Cave. No matter, he'd get there when he next had the chance.

Waiting until the right moment to cross the deck, he tried to signal to his team he wanted to talk with them. It took a few minutes to get everyone's attention, but eventually they were gathered in the semblance of a group on the port side, leaning against or standing beside the bulkhead as determined by the angle of the deck. They huddled as close as they could to hear Armstrong. His words were almost drowned out by the din.

"Men, Hall's watch is topside workin' on stowin' the sails. We hope they'll be done soon, so captain can head her into the wind, and she'll stop heelin'. I don't know about you, but I've had about enough of it. We'll get some relief when they're done, but we'll have to work until they can take over, and that's all there is to it. Also, until we stop heelin', Fred, you work with me, and Brian, you with the others because there's no way Fred can get coal enough from the starboard side for two firemen. I've been watchin', and I can't see we're gettin' the same amount of coal from both sides, so she won't be trimmed properly. Don't worry, Brian. We'll swap you and Fred every thirty minutes or so. The trimmer serving three firemen will have the worst of it. All right, lads, hop to it."

Brian Mitchell and the other three firemen went back to work.

"Fred," said Armstrong. "We'll get my furnaces stoked again, then you swap with Brian. I'll go to the engine room and find Mr Fletcher to see if there's a plan."

Fred nodded, waited until the time was right and headed for the starboard bunker. Armstrong waited until he returned. When the deck was right, he and Fred Stoker headed over to attend to his three furnaces and were pleased to see the men had given them some attention while he managed his shift, but he would need to spend some time getting them burning properly again. The for'ard crew and bunkers would have to wait. There would be much more trouble if his fires went low - the perils of watch management.

Armstrong had become so absorbed in attending to the fires, he hadn't noticed the heeling had reduced, and the pitching motion had increased. They must have got the sails down and headed her more into the wind. It meant they would be riding the waves bow on, so there was more risk now of being thrown against the furnaces when she pitched forward. *No way to make a livin'*, he mused.

Stopping briefly, he checked on the men. Brian Mitchell had more than his work cut out for him providing coal for three firemen, and two of the firemen were sometimes standing idle waiting for coal. *Time to change it,* he thought. *Poor Brian. Wasn't much of a deal for him. Worked with three firemen and then the plan changed.*

It was easier now as they could gather against the bulkhead behind, and he signalled them to get together. "All right, time to go back to one trimmer, two firemen. Take a few minutes rest, get some water. I'll go for'ard to see what the plan is now the sails are stowed."

There was no need to change the arrangement now for the for'ard crew. They'd been two firemen to one trimmer all along. He'd need to check the starboard bunkers later. He wasn't sure how they'd work out how much coal had been taken from each side.

It was hard work getting to the engine room. One moment he'd be climbing a hill, the next he'd be falling down it as the big ship rode the waves. *Better now,* he thought. *This is how a steamship is meant to sail.*

Cave and Fletcher were both at the engine. The greaser was with them, and they all seemed intent on whatever they were doing and failed to notice his arrival.

Armstrong thought to stand quietly nearby and listen. Almost immediately, he realised the futility of the thought. The noise from the engines was ear shattering. They were noisier than usual, and Armstrong reasoned the gearing must be taking a beating as theiler was alternately pushed in the water and lifted from it as the ship wallowed in troughs and crested waves. He was about to shout to announce his presence, when the ship moved violently, and he fell into Fletcher.

A startled Fletcher stood too quickly, and knocked Armstrong to the deck. Fletcher hurried to help him to his feet.

"No harm done," shouted Armstrong. "Is there a plan now the sails are stowed?"

"How do you know the sails are stowed? Nobody told me that," shouted Fletcher.

"Different motion of the ship. Only just happened."

Fletcher looked to Cave and nodded. "That's why," he shouted.

The four men stood without speaking for a few moments, Armstrong wondering about a plan, and the others surely thinking about the implications of "That's why."

Cave looked at Armstrong and shouted, "I understand most of Hall's men have been on deck with the sails. Once they have had a rest and something to eat, they'll relieve you."

"How long?"

Cave shrugged.

"Can you spare the men that didn't go topside? They can at least help. My lads have been at it since the forenoon watch. We could use whatever help you can give us. Where's Mr Hall? Did he go topside?"

Fletcher shook his head. "There's Hall and two others didn't go topside."

"We could sure use them."

Fletcher looked at Cave, who nodded.

"Anything else?" shouted Cave.

"Yes, Mr Cave, could you arrange for some food to be sent down. My lads would sure appreciate that and bein' relieved when possible."

Fletcher looked at Cave, who nodded again.

"I'll arrange the food now," shouted Fletcher and left the room making allowances for the pitching of the ship.

"Thank you, Mr Armstrong. The food we can do, but the relief will take longer," said Cave and turned back to the engine.

Armstrong headed back to the for'ard boiler room. *At least he could tell the crew there'd be some food and some help. It wasn't much, but it'd have to do.*

He finally got back to the aft boiler room and set to, stoking his furnaces. It was harder for him as during his absences, the fires would go down, and he would have to stoke them quickly to get them firing properly again.

Nonetheless, it wasn't long before Brian Hall and two of his men came into the room with biscuits and more sweet water.

"Is this the best you can do?" queried Armstrong, shaking his head.

"No fires," replied Hall, shrugging.

"Get one of your men to take half of the food for'ard."

Hall nodded and dispatched a man.

"Whatever job your other man does, get him to relieve one of mine."

Hall dispatched the other man to relieve a trimmer.

"Where the hell have you been?" asked Armstrong once the man was out of ear shot.

"None of your business."

Armstrong shrugged and went back to his stoking.

Hall stood there for a few moments until his man came back from for'ard.

"Go and relieve one of the for'ard firemen. I don't care which one. Pick the one that looks the most tired."

He waited a few moments longer. Armstrong's relieved man sat with his back to the aft bulkhead, clearly grateful for a break and for the biscuits and water.

Hall turned and headed for the ladder.

Armstrong watched him go and shrugged again. *Mr Cave, you've got a problem. No, Mr Cave, you've got a big problem.* He then tried to work out how he would relieve his two teams with one extra trimmer and one extra fireman.

28

The Ship in a Storm – the First Officer

Price, Hosking, and Patterson – the officers, and the captain headed for the companionway to the saloon. It was supper time, but Price knew there would be no supper with the captain's orders for no fires.

They used the companionway double doors to stop as much water as possible following them, but success was limited. Arriving on the next deck, they stood in a group, dripping water onto the deck, adding to that which had followed them in.

The only light available was provided by the continuous flashes of lightning coming through the skylight. The first-class saloon was empty. A few items that had been left by passengers skated back and forth along the carpet, now the motion of the ship was more forward and back than side to side. Cups and books figured amongst the scattered items. There was a terrible smell of sick in the room, but Price couldn't tell if it was in the room itself or coming from the adjacent cabins.

"Get the stewards to clear up this mess, Mr Price. This won't do at all. The water, too and if any passengers have been sick in here, that will need to be cleaned as well."

The officers presented a sorry, bedraggled sight in their skins and sou'westers. The captain removed his sou'wester and the others did the same.

"Mr Hosking and Mr Patterson, go by the galley and get yourselves some biscuits. They'll do until the storm passes, and we can do better. Then get some rest. Mr Price, you have the ship. Please check on all the passengers' quarters and have any mess cleaned by the stewards. I will relieve you when I have eaten, rested and made myself presentable. Good night, gentlemen."

The other three officers watched the captain walk off, trying unsuccessfully to maintain balance against the pitching ship. He halted near the doorway to his cabin as the angle of the ship became too steep to climb, waiting until the ship crested a wave before entering.

"I'm sorry, Mr Price, but we'd best go," said Hosking.

"Of course," said Price. "Be off and do as he says. There'll be more to do before this night or the storm is done, so get some rest while you can."

He watched the men do their best to walk away. Like the captain before them, they discovered walking below decks was no simple matter, and they had to judge their walk to coincide with a more level deck. They were still hurled from side to side as the ship was battered by wind and wave. As they walked, the deck would often be higher or lower than anticipated, such that a foot would meet the deck sooner or later than expected. Their walk had a strange rolling motion that Price thought he might find comical if there wasn't so much danger.

Price had expected the captain to give him the ship. The captain was responsible for the ship, and he needed a rest as much as anyone, so it was better he took it now. Sleep was Price's enemy. If he sat and went to sleep, he would be derelict in his duty, so it was best he kept busy.

He walked past the cabins located off the saloon, putting his head close to the wall for a while, in case he could hear anything unusual. After several sharp contacts with the wall, he decided against the practice. He hoped anyone in need of help would come looking for it. *Where were the stewards? They should at least be checking on the passengers, making sure night pots were emptied. Where to empty them was a problem. It would be impossible to throw anything over the side in the wind.*

If he was going to wander through the rest of the ship, he would need a lantern. He knew it was dangerous, but he had no way to see without one. There would be one in the galley, and the best way to get it would be to go back topside, cross the deck and go down the companionway to the engine department's quarters. *That might be the best way, but it's not the only way.* He went up the passageway that led to the galley. He should have gone with Hosking and Patterson. He could only sense he was moving forward, and it was very difficult being hurled about in the dark. *Maybe, the external option had been the best.* Nonetheless, he eventually found the galley and thanks to the skylight and lightning, found a lantern and some flints. It tested all his patience to get it going. He found some biscuits and sat on the deck to eat them, before setting off to explore the ship.

It was no surprise to find things in the second-class saloon the same as in first class. Some items scattered about clashed with the furniture and the walls. *Was the engine department the only one active? Where was everybody?*

He went down the passageway to the for'ard crew's quarters. He was really tired now. It was warmer in the ship, hard work to get about, and the last twelve hours or so were getting to him. It was harder to walk with the lantern too. He now had only one hand to protect himself as the ship lurched and shuddered. He would also need to check on the lookouts.

The lantern swung from side to side, and he had to be careful not to break it as he headed down the ladder to the crew's quarters. He found the chief steward sound asleep and snoring in his bunk.

"Mr Hughes, Mr Hughes," he called, shaking the man.

"What is it? What is it?"

"Have you seen to your passengers?"

Hughes sat up, rubbing his eyes and squinting to see Price in the light from the lantern.

"Yes, Mr Price. We went around and made sure everyone had some water and biscuits. Some passengers, mostly first class, complained they wanted some proper food, but most were too sick to bother. Many of the cabins were a mess, Mr Price. Sick and whatever scattered everywhere. We'll have a proper mess to clean when the storm passes. Two passengers have fallen. One had a broken arm and the other a nasty wound on her head. They're in the surgery. Surgeon says he'll keep them there until the storm passes."

Price nodded.

"Where'd you get the lantern, Mr Price? We've been working in the dark and right hard it's been."

"Mr Hughes, the captain wants the saloons cleaned up."

"We've done all that already, but it'll do no harm to do it again, Mr Price. Be easier with a lantern, of course."

"Well, the captain's gone to his cabin, and it might be best to wait until morning. As soon as it's dawn, have your washers and stewards do their best to clean up what they can in the closets, passageways and saloons. I don't think the storm will be done by then, but it'll be easier with whatever light the day can provide."

"Very good, Mr Price. What time is it now?"

"I don't know, Mr Hughes. Only the storm is ringing the bell at the moment. There're lookouts, but they'll have their hands full. I'll do my best to come back and wake you before the captain is back on watch. If I don't, be sure you are up at dawn. Good night."

"You look tired, sir. You get some rest too, sir. Good night, Mr Price."

Price went through the battle to get to the engine quarters. He was surprised that if anything, the storm had become worse. The ship pitched more violently.

He found the engine quarters almost fully occupied. He knew many of the crew had supported the sailors, but that was hours ago. By the light of his lantern, he saw Hall curled up and sleeping. He didn't know the man, just knew he was the leading fireman on one of the watches.

Turning back, he climbed the ladder down to the engine department and went through the passageway to the engine room. Both Cave and Fletcher were there.

"Mr Cave, Mr Fletcher. Anything to report?"

He saw a worried glance between the men.

"Aye, sir," shouted Cave. "The driving chains are taking some punishment with the screw going in and out of the water. The propeller speeds up when it's out of the water, then slows down when it goes under. Things're getting hot, sir. I don't like it. Greaser's been working hard, but we're not sure if what he is doing is helping."

"What can we do?"

"Disengage the engine and put her under sail is all I can think. She'll go better when the sea dies down. It's the waves, sir."

"How long before there's any damage?"

"I don't know, sir. It's been getting hotter for the last two or three hours."

"Why didn't you tell me before?"

"Thought you might have your hands full, sir."

"Not if the ship is at risk. Don't let this happen again."

Price thought for a few moments, then nodded. He'd have to tell the captain. He couldn't make such a decision without consulting the captain.

"I'll see the captain, but to be sure you understand me, don't let this happen again."

He climbed to the next deck and was about to go to the captain's cabin when he thought it might be best to check on the lookouts. He wasn't far from there, so he could do a check and not take too much time. The captain might ask about them, so it would be best to know. Perhaps he should have made Patterson one of the lookouts. That would surely have satisfied the captain as a suitable punishment.

The lantern cast shadows about as he headed down the passageway into the saloon where the weak light revealed four men sleeping on the deck. They were dressed in the scrappy clothes of sailors, and the men and the deck around them were soaked with water. It was hard to see their faces in the poor light cast by the lantern. Neither his presence nor the lantern had woken them which Price took as testament to their fatigue.

Nudging one of them awake with his shoe, he asked, "What are you men doing here?"

The man awoke quickly, blinking in the light of the lantern.

"What's that, sir?"

"What are you men doing here?"

"Lookouts, sir. We're rotating every hour, so it's not worth while going back to the quarters. We sleep here then go out when it's our turn."

"How do you know when it's your turn?"

"We've got an hourglass, sir." He pointed to an hourglass nearby. All the sand was at the bottom.

"Must be our turn now, sir, by the look of it."

He nudged another man awake, and they headed up the companionway. Price followed, after putting the lantern into a gimbal near to the steps. Best to keep it burning. Its job wasn't done yet.

They went between the doors and then braced themselves as they opened the outer doors. The wind tore at them, and they were instantly soaked by a wave. Price was right, the storm was worse.

The group floundered its way aft, holding onto any purchase to prevent themselves being swept away by the wind and water. Price looked for'ard and saw nothing but blackness. Then, as his eyes became accustomed, he could make out the lines of a wave. The angle of the deck became steeper and steeper as the ship ploughed into the storm. The ship clawed its way up the wave, and Price was momentarily grateful the captain had ordered all the crew into the ship.

He then dragged his eyes off the wave and tried to find the lookouts. The two men that had come with him stood at the aft rail, holding the rigging. There was no sign of anyone else. He joined the men. The angle of the ship was such that he wondered if the ship could slide backwards. When they reached the summit, the ship paused momentarily, then the wave rushed past the ship's sides, and as the ship fell, it engulfed the aft of the ship.

Water thundered about the group huddled there. The force of the water was massive, and it was a struggle just to hold on. Their feet were swept off the deck, and only their grip held them against the wave. There seemed no end to the water as the wave flowed past, their fingers numb, their energy sapped, and only desperation stopping them being swept along with the water.

In the few moments of respite, as the ship started climbing again, the men beside him shouted, "Aart! Michael! Aart! Michael!"

There was no answer. Price hadn't expected one. The men were gone. He signalled to the other men to follow him, and they hurried back to the companionway. The just got in before another wave thundered across the deck.

Nothing was said as Price fetched the lantern down from its gimbal. He looked at the men. "Were the men Aart Jansen and Michael Wilds?"

"Yes, sir. Did you know them well?"

"No, not well, but well enough. I'm sorry. I'll tell the captain. Stay here. No more lookouts until you hear from me."

"Will the captain want us to go back out?"

"I hope not."

"I wonder when they went?" asked one of the men.

"How long had they been out there?"

The same man shifted on his feet, looking down. None of the men spoke.

"The hourglass was empty, so it was more than an hour, wasn't it?"

The man Price had nudged awake said, "We tried using the glass outside, but it was useless, so we decided we'd keep it in here, and the men outside would come in when they thought an hour was up, or we'd go out if we woke. We set the glass before we slept, but it was always empty when the lookouts came back."

"What's your name?"

"Lucas Foster, sir."

"Don't worry, Lucas, it could have been any of you. It's not your fault, but they could have gone any time in the last hour. There's no point in looking for them was what I was thinking."

"We could turn around and try, sir. We've got engines, sir, so it might be possible."

"No. There's some trouble with the engines, so there might be only sails shortly."

"Trouble, sir? What kind of trouble."

"No matter, Lucas. You men wait here while I see the captain."

"Beggin' you pardon, sir, but it'd be suicide to keep lookouts."

"I know that, but it's the captain's decision. Wait here."

He placed the lantern back in the gimbal before turning and heading for the captain's cabin, leaving the men slumped about the deck, casting fearful looks at each other.

Price had to knock several times at the captain's door before he was requested to enter. A lamp burned in the cabin. The captain was dressed in some sort of nightgown and cap that looked incongruous compared to Price's wet weather oilskins.

"What do you need, Mr Price?"

"The engine driving chains are overheating due to the propeller being lifted out of the water by the waves. Mr Cave suggests we shut down the engines and use the sails before there's any damage."

"Is that all, Mr Price?"

"No sir. We've lost two of the lookouts overboard. We don't know when it happened."

The captain nodded.

If Price had expected any emotion, he didn't get it.

"What sails are set?"

"A storm jib, sir."

"Will that be enough?"

"I hope so, sir, but we won't know until we stop the engines."

The captain nodded again.

"Tell the chief to disengage the engines, then see if the storm jib holds her. If it doesn't, re-engage the engines and add another jib and keep doing that until she holds."

"I don't think we can do that in the storm, sir."

"Ah, then I suggest you ask the bosun for his help and advice."

"Yes, sir."

"And, Mr Price, how many lookouts are left?"

"Four, sir."

The captain's face was impassive. Price thought it was as though he asked how much coal was left.

"I don't think we can ask the men to go out there, sir, either to set the sails or to be lookout."

"It's not your decision, Mr Price. The safety of the ship is of utmost importance." The captain walked over and consulted his nearest clock. "It's about an hour to daylight, Mr Price. I'll grant you the danger to the men is highest at night and the benefit perhaps least, but we can under no circumstances dispense with the lookouts during the day. We could be heading for the coast of France for all we know. I will relieve you at 0700. Good night, Mr Price."

Price started to leave, but turned back.

"What is it, Mr Price?"

"It's about the men we lost, sir. One was a married man. He had children. The men were related. It'll be hard for the family."

"That's probably true, but it would be good if you could get to the point."

"Perhaps we should have a service for them?"

"Mr Price, I do wish you would maintain some perspective. Sailing is a dangerous business, and there is no room for sentimentality. The men are gone, and unless we find the bodies trapped in the rigging, there are no bodies for a service. Their families will do the grieving, and that's as it should be. They won't be the first, nor will they be the last. Our job is to sail this ship and to keep as many alive on this voyage as God will permit. We may all join those men before this night, or this voyage is over. Forget the dead and worry about the living. Good night, Mr Price."

Price left the captain's cabin, glad the lookouts would have some respite, but fearful for them once they were posted again. As he stumbled across the saloon, he was relieved he hadn't sent Patterson as a lookout. It would have weighed heavily upon him if Patterson had been one of those lost. *Not sure the captain would have been the least troubled. Perhaps it was an appropriate punishment to lose your life for failure to be on time for a meeting.*

When he reached the saloon, he found all the men were asleep. Price didn't think he had been gone so long. He wondered if he should wake them. He decided to leave them. Perhaps sleep was better than anything at the moment. Besides, he had to find the bosun and consult with Cave. The long night weighed heavily upon him.

Returning to the crew's quarters, he found the bosun sound asleep. He hated to wake him, but the bosun was instantly awake. Price had done no more than call his name.

"Trouble, sir?" asked the bosun.

"Yes, Mr Merchant. There's plenty to go around. There's trouble with the engine's driving chains, so the plan is to shut the engines down and proceed under sail."

"Under sail, sir?" The bosun couldn't hide his surprise.

"Only as many jibs as we need to hold the bow. There's a storm jib there now, and it may be enough. So, the plan is to shut down the engines, see how she holds and add jibs until she does. We'll keep the engines going until the necessary jibs are set."

"Very good, sir. We can do that."

"There's more, Mr Merchant. We've lost two of the lookouts overboard. The storm is very bad, so it won't be easy to set the jibs, and we don't want to lose any more men."

"If it was easy sir, the passengers would do it."

Price permitted himself a smile.

"How many men will you need, Mr Merchant?"

"Well, sir, if you'll help, we'll need a helmsman and three good sailors."

"All right, wake them and send them to wait at the companionway. You come with me, and we'll see Mr Cave and work out how we stop the engines and add jibs until she holds."

"About the men we lost, sir. How did it happen?"

"I don't know, Mr Merchant, but I can guess. We went topside to check on them, and they were gone. The waves and the wind are gale force, so I expect one of the men got into trouble, and the other tried to help him. It's very dangerous out there, Mr Merchant, so you tell your men to be careful."

"No need to do that, sir. They're paid to take risks, and they know them."

"Very good, Mr Merchant. I'll wait for you."

It seemed only a matter of moments when the bosun joined him. "Ready, sir."

They went up the ladders, with Price and Merchant heading for the engine room and Merchant's men waiting at the companionway for them to return. Cave and Fletcher looked like they hadn't moved since Price was last there. Price told them about the captain's decision.

"I can disengage the engines, sir, but how will I know if the bow is holding?"

"We'll use the communications pipe."

Cave shook his head. "It's full of water."

"Can we empty it?"

"Only if we unblock both ends at the same time."

"How about you unblock your end and leave it unblocked?"

"Yes, sir. That will work, sir. Although, I won't need a bath for a while."

"Can we wait until daylight, Mr Cave? This'll be easier in the daylight," asked the bosun.

Cave shook his head. "Best to do it soon. The driving chains are too hot already."

"All right, Mr Merchant. Let's take your men on deck. Mr Cave, stand by the communications pipe. I'll tell you when to disengage the engines."

"Very good, sir," said Cave. "Good luck out there, sir."

Price and Merchant hurried off.

They found the sailors and helmsman waiting at the companionway to the deck. They clambered up and once again used the double doors to avoid water flooding in. The sailors remained behind as they wouldn't be needed if there were to be no extra jibs. Merchant, Price, the helmsman and one of the sailors went out into the storm.

It was bitterly cold, and the wind and the waves had increased from when Price last saw them. Price found he was glad it was not yet daylight as he was sure the elements would be more terrifying if he could see them.

The four men battled their way to the wheel. They were almost fighting each other for something to hold onto and avoid being swept away by the wind and the waves. Communication was impossible as anything they tried to say was torn away by the wind. Still, they all knew what had to be done, so there was some coordination about their efforts. Three men held the wheel while Price untied the lashings. The wheel sprang free, and the men fought it as the rudder was pushed about by the waves. Price knew they wouldn't be able to hold it for long, so he grabbed the communications pipe, removed the plug and screamed, "Disengage! Disengage!"

A wave broke over them. Price tried to cover the pipe, but some water went in. *Might be a good thing. At least Cave knows I'm using it.*

The bow of the ship started falling away from the wind, and the men on the helm fought to hold it and bring it back. *Don't go past the wind! Please don't gybe it!*

The bosun signalled they needed another jib. *Damn! This'll be tricky.*

Price nodded, lashed the wheel again, and the bosun went to get his other men. The men came out and went to the stowed jibs. Price saw they were going to raise the outer jib. They'd need the engine. He picked up the pipe and shouted, "Engage! Engage!" This time, after a few moments, they actually felt the engine engage as the ship started to make way again.

Good! Well, maybe. Now, Price had to remove the wheel lashings and quickly help with the wheel to point the ship into the wind. The men on the extra jib waited until the storm jib started to flog and then moved quickly to hoist the extra one.

There were a few anxious moments as the bow of the ship looked as though it might cross the wind, such that the sails would be hoisted on the wrong side. The helmsman and the sailor were good at their job, and the bow swung back as the jib was raised. They let the bow fall off the wind a little, and Price lashed the wheel. The ship held steadily. Price lifted the pipe and called, "Disengage! Disengage!" Once again, some water found its way into the pipe. Price imagined Cave getting an earful.

They waited, but the ship held steady. The extra jib was enough. Time to lash the wheel and go below. The men fought their way back to the companionway.

Day was breaking and Price looked about him before leaving the deck. There was just enough light to reveal the power of the elements. The two jibs were full and taut down the port side, giving testimony to the sail maker's craft. The rigging screamed in protest against the wind which howled as though in frustration at its inability to destroy the ship. The sea was chaotic, and waves came from three parts of the compass, but the biggest ones were from the west. The ship crawled up another wave, going up the side rather than into it as it had when the engines were running. Water churned all around them, and Price briefly wondered about the animals. As he closed the storm doors behind him, Price decided to have one more go at convincing the captain to sail without lookouts.

Even as he thought of it, his heart sank. The captain wouldn't relieve him until 0700, so the men would need to be on lookout until then.

Price went down to the crew's quarters to tell the chief steward it was time to clean the ship. He knew it was a waste of time, but the captain had given his orders. Then, he went to the saloon to wake the lookouts. Again, the captain had given his orders. He told the men to take some rope and to tie themselves to the ship.

"What if she goes down?" asked Foster, a look of anguish on his face.

"Then you'll be lookout forever," said Price and was gratified when the other men laughed. *No time to lose your sense of humour,* he thought. *Lose that, and we could lose hope.* Whatever else, he was dealing with very brave men.

29

THE SHIP IN A STORM – THE CHIEF ENGINEER

Cave sat, waiting patiently for the call down the communications pipe to disengage the engines. The pipe came down the bulkhead near where he sat, so it wasn't hard to hold the pipe, ready for the call. He'd already taken the plug out and emptied what he could of the water. Maybe that was a waste of time. More would come when the plug was removed at the other end.

He thought perhaps he had missed the call when water gushed from the pipe. Once the flow ceased, he put the pipe to his ear. Wind whistled in the pipe. He prayed he'd be able to hear Price. Just then, he heard a faint, "Disengage."

Disengaging was easy. He had only to shut off the steam to the engine. It would be harder if they had to re-engage. He thought he'd best be ready. He signalled to Fletcher and the greaser. They stood ready to turn the wheels so the crankshaft was horizontal. Until they had done so, he couldn't re-engage the engine. He glanced over. The two men made hard work of it. He wished he'd got extra men from the engine room. They might have to do this several times if they needed to add more jibs. He looked again, and Fletcher signalled they were ready.

Waiting, waiting with the pipe and getting soaked for his trouble. Then he heard, "Engage! Engage!" It was clear this time, so he decided he was getting used to hearing the words over the wind.

He re-engaged the engines. *Slowly does it. Not too fast, not too soon. Don't break or blow anything.* He could see the pace building up, and he increased the flow of steam. He was worried about the driving chains, too. *They'll be more fragile on re-starting.*

It wasn't long before he had the steam back, so he concentrated on the pipe. He heard, "Disengage! Disengage!" He turned off the valve again and signalled to Fletcher. *How many more times will we need to do this?*

He sat for a while and realised no more water had come from the pipe. Price must have plugged his end again, so perhaps the extra jib was all that was needed. Still, he'd better sit and wait, paying attention to the pipe.

It was warm in the room, and fatigue started to take hold. He still held the pipe but stood up and hopped from foot to foot. Fletcher and the greaser waited. He wondered how long he could fight sleep when the bosun stumbled into the room. Cave had been fighting the movement of the ship from only one position. He realised how hard it must be for crew like Merchant who had to move about the ship.

"Mr Price says all is well, Mr Cave. She'll hold with the jibs until the storm passes. Are the gears all right?"

"I believe so. They'll cool down now. I'll discuss with Mr Fletcher as to whether we need do any more than wait."

"Very good. Time to rest for you and your men, then."

Cave nodded wearily, and the bosun left. He saw Fletcher watching and signalled him over.

"You and Fred can leave, Bruce. Find something to eat and get some rest. I'll finish here. Just leave some space for me on the bunk in case we have to share it."

Fletcher nodded, and he and Fred Barret disappeared down the passageway.

Cave went to find Armstrong. He found him in the aft boiler room and signalled to him to come out into the passageway. Armstrong left his furnaces and joined Cave.

"No engines for a while, Mr Armstrong. There's some trouble with the driving chains, so we're running under sail."

"For how long, sir?"

"I don't know. Until the storm passes. Mr Merchant was just out there and says it shows no sign of abating. I'll get Hall to bring his team down to relieve you."

Armstrong nodded. "That would be good, Mr Cave. The lads are exhausted."

Cave headed off to find Hall. He climbed the ladder into the engine crew's quarters. There was enough light coming from the skylight to see the men sleeping in the room. He knew Hall's bunk and had no trouble finding it.

"Hall! Hall!" shouted Cave, waking more than just Brian Hall.

"What is it? Can't you see I'm sleeping?"

Cave stood back, staring down at the man, his dislike intensified.

"Aye, I can see that, and I'd like you to take your watch."

Hall blinked in the half-light. "It can't be my watch. It looks like it's only dawn."

"Hall, it's your watch, and if you don't get yourself and your men to the boiler rooms in the next five minutes, I'll have you all thrown overboard. I hope I'm making myself clear."

"Yes, sir. Certainly sir," mumbled Hall, hurrying from his bunk.

"Starboard watch! Let's go!" he shouted, no doubt trying to add some sense of authority and responsibility to the order.

"Can we get something to eat before we go, Mr Cave?"

Cave shook his head. "I'll send something down. Get on with it. You should have taken the middle watch and given the other men a break."

"My men helped the sailors, Mr Cave. They were in no condition to take that watch."

"And you, Mr Hall? Who did you help?"

"I put some men on Mr Armstrong's watch."

"And you, Mr Hall? Who did you help?"

Cave realised the room had gone quiet, and the men were listening, but he didn't care. He was past exhausted and felt nothing for a man who had a good night's rest while the rest of the ship battled with the storm. Then he saw Hall staring at him with visible hatred. *I'll have to let it go,* he thought. *Not in front of the men.*

"Damn it, get on with it, Mr Hall. You might as well see the cook and get your men some biscuits." He stretched out on a spare bunk and fell asleep.

30

THE SHIP IN A STORM – SAILING AS BEST THEY CAN

It was morning, and in spite of the storm, the crew on the ship set about their allotted tasks as best they could.

Price, the chief officer went to his quarters and woke Hosking, the first officer, warning him the captain would be up and about soon, and Hosking should do an inspection of the ship. He left Patterson, the second officer, to sleep. He looked at his own bunk longingly as though he wanted to stretch out on it, but couldn't as he was yet to hand over to the captain.

Hall took his watch below and relieved Armstrong. No words passed between the men, other than Armstrong telling Hall the engines were not in use and may not be for some time. There was no engineer to give advice, so all the furnaces were maintained, but were allowed to die down. It didn't take all the men, and Hall was down by two men anyway, so he organised his men such that they could rotate and take a rest every hour or so. Hall snapped at his men, making pointless orders and taking out his bad mood on anyone he could, clearly still seething about Cave.

Armstrong took his men back to their quarters. He didn't need to send Hall's men up for'ard to find other bunks. There were enough spare bunks. Everyone was exhausted, and it wasn't long before the quarters resounded with snoring.

The chief steward organised his men into patrols. Their first task was to find anything that needed attention then organise a team to address it. They found the ship a shambles. In addition to the tasks in the saloons ordered by the captain, almost every cabin needed to be cleaned. There wasn't crew enough, so the passengers had to help. Some passengers wanted their rooms left alone as they were too sick to help, and the crew had no choice but to comply. Nearly every passenger was seasick. Those that weren't were only prepared to clean their own cabin, if they had shared with someone who had been sick.

The crew found that if you weren't sick before you went into the cabins and the closets, you were soon after. The ship continued to pitch and yaw, so filling and emptying pots and buckets meant there was plenty of spillage for the bilge. All the crew needed to be cleaned themselves after they had finished cleaning the ship and were granted permission to use the baths. They didn't take a bath, just rinsed themselves and then cleaned the bath afterwards.

Even the crew that were seasick had to help. There was no relief from the sailor's common enemy, so the crew often had to clean up their own mess several times. They found the sick feeling could only be managed by lying down, so they took it in turns to work for a while, then lie down. The process didn't help productivity, but it got the job done.

Fires were still not allowed, so there was no hot food. Most people, crew and passengers alike, were averse to food of any kind, but there were some passengers who were not troubled by the conditions and complained about their poor treatment. They presented themselves in the saloons at breakfast time, only to be told there would be no hot meals until further notice. There was talk of sending a delegation to the captain.

The bosun tried to find the passengers who had expressed interest in the animals to ask for help in attending to them, but he was told the passengers were indisposed. He arranged for two of his sailors to do the job. It still wasn't easy to cross the deck, so like the stewards before them, the sailors' first task was to find out what needed to be done.

First, they checked the pens and the stalls. The cow was in poor condition, lying on its side and groaning which in turn distressed its calf. The sailors weren't sure if it was seasick, just sick, or hungry. They would have to find someone who knew about cows. There seemed to be plenty of chickens and ducks, but they had no way of knowing if some were missing. There was plenty of squawking and clucking when they spotted the men, so a decision was made that food and water would do the job.

The oxen were in a sad state. They had obviously fallen many times and were jammed against the port side of the stall. At least one was dead. The sheep didn't look too good either, but the pigs looked best of all. "Natural sailors," one of the men said, as they headed back to see the bosun with their report and to develop a plan of action.

Returning through the companionway, the sailors found the bosun talking with the chief steward. They compared the storm to others they had endured. The sailors explained the condition of the animals.

The bosun sent one to fetch the surgeon and the other to get some more sailors to help take food and water to the livestock. "We can't leave them hungry and thirsty," he said. "If we do, they'll die for sure. And, just don't throw the food and water willy-nilly into the stalls. If you do, it'll be trampled or washed overboard. Put it in the troughs and if they're dirty, clean them out first."

The surgeon returned with the sailor and asked the bosun if he really wanted him to attend to a sick cow.

"Yes, I do," said the bosun. "We need the milk for your passengers, so it's probably your job anyway."

"Where is it?"

"Out there," said the bosun and jerked his thumb towards the companionway.

"All right," said the surgeon and headed for the weather deck.

"Go with him," said the bosun to the sailor. "It's not safe out there, and I think we need a surgeon more than a cow."

The sailor hurried after the surgeon, helped him to cross the seething, tossing deck and stayed with him while he checked the cow.

"Needs milking," said the surgeon.

"Can you do it?" asked the sailor.

"Who normally does it?"

"Beats me."

"Yes, I can do it. Pass me that stool and that bucket then help me get her up."

"Can't you do it with her lying down?"

"What's your name?"

"Sam Burgess."

"Ever been on a farm, Sam?"

"No, sir."

"I thought so. We might have to tie her onto the stall, to stop her falling as the ship tosses. She'll want to get up. She'll know I'm going to milk her. So, we ease her up first then get her up against the port side."

The surgeon and the sailor got the cow up. They held her against the port side of the stall.

"Forget filling the bucket," said the surgeon. "I'm going to waste the milk. No one will want it any way. She'll have more, later. Tell the bosun to find out who's been milking her and tell them to do it twice a day, no matter the weather."

He sat on the stool and set to work on her teats while Sam held the cow against the stall. It was lucky she wasn't big. Milking wasn't as hard as staying on the stool. Nonetheless, the job was done. The cow bellowed its gratitude and slid back down to rest on the deck. The men put the stool and buckets in their holders for safe keeping and battled their way back to the saloon deck. The surgeon was soaked and shivering from the cold. He didn't say anything to the bosun but rushed away, perhaps to get warm or perhaps to avoid being asked to do more.

"What was it?" the bosun asked Sam.

"Needed milking."

"Who normally does it?"

"That's what surgeon said to ask you."

"I suppose somebody's been doing it. Thanks, Sam. Go and help the men to feed the animals."

Price went out on deck to check the lookouts. He found two men tied to the aft rigging and being thrown about like rag dolls. They didn't appear to be looking out for much, just fighting to stay alive in the elements. He checked the compass. The *Lady Grace* was on 250. Returning to the saloon, Price found the captain on an inspection tour. He was once again dressed in his sou'wester and oilskins.

"Ah, Mr Price, I have been looking for you. I will take the ship. What's our heading?"

"250, Captain."

"Good. No, excellent. Have you been able to fix a position?"

"No, sir," said Price, shaking his head.

"Speed?"

"No, sir."

David Hosking, the first officer arrived, looking shaved, refreshed and also ready to go outside.

"Ah, Mr Hosking. I've just taken the ship. You and I shall take the helm."

Price waited and watched them go then headed off to the galley for something to eat before going to the officer's quarters for some much-needed sleep.

The captain and Hosking came through the outer doors and were nearly swept off the deck by a wave. Sleep and time away from the storm had perhaps robbed them both of the alertness they would need to stay alive on the weather deck. Soaked, grabbing handholds where they could, they went to the helm. It was obvious the lookouts were in distress. They were tied to the rigging and looked more dead than alive.

Ignoring the lookouts, the captain inspected the compass and the lashing on the wheel. He nodded, as if to acknowledge all seemed in order. He motioned to Hosking to join him.

"Tell the lookouts to get off the deck."

Hosking looked quizzical, as though he wasn't sure he had heard properly. The captain's words were torn from him by the wind as he spoke.

"Just to confirm, Captain, the lookouts are to go in?"

The captain nodded.

"We're going in, too, Mr Hosking."

The four men made the hazardous return journey. Several times the lookouts needed help to make the trip. Once inside, soaked and bedraggled, the four men stood on the saloon deck dripping water.

"Mr Hosking, I shall put you in charge of the lookouts. It is no longer necessary for them to remain on deck, but I do require one of them to go on deck every half hour and scan the horizon. Our heading is good, and we may have nothing to fear. They are also to check the sails and the wheel lashings. Thank you, Mr Hosking. Please so inform the men."

Hosking turned to inform the men, and they were already stretched out on the saloon deck, fast asleep.

The captain finally got a sighting around mid-afternoon and was able to plot their position. They were about one hundred miles further west than their intended course, but that was an excellent result as there was more sea room to the west.

It was now a matter of waiting for the storm to pass and hoping they didn't hit another vessel. There was always a risk of collision as many vessels passed through these waters, but the sails and the course had kept them away from land. Land was always the bigger threat.

Another day passed before the storm blew itself out. There was almost no activity on the ship as passengers and crew alike focussed on comfort. The *Lady Grace* ploughed on, sailing well with two jibs. While the two jibs held, the sailors could confine themselves to the animals' welfare. They couldn't find who had been milking the cow but eventually coerced the surgeon to coming back and showing them how.

Price and the captain shared the ship, four hours on and four off. There wasn't much to do. Check the clock, the compass and the speed and take a position when possible. Patterson stayed with Price and Hosking, with the captain.

The boiler room watch system reverted to how it had been when they left Southampton. They had to work longer watches, but after a few cycles, Armstrong and his men once again had the forenoon watch. The men had all listened intently when Hall confronted Armstrong in their quarters about returning to the pre-storm watches. No one disagreed when Armstrong chose not to make an issue of it. It was as though everyone agreed a fight with Hall was one-sided.

On the morning the storm had passed, it was dawn and the lookout came out to check the horizon, the lashings and the sails. The lookout hurried below to wake the bosun and to tell him the storm had passed. They went on deck together.

A hint of the sun was in the eastern sky. There were a few high clouds, and the breeze was brisk. They stared in wonder as the sky gradually became pink. There was still a big swell running, so the ship was still yawing, but nothing like it had been. There was some more north in the wind, and the bosun would have to adjust the sails, or they would head off course. Such a change would require advice from the officer of the watch, so the bosun hurried below to find who it would be.

Everything on the ship could now return to normal.

31

THE STORM PASSES

William had not long come off watch. He had trouble getting to sleep. His watch hadn't been busy - just keeping the fires burning. So he was pleased when the bosun called into the engine quarters, "All right lads, starboard watch on deck to man the sails. Be quick now, wind's a wasting!"

It was a chance to go topside and get away from the damp and the smell. Some of the men had been sick in the room, and only token efforts had been made to clean up. Hall lay still as his watch departed. Fletcher wasn't in his bunk. He was probably down with Cave worrying their way through something. The bosun looked as if he was about to say something to Hall, but then turned and went topside with the men.

Once on deck, William sucked in great lungfuls of the clean air. The contrast with below deck could not have been starker.

The sun was already up and while the breeze was cool, there was welcome warmth from it. William enjoyed watching the ship's normal weather deck activities resume.

The bosun came up on deck with some sailors and set the jibs to take advantage of the wind. There was no doubt the ship would soon return to the course they had been on before the storm, but it didn't travel well with the sails flapping and bouncing. It was cold but pleasant enough on the weather deck. The bosun and the men stayed there and awaited orders from the officer of the watch.

It wasn't long before the captain and Hosking came on deck with a helmsman. He spotted the bosun and signalled him to join his group. There was a large swell, and it was still uncomfortable to move about, but no water broke over the deck. Nonetheless, the captain seemed to have regained all his vigour and set about giving orders. William watched and listened to him take charge.

"Mr Hosking, remove those lashings. Helmsman, take her to 195. Mr Merchant, all the sails if you please. We can take advantage of this breeze. Mr Hosking, tell the chief steward to restart the fires and prepare some hot meals for the passengers and crew. When that's done, all the cabins and bunks are to be aired and cleaned. Tell the chief engineer, the working decks are to be cleaned and the bilge emptied." The captain appeared thoughtful for a moment and then said, "That's all, Mr Hosking. Off you go."

"All right, lads," called the bosun. "Four teams, same as before. Two on deck, two aloft. We'll do the mainmast first, then for'ard and aft."

The men set about their tasks without further bidding. Their last task had been to get the sails down at the start of the storm. By any comparison, raising the sails in these conditions was easier. It seemed no time at all had passed, and the ship was under full sail.

The *Lady Grace* skimmed across the sea. She seemed to lift her skirts and prance around, across and between the waves. She still heeled when a wave caught her, or a swell and the wind combined to push her over, but she seemed to shake herself coyly, before reengaging the sea in the next joust. Unlike the storm, this sea was no match for the *Lady Grace*. She was in her element and sailed as if she knew it. William decided this ship preferred sailing to steaming, and he was on her side. He smiled to himself. *The conditions have to be like this, though.*

William loved to be on deck. Once the swell settled down, the ship no longer carried a cargo of seasickness. Passengers sometimes strolled on the deck and although the crew was kept well away, the men were close enough to admire the smart outfits of the first-class passengers. The girls were pretty too. Many looked like Hannah, and William wondered if she had completed her journey. It wasn't time to thank her yet, as he hadn't reached his destination, but if he was here through anyone, it was certainly Hannah. *And Mary? What of Mary, now? Did she think of him at all?*

There was no more need for a starboard watch in the boiler room. William overheard Cave and Fletcher agree to split Armstrong's watch into two, and Hall's watch worked with the bosun and the sailors. Some of the men had to move into the sailors' quarters and William was delighted to find he was one of those. He didn't see Hall anymore and was glad of it. He bunked near Eddie and learnt more about sailing every day. Perhaps this life at sea was a good one, and it might be the thing to choose. Perhaps when they reached Australia, he would stay as a sailor on the *Lady Grace*.

One night, after supper, William and Eddie went on deck. The breeze was still brisk, and the ship sailed steadily towards its destination. It was like she was being pulled towards Australia, and there was nothing she could do about it. William really liked how the ship kept sailing day and night and reaching Australia was only a matter of time. It wasn't yet dark, and the men watched the phosphorescence off the bow and laughed at the porpoises dancing in the bow waves. The *Lady Grace* ignored them, and that seemed to upset the porpoises. They would dive through the bow wave, turn and come around to do it again and again as though challenging the *Lady Grace* to go faster. Some of the passengers had children with them who squealed in delight at the mammals' antics.

"How long have you been sailing, Eddie?"

"Oh, about ten years now."

"Will you always be a sailor?"

"Like I said when we met, I'm done with sailin' ships. I suppose it's better to be on a ship like the *Lady Grace*, but even though I've signed on her to learn somethin' different, I'm still a sailor. No, I'd like to do somethin' else. I'd really like to stay ashore, be safe and spend time with my family."

"I'm thinking of being a sailor."

Eddie laughed which made William blush.

"I've been on ships older than the *Lady Grace* that didn't survive as well a storm like we just had. We were lucky to have new sails, ropes and riggin'. Makes a big difference. We'd have lost a lot more men on an older ship. No, Bill, find somethin' safer. Meet a rich girl, marry her. There's a better idea."

Well, Mary wasn't rich, thought William. *At least, as far as I know she wasn't.*

The men stood in silence for some minutes. William was unsure what to say. He felt embarrassed about blushing and was glad it was too dark for Eddie to see.

"It's dangerous out here, and the pay is hardly enough to make it worthwhile. I'll give you that it has its moments. Now, is a good example, but I've been in two serious wrecks and countless near misses, Bill. Man's probably lucky to be alive."

"I'd like to hear about it."

"Out here? Won't it make you scared?"

"Scared was taking the sails down."

"I'll grant you that."

"So?"

Eddie smiled, wide enough for William to see in the darkness.

"Two or three years ago, I was on a brig called *Cawton* out of Scarborough. We collided with another brig called *Mersey*, out of Shields. We'd both come from the north, laden with coal. There aren't big crews on those ships, so it's easy not to see another ship until you are on it. We lost our bowsprit, but the *Mersey* looked like it was in real trouble, so most of the crew left the ship and came on board with us. And that wasn't easy, either. They were lucky, I can tell you. Waves were huge."

"Why didn't all the crew leave?"

"Well, some thought they'd be all right. Others were too scared to cross on the ropes. It's terrifying, Bill. No one knows what to do. Any decision you make can be a bad one."

"What happened to the crew that didn't leave?"

"We all watched the *Mersey* drift onto the Goodwin Sands, and it wasn't any time before she was a total wreck. The men screamed for us to help, but there was nothing we could do."

"Did you leave them?"

"We had to. We couldn't do anything. They'd made the wrong choice. Should have joined us when they had the chance."

Eddie was silent for a few moments, then continued.

"We managed to jury rig the *Cawton* and get her to port, but there were many nervous hands on board. The captains would have nothin' to do with each other, each believin' themselves to be in the right."

"The captain of the *Mersey* joined you? I thought he was supposed to stay with the ship?"

"Cargo ship. Everyone gets to make his own decision."

"Who was in the wrong?"

"Who knows? I'm sure they had an enquiry, but I was long gone by then."

"If you were on the *Mersey*, what would you have done? Would you have crossed?"

"Dunno, Bill. No one knows what they'll do until they have to do it."

"You said there was another one," said William, eager for more.

"Well, just last year, I was on a schooner called *Intrepid* out of Newcastle headin' for London, and we sprang a leak. Didn't matter what we did, we couldn't stop the flow of water. It was dark, and we couldn't really find what was wrong. Captain kept at us to fix it but fix what? We couldn't find anythin' to fix. So, even though it was night, captain stuck her on a compass headin' for the land."

"The land? Wouldn't you want to stay at sea?"

"No way. She was sinkin'. She sinks, we drown."

"But, if you hit the shore, she breaks up and you drown anyway."

"No. Captain headed for a beach. At least, we were all hopin' he did. But, that had us all nervous as we got close. We could hear the waves on shore, but couldn't see what we were gettin' ourselves into."

"Were you scared?"

"Of course. Everyone's scared of the unknown. Anyway, next thing she hit the beach at Cromer, and we were all in the water. Luckily, we got ashore, thoroughly wet and sorry for ourselves. The locals took care of us. At least, they gave us some warm clothes and somethin' to eat."

"They'd do that for you even though they didn't know you?"

"Aye, that they did. Might have been sailors once themselves. Doesn't always work that way. I've heard of ships that went ashore in the Pacific, and the crew themselves became somethin' to eat."

"I don't believe you! People don't eat people."

"Best not to find out, Bill. Well, that's a big enough day for me, so I'm off. But Bill, there's always somethin' better than being a sailor. And it's not bein' a trimmer, either."

They both headed for'ard and went below.

The wind continued to favour the *Lady Grace,* and she sailed on day after day. Sometimes, the men were called to adjust the sails to suit the wind every hour or so, both day and night. The officer of the watch was always keen to get the best out of the sails and the ship.

There were never times to relax. If they weren't adjusting the sails, they cleaned the ship. On fine days, they dragged their bedding on deck at least once a week and aired it. The engine department and sailors had to keep their own quarters as clean as possible. The watches took it in turns to clean out their quarters and the water closets. There was some feigned and some real anger as to how well the job was done.

William was glad he was up for'ard. The sailors seemed to know better how to look after themselves and their quarters. He supposed it was because they didn't get as dirty, not working with the coal.

One evening, he was on deck and remarked to Eddie the weather seemed to be getting much warmer. He wondered how that might be happening.

"World's a funny thing, Bill. It's a great big ball that's cold at the top and the bottom and hot in the middle. We're headin' for the middle, and we get closer every day. Another thing about the middle is, it sometimes doesn't blow, so if that happens, the captain'll use steam to keep her movin'. He's had a good run so far and hasn't used much coal, so he won't be afraid to use some to keep her movin'. You might be trimmin' again, soon."

William's heart sank.

"When do we get to the middle?"

"It'll only be a few days, now, I think."

"Is the middle half way to Australia?"

"No, Bill. The middle is about a quarter the way there. Don't worry, there's plenty of sailin' left."

As was their custom, they went up for'ard together and went below.

William woke during the night. At least, he figured it was the night. The usual rattle of snores and farts came from the bunks around him. The motion of the ship was different. It seemed to roll about, unlike the gentle fore and aft motion he had become used to. He sat up. No one else stirred. There was no lamp, and he wished he was back in the engine quarters so he could tell from the skylight if it was really dark outside. He thought it worth a look on the weather deck. He rolled out of his bunk and felt his way to the door.

"Who's that? Who's up?" called a voice in the darkness.

"It's Bill," he said, without thinking.

"What the devil are you doing?"

"I'm going for a piss."

"For Christ's sake, use a pan."
"I can't find one."
"Get on with it, then."

He stumbled about, bumping into a few more occupants and incurring their anger before finding the ladder and reaching the weather deck.

There wasn't a breath of wind, and the air was heavy with moisture. The ship fell about, rather than skimming across the waves. The sails slapped and banged against the masts, stays and shrouds. He wondered why the engines weren't being used, like Eddie had said. He guessed the wind had dropped only recently, and their furnaces weren't properly stoked yet. He looked at the stars above him as they glittered and winked at him. His mother had told him stories when he was young about where they had come from. Whoever made them, sure had his work cut out. He was musing all this when there was a commotion behind him.

"Ah! There you are," called Eddie. "Time to take the sails down. Go below and fetch the lads from the engine quarters. We'll need them, too."

William did as he was bid and shortly returned with the rest of his watch. Hall remained snoring on his bunk. William was careful not to disturb him.

Stowing the sails was both harder and easier in windless conditions. The ship fell and slopped about, first one way and then another. The men who were aloft had no real idea of what motion to guard against, so it was harder to hang on and work at the same time. On the other hand, the wind wasn't trying to tear them from the rigging, so it was easier to climb and move about. But it was dark, so everything was touch and feel.

There was a terrible cry when someone fell. Just a call of distress and a thump as a body hit the deck. It wasn't anyone working near William, and those working made no move to climb down, just kept on with their jobs.

It wasn't until they finished the mainmast that they found one of the sailors had fallen. Like Eddie said, sailing is a dangerous business. The bosun said he'd broken a leg, was lucky to be alive and would be useless for the rest of the voyage. He'd been taken to the surgery.

The teams finished stowing the sails and this time left no jibs. William guessed any sail would be an impediment with no wind and under steam. The bosun told the engine crew to report to the engineer on watch, and the ship would steam until the wind came back.

32

Trouble in the Boiler Room

William went below with the others. He didn't want to go back to trimming. He liked being topside. Liked the wind, the action, and liked the men. Most of all, he liked being away from Hall. He sighed as they all went down to the boiler room. Things would have to go back to normal. Armstrong had been running a split watch, but now that all the boilers were needed all the time, both Armstrong's and Hall's watches would be needed.

The men presented themselves in the boiler room. The room seemed much warmer. William guessed now the weather outside was hotter, it would be hotter in the boiler room, too. The heat was exhausting, and there were always one or two men drinking from the barrel.

Hall was in charge. William guessed Hall and Armstrong had managed a watch each, using Armstrong's men.

"Well, lads," said Hall. "Welcome back. I heard you boys would be back soon. Things're back to normal. And how are you, Bill? Ready to do some trimming, no doubt?"

Hall dismissed Armstrong's men, and his own men set themselves up in the for'ard and aft boiler rooms without being told. The other men had done a good job, and it was just a matter of keeping the fires well stoked and raked. The ship was already under steam, the engines banging, the drive chains rattling and the steam hissing. Things might have been back to normal, but the pace was harder with all the boilers going. It was clear the captain was going to take advantage of a lack of wind and push the ship harder under steam. It wasn't long before all the men in the boiler room were shirtless, perspiration pouring from them.

William was hurrying from the bunker with his wheelbarrow, keen to deliver the coal to the firemen. Suddenly, his legs locked around his ankles and he pitched forward, smashing his forehead on the edge of the wheelbarrow. He lay still for a few moments, dazed from the blow to his head and wondering about the cause.

Looking up, he saw Hall grinning broadly, tapping the handle of his shovel. As he wondered what that meant, he felt himself hoisted to his feet by Vince Alexander and Alan Coe.

"Christ, Bill. Are you all right?"

William tried to nod, to look at his mates, but his vision was blurred.

"Christ, Bill. There's blood everywhere! We've got to get you to the surgery."

"Take him," said Hall. "Shift's nearly done, anyway."

"Here, Vince," said Alan. "I'm bigger, I'll take him, and you tend to the furnaces."

Alan Coe hoisted William onto his shoulder, left the boiler room, climbed the ladder to the next deck and walked down the passageway to the surgery. The surgeon was already at work, still tending to the man that had fallen earlier from the shrouds.

William noticed a sharp smell on entering the room. He'd never been to a doctor, so had no idea what to expect. There was a lighted lamp, and a port hole that allowed some light from the imminent dawn. The surgery was a small room. It contained two beds for patients, a bench where the surgeon could perform minor operations and a desk and chair for the surgeon. There were shelves and cabinets around the walls that were filled with a variety of bottles and jars.

"One at a time!" said the surgeon, but did a double take when he saw William's face.

"Lord. What's happened?"

"I think he's hit his head, sir, doctor, sir."

"You wait," said the surgeon to the sailor on the table. "I'll check this man before I finish with you."

The surgeon told Alan to put William in his own chair, grabbed a bowl, put some water in it and washed William's face. There was a severe gash on his forehead, bleeding heavily. There was so much black dust he had to wash the area several times before he could identify the source of the blood.

"You're going to have to wait longer," he said to the sailor. Then turned to Alan. "And you're going to hold your friend while I put some stiches in this cut."

"Will it hurt?" asked William.

"Of course not. What do you take me for? A butcher?"

"If it's not going to hurt, why does he have to hold me?"

"Sense of humour, eh? Good. You're going to need that. Hold him."

Alan stood behind the chair and held William's arms.

"What are you doing?" asked the surgeon, standing in front of William and holding a needle he had threaded with some cotton.

"Holding him," replied Alan, looking bewildered.

"And, why do you think you are holding him?"

"Well, you said it won't hurt, but I think it might, so I think I'm holding him so he won't hit you."

The surgeon laughed. "No, you're meant to be holding his head, so he doesn't move it all about the place. So, you stand to one side, place a hand on either side of his head and hold it firmly. He will try to move his head, but don't you let him. It's funny, but people don't like being sewn up."

The surgeon looked at William. William hadn't been able to see him clearly before due to the blood. His face was not unkind. He had a shock of white hair and a big walrus moustache that William really liked. He wore a clean, white jacket.

"What's your name, lad?"

"Bill, sir."

"Well, Bill, I'm going to put three or four stiches in that wound of yours. It'll hurt a little, but more if you move your head about. I'm going to pass the needle through the skin on either side of the wound and pull the skin together. I'm sure you've seen your mother use a needle. Then, I'm going to put a bandage around your head and put you in that bunk over there to sleep for a while. You'll have a headache when you wake, but that will last only a day or so."

He jerked his thumb at the sailor lying on the table. "He might walk with a limp for the rest of his life. Which do you think the girls will like best? A man with a scar, or a man with a limp? So, you think about that while I get the job done."

"Will I really walk with a limp?' asked the man on the table.

"I said might, so not if I can help it," said the surgeon.

Alan held William's head, and the surgeon put four stiches in the wound. *He was right, it really didn't hurt at all. Well, not much.*

"Now, let's get him cleaned up and then give me some help to put the lad into the bunk, and you go back to your watch," said the surgeon to Alan. The surgeon stripped William of his clothes and sponged him down with some cloths. Alan looked embarrassed.

"Not having you ruin my bunk," said the surgeon.

The surgeon and Alan put William into the bunk. There were sheets under and above him, and a pillow which he had never used before. It was a few moments before he realised there was no smell from the bed. No, that wasn't right, there was a different smell, not unlike the soap he used when he and Pat visited the bathhouse in Dublin. *Was this how rich people lived?*

"Come back for him tomorrow. He won't be able to work for a day or so, but he'll be fine by then. And tell your watch supervisor to be more careful with his men. We don't have enough for them to be falling down or over, whichever it is." He looked briefly at the man behind him and at William in the bunk, before looking back at Alan.

"Yes, sir," said Alan.

William wondered what Alan would say to Hall. He expected not much. Hall wasn't a man to receive such a message kindly, so Alan would likely say nothing.

As he dozed off, William realised Hall must have put the handle of the shovel between his legs. It was no wonder he pitched forward. *What was he to do?* If Hall was going to raise the stakes and do things that put him in the surgery then there was no doubt, worse was to come.

As Eddie said, "There's plenty of sailin' left"

He wished there wasn't. He was more than ready for this voyage to be over and to see the last of Hall.

33

THE SHIP'S SURGERY

William woke in unfamiliar surroundings with a severe headache. There was light in the room from a porthole near his bunk. The ship moved steadily. He knew it was under steam. He looked around. The surgeon sat at a desk, perhaps working with some papers. He remembered he was in the surgery.

"Doctor," he called, and he thought loud enough, but the man seemed not to hear. "Doctor," he called again, and still the man didn't stir.

William decided the doctor was asleep, and he would have to look after himself. He lay still for a while longer, enjoying the solitude in the room. He'd become so accustomed to sleeping in the crew's quarters that the absence of noise was a welcome change. After a few minutes, he moved the blanket, sat up and swung his legs out of the bunk. The act of sitting up caused his head to swirl, and he felt very dizzy.

The doctor noticed him and hurried over. "What is it, Bill? Why didn't you call me?"

"I need a piss, sir, but I don't think I can make it to the closets."

"No," said the surgeon, "and nor should you try. Here," and gave William a dish.

"Try to keep your aim true. Most can't."

William thought he did a creditable job, put the dish on the deck and was grateful to lie down again.

"Are you hungry?" asked the surgeon.

"How long have I been asleep?"

"A bit over a day. That was a pretty bad knock to your head. Your friend came back this morning to fetch you, but you were sound asleep, so I sent him away. He said they'd be needing you on your watch, but I told him they'd have to manage without you."

"How's the sailor with the broken leg?"

"He's still here, and he'll be all right, at least as far as I can tell. Takes a while to work out, though. If there's no complication, he'll keep his leg. I think in addition to walking with a limp, his sailing days might be over."

William looked at the other bunk, but there was no movement.

"Don't worry, he's sound asleep. He woke up a few hours ago, had something to eat and went back to sleep. I think he likes it here. He's not much company for me, though. Neither are you, for that matter."

"I'd like something to eat."

"Don't worry, I'll be back." The surgeon came back a little later with a bowl of broth and some bread. "Cook says he's glad to hear you are all right. Said to tell you the first-class passengers will eat this for lunch. He hopes you'll enjoy it. Best if you try to sit up again, or you'll wear most of it."

William gratefully accepted the surgeon's help to sit up and to eat. A few mouthfuls told him how hungry he was, and the broth and bread were gone in no time.

"I heard there's wind, and they're busy unfurling the sails," said the surgeon. He put his hand on William's shoulder to prevent him getting up. "They'll work out how to do it without you. Another day here won't do you any harm."

He pushed William down and covered him lightly. There might be some breeze, but the heat from the equator made the room uncomfortably hot. "How did you do it? The accident, I mean?" asked the surgeon.

"I don't really know," said William, but didn't look at the surgeon.

"That's not much of an answer, and you've had some time to think of one. You'll have to do better when the chief engineer asks you, and he will ask you. You have to decide whether to tell the awful truth, or a good lie. It's up to you. Anyway, I see injuries like that when trimmers fall over a piece of coal."

"Why are you helping me?"

"I don't think I am. If I was to really help you, I'd go to the chief engineer, but I don't think you'd like that. I think I'm just giving you your options. When Alan came this morning, he was very glad to find out you are all right and muttered something about all the men on your watch being worried about you. I asked, 'Was it about the injury?' and he replied, 'Not just that.' So, Bill, take another day of rest and with the ship sailing again, you might be out of harm's way, at least for a while."

"Yes, sir. Thank you, sir," said William and drifted off to sleep. He woke several more times, mostly for a piss, but once for something to eat. The surgeon was always available to help and always at his desk.

Finally, the next morning, the surgeon told him, "Captain's been by, looking to see why his men are malingering. He agreed a broken leg was an impediment to skilful sailing, but failed to see how a bump on the head was enough to keep a man off watch. I told him I'd release you this morning, so that's how it's to be. I suggest you go find your bunk and hole up there as long as you can. Take your time, Bill. You might feel better at the moment, but I can't guarantee how you'll feel swinging on a rope a hundred feet above the deck. I hear you are handy both in the boiler room and on the deck. I know it's dangerous topsides, but it might be more dangerous for you below, so stay away from there as long as you can. You will need to come by each day for me to check your bandage, but that won't take long. Let's get you dressed."

He picked up a parcel from the corner and passed it to William. "These are your clothes. I've had them washed. Can you dress yourself?"

"Aye," said William, taking the parcel. He was unsteady and had to balance himself against the bunk a few times.

When he had finished, the surgeon handed him his boots. "You'll need these, too."

"Aye," said William and pulled his boots on.

"Off you go, Bill and good luck."

The surgeon shook William's hand, and he went for'ard unsteadily up the passageway. He decided since they were sailing again, he should go back to the sailors' quarters. There was no one there, and he slipped into his bunk. He still didn't feel right, so he thought it best to take the surgeon's advice and stay there until someone found him. He was awoken by Eddie and some of the others returning from their watch.

"Here he is," said Eddie, once he realised William was awake. "We've missed you, right enough, but we've agreed to cover for you until you are right. The bandage looks impressive. What happened in the boiler room?"

"Tripped on a piece of coal."

"Sounds about right. Happens all the time. Do you need anythin'?"

William shook his head.

"Well, ask if you do. We're all happy to help and want you back as soon as you can make it." He patted William on the shoulder and left him to sleep.

He woke to the sound of men moving in the room. "Are we on watch?"

"Yes," said Eddie. "Are you able to join us?"

"I'd like to."

"Come on, then. You'll like it topside. There's a good wind from the east and she's sailin' well. We're just workin' the settin's, and there's enough of us to do that without you, but like I say, it's nice up there, so come and enjoy it."

"Where are we?"

"We've left St Paul Rocks in our wake and are on our way to Trindade Island. They tell me we're a few days out. The wind has held so far. It's been steady and strong. Come on."

William got up, feeling dizzy, but ignored it. Even by the light of the lamp, Eddie could see he wasn't right.

"Are you sure that coal didn't hit you on the head? You don't look right. Maybe, you should go to see the surgeon?"

"No, I'm all right. Let's go."

The men clambered up the ladder and out onto the deck. The weather was cooler, the wind was brisk, the sun invigorating. William was glad he had come out. They saw the bosun standing near the mainmast, and Eddie and his men went to join him. William stayed with the group.

"No," said Eddie. "Stay here. I'll get you if we need you."

The bosun looked over, saw him and waved.

"Bosun wants me to come," said William.

"No, he doesn't," said Eddie firmly and walked off, joined the bosun, spoke with him for a few moments, turned to William and signalled him to stay.

William eased himself down against the side of one of the hatchways, enjoying the feel of the sun and the motion of the ship. He looked up and marvelled again at the expanse of canvas. Beyond the sails was endless blue sky and only a few wisps of puffy, white cloud. Every now and again, there would be a spray of mist from the side. It was cool and smelt of the sea - salty and fishy. The deck was clean, hard and rough under his hands. As he watched, the deck crew adjusted the settings, and the *Lady Grace* sailed better.

Eddie's an asset to the bosun, thought William. *And a good friend to have, too.* He fell asleep and woke to Eddie shaking him gently.

"Let's go and get somethin' to eat."

"I don't think they'll have anything for us right now."

"Doesn't matter. When you're a sailor, you get to eat when you can and we're ready to eat now." Eddie reached down and helped him to his feet. "Come on and be careful of the ladder. We don't want you fallin' off one of those."

They all went below, got some food and went to their mess. Unlike the engine room crew, the sailors had a separate mess. Eddie made sure he and William sat a little away from the other men. William looked around. The thought crossed his mind that his being alone with Eddie might have been engineered.

"So, what happened in the boiler room?" asked Eddie.

"Like I said, I tripped on a piece of coal."

"That's not what I hear. Ship's like a village, Bill. Everyone knows everythin'."

William shrugged and waited.

"I don't know how old you are Bill, but you don't look that old to me. You have to be careful. You're dealin' with a grown man here. He's bigger, faster and meaner than you. I know the bosun would keep you with the sailors if he could, but they'll need steam again if there's no wind or headwinds. If they need steam then you'll have to go back to the boiler room." Eddie paused.

William looked at him, wondering why.

Eddie went on. "I hear the lads on your watch plan to keep an eye on you. Story goes they feel responsible and should have been more watchful. They'll help if they can, but it's still up to you. You watch him, Bill. Don't ever take your eyes off him. There's still a long way to go. And Bill, keep sayin' you fell over the coal. There's no value in askin' for help. The system is not there to help, it's only there so they can say they have one."

William nodded. "Thanks for your help, Eddie. And thanks for your help topside. I think the bosun wanted me to work."

"No, he didn't. Do you want to know what he said?"

"No, I don't. Well, all right, tell me, even if it's bad."

"He asked if you were all right. I said, 'Not yet.' He replied I was to take good care of you. He said you're worth any two other men."

William looked surprised.

"He didn't mean me as one of those two men, of course! Told me I'm worth my weight in gold."

They laughed together.

The *Lady Grace* continued for the next two days under sail. The sea was benign with very little swell, and the wind continued to blow steadily from the east. The passengers were often on deck, walking, washing and sometimes playing games. William helped with the sailing where he could, but mostly spent time just being on deck and felt fitter and stronger every day.

One day, the crew caught one of the porpoises that made occasional visits to the bows. William hadn't taken much notice until he heard a commotion. He hurried for'ard to discover the source of the fuss. They'd harpooned it, and it writhed as it fought its captors. It was dragged to the side, and the sailors used some gaff hooks to secure it and drag it on board. Some of the passengers and their children had come over too, but interest turned to anguish, and they were distressed by what they saw.

The children all looked distressed and one of them cried out in dismay, "Mummy! Do you hear it? The poor thing. It's making noises. Stop them. Please, stop them. They're hurting it."

The sailors didn't care as they dragged the poor mammal on board and clubbed it to death. There were no more porpoises chasing the ship after that and the captain forbade any more fishing when the passengers were around.

Another day passed and during the following night, William was shaken awake by Eddie. "We're all aloft. Headwinds have arrived. Sails are comin' down and we're back under steam."

34

THE CONFRONTATION

The helmsman manoeuvred the ship to reduce the pressure on the sails so they could be stowed. It meant the ship was out of synchronisation with wind and sea, so it flopped and fell about, causing the usual difficulties in getting the sails down. William forgot about his injury and helped where he could. He tried to go aloft, but the others wouldn't let him. He was confined to the deck for a while yet.

It didn't matter. The sails were stowed soon enough. But the steam wasn't up yet, so the *Lady Grace* continued to flop and fall about. Even from the deck the crew could hear the crash of items that weren't stowed properly.

William and his watch headed for the boiler room. Descending the ladder was harder than usual as the ship pitched about. Fletcher met them at the bottom of the ladder and walked with them into the boiler room. William hadn't seen Hall since the night of the accident. The men looked at each other, but neither man said anything.

"We need to get the steam up quickly lads and get her under way. The passengers will have a very bad time of it. The wind changed without warning, and this is what we have, so work quick as you can." Fletcher turned without saying anything further and headed off to the engine room.

The men set to with a will, and they could soon hear and feel the throb of the engines. It wasn't as hot as it had been the last time his watch had been here, but William hadn't spent much time on the watch either.

After a while, Armstrong and his watch came and with the handover complete, William climbed the ladder out of the boiler room. He decided he was back with the engine crew again, so he headed back for the engine quarters. Most of the men had food, so he went and got some. He came back and found a spot to sit. Alan Coe sat opposite him.

"All good, Bill?"

"Yes, Alan. Thank you. All good."

William looked along the table. Hall sat with an empty space opposite him. William decided that now was as good a time as any. He picked up his mess kit and went and sat opposite Hall who looked up, surprised.

"Mr Hall," said William.

"Smith," said Hall, looking apprehensive.

"How are you, Mr Hall? I haven't seen you for a while."

"I'm good, Smith. And how are you?"

"Matter of fact, Mr Hall, I haven't been well."

Hall looked nervously around, obviously wondering where this was going.

"Ask me why I haven't been well, Mr Hall. I'm sure you'll want to know."

Hall looked up, obviously anxious and furious all at once.

"I don't give a damn about you, or why you haven't been well, so clear out and stop bothering me."

"You don't care? What, with me being on your watch and all?"

Hall grabbed his mess kit and started to get up. He felt hands on his shoulders, pushing him down. He looked back. Alan Coe stood behind him.

"Begging your pardon, Mr Hall, but you might want to hear what Bill has to say."

"All right," muttered Hall, "but make it quick. I don't have all day."

"Well, Mr Hall," said William, "as I was saying, I've not been well. As it turns out, I fell over a piece of coal and cut my head. I spent some days in the surgery. I'm better now, you'll be pleased to hear. When the surgeon found out what had happened, he expressed surprise the boiler room was such a dangerous place. I told him it was a terribly dangerous place."

"Are you threating me, Smith?"

"Of course not, Mr Hall. Just letting you know the boiler room is dangerous for everybody. If you didn't know that already, of course."

William picked up his mess kit and headed for the door. He looked back before he left the room and saw Hall turn, obviously to tell Alan Coe to get out of the way, but the man was no longer behind him. Hall sat fuming, looking like he didn't know what to do next. Then he too, picked up his kit and stormed out the door, pushing William aside as he did so.

When William came back from the galley he fell into his bunk. He was tired after working hard on his shift and exhausted after his confrontation with Hall. He'd done it on impulse and hoped it would pay off, but doubted it would. His da had told him once you could rely on a dedicated enemy much more than you could a dedicated friend.

Hall came back and sat on his own. Alan had gone back to sit with Vince. William could hear them whispering.

"I can't see any good coming of this," said Alan Coe.

"I know, Alan. But look around the room. It's Hall that's on his own now, not Bill," he whispered.

William rose on his elbow and looked. There was nothing friendly about the attitude of the men in the room towards Hall. They looked at him with open hostility. He lay back down and went to sleep.

Jim Huston woke him. "My turn," was all he said.

William wished he'd woken earlier. There was no time to get his meal, and he would have to content himself with some biscuits. He looked around and saw all the other men on his watch were still there. He guessed they were all tired. Hall had stopped taking care of his watch. A good watch leader would have been up and organising his men in good time to be properly fed before going on duty. *No matter*, he thought and hoped they would be sailing again, soon.

They steamed into the wind for the next few days and everyone's nerves were on edge. The ship bashed into the wind and the waves. A sailing ship would have gone miles off course, tacking to and fro, using the wind however it could. The motion of the ship was every bit as uncomfortable as they had endured during the storm, perhaps even more so. Waves punched the ship on the bow, rather than the bow rising over them. The whole motion involved incessant jarring and shaking.

Once again, the passengers and crew alike were afflicted by seasickness. The ship stank of it, and the smell of it made things worse for everyone. They all prayed for a change of wind, but no one seemed to be in favour with the Lord. William decided the collective prayers of the good people on the *Lady Grace* were insufficient to change the wind.

William was wary on his watch, keeping an eye out for Hall and what he might try next. Hall left him alone to tend to his firemen. The watch had become routine. It was an unhappy watch, no laughter, no lightness, all drudgery. The heat was less each day as they moved away from the line, but the wind continued to come from the south-east. William overheard Fletcher and Cave saying the captain was fretting about the coal consumed to steam into the wind.

Everything had been well enough until the starboard watch came on shift on the fourth day of steaming. The bashing, jarring and shaking was terribly unsettling. Men who were normally easy-going, found reason for fault. There were frequent exchanges of harsh words between the firemen and the trimmers. There was resentment from the watch for Hall, too. The men were angry he failed to wake them in time. At best they received one good meal a day, and it wasn't before they went on watch which was when it was needed most.

Lucky Gordon put his coal in the wrong place for Hall who had swung his shovel to gather another load. His shovel missed the pile of coal and Hall fell forward.

"Sorry, Brian," muttered Gordon and stooped to help Hall regain his feet.

Hall didn't hesitate. He swung a fist and caught Gordon on the chin. Gordon fell sideways into the furnace wall. There was a sharp cry of pain. He tried to push himself off with his hands and burnt them in the process.

"Damn you, Hall," shouted Gordon and charged at Hall. He was short, but thickset, so Hall was startled by the attack and not ready. Both men fell to the deck, each trying to punch the other, but thwarted by the darkness, the motion of the ship and the coal lying about. The rest of the watch grabbed at the men, trying to pull them apart.

"Let us finish it!" cried Hall, clearly relishing a physical confrontation. "There's no one but us to know, is there?"

"He's right," agreed Gordon. "I'm happy to finish it, and now is as good a time as any."

The other men looked at each other, shrugged and stood back, leaving the antagonists some space.

Hall was prepared now and circled Gordon, fists at the ready. He dropped his fists slightly, as though setting himself to a better position and without warning, charged at Gordon.

Gordon had once told William he earned money when he was younger, challenging older, more experienced fighters at fairs. It was clear to William as Hall charged, that Gordon was ready. He stepped slightly to the side and drove his right fist into Hall's face. The blow stopped his momentum and as though the *Lady Grace* was in Gordon's corner, the ship steadied at that moment. Gordon reached out with his left hand and took hold of Hall by the shirt. Hall's nose was crushed, blood already pouring from it. Gordon waited for a few moments, looking at his antagonist, perhaps wanting the fight to continue.

William thought Hall looked bewildered.

"You should take better care of your watch, Mr Hall," said Gordon, drove his right fist again into Hall's face and let go with his left. Hall fell to the deck.

The other men looked stunned. One of them said to the man beside him that of all the men on the watch, Gordon was the last he expected to retaliate.

"Like he said," muttered Gordon. "There's no one but us to know, is there?" and walked over to get himself a drink of water and to rub some fat into his burnt hands.

"The surgeon might need to find out," said Vince Alexander.

"I think he's expecting it," said William.

"Let's just move him out of the way and get on with the watch," said Alan Coe. "It can't be long to the end of the watch, anyway. Jim, I think we three can manage. What do you think, Vince?"

"Aye, I think we can. Mr Hall will awake with a headache and a nose that points sideways, but other than that, he'll be all right. What'll we say happened? Can't say there was a fight, can we?"

"Best not to. Like Bill says, these are dangerous places, so best to say he missed his footing and fell into a bulkhead."

The men all nodded, then moved Hall near to a bulkhead and returned to their jobs. When they heard the men arriving for the next watch, Coe collected Hall, put him over his shoulder and said, "I'll take him to the surgery."

Armstrong stopped him and said, "What's happened?"

"Fell over, Mr Armstrong. I'll take him to the surgery."

"He looks out to it."

"He is."

"Best get on with it, then."

"I'll go with you," said William.

"Good idea, Bill. I'll be fine on my own, but I think the surgeon will want to make sure you're all right."

When they arrived at the surgery, the surgeon was seated at his desk. He looked up when he saw Coe carrying a body.

"Alan. Who's this?"

"Leading fireman Hall, sir."

"Put him there. You're used to the drill, now. What happened?"

"He fell into a bulkhead, sir."

"Let's look at him."

The surgeon adjusted the lamp to better see his patient. Hall moaned softly. The surgeon got a bowl with some water and cleaned Hall's face as best he could. The coal dust was ingrained. It was just as well he was still unconscious. The cleaning process would have been painful.

"When did this happen?"

"Not long ago. Near to the end of the watch, sir."

"How're you Bill?"

"I'm fine, sir."

"You have anything to do with this?"

"With Mr Hall falling into a bulkhead? No, sir."

"Well, gentlemen, I'd say the bulkhead has a pretty good right, if I'm not mistaken. He'll be back at work in a day or so. I'll keep him here, and I'll tell Mr Fletcher there was an accident, if he asks. He probably won't. Some questions don't need to be asked. The answer is already there. From what I hear about this man, no one will care if he's absent from his watch, and he'll be carrying a grudge along with his other responsibilities when he returns."

He looked at William. "Nice to see you, Bill. You haven't been to see me." He put out his hand, as though to shake William's.

William responded automatically and held out his hand. The surgeon didn't shake, but took it, inspected it, nodded, smiled, then shook. He turned and looked at Hall.

"Not a pretty sight is it? Most people have the ability to make someone's heart beat faster, but it's hard to imagine such a capacity in this man. I'll try to straighten his nose before he wakes, but I warrant he'll be wary of bulkheads in the future. Off you go then. Bill, call by another time so I can check your wound is healing properly."

"Yes, sir. I will, sir."

William and Alan turned to go. At the door, William looked back to ask when he should come back and could see Hall was not far off being conscious.

He was about to ask the surgeon for a time and overheard the surgeon say to Hall, "I might just wait until you wake before I try to straighten your nose. Of course, there's the matter of the Hippocratic Oath, but I'll hide behind the fact that someone else did the harm first. Probably won't be able to straighten it anyway. No matter. I'm sure you'll want me to try. You're not as big as I thought you'd be, but it's good someone has brought you down a peg or two."

Alan waited for him outside the door, so he thought it best to leave before the surgeon realised he was still there.

35

Another Storm

Around mid-morning, the wind swung to the west, and the order was given to hoist the sails. William and his watch hurried on deck to join the sailors, and he was astonished to find it was cold again. It was a well-practised drill now, and the sails were all up in no time. Thankfully, he wasn't cold for long. The bosun told the engine crew they could go below and finish their sleep if they wished. The sailors had to remain nearby.

"The wind is swingin' from the west to the south-west and back again," Eddie told William. "We'll have to keep adjustin' the sails. You'll have to learn how to reef them. We're in the 'Roaring Forties' now, so the captain will want to use the wind. It's why they come down here. It's another thirty days or so to Melbourne, so the more the ship can take advantage of the wind, the faster she'll go."

"What's a reef?"

"See up there, Bill? See the points on the sail where you can see rope threaded through it? You can pull those ropes down and the sail with it. You tie them to the spar and reduce the amount of sail. She'll sail better in a strong wind. It's hard to do if the wind is too strong, though."

There was only an hour or so before his next watch, so William decided to stay with Eddie until it was time to go below for supper. It was cold in the wind, but the sun was out, and he enjoyed looking at the sky and the waves. The *Lady Grace* didn't like it so much when the wind came directly from behind. The aft sails stopped the wind reaching those for'ard, and the ship started bouncing about.

"She's better if she can sail with the wind aft of the beam, but sailors and helmsmen will have their work cut out makin' adjustments as the wind swings. Captain might even be wishin' for a storm. If there is, the wind'll be right behind us, and there'll be plenty to go around."

Early the following morning, the captain got his wish. The wind had been steadily increasing from late evening. The sailors and some men from the engine room, including William, were busy either adjusting the angle of the sails or reefing them to reduce the sail area. Eddie warned the men it wouldn't be long before they had to stow at least some of the sails. He'd been through several storms in the Roaring Forties and told them the captain was likely to keep some sails up, no matter what. He told them it wouldn't be long before they all wished themselves off the ship. With the wind aft, the waves and the ship would be pushed along by the wind, and the *Lady Grace* would find herself threatened by huge waves from behind.

Not long before William was due to join his watch, Mr Patterson came through requesting all fires and lamps be extinguished.

William went below, got something to eat and joined his shift in the boiler room. There was plenty to do. Captain had ordered all the fires to be put out and the boilers cleaned. Fletcher supervised the operation and fretted the whole time the fires were out. It wasn't as though they needed the engines, but William heard him say, "It just isn't right for a steamship to be without steam."

No one knew when Hall would be back, and no one missed him. Alan Coe and Vince Alexander shared the job of leading firemen for the watch. They took it seriously and made sure their men were awake in time for a meal. The mood in the aft boiler room was noticeably better. There was some surprise there hadn't been any questions about Hall's accident, but the men agreed it was for the best.

William came off his watch wet and dirty after cleaning the boilers. There was still some work left to do, and he and his watch were pleased to pass it on. The motion of the ship had become more violent as the night progressed, and the movement for William was a whole new experience. He resolved to go on deck and see what was happening. He hoped he might be able to stand in the rain or a wave and rid himself of some of the grime.

Some sailors were gathered in a bedraggled, wet and shivering group at the bottom of the ladder.

"You be careful out there, Bill," muttered one of them. "Best not to go alone."

"I just want to wash away some of the grime."

"You'll go with it if you're not careful."

Climbing the ladder to the deck proved to be a bigger challenge than he imagined. He was bounced up and down, left and right. At last, he emerged through the hatchway to the deck. It was almost impossible to see with the dark clouds low to the sea, and the spray whipped up by the wind from behind and thrown across the ship. He looked behind and was startled to see a huge wave looming. It seemed certain to break over the ship, but then the *Lady Grace* seemed to be lifted by it as it raced underneath. Then, as it passed by, she slid down the back of it. Not all of the sails were up, and those that were, had been reefed. The jibs snapped and cracked as the sails behind them stole their wind. The ship had no orderly movement, not heeling as it was in the last storm but bouncing about, as it was pushed by the wind or the waves.

William was soaked and cold as he clambered back down the ladder.

"Mission accomplished?" asked the sailor.

"Aye. And then some." He made his way back to the bunk room for biscuits and water. There was no way to dry himself, so he stretched out on the bunk and was soon asleep. A sailor shook him awake.

"Bill! Bill! They need your help. Captain wants some of the reefs taken out."

"Reefs taken out? Taken out?"

"Aye. He wants more speed. Says the ship can do it. Eddie wants the men from your watch to help."

William could hear the sailor moving about, waking the rest of the men. The men from the starboard engine watch and the sailors clambered up on deck. Eddie spotted them and hurried over.

"Good! The usual drill. Two teams each on the deck and aloft. Captain wants reefs taken from the sails. Hop to it, lads. The wind is stronger than you're used to, but she's not bouncin' about as much. Foremast first and work your way aft. That way, the sails will give you some protection from the wind."

Things looked no better to William than when he was last on deck. If anything, the wind was stronger and the waves larger.

Big waves behind the ship pushed it along, and the wind created surface spray so everything on the weather deck was drenched. Nonetheless, standing looking at it didn't get the job done, so he and the others got on with it.

The men swarmed over the foremast, and the reefs were taken out quickly. William decided they would be hard to put back in again and hoped it wouldn't be his problem. He was still not accustomed to swinging in the footropes, nearly a hundred feet above the deck. The aft wind pushed them into the sails, so there was some measure of comfort, but the ship still pitched wildly to port and starboard, so there was every chance of being flung over the side. He still didn't look down and kept three points of contact at all times.

When the job was done, and the extra sail area was filled, the ship travelled faster. The men had no doubt though, that if the wind increased, the sails would need to be reefed again. The engine-room men clambered back through the hatchway to the welcome warmth below, but were hit immediately by the smell of sick. It was pervasive, and the men headed for their bunks to lie down and avoid becoming sick themselves.

The port watch came into the quarters and demanded their bunks. The starboard watch vacated them and headed for the boiler room. Only half the furnaces were alight and those burned low, so there was little to do on the watch. Coe and Alexander shared the work around so most of the men had a chance to rest along the bulkheads for most of the watch. The motion of the ship was more suited to a steamship since the ship sailed upright most of the time. But William heard it was very uncomfortable for passengers and crew alike, as the ship bounced more than glided.

Their watch was done, and the men went via the galley to get a handful of biscuits. It would do for most of the men as no one was well enough to eat much, and the fires were out anyway. They'd hardly got to sleep, and a sailor shouted in their quarters.

"Captain wants the sails reefed. All hands on deck."

The men scrambled up to the deck. They hadn't thought about it before they arrived on deck, but now it was dark, the job was much more dangerous. Eddie, the bosun and the sailors were already there.

"Same teams, hop to it lads. Helmsman is ready to bring her around to take the pressure off the sails, but you'll need to be quick. He'll bring her up, you reef the sail, and he'll drop her back again. Once for each sail. He'll keep doin' it until the sails are all reefed."

The men did their best to work in the darkness, but it was painfully slow. The helmsman brought the ship up many times, and the sailors weren't ready. They all had to be ready at the same time. It was no good calling instructions. No one could be heard above the sound of the waves and the wind in the rigging. Each sailor took his position and attempted to reef the sail as the ship came up to the wind. If the other sailors weren't ready, then nothing would happen, and it became a waiting game until they were.

Hours went by as the men struggled with the sails, the cold, the wind and the motion of the ship. Frozen hands and feet contributed to the misery. At last, the job was done, and the men struggled below more dead than alive. Uncaring, they collapsed on their bunks. William was aware their watch must be soon, but hoped they had enough time for some rest.

William was dreaming. A sailor shouted that the captain wanted the reefs taken out of the sails. He felt a hand on his arm and marvelled at the realism of the dream. It was still dark, but he could sense men moving.

"Captain wants the reefs taken out. All hands on deck."

There were curses and groans and some suggestions of a task for the captain to perform on himself.

"Come on, lads. The job has to be done. Captain's orders."

This can't go on, thought William. *The crew will be dead before we get to Melbourne.*

Once again, they clambered up the hatchway and into the darkness, and took the reefs out of the sails. The reefs were easier to remove than to apply, so the job was quickly done. The men were careful, though, as fatigue was an unwelcome addition to the dangers of the darkness, the wind and the cold.

There was some light in the sky when the men finished. William looked around at the sea and the sky. *It might be just as well to do the job in the dark,* he thought. *If anyone fell off at any time in this, they'd never be seen again. At least, at night, you wouldn't know and panic.*

The surface of the sea was mostly white. The work of nature and the ship's wake were indistinguishable. The wind howled and tore at them and William was anxious to go below.

Men had no right to be here, challenging the sea, he thought. *Ships seem so large, but compared to the ocean, they are nothing. Not only that, the sailors are so daring, believing they can survive out here. No wonder so many people and ships are lost at sea with storms such as this lying in wait. Why did people chance their luck more than once? Surely, that was tempting fate.* He no longer thought of being a sailor.

The skylight showed a figure on Hall's bunk when they got back to their quarters. While the starboard watch worked on deck, the port watch pulled a double watch. There was no ill feeling.

"We wouldn't have swapped with you anyway," one of the port watch men said.

"We wouldn't have swapped with us, either," said William.

36

SOME TROUBLE WITH THE SHIP

The storm blew itself out after a few days, and the wind then had more south in it. The direction was welcome as the ship sailed much better with the wind aft of the beam. The wind also dropped in strength, so all the sails were hoisted, and the *Lady Grace* sailed like a lady again. The fires were started, hot meals prepared, the bunkrooms, the ship and the bilge cleaned out, and some hardy passengers strolled the deck again. There was excitement as Melbourne wasn't too far away now.

Hall looked terrible. His nose was horribly misshapen, more to the side of his face than the middle. Both his eyes were black, and there was visible bruising on every part of his face. The rumour was going around he might have hit the deck as well, when he fell. The watch agreed while they were sailing, it was better for Hall to remain in his bunk. Well, not so much his bunk, but not in the boiler room. It was Fletcher's idea, the watch agreed, and when Fletcher told Hall, he just grunted. Everyone took that as assent.

Then, the inexplicable happened. The wind dropped, and the *Lady Grace* was becalmed. It was unheard of in these waters. Ships mostly struggled with too much wind, never not enough. The captain decided they were too close to Melbourne to lose time, so he ordered all the furnaces stoked, and they would steam the rest of the way, if need be.

Once again, the engines were on full, and the *Lady Grace* steamed through a windless sea. Everyone agreed the captain to be wise, and his decision to be excellent. The sooner they reached Melbourne, the better. Fletcher reluctantly brought Hall back on his watch. They needed all the men to keep the furnaces fully stoked. Hall was still not well, but no one said anything about him not pulling his weight. Lucky Gordon trimmed for him, and not a word passed between them.

In the engine room, Cave looked worried, and he and Fletcher agreed something was not right. The ship shook slightly as though the shaft bearings were worn unevenly, or maybe a propeller blade was loose. The captain dismissed the concerns and assured the engineers the sails would be used again as soon as the wind came back. The captain should have worried, too.

It was on the middle watch that a huge crash sounded through the ship. Those who hadn't heard the noise were reliably informed by those who had, as to its cause. Passengers were out of their bunks, as were most of the crew.

"We've hit a whale!" one lady called.

"We've hit an iceberg!" called another.

"Saints preserve us!" cried a third.

Price, the chief officer was on watch and called to the engine room on the communications pipe.

"What's happening, Mr Cave?"

"It's Fletcher, sir. I don't know, sir. It came from under the ship. I doubt we hit anything. I think the propeller shaft is broken near to the engine room. I had to shut the engines down as they were racing, so I think it's the shaft. I've sent Andy Couchman down to check. If it's not the shaft, I don't know what it is."

"All right, let me know when you find out."

"Yes, sir."

The *Lady Grace* flopped about on a windless sea. There was a big swell, though the waves were small. It meant the ship would turn around slowly, pointing first one way and then another, all the while heeling from side to side as the swell came from one side and then another.

Many of the passengers were on deck, trying to find out what was happening. Most were rugged up against the cold. Those who weren't stood shivering, refusing to go below and convinced the ship was sinking. Some had brought lamps, although the dawn was not far off, so they were not effective. A few had clustered near the helm and pestered Price about what happened. He tried to reassure them, but it was hard to do when he was waiting to find out himself. The communications pipe whistled. Price grabbed it quickly. The passengers pressed forward eagerly, hoping to overhear.

"Mr Price?"

"Yes, Mr Fletcher. Do you know what happened?"

"Yes, Mr Price. The shaft has snapped in the hollow section near to the engine."

"Can you fix it?"

"I don't think so, sir. I'm going down with Couchman now to have a look myself."

"All right. Let me know. I'll tell the captain. You'd best wake Mr Cave."

William and the others on his watch had heard the loud bang and worried the ship had struck something. Some of the men wanted to hurry on deck, fearful that if the ship went down, they would go with it. Vince Alexander went to the for'ard boiler room to see if they knew anything. He came back and told them Jim Woods had gone to the engine room and been told by Fletcher he thought the propeller shaft was broken. The watch agreed Vince should go back to the engine room and find out whatever he could. In the meantime, the watch should stop stoking the fires. They should all be ready to quit the boiler room at a moment's notice in the event the ship was holed.

Couchman and Fletcher took a lamp and climbed down into the bilge. The smell was terrible, and Fletcher remarked to Couchman, "It's supposed to be perfume to a sailor's nose."

"Well sir, it's telling us the ship's not leaking, and that's got to be good news."

They reached the bilge and they could immediately see the shaft was broken.

"Like I said, sir, it's a clean break. Maybe we could rivet a sheaf around it? There's not much room to work here, but it might be possible to fix it well enough to get to Melbourne."

"It's either that, or wait for wind. It'll do no harm to try. It'll be better to have the engine when we dock in Melbourne, anyway. Have we got some thin plates we can use for a sheaf?"

Fletcher held up the lantern and studied Couchman. "You don't look so good."

"It's the smell here and the movement of the ship, sir. I'm not sure about it being perfume. I'm sure I wouldn't want my lady to wear it. I'll be all right once we start to work."

"All right. Let's get out of here. You find what we'll need for a repair, and I'll get Cave and Barret."

As they came up the ladder, Fletcher said, "I'll see if the bosun can empty the bilge. I'm sure that will help."

"Very good, sir," said Couchman, hurrying away to get what they would need.

Fletcher went to the bunk room to get Cave and Barret. Neither of them was there. Surprised, Fletcher returned to the engine room and found both Barret and Cave.

"Ah!" exclaimed Cave. "There you are. Captain's wanting a status report."

"How did you know we have trouble?"

"The whole ship knows. Can we fix it?"

"Couchman thinks so. At least, he hopes we can fix it well enough to get to Melbourne."

"Captain says the wind is picking up, so we'll be able to sail. I know he'll be pleased if we can fix it, though."

"So will anyone that's sailed into Melbourne."

William and the others were leaving their watch when the order came down to help raise the sails. The men were glad to do so, as it had been nerve-wracking waiting in the near darkness for further news about the ship.

The sails were soon up. The bosun and the sailors were kept busy adjusting the settings of the spars and jibs as the wind swung between west and south-west. It was a good, stiff wind, and the *Lady Grace* was once more underway for Melbourne.

William and Alan Coe were asked to help pump the bilge. They'd done it once before, and it wasn't their favourite job. They attached an extension to the bilge pipe on the deck, aft of the ship, so the contents of the bilge would pump over the side and into the sea. Once the extension was attached, one of the trimmers would go below and ask the engine room to start the bilge pump. They hoped there would be enough steam, as the furnaces had been allowed to run down for several hours. Of course, all the engine room staff were in the bilge, attempting to fix the shaft, so there were several attempts to get the bilge pump started. Eventually, they got the pump going and filthy, smelly water erupted from the pipe, falling into the sea. Any passengers and crew on the deck wisely moved towards the bow, upwind. It took nearly an hour to empty the bilge.

"At least, the lads in the bilge won't have to deal with that," said the bosun watching the water pump over the side. "The steam pumps are a wonder. We used to do that by hand. I look at things like that on ships and wonder if wonders will ever cease? Ships are getting better all the time and the sailor's job, easier." He had the good grace to smile at the men around him. Most of them looked like they disagreed with him, but no one said anything.

It took a day to fix the propeller shaft and several hours to get up enough steam to test the repair. Fletcher and Cave drew straws to see who would remain in the bilge and watch the repair to see how far they could push it. Fletcher lost and stayed behind once the test started. The repair was still intact at half speed, and Cave recommended they neither strain nor test it further. The wind was still good, so they let the furnaces die down again and continued under sail to Melbourne.

The next morning, there was a buzz about the ship. The captain had told the passengers over breakfast, if the wind continued, the ship was about seven days out of Melbourne.

William and the starboard boiler-room watch were more or less permanently assigned to the sailors. They were busy at all times of the night and day resetting the sails. It often seemed the officer of the watch called for the sails to be adjusted just so the sailors could be given something to do. Many times the sailors would adjust the spars, only to return them to where they were within the hour.

Still, the news they were so close to Melbourne lifted even the sailors' spirits. Those who had been to Melbourne were pressed time and again during mess to tell what they knew, and what the men could expect.

The crew heard a special supper was planned for the passengers that night. They heard too, the crew would get whatever was left over, so they were busy drawing lots without knowing how much food would be left. Eddie told William such things always happened, and often the crew got nothing.

As darkness fell, a magnificent sunset appeared behind them. Everyone agreed it was a great omen. It was a beautiful, warm evening, and the wind was warm enough to stroll on the deck in comfort. Some musical instruments were produced, and the crew could hear the chatter, laughter and music from the passengers' saloon. It was one of the rare times the men hoped for sail and setting changes so they could peek through the skylights as they went by. Those that did were astonished at the finery the passengers had managed to bring.

The ladies were dressed in fulsome, colourful dresses and bonnets, and the men looked resplendent in suits. There was an area for dancing, and it was packed with enthusiastic revellers. A few of the men lingered too long and caught the sharp edge of the bosun's tongue. It didn't pay to rile Mr Merchant, the men agreed.

37

The Fight

The next morning, William went on deck to see what was happening, since they hadn't been called out at all during the night. It was so magical, he wondered if he might miss a sailor's life, after all. The *Lady Grace* cleaved through the waves, pushed along by a strong sou'wester. The sails were full and firm. The only sounds were those of the sea breaking against the hull. Sometimes, there would be a bump as a rogue wave hit the hull from an unexpected direction, but mostly the ship glided along as though being pulled by an invisible thread.

William leaned against the rail at the bow and thought about the previous evening. He'd been keen to hear about the gold, but was afraid to ask, in case it gave his real intentions away. No one ever mentioned it. He wondered why. Did they all plan to jump ship in Melbourne? Or, was there no gold?

He could see the shore in the distance. There were tall cliffs, and the waves pounded against them. He couldn't hear them over the noise of the ship, but decided it was no place to be. A ship would be crushed and broken in moments on such a savage shore. He thought of Eddie's stories and shuddered.

He stood near the bow, gazing at the sails and filled with admiration for man's ingenuity when he felt a presence beside him. He turned casually to see who it was. It was Hall, coming at him with a belaying pin. Hall swung and William ducked. The pin whistled over his head. William looked around quickly. He couldn't see anyone else and knew the men at the helm couldn't see this part of the ship. Panic gripped him. He would have to face the man alone. This couldn't be happening.

William could feel the hatchway cabin at his back. He was trapped and looked about for any way to escape. There was none. "What are you doing, Mr Hall? This makes no sense. Aren't you better to leave things alone? We're nearly in Melbourne."

"Aye, and that's why. There's not much time left to finish this."

"Finish what? What have I done?"

"Done? What do you mean, what have you done? You're a fool, Smith. You'll pay now for what Gordon did, and he'll pay later."

"What Lucky did wasn't my fault!"

Hall made a feint with the pin and laughed when William ducked. "Why don't you stand still and get it over with?"

William again looked quickly to his left and right.

Hall laughed. "You're trapped, aren't you? No Eddie or Fletcher, now. Just you and me. It was always going to be like this, Smith. Just you and me."

William was desperate and terrified. He ducked when Hall feinted again.

Hall laughed. He was clearly enjoying himself. "There'll be no help this time, Smith. Best you say your prayers. You've no time for anything else."

Hall's face changed. A look of determination came over it, and William knew he was about to attack. The wind shifted, and the *Lady Grace* heeled sharply. Hall nearly lost his footing and had to take a moment to regain his balance. William did the only thing he could and leapt for the shrouds. He was surprised how quickly Hall followed, as he'd shown no inclination to work with the sailors at any time during the voyage.

"Think you know your way around up here, do you? I was born up here, Smith, and you'll not get away this time."

William was younger, fitter and not encumbered by the belaying pin, so he could use both hands to climb. He moved away from Hall quickly. He got to the mast and started down the shrouds on the other side. Hall saw what was happening and started climbing down his own side, clearly hoping to re-engage William on the deck. It was a race, and William used every skill he had learned to reach the deck first. His only hope was to reach Hall while he was still in the shrouds. Hall would use one hand to hang on in the shrouds and be less able to swing the belaying pin.

Grabbing a belaying pin to use as a weapon as he ran past the foremast, William reached the other side of the ship, just as Hall stepped onto the rail. His knees were bent through the shrouds, and William bashed Hall as hard as he could on a kneecap with the pin. Hall cried out with pain and swung his own pin at William. It connected with the shrouds and became entangled in them, falling to the deck. William reached down and picked it up. As he did, he realised his mistake. Hall leaped from the rail and onto William's back. They fell to the deck together, Hall trying to wrest a pin from his grasp.

William now had pins in both hands and could only try to bash Hall with them. Hall was surprisingly strong and wasn't in any way hindered by the injuries received in his fight with Gordon. William's only advantage was that he had two pins and Hall had none, but Hall's hands were both free, and he used them to batter and punch William wherever he could.

They writhed around in a tangle for a few moments when William saw one of Hall's knees within reach. He hoped it was Hall's injured knee and put all his effort into bashing it as hard as he could with one of the pins. Hall bellowed in pain and rage. William hoped someone would hear and come to help. He was already tired and no match for Hall's weight and strength. The wound on William's head had re-opened and blood was pouring into his eyes. Hall used both hands to protect his knee, and William took the chance to slither away.

"Damn you, Smith! You'll pay for that!" Hall tried to stand, but fell as soon as he put his weight on his injured leg.

Moving further away, William stood and wiped the blood from his eyes with his sleeve. He tightened his grip on the two pins and took a step towards Hall. He stopped. He'd be a fool to attack Hall, even in his weakened condition.

Hall pulled himself up against the rail. "Come on, Smith. Where's your guts? Need someone to help, do you?"

The *Lady Grace* lurched, and William slipped and fell into Hall. Hall struck immediately with his fists, and William tried to hit him with a pin. One of the blows caught William on the shoulder and as he fell, he struck Hall on the side of the head, stunning him for a few moments. Hall was holding the rail, trying to stop himself from falling. He failed, once again collapsing into William.

William was surprised that the blow to the head had taken some of the fight out of Hall. He tried to hit William, but the blows were weak and directionless. William stood, looking down at Hall. "Enough, Mr Hall. Isn't it enough? Please, can't we stop this?"

Hall looked up and tried to get to his feet. His knee couldn't take his weight, and he fell. He crawled across to the rail and pulled himself up. "Please, can't we stop this?" mimicked Hall in a high-pitched voice. "You're a baby, Smith, and babies have no place on ships."

He tried to push himself off the rail, but the *Lady Grace* lurched again, and Hall fell backwards over the rail. He had the presence of mind to grab the shrouds as he fell. He was hanging off the side of the ship, legs dangling, trying desperately to get some purchase with his good leg.

William rushed to help him. "Give me your hand, Mr Hall. I'll pull you back on."

Hall reached out, and William tried to pull him up, but he was too heavy, and William was too tired. "I have to get help, Mr Hall. Can you hang on?"

"Give me one of the pins, and I can use it to anchor myself. Then I'll be able to hold on."

William released his hand, reached down to the deck, picked up one of the pins and passed it to Hall who had managed to get a foothold with his good leg.

"Well done, Smith. Now, help me to secure it."

William leant down, and as he did, Hall reached up and grabbed his shirt front.

"Like I said, you're a fool, Smith. Say hello to the fishes for me."

He swung at William's head with the pin, still holding his shirt and supporting himself on his good leg. It was a solid blow and William collapsed against the rail.

Another rogue wave hit the ship and Hall, still trying to hold onto the pin and William's shirt, could not hold his own weight. His hand let go of William's shirt, and he tried to grab the shrouds while still holding the pin. It was impossible. William, blood pouring from a new wound on his head, tried to grab his arm and help him get to the deck, but instead of accepting the help, he swung the pin again at William's arm. The blow forced William to let go, and Hall slid off into the sea.

Staring in horror, William turned to alert the helm that a man was overboard and fell straight into Eddie.

"Steady, Bill. Steady does it."

"Eddie! Eddie! Hall's overboard! We have to turn the ship around!"

Eddie was holding William by the shoulders, so fiercely it hurt.

"What are you doing, Eddie? We have to help him."

"Think about it, Bill. You look like you've been in the fight of your life. He won't know how to swim, and even if he did, his legs won't work. By the time we turn the ship around, he'll be long gone, and you'll have some explaining to do."

"How do you know his legs won't work?"

"I wondered where you were, so came on deck to see if you were here. I saw you trying to help him and him hit you. I don't think he wants your help. No, Bill, it's good riddance."

"We can't leave him, Eddie. That's murder. Please let me go. I have to help him."

"What are you going to tell them, Bill? Hall attacked you, you fought him off, and he fell overboard?"

"You can tell them what you saw!"

"How do I know what happened? Like I said, I saw you helping him, and he hit you. Then, he fell into the sea. What will they think? That he attacked you or you attacked him? Men fall overboard all the time, Bill. Captain won't worry about arrivin' in Melbourne with one less man on board, and neither should you. I need to get you to the doctor. Your wound's opened up again."

"It's so heartless, Eddie. I wished him no harm. I hit his leg to disable him, not to kill him."

"That might be the case, but he would happily have thrown you over the side and told no one about it. Be glad it's him and not you. Besides, you tried to help him, but he wanted to continue the fight. If Lucky Gordon hadn't belted him, he might have been too quick for you, and it might well be you feedin' the fishes. Come on, Bill. Let's go and have breakfast. That's why I came to get you. It's too late now, anyway. He's already a long way behind. Come on, lad. Pull yourself together. I don't know if anyone has tried to kill you before, but you sure shouldn't be feelin' sorry for him."

"It must be a horrible way to go, Eddie. Out there alone in the sea."

"We all have to go some way. That's as good as any other. He's probably been pushin' people around for years. Men like that don't last long. They usually meet someone like Lucky Gordon and learn their lesson. I suppose he realised he was no match for Gordon and decided to take out his vengeance on you. He sure got that wrong."

"I wonder if he's watching to see if the ship turns around."

"I doubt it. Probably sank straight to the bottom. There're sharks down here, too. Lots of 'em. Enough, Bill. Just be grateful you're still with us. The man's not worth another thought. Let's worry about you, because I think you need some worry. Let's get you to the doctor."

"I'm not going to the doctor. I don't want any questions. My head hurts, but I can clean the blood away, and there'll be no questions. I don't want anyone to know about this."

Eddie shrugged. "As you wish. It's your head."

They both walked to the hatchway. William looked back once, but Eddie not at all.

38

Melbourne at Last

The men were excited at breakfast. The news was the ship would be in Melbourne the next morning. There was talk the passengers would have another fine supper that night, the last before docking. Again, the men drew lots to settle who would share the remainder of the passengers' meals, even though little had remained the last time.

One of the men asked William why he looked so unhappy when they were certain to arrive the next day. He replied that he was sick, and the man reassured him he would feel better once he had dry land under his feet.

The supper that night was a sombre affair. There was music, laughter and dancing, but not as many of the passengers wanted to participate. It had been a long voyage, and many were too enthusiastic to be arriving in Melbourne to be excited about anything else. William and some sailors stood on the deck and watched.

There was plenty of very fine food left over, and the crew were advised to go to the galley and help themselves. Many did, but William found he was too upset by the morning's event to even be hungry.

The ship was still sailing, so William was bunked up for'ard with the sailors. He left the deck and went back to the mess where the sailors went to get their food.

Sailors returned from the galley with plates filled with potatoes, rice pudding, pork, chicken, bread and even pickles that had been given to some of them by a passenger. Everything was piled high on their plates. Some had a mug of ale or wine. There was much shouting and laughter as they compared their booty.

Unable to join the fun, William left the mess, went to the sailors' quarters and found Eddie lying on his bunk. Eddie shook his head slightly when William approached which he interpreted to mean Eddie didn't want to talk about Hall. That was no problem. He didn't want to talk about him either.

"What do we do when we get to Melbourne?" he asked.

"Well, passengers go ashore. Then, they may ask us to help with any cargo, then we go ashore."

"How long will the ship stay there?"

"Depends. They'll try to get cargo and passengers to go back to England. They have to stay a few days while the agents work on that. They can't advertise before we arrive. Sometimes, if ships overtake you, there's advance warnin' of arrival, but we haven't seen any ships goin' that way, so we'll be a surprise when we arrive. Then there's the matter of the broken propeller shaft. They'll have to get that fixed permanently."

"What do we do while all that happens?"

"Most of the men will go ashore and get drunk, especially if they give us all the money they owe us. Sometimes, they don't give us all of it, so we'll come back. Some men will try to jump ship, and get to the goldfields. There's rumours goin' around most of the gold is gone. That might have been started by the shippin' companies, of course." Eddie laughed.

"Do you think there's any gold left?"

"Dunno. Some men make it, and some get caught and brought back. I haven't met anyone who made it, so I don't know how they go. I expect there's still gold. No reason not to be."

"Where will the men stay when they're not on the ship?"

"Oh, there's places," said Eddie, uneasily.

"Can we stay on the ship?"

"If we want. They'll want some men to stay, but it's mostly the stewards and washers who give the ship a thorough cleanin', gettin' ready for the next passengers. Sailors and engine crew mostly go ashore and spend their money. You can come with me, if you want, at least for a while. Have you ever been drunk, Bill?"

"No, but I've seen people that were drunk. My da was drunk sometimes."

"Not the same as being drunk yourself. And you can't blame your da for drinkin'. The good Lord invented drink, and it's not a good idea to go against His noble intentions. I don't want to be the one to teach you, but like I say, you can come with me for a while, if you want. You can't stay if you won't drink, though. The men won't like it. They'll say, 'You can't trust a man that doesn't drink.' But there's time enough to worry about it, so put it out of your mind for the moment. We have to get there, first."

The *Lady Grace* sailed on.

William was woken during the night to join his watch. The captain preferred to go into Port Phillip under steam, rather than sail, so the furnaces had to be stoked and steam made ready. As they assembled in the boiler room, it was obvious Hall was missing.

"Has anyone seen Hall?" asked Vince Alexander.

It was the question William had been dreading and was glad of the partial darkness that covered his unease. No one said anything.

"Someone has to find him," said Alexander. "I'll check with Fletcher."

The men did the best they could, since without Hall and Alexander to stoke the fires, the load fell to the other firemen. As it turned out, they were wasting their time anyway. They wouldn't need full speed.

Alexander came back. "Fletcher says he hasn't seen him. He said the repairs mean we can't do more than half speed. He said they'll only want three boilers, like when we left Southampton, so our watch can work with the others on the for'ard furnaces. I said if we did that, we wouldn't need Hall. In fact, we wouldn't need us all, but he laughed and said we should stay. Might help build up a thirst. He didn't seem worried about Hall. It's odd. I wonder what's happened?"

They all left to join the for'ard crew.

At one point, several of the men stopped for some water, and William overheard one of the for'ard firemen ask where Hall was. "No one knows," was the reply, and it didn't raise any further comment.

Perhaps Eddie was right, thought William. *Just another missing sailor.*

On the one hand, he was glad Hall was gone because there was no more threat. He could come on shift and not worry about what might happen. On the other, he'd allowed Eddie to talk him out of helping Hall. It didn't matter much what had happened, he'd murdered a man.

His watch came off shift, had breakfast and went to the weather deck. It was a beautiful morning, and many of the passengers were there as well. The ship was close to the land, and the first close sight of Australia was a shock to many. They couldn't see it too well from the distance, but the foliage looked anything but green. William overheard a passenger who had been to Melbourne before say, "It's more blue than green."

Eddie stood beside him. No one else was close enough to them to overhear.

"No one's worried about Hall at all," said William. "A sailor's life is not worth much."

"I have some news. I overheard bosun talkin' to Mr Price. Armstrong reported Hall missin'. He and a couple of others searched the ship, but couldn't find him. Said Hall'd spent most of his time on his bunk after the accident, and Armstrong had to find another bunk to sleep on, so he couldn't be sure when he was last seen. Surgeon said he might not have recovered after fallin' and hittin' the bulkhead, might have been disoriented and gone on deck durin' the night, thinkin' it was the boiler room and fallen overboard. Armstrong wasn't sure that was right, but couldn't offer any other idea. Captain said if he wasn't on the ship, then he was overboard, and that was good enough for him. Said he was only responsible for the livin'. The dead could take care of themselves."

Eddie stopped, looked at William and added, "I don't think Mr Price agrees with the captain, but me, I'm on the captain's side."

"Do you believe in God, Eddie?"

Eddie shrugged, "Sometimes."

"Will God punish me because I killed Hall?" William started to cry.

"Punish you? Why, I think He'll thank you. Why do you think God will punish you?"

"Well, a man was run over by a coach in my town. The driver stopped, looked back, laughed and drove off. I asked my ma why he didn't care." He wiped his tears away.

Eddie thought he looked very young and very vulnerable, not at all like someone who had come out best in a fight to the death.

"'There's laws for them and there's laws for us. But no matter. God will get him when he dies,' my ma said. Does that mean God will be waiting for me to die?"

"Depends on what you think about God. I think God decided the world had seen enough of our Mr Hall, and it was time he came home for his punishment."

Eddie reached out and gripped William's shoulder. William winced.

"Sorry, Bill," and dropped his hand. "I'm sure God only punishes those that deserve it. You don't. Never have, never will. You need to forget about Hall. He would've forgotten you, by now."

After a few moments of silence, William asked, "What'll we do now?"

Eddie looked surprised and replied, "About Hall? Nothin'."

William looked at Eddie and shook his head.

"No, what'll the ship do now?"

Eddie laughed and so did William.

"That's better. They'll sail her past the heads, wear her or tack her, depending on the wind and come up to the land on the other tack. When we're close, they'll lower the sails and bring her in under steam. It's a narrow entrance and the channels are tricky once we're inside. They'll wait for an incomin' tide. No point in pushin' her too hard with the broken shaft and all."

It wasn't long before the bosun ordered the crews to the sails, ready to adjust the spars and the jibs as the helmsman swung the ship through the wind. William was glad to have something to do. It took his mind off Hall. Only he and Eddie knew for certain that Hall was dead, but it surprised him that apart from Armstrong and maybe Price, no one was in the least bothered that a man was missing.

After a while, William realised most of the morning had gone, and he would be back for his watch in the boiler room. He would not be on deck going into Melbourne, and he was disappointed. He was about to say something when the bosun came up.

"Eddie, you'll need to keep the sailors and the engine crew on deck. If anything goes wrong with the propeller shaft, we're going to need the sails at short notice. Send them below for something to eat now. Once we enter the bay, they'll not be able to stand down until we dock. Captain says we'll lower the sails in about an hour."

They'd hardly started their meal when they were ordered on deck again.

"Captain says we're going too fast and we're getting too close. He doesn't want to use steam until the last minute, as he doesn't want to overwork the repair. We're going to have to tack back and forth for an hour or so."

The first tack was easy, as it was just a matter of bringing the ship up on the wind and adjusting the spars and jibs. As the ship started to head back the way it had come, some of the passengers who continued to brave the heat on deck, complained they didn't want to go back to England yet.

After about thirty minutes, they swung her around again and started heading back towards Melbourne. It was hard work with the spars and jibs, and the crew hoped they didn't need to do this too often.

Thirty more minutes and they could feel the engines running. The bosun came and ordered the sails lowered and stowed. They were heading into the bay at last. Most of the passengers were on deck, pointing excitedly at items of interest on the shore. The sun was now very hot and almost overhead. Many of the ladies had parasols, and others standing behind complained they couldn't see through them. Some of the sailors climbed into the rigging. It was a festive atmosphere. Some families hugged each other, and some cheered, as though surprised to have survived the journey.

The bosun made sure the crew were aft and away from the passengers when they were not busy with the sails or rigging. All the officers were at the helm, and all looked anxious. William overheard Price say surely the pilot boat had seen them and would be there soon with a pilot to help them find the right channels.

Just when it seemed they would have to put out to sea again and wait for the next day, the pilot boat came out from near the heads. It pulled alongside, the ladder was lowered, and the pilot ascended briskly. The crew hovered nearby so they could hear what was happening.

"Well done, Captain," the pilot said. "We've been watching you for a while. We couldn't be sure you wanted to come in today. When you lowered the sails, we thought we'd better check."

"Aye, we want to come in today, if you please. This is the *Lady Grace* out of Southampton, and we've a broken propeller shaft, so we want to get in and moored as soon as possible."

"Broken?" asked the pilot, raising an eyebrow. "How are you steaming, then?"

"We've done some temporary repairs. I would recommend no more than half speed."

"Right you are, sir. I'll take the helm, if that's all right with you. Easier to steer than explain." Without waiting for a reply, the pilot took the helm and started talking about what he was doing.

"Captain, see that narrow opening dead ahead? That's where we want to go. Slow and steady is best as it's very narrow. Can't be too close to either port or starboard. You were wise to wait for an incoming tide, but we still need to be careful. We'll steer slightly to the starboard side of the heads, and once we are through, we'll swing her to about ninety degrees. Slow and steady is most important. Get your engineer on the communications pipe. He'll have to be quick when we need him."

William looked at the officers. If the pilot was trying to make himself indispensable by making the officers nervous, he'd done a good job of it.

The crew and officers clustered aft were silent as the ship came through the heads. It seemed to William that all he had to do to touch either shore was to reach out. He marvelled the ship could fit through and was glad they were under steam. There were two visible wrecks, one on the port side, and the other on the starboard.

The pilot glanced briefly at the captain. "Interesting, sir? I'm sure you're wondering about them? How did they happen, you must be thinking?" He was greeted by silence.

William thought perhaps no one, but least of all the captain wanted to know.

The pilot went on, anyway. "The one on the starboard side is a barque named *Isabella Watson*. It happened about two years ago. She'd sailed out of London fully laden with cargo and about seventy passengers and crew. The pilot was late getting to her, and the captain decided to bring her in anyway. He should have stayed at sea. She got caught in a sudden squall. Hit the rocks near the stern on the starboard side. She had no chance. They got one lifeboat away safely, but the next was swamped."

"Was there any loss of life?" asked Patterson, the second officer.

The pilot glanced at him briefly as though to determine the source of such a silly question.

"Of course. She lost about ten passengers and crew. I was there. We managed to get some lines to the ship and pull people ashore." He stopped as though reflecting on the dangers of sea travel.

"You were there, you say?" said the captain. "Were you the pilot?"

The pilot shook his head. He didn't seem the least affronted by the question. Perhaps he was accustomed to it.

"No, another pilot. There's a few here. Too many, sometimes, I believe."

"And the other ship?" asked Hosking, after a few moments.

"The other one was the *Will O' the Wisp* and was wrecked about a year ago. She was a clipper schooner trading at the time between here and New Zealand. Captain had been here before and didn't bother with a pilot. Thought he knew what he was doing. Sailed too close to the eastern side of the west channel and hit a sand bank. It was completely wrecked, as you can see. We'll stay well away from there. Eastern channel will do us fine."

There was a pause as if the pilot expected more questions. Everyone was silent, probably still overawed by the narrow opening and the tragedy of the shipwrecks.

"There's lots more, of course," continued the pilot. "Probably hundreds by now. They get wrecked and washed away. Waste of life and money, if you ask me. Pilots are here to be used. Might cost some money, but nothing compared to the loss of ship, cargo and passengers. Imagine sailing all the way from England and wrecking your ship in sight of your destination."

William imagined it and shuddered.

The pilot started to steer to the starboard. Dusk was upon them, and it was harder to see. It didn't seem to matter to the pilot who moved the wheel with confidence. "Maximum speed is half speed, Captain?"

"Yes."

"Then ask your engineer for half of half, if you please."

The ship slowed, and the pilot tried to line up landmarks on the north and south of the bay. He nodded to himself when he deemed the moment to be right, then swung the *Lady Grace* to port, finally heading her directly north.

"Half speed now, if you please, Captain."

They continued in silence for a while.

"There's nowhere to dock, Captain. We'll have to anchor off Gellibrand Point, and the lighters will take you ashore. I'll see you to anchor and present my bill to the purser for payment. The lighters will negotiate their rates with you and your passengers. They'll gather around like fleas on a dog. Tell your passengers not to go ashore tonight, unless they have to. They'll get a better price in the morning. Everything is cheaper in the morning when they'll have time to shop around. Might be safer, too. The passengers will be able to see where they are going and what they are stepping in come daylight."

After about an hour of steady steaming, they could see a forest of masts, and the pilot spoke again. "Your men have done a good job with the repair, Captain. Please have your crew ready with the anchors."

The captain turned to Price and nodded. Price turned to the bosun and nodded. The bosun selected several men and hurried for'ard.

The pilot guided the big ship expertly into a space and said, "Drop anchors, if you please, sir."

Price called to the bosun, and they could hear the chains rattling as the anchors dropped.

"Steady astern, please Captain, until she holds."

The *Lady Grace* settled back, the anchors lodged firmly, and the voyage was over. Like thousands before him, William stood at the rail and looked at Melbourne some distance away, shrouded by dusk. Some distant lanterns glimmered, there was the faint sound of music, the clattering of carriages and horses, some shouts and laughter. William realised some of the shouts were nearby, as the lighters pulled alongside and called for any passengers or goods to be taken ashore. He saw the pilot walking away from the helm and guessed he was off to see the purser. Later he saw him clambering down the ladder to his waiting boat which was soon lost to sight in the throng.

There was a huge commotion on the deck as some of the passengers who were familiar with the process, negotiated with the lighters. Others were confused and begged the officers for help. William tried to find Eddie who was the only constant now for him, and at least, someone to lean on for help.

The din and disorganisation were terrible. There was noise from the passengers who hugged and kissed family and friends alike. William could hear passengers promising to catch up ashore or back in England, as the case may be. There were tears and shouts, and some even expressing surprise to have survived a journey that had not been successful for many others they knew.

William once again wondered at what he had done by joining the ship, and what the future might hold for him.

The captain issued orders to Price, Hosking and Patterson. Price spoke to the bosun who called in his booming voice for the crew to meet in the engine crew's quarters. The crew hurried below to hear what the bosun would have to say. When enough of them were assembled that those who heard could tell the others, it was Price, not the bosun, who spoke.

"Well done, men. It was a fine voyage, and we're all pleased to arrive. We have the business of the propeller shaft to attend to, so we'll be here for a few days at least. See the purser, and he will give you some of your money. Captain wants you all to go ashore, either tonight or in the morning, but report back day after tomorrow for further instructions. If you plan to go ashore tonight, don't compete with the passengers for a lighter. Wait until those that are going are all gone."

"What about the cargo?" someone called.

"It's organised, and you'll not be needed," said Price and left the room.

William saw Eddie talking to a group of men and joined them.

"Like I said, they won't give us all our money because they want to make sure we come back. I'm goin' ashore tonight and anyone that wants to join me is welcome."

There was a clamour of assent from the men and Eddie spotted William.

"How about you, Bill? You want to go with the flow?"

"No, Eddie. I'll come ashore in the morning."

"It'll be cheaper tonight. I'll negotiate the lighter and get some money from all of you. Tomorrow, you might have to pay it all yourself."

William laughed. It was good to laugh. "All right, Eddie. I'll go with the flow."

Eddie gripped William's arm, laughed out loud, and the men all laughed with him. William thought how much he enjoyed the company of those men and their laughter and wondered if that moment would map the rest of his life. He was grateful that destiny had put him on the *Lady Grace* and just as surely now put him in the company of these men, and he hoped, in a land of opportunity.

His thoughts were swamped by the laughter of the men being told a story by Eddie of the last time he was in Melbourne. William had no idea what they were laughing about, but joined in the laughter anyway.

"Laughing beats crying, and that's for sure," he said out loud, but no one heard. It didn't matter. He was in Australia, at last.

He thought of Mary and his family. Would he ever see them again? What of little Jimmy? Would he remember he had a big brother? He missed little Jimmy and hoped he was all right. They were now so far away. It wasn't easy to get to Australia, and it would be no easy matter to go home.

And what of Hall? He had killed a man. He would have to live with that for the rest of his life. He could console himself with the thought that it was an accident, but the fact was that a man was dead, and he'd killed him. A wave of shame and fear swept over him, and he was glad no one noticed.

There was only one way he would cope and that was to consider the past was now behind him, and the future yet to be discovered. William was determined to force himself to forget the past and make the best of the future. One day he might go home, but he knew that if he did, Mary would be long gone. She'd be a fool to wait, and he'd be a fool to expect she would.

No. Australia is the future.

About the Author

Peter Clarke is only one of many Australians who are intrigued by the stories of the immigrants who helped create a nation. Where did they come from? Why did they come? Why did they stay?

Born in Mudgee and raised in the Blue Mountains, Peter is familiar with the challenges of drought and fire, but these challenges are nothing compared to those faced by the early pioneers.

A working life in the computer industry has not in any way prepared Peter to write about the pioneers. However, a lively interest in early Australia and an adequate Irish heritage has contributed to a curiosity that has only been in part satisfied by several trips to Ireland. Thus motivated, Peter used the new technology to surf world history and events, to create a story of one man's journey which reflects the difficulties of the time.